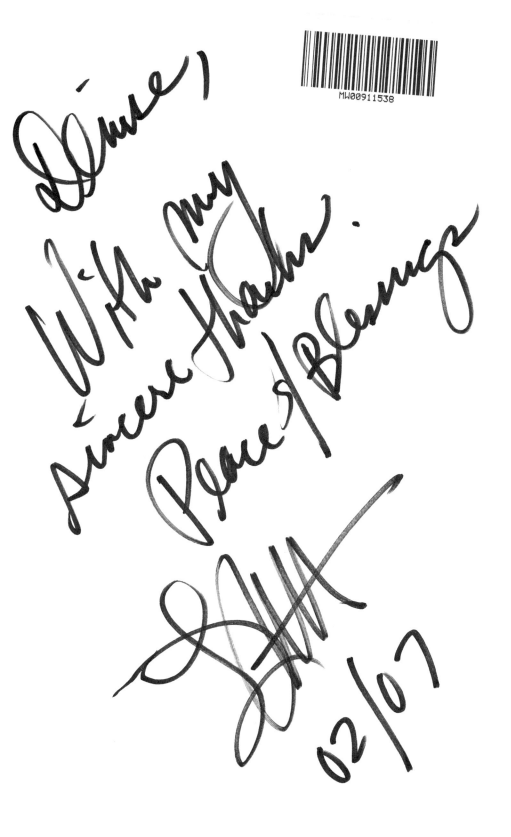

LETTERS FROM THE MINISTER

by

L. Mack Mossett, III

Bloomington, IN  Milton Keynes, UK

authorHOUSE®

AuthorHouse™
1663 Liberty Drive, Suite 200
Bloomington, IN 47403
www.authorhouse.com
Phone: 1-800-839-8640

AuthorHouse™ UK Ltd.
500 Avebury Boulevard
Central Milton Keynes, MK9 2BE
www.authorhouse.co.uk
Phone: 08001974150

First published by AuthorHouse 8/28/2006

ISBN: 1-4184-1428-X (e)
ISBN: 1-4184-1427-1 (sc)
ISBN: 1-4184-1426-3 (dj)

Library of Congress Control Number: 2004091967

Printed in the United States of America
Bloomington, Indiana

This book is printed on acid-free paper.

ACKNOWLEDGEMENTS

There is something very special about "firsts," in that they encompass almost every aspect of an individuals being. The first of anything requires so much of everything that very often one feels completely spent after the trauma and triumph of a first experience. And although the thrill of conquering a personal Everest is often celebrated alone, the sojourn to the peak is never solely traveled.

Writing my first novel required me to pull from every part of everything I ever knew; every memory, every experience, every emotion ever felt, every aroma inhaled, every good and bad taste that ever traversed my tongue, and in retrospective contemplation, I was never alone. So many people have written on my heart, in some way over the years, and I must thank them for being pieces to a puzzle that finally became a legible arrangement of prose.

My wife was, and is still my foremost critical and honest editor, and with dexterous care she helped validate my work. I am grateful to her for giving me the time and support to focus on my creations, allowing the side of my brain that does that, to do that comfortably. I thank my mother for cultivating a love for reading in my soul. I will never forget the nights we read *I Wish I Had Duck Feet*, by Dr. Seuss together. And to my son and daughter, who know I wrote a book and all, but still simply think I'm great for making the best fried rice in the universe, thank you. Because when all is said and done, that's all that really matters.

CHAPTER 1

Angela Johnson Hebert stood in her mirror at 8:30 in the morning, as she had done almost every day for the last fifteen years. Though life brought its daily satchel, of twists and surprises, this portion of her day remained the same. She liked it that way. Her mastery of emotional camouflage evoked belief amongst the masses that her life was relatively uneventful but that was far from the truth. She caught her own gaze, and saw eyes that were tired with experience for they had seen exuberant joy and melancholy sadness often within the same glance. The light of her eyes reflected the remnants of disappointment and the pain of lost love. But they also glistened with hope, rejuvenating freshness, willing encouragement, and self motivation. They were windows to the unique ability to find calm in chaos. The image in the mirror did not remind her as much of the fragility of her life but more so of the double-existence her life's choices had required.

She was married to one of the most prolific preachers of the era, lived in a million dollar home, not purchased at the expense of the church members, and had two clueless children who were routinely showered with wishes conjured beyond the dreams of the most imaginatively spoiled child. Her life was an amalgamation of textbook fairytale and American dream. The European S.U.V, and high-end sedan, were both complimented by a hot little Jaguar convertible for the weekends. All waited at the ready in her circular driveway.

Angela had more than most women could ever ask for. Her undeniable beauty was a fact never contested. Straight, jet-black hair down to the center of her back gently caressed a flawless face and oval eyes. She was unique, in that her dark, rich skin seemed a contradictory match to her virtuously straight hair. But it was just another special quality that made

3

her who she was. Her smile was radiant and unforgettable, and every man that she had ever met could bear witness. Her hands were hands of privilege after sacrifice, historically soft and impeccably manicured. They were willing hands. They were working hands. They were hands that were busy not by requirement, but by choice.

Those peering into the window of her world concluded very simply that she had "arrived," and done so in style. She had been placed on a pedestal that brought her both praise and envy and she had learned to handle both with impeccable, though often painful, grace. There were those who constantly sought the opportunity to chip at the armor of the family crest that she had worked so hard to create, but Angela had managed so far to keep them all at bay. Only one person really knew the life she lived. Only one person knew who she was beyond the mirror. The Minister. Only he knew her most intimate concerns, her worries about the effects of time and place on her body, the ramifications of sacrificing her promising career, and how the hidden fragility of her psyche was slowly coming to the surface after years of fabricating mental walls of protection. He had broken through years ago and over time, made himself her main source of validation. That was his goal, and that was his success. At least, that is what he believed.

It was Sunday, and unlike the weekdays when Angela prepared the children for school before she dressed herself, Sunday the system was reversed. She took time for herself. A long hot bath was complimented by the casual reading of a new novel. An exotic china cup and saucer set held hot tea as it sat on the side of the bath tub while lavender incense burned slowly bringing her mind to submissive relaxation. Allowing herself to fall deeper into the caress of the silky bubbles, she closed her eyes after taking a sip of the now warm tea. She used her Zen breathing techniques learned in her weekly yoga class and further quieted the whisper of the popping bubbles of her sudsy retreat. It was well-orchestrated peace and solitude. Then reality came through the door like a freight train.

"Mommy, Mommy Brother won't let me watch Nickelodeon!" Angie's five year old, Shelby, came booming into the bathroom with her irritated announcement, whined in high soprano. And right behind her raced her big brother, Ed Jr.

"Mom, she always gets to watch whatever she wants in the morning!" he contended.

"No, no, no, I was there first," Shelby interjected.

"No you weren't in the kitchen first!'

"Yes I was–"

Ed, Jr. raised his hands as if he were addressing a jury with opening arguments. "Mom, I came in and got some cereal, and when I was walking over to the table, Shelby ran in there and turned on the TV, but I was already in there coming out of the pantry–"

Just as dramatic and never out done, Shelby, "No, Mommy, he was... he... Eddie—" Her shoulders were raised and her hands operated in sequence with sound as she struggled through the giggles to her rebuttal.

"Where is your father?" Angela demanded, interrupting the theatrical litigation.

"Who?" A stunned Eddie replied, as if he wondered whom his mother was talking about.

"Your father!" She sternly repeated. "You know, the man you sometimes see around here; the black guy with the same last name as yours."

"Oh," Ed said with an ear-to-ear grin developing and forming an almost exact duplicate of the unforgettable smile of his mother.

"Dad's in his office. I knocked on the door, and he said 'Go ask your mother' before I even said anything. I guess he was busy or something."

She sighed the 'here we go again' sigh, realizing that it was time to jumpstart back into "Mommy Mode." The children stood there with goofy looks on their faces. They were simply holding up their end of the family bargain that called for them, and every other child in the universe, to maintain mischief and high jinks on a regular basis. Their mother, of course, was not amused and was going to soon address their issues with the short end of a "strap," as her grandmother used to call it. That was her side of the family bargain.

"Okay will you guys get on out of here so I can get dressed, and both of you cut it out because if I have to come in there, somebody's gonna get it. Now, I mean it. Go, and I don't want to see you until I want to see you!"

The children quickly exited, continuing to mumble the argument, and then racing down the hallway towards the kitchen. They were typical that way. There would be momentary harmony and then it was guaranteed that some new issue of contention would formulate and surface.

Angela quickly sponged off the excess suds on her milk chocolate body and used her toes to flip the switch to drain the tub. Solitude had been effectively terminated. She draped herself in a white Channel, cotton robe and walked down the hall drying her face and hair, while calling her husband's name, to which there was no immediate answer.

"Ed!"

The Minister was safe behind his desk in his well-appointed office. He had always had an idea of what he wanted his home study to look like. He was a traditionalist in that manner. Deep, dark, manly wood surrounded him with several bookcases filled with biblical commentaries as well as several novels and autobiographical works. His library was quite impressive in terms of balance. One could find works as traditional as Ernest Hemingway and as contemporary as E. Lynn Harris. He had loved Hemmingway since he had read "The Pearl" in his 9th grade English class. He loved Hemmingway's direct approach to descriptive exposition. Cold nights were simply described by saying, "It was cold." There was no need for controlled comparative thought. It was simply the coldest night the reader could ever think of or remember from personal experience. It was nothing more, and nothing less.

The other course he loved was Geography, and his love for discovery and travel was also well represented. A myriad of framed photos and artifacts from India, Asia, Central Europe, the middle-East and Africa were strategically placed on the walls and in display cases. Not only were there religiously referenced pieces but also works of art that could be appreciated by any non-discriminating generalist who simply admired something appealing, and respected the creative efforts of the artist. He prided himself on his open-minded approach to life, and that was one of the many reasons he was such a sought after minister.

He was embraced by the masses because he focused on understanding them first and then offering them the Gospel. Unlike many of his contemporaries, he was not an unbending fundamentalist who forced his convictions and beliefs on anyone. He believed in the persuasive power of the Gospel, and felt it was imperative that he address the obvious needs of the people before offering them solutions for the souls. The Biblical story he often referenced was one in which Jesus miraculously fed 5,000 hungry people. In it, Jesus understood and serviced a very basic human need; hunger, before attempting to levy life-altering mandates of spiritual and moral behavior. "A sandwich before salvation is always helpful," was the way he sermonized the thought.

The church he pastored was growing by leaps and bounds. His impressive style of preaching and teaching was establishing a national reputation, thus increasing an already weighty travel schedule. Something else was also growing by leaps and bounds, an inner appetite that searched for satisfaction far beyond his weekly sermons and his struggle to satisfy that hunger often gnawed at the very fabric of his being.

Angela burst through the double doors of the office, interrupting his pen mid-sentence. She could do that. It was called the 'boundary-free privilege of a black, female spouse!'

"Ed, why did you send the kids back there? I was taking a bath. Don't I deserve a moment's peace? Come on." One hand was on her hip and the other massaged her towel wrapped head. She was right, and had not paused for a breath between sentences yet. Her role as functional hub of an active family was monumental and unending yet she handled things with such grace and style that one might mistakenly think her job was easy. The reality was that her job was becoming more and more difficult everyday.

The Minister abruptly placed his open palm over the paper on which he was writing as he lifted his head, looking over his reading glasses.

"Oh, I'm sorry, baby. What did you say?"

"What I said was, 'why did you send the kids back there?' Junior said he knocked on the door and you just told him to come back there to me."

Angela wasn't angry, just frustrated. She knew how engrossed her husband could get in his work, especially his writing. *But just what was he writing?* She was sure he had completed his sermon for this weeks church service, and though it was not unusual for him to write down a few last minute notes on Sunday morning, he was usually more "mentally available."

When he looked up at her, she could see something different in his eyes, and the fact that his right palm was conspicuously covering the document on his desk alerted her to the privacy of his composition. In all his brilliance and eloquence, the Minister had one of many common male imperfections, over-zealous-assumption. Like most men, he assumed that the woman he loved was unaware of his surreptitious behavior and covert improprieties. Over the years, Angela, like most women, had turned her back on numerous issues that probably should have been grounds for divorce or at least separation. Sometimes he knew that, other times he really just thought he had her fooled.

No longer waiting for a response, she rolled her eyes and eased out the door, closing it with a recognizable slam, clearly expressing her frustration. She could not help but fight the guttural feelings of inquisitive intuition trying to overtake her as she walked toward the kitchen. *What was he up to now?* She forced the thoughts to the back of her mind and pressed forward to the task at hand, the children.

As a mother and a former corporate executive, having sold her interest in the multi-million dollar Public Relations firm she partnered, she knew how to compartmentalize her emotions and focus on the immediate issue. There would be another time to deal with the Minister and his secret note writing. She thought about her grandmother who often said, "Don't worry baby, 'cause what's done in the dark will eventually come to the light." She would be patient for now, and wait for the sun to rise on the secret beneath her husband's hand.

CHAPTER 2

Reverend Doctor Edward Alan Hebert was quite a man. Charisma poured from his being like a mighty river. He stood just a hair below six feet, but his muscular build made him sometimes seem even larger than life. His eyes were deep, contemplative and complex, yet there was an uncanny innocence about him that drew people. He was not just approachable; he was magnetic. Uncommon softness and genuine gentleness balanced his strength.

Powerful broad shoulders led to well-developed biceps and forearms covered with a boldly masculine amount of hair, but his hands were soft and un-calloused. When shaking hands with his father-in-law for the first time nearly twenty years ago, Angela's dad commented on the softness of his hands, warning her that his soft hands meant that he was a stranger to hard work. The Minister worked hard with his head, not with his hands. And well beyond that, his hidden passions required subtle palms that delicately suggested his desire and a touch elusive enough to give rise to the recipients most private sensitivities.

He had come from a family of considerable means, yet he was a "self-made" man. He had decided who and what he would become and persevered toward his goal. An undergraduate degree in Communications, a graduate degree in Ministry and Religious Counseling, and a PhD in Psychology were all systematically completed. There was a consistent undercurrent of confidence that made him feel that there was nothing he could not do, no goal he could not attain, no challenge he could not face and ultimately conquer. Throughout his career, he welcomed those who sought to find ways to block his progress, as he would always find ways to overcome any obstacle. His congregation revered and prized him for this attribute, but there was an undeniable fragility in his spirit.

He often preached, as most contemporary preachers do, citing ideas and quotes from

St. Paul's New Testament epistles to the early churches of Rome, Ephesus, Philippi, Thessalonica, Corinth, and many others. While completing his doctoral dissertation the Minister had engaged and studied extensive research that sought to explain St. Paul's 'thorn in the flesh' concept of a nagging issue of particular sin or pain that would not go away. The essence of one of his sayings stated, '*when I would do good, evil is always present...*' It was interesting that in a dissertation that discussed the psychosis and paralysis of manic depression, he referenced such a popular biblical figure. But the Minister definitely had a locked closet in his mental house, one that he tried with capricious success to keep closed. And only one person knew the delicate imbalances and thorns beneath his flesh. Only one person saw the real weakness behind the strength and the lie behind the most honest brown eyes. Only one, of the many who loved him, knew the roughness of mind that resided beneath the soft curly locks that crowned his head. Only one person saw the child in the man, and the pain in the passion. And that one person was not his wife Angie.

> *He wrote: The pleasure of meeting you yesterday was mine. You are a song that just keeps playing over and over in my head, and judging by the dream I had last night I must play your tune again. I am now caught in the rhythm of your enchantment, and the beat goes on.*

He placed the note, written on ivory parchment, in the pages of his Bible, and leaning back in his Italian leather chair boasting a mischievous smile. *Let the games begin.* He thought of the excitement, the risk, and the triumph of placing another beautiful person into his palm. He took a brief moment to savor his thoughts, but little did the Minister know that this very well might be the last game he would ever play. Underestimating the grasp of personal passions can be terribly dangerous. He knew that. He understood that. He struggled with himself because of that, and as evil often prevailed in the wrestling matches of his mind, the comments of St. Paul slowly faded to black in the recessive alleys of his thoughts. *"When I would do good, evil is always present."*

CHAPTER 3

Ivy Page answered her phone on the first ring because she knew exactly who it was, and because she was just anal like that. Only one person would call before 8:00 a.m. on a Sunday morning. Only one person called at a moment's impulse without regard for time or convenience. As a matter of fact, an early Sunday morning was quite considerate on her part, as Ivy had lost count of the numerous pre-dawn calls she had received from her best friend in the world, Gemma.

They had met on the first day of their freshman year in college and become inseparable. A housing assignment error had brought them together and they would not be torn apart. Normally, the housing counselor placed students with the same or similar majors in dorm rooms together. The goal was to help ensure compatibility, in terms of home dwelling, but to also possibly create a situation where students could tag team and assist each other in managing the rigorous academic challenges of college life. But how this Theater Arts major, with nothing but Broadway on her mind and this Pre-Law student who was going to will her way to the Supreme Court wound up in the same bunk bed crammed dorm room is still an unsolved mystery.

They had no courses together, and on paper nothing in common, but what they shared was a common soul and a desire to be the best of the best. The bugs of aspiration, inspiration and dedication, had bitten them both, at very early ages. That and many other issues they discovered, many of them deeper than either of them would ever admit, had bonded them for life. Now they had grown up and although things were very different, there were still issues that remained the same. Though they lived more than two hours away from one another when Gemma was home, and had very separate lives, they were so much alike that one could often predict the others thoughts before they were verbalized.

Gemma's aggressive attitude and no-holes-barred spirit had coined her nickname, *Geronimo*. She was easily excited and did not always think things through completely before diving into a task. She was easily influenced by emotion and sometimes turned her head to facts, often engaging in a self-invented version of reality. Her first marriage was a prime example.

"What girl?" Ivy said rolling over without even opening her eyes.

"How'd you know it was me?"

Ivy could almost hear the smile on the other end of the line; an infectious smile that always made her smile, and then laugh until her sides ached.

"I knew it was you because it could only be you at this hour. You're the only one with no respect for my sleeping patterns. You never have." She yawned. "But I'm glad it's you *Geronimo*," she whispered with a smile of her own in full development. "What's going on, girl? Welcome home, I think."

"No, no, no girl! What's going on with you?" She retorted excitedly without even addressing Ivy's salute.

"What do you mean?" Ivy sat up now, her fluffy down comforter slipping just below her shapely breasts. Ivy was not sure but she had strong suspicions about Gemma's, "I'm gonna tell yo' Momma tone." Gemma had skipped the pleasantries and gotten right to the point.

"Well, I just happened to be downtown yesterday on 5th Avenue to be exact, and I saw something very interesting. Yes, I think I happened to walk right past *Tuscany a Roma*." She paused, waiting to see if Ivy was going to interject and come clean, but in her heart she knew that was not Ivy's style. She was a lawyer, and a very good one at that, and she knew how to secure pertinent information while maintaining a poker face that would stump even the most insistent inquisitor. So Gemma continued. "I looked in the window at just about 2:30 in the afternoon and I saw two people having quite an intimate lunch."

"Gemma please, lots of people go there for lunch. You know that. It's one of the hottest spots in the city, off the beaten path. And I guess you *are* back." She tried to subtly change the subject but Gemma was not budging.

"Yeah, but the two people I saw yesterday looked like they were having each other for lunch. I don't think they even knew what they had on their plates. And that, 'off the beaten path' comment was quite a Freudian slip counselor," Gemma jovially specified.

There was a moment of silence, like that just before Catholic confession. Gemma waited quietly, but her anticipating smile screamed loudly through the receiver. And then Ivy came clean.

"Girl, he is too much," Ivy said as she slipped out of bed and headed to her kitchen to start coffee. Her smile too, was now ear to ear as she shook her head and giggled, swaggering her way down the hall. "And what were you doing in the city yesterday? And why didn't you call me and tell me you were home?"

The two spoke to each other regularly despite Gemma's travel schedule, which often had her out of the country for weeks at a time. Ivy's caseload often consumed her as well but they kept up with each other's lives as if they were next-door neighbors. E-mail and cell phone text messaging seemingly had been invented especially for them, and over the passing years they had burned up the electronic airwaves trading stories worthy of the hottest tabloid scandal.

Gemma finally released the exuberant scream she held inside. It was a scream and laughter combination of the type that only *Geronimo* could produce. After they settled down, Gemma did not know where to begin with the questioning. She wanted details.

"Where, how, when, what?" Gemma's thoughts and questions were going a mile a minute, and her mouth was unable to keep up.

"One at a time, Gem. I—," Ivy tried to interject.

"Wait a minute Ivy; isn't he married?"

"Yes, he is married, and if you'd give me a moment, I might just tell you all about it! It's not what you think." Ivy tried to steady her excited friend, knowing full well that it was exactly what she thought.

"Okay, my best friend in life is having an intimate lunch with Donavan Davis, 'Triple D' as he is known in some," Gemma purposefully cleared her throat, "circuits, in one of the most romantic little hidden restaurants in town. When I look in the window, I see your eyes locked on his as if he held the answer to the deepest philosophical questions on earth, and you want me to slow down? Girl, what is up with that?"

The friends erupted into vivacious laughter, like twelve year old girls share at slumber parties making confessions about their secret crushes, and finding that their cohorts are in full agreement with their selections. But the slumber party girls were all grown up now, and lived in the very small world of African-American affluence, yet the same childhood cohorts might very well be in concert with the conversation.

Ivy knew that there was quite a bit to be told about her interaction with her lunch date, and there were depths to her interest that even she had yet to discover. She usually shared everything with her best friend and this time should be no different, but Donovan was a uniquely different specimen of manhood. There were complex layers of character that would slowly be discovered, so having only been introduced to the tip of the iceberg that would eventually consume her, Ivy would tell what she knew. And she liked what she knew.

Donavan "Triple D" Davis was one of the NFL's pride linebackers. With a towering frame standing 6 foot 4 inches dressed in 255 pounds of lean muscle, he moved on the field like molten lava forcefully spewed from an active volcano, systematically destroying everything in its path. He was quick, thoughtful and intuitive, but his talents were special beyond the field. This beautiful raw specimen of masculinity had graduated Magna Cum Laude from the Naval Academy, and successfully completed a two year assignment on a medical research vessel before entering the NFL draft. That might have been destructive for any other professional athlete's career but not this one. His skills had been pricelessly honed and the team that secured him knew that they had acquired a prize. He was a marketing and promotions dream, and all teams knew that in this era competition, business success or failure depended on much than franchise wins and losses.

Donovan had done everything right. After six successful seasons, his agent was currently in big money trade negotiations with the New York Giants. He was married to Lydia Lombard, a social butterfly in all the right clubs and who was regularly visible at all the right charity events. She spent her husband's money unquestionably well and probably could have won a Miss America pageant on her worst hair day. They were the perfect portrait: he, tall and chocolate and she, voluptuous and fair-skinned. Her Creole parents would have vehemently disapproved of her dark-skinned spouse, but his eight-figure salary and seven figure signing bonus that he generously shared with them seemed to squash even their generational prejudice.

Money has always been, and always will be, a means of both categorical separation of classes and the underwriter of prejudice. But it has also had the historically unique ability to bring together those things and people who might otherwise remain indomitably disconnected. Such was the case in the Davis' situation. A gap had been bridged that may have otherwise never been crossed.

The truth was that **Donavan** was quite impressive in several facets of his life. However, he **was not** nicknamed "Triple D" for his defensive

14

skills on the gridiron. He had a life outside the lines; a life known by only a select few, and admired probably, by even fewer. But as far as Ivy and the adoring, naïve public knew, he was perfect.

In typical "opening argument" fashion, Ivy began slowly. "Gemma, this whole thing is kinda crazy. I really wasn't looking for anything like this! I was at a charity event that the firm sent me to last Thursday night, bored as usual but going through the motions. You know, hobnob, hobnob, air-kiss, air-kiss. Finally I sit down to cut into the rubber Chicken Kiev and guess who the keynote speaker was?"

Geronimo jumped right in, "Donavan Davis."

"Donavan Davis," Ivy confirmed. "He was magnificent. I never knew any one man could be so knowledgeable but down to earth in his delivery. I knew he did a lot of endorsement ads and PSA's, and things like that, and I just figured he was the "chosen jock" of the day, but he was down-right captivating, and I was on the edge of my seat throughout his speech."

"What was he talking about?" Gemma quickly interjected.

"Hell, I don't know. I think I was on the edge of my seat because my panties were wet."

The two erupted in laughter and Gemma conferred her thoughts about how fine Donovan was.

"After the event, people were still milling around, brown-nosing and whatnot, and here comes Mr. Davis. He bought me a drink and we started talking. Before I knew it, it was 2 a.m. and we were making plans for lunch."

"Where was his darling little wife while all of this connecting was going on?" Gemma asked. "I hate her; she's so perfect," she echoed with a jovial coo.

"I saw her earlier in the evening but I think she left for another event just after his speech."

"And then he moved in for the kill, or was that you counselor?" Gemma said sarcastically.

"No it wasn't like that at all, Gem. I never felt like he was hitting on me and I definitely wasn't hitting on him. He was just a sophisticated man having a great conversation with the finest, most sophisticated female attorney in the building."

"I know you're right!" Gemma quickly retorted in a way that only she could, and the ladies again burst into laughter.

They were good for each other that way. They were two confident African-American women who supported each other completely and pumped one another with a plethora of compliments. Their friendship was both rare and necessary for the survival of self-esteem that was often challenged and battered in an often, unkind world. Their professions were subjectively ruled by a very narrow congress and though their skills made room for them, they both knew that there was an ever-existing knife that sought to cut away at their stations to make room for the newest and freshest rising star. So they sharpened themselves by securing esteem built foundations of confidence.

Gemma was definitely interested in the juicy details of the story, but there was a hint of worry in her heart. She knew that her friend Ivy could take care of herself and that she had had her share of flirtatious moments with married men, but nothing ever came of them, to her knowledge. Ivy believed in that *what goes around comes around karma* so she had made her feelings clearly known about the taboo of relationships with married men. But Gemma, Ivy's *Go for it alter ego*, could sense deeper possibilities with this guy. And the possibilities could be painful. Gemma admired her dear friend's strength, perseverance and independence, and she did not want to see any of those fine qualities sacrificed for the sake of blind romance. That was her character flaw, not Ivy's.

Ivy had seen her share of pain. Born to an unwed mother, she had been taken in by her, now deceased, aunt and uncle. They did not have much, but they gave her all they had, and that was a world more that most parents with the means were willing to share. Their wealth was not in substance but life lessons that would help navigate her course. They were lessons that were not simply taught, but lived thus becoming a well-woven thread in the very fabric of her being.

Henry Lee Ivy Page had instilled in his niece a pride motivated work ethic that was matchless, and there was a unique intensity about Ivy that gave her the ability to plow through adversity and overcome obstacles. He had helped her to digest and make functional the fact that she could do anything she set her mind to accomplish, and that she was special. She really was special, in ways that her uncle did not realize but her aunt did. Ivy had an uncanny way of causing people to fall in love with her.

She was definitely beautiful, and she knew it. So did everyone who encountered her. Ivy had made that discovery, like every other pretty girl, when she found that she could change a mind or opinion in her favor by a simple bat of her eyes and the hint of her smile. Aunt Cindy taught her how to use that gift to her advantage. "Use everything God gave you, baby. Everything. A man will give his last dollar to a pretty woman, just 'cause she's pretty, and if you just smile and say thank you, he won't feel slighted," her aunt once told her. Aunt Cindy was pretty too. It was more than that though. Ivy was more than a pretty face and a lean body.

Something glowed inside her like a flame that could not be quelled. It was a flame that could warm a cold heart, but burn an uninvited intruder.

CHAPTER 4

Ivy Page had learned how to use her attributes yet there were still depths of her essence she had yet to discover. She had learned to use some of Aunt Cindy's lessons early in life, and had greatly reaped the benefits. Her uncle of course, just like every father of a beautiful daughter, was the first victim of Ivy's intense eyes, and from there the list was endless. Countless men had fallen under her spell; boyfriends, professors, athletes, even ministers. Two things however, set her apart from most other beautiful women who know they are beautiful. She never abused the privilege of her looks and she was fearless to a point of default. Her uncle planted a seed of pride and self-worth that, over time had grown into a tree of confidence.

Uncle Henry had also taught her to confront and control her fear, and to defend herself, at all costs. Aunt Cindy always disapproved of the "unlady-like" lessons in self defense often saying, "Henry Lee Ivy," she called him by his full name when she was serious. "Don't you turn my princess into no brawlin' man!" But Henry reminded her that he didn't have a son so Ivy had to be his "man-girl." He was determined that his years of boxing and wrestling in the U.S. Navy would not go to waste. He was committed to impart every ounce of his knowledge to his pride and joy, and it would not turn her into a "brawlin' man." It would make her stronger. He and Aunt Cindy were extraordinary parents in that way, as they valued most what they could give, not what they could keep. So, often after Aunt "CC" had gone to bed, or at least after they thought she had gone to bed, Uncle Henry took his pretty little niece with the piercing, resolute gray eyes, fighter eyes, down to the basement for a few rounds of training. He promised her that one day the lessons would be valuable. That day came her senior year in college, when she nearly killed a man after a rape attempt. The strength she exhibited that night was unreal. Uncle Henry would have been proud, but Ivy never told him.

Ivy had been convinced by one of her long time friends to attend a party thrown by a few graduate frat brothers for one of them who had recently signed with a pro football team. They had chartered a yacht and were planning an over night harbor cruise. It sounded fun and with their budget, she was sure that the food would be good. What Ivy did not know was that she and a few other girls were going to be the entrée for the evening.

When she arrived at the marina she could hear the music blaring but she did not see the numbers of party guests one might expect for such an occasion. She asked her friend Yavonne where everyone was and if she was early. Yavonne told her that she was right on time, and that this was a special private party for just a few close friends of the frat guys. Ivy's intuitive antennae raised itself and a sense of discomfort overcame her. Her first thought was to walk back to her car, get in it and go home. But Yavonne convinced her that everything was fine and that she should be honored to have been included in the event. These guys were the right guys to know. It was almost guaranteed that they would be loaded one day, and it is always good to know financially influential people at the humble beginnings of their careers. She flattered her with statements about how highly thought of she was by the guys, even though she did not know any of them personally. But they knew her. They knew her very well, thanks to Yavonne who made it her business to be in everyone else's business.

Yavonne was the girl in every group of girlfriends who is not as pretty, not as smart, a little bit heavier, lies about her family and has an unrealistic view of self, has a mouth that never stops, and who lives vicariously through other people. Her claim to fame lies solely in association, so she constantly seeks to make alliances with those who she believes will make her more attractive. For her, it is never what you know; it's who you know. Meet Yavonne Gaines. She was a soldier at war with her own significance, and the evening's ensuing fiasco would be another lost battle.

When the yacht set sail, Ivy noticed that there were exactly eight passengers on board; four guys, four girls. Ivy knew only Yavonne. Yavonne knew all on board. As the night wore on, introductions were made, songs were played, dances were danced and the Dom Perignon flowed. And then with mysterious convenience, everyone was gone. When the music faded and the champagne stopped flowing, it became obvious that the evening's plans had not been fully disclosed.

There were four very private areas on the well-appointed yacht, each with sleeping arrangements, and the new member of the NFL had plans for the master suite. Ivy's antennae elevated again and suddenly she felt cornered, as it all came together. She was Yavonne's ticket to the party. She was the prize to be presented after several successful college seasons on the football field. She was part of the NFL welcome package, and that was why Yavonne knew everyone on board. She was the recruiter of the female entertainment for the night, and Ivy was the trophy presentation.

Ivy again scanned her surroundings and saw no one. It was amazing how a boat so relatively small, suddenly seemed like a huge ghost town. The romantic sound of the waves splashing against the side of the craft had lost its calming affect, now sounding more like the menacing rhythm of heavy footsteps in a deserted parking garage. They thumped against the hull echoing the cadence of Ivy's increasing heart rate. And then he came toward her, telling her how he had been watching her and how Yavonne had promised that she could get her to the party. Yavonne had scored big points with the guys this time, but her willingness to sacrifice her friend only reaffirmed her shallow character. Ivy smiled, all the while trying to plan her escape, but there was no escape as he grabbed her shoulders. The enormity of his palms netted her arms as well. She felt her breath escape as he placed his large mouth over hers and jammed his tongue so far down her throat that she nearly choked. She was determined not to cry as she mentally kicked herself for even dealing with Yavonne. She knew she should not have trusted her.

He wrestled her out of her top and his excited drunken state made him unaware of Ivy's resistance and lack of fear. He had done this to many women before her, most of them at an invitation they found difficult to refuse, and he would do it again. It was his right, after all. He was a star, and destined to be an even bigger star. Any woman should be honored to be in his company. Training for nights like this had begun in the neighborhood Pop Warner leagues years prior. This was a reciprocally appropriate reward for every yard he ever gained, and every rousing cheer he had ever evoked from the crowd. This was for the National Championship, dammit!

When he stood back, momentarily releasing her, to remove every stitch of his own clothing and reveal his muscular physique, Ivy knew that this was her only chance to make a move. His arrogance dictated that he disrobe first to offer his victim an uninhibited view of what many had underscored as physical perfection. He was an impressive physical specimen, with muscle seemingly stacked on muscle, like decorative frosting on a tiered cake. By looking at him, she knew that there was no chance of overpowering him and there was most definitely no place to run.

But she found consolation in the memory of Uncle Henry's words, "They may beat you, but you make sure they know they were in a fight." And that was exactly what she was going to do, stay and fight. She would not simply resign to defeat, knowing that the key to survival on this floating nightmare was going to be timing.

The star jock closed his eyes and stretched as if to say, "*Ready or not, here I come*," and it was at that very moment that Ivy balled her gnarly fist and struck him with all her might, dead in the throat. He could neither speak nor give chase. He immediately fell to his knees, both his hands wrapped around his throat. Ivy had learned from extra-curricular self-defense classes taken in high school that a swift blow to the throat could temporarily collapse the esophagus causing paralyzing pain, to which there could be no immediate defensive response. The theory had been accidentally confirmed in one of Ivy and Uncle Henry's sparring sessions in the basement. It had taken him several minutes to recover. The proof of the hypothesis was again confirmed as the giant brut struggled to breathe. For a moment, she stood still and fought off an oncoming grin, as she was surprised at her own precision and the dependability the tactic. It actually worked and luckily, she still had her wits about her for one very simple reason. She had not been drinking that night. Ivy hated champagne, especially Dom Perignon. Unlike her friend Yavonne, labels had never impressed her, and beyond that, it simply did not taste good to her. Alcohol, in general, had never really been her forte.

Then with one hand still clutching his throat, he ineffectively reached to grab at her but Ivy lunged for a knife she had seen on an elaborately decorated fruit tray. She grabbed it, and realizing again that there was nowhere to run, she grabbed him by his manhood and held on like there was no tomorrow. He was dumbfounded. She gripped him like a vice with her left hand and forced the blade of the knife at the base of his member with her right. He shivered in fear as she ordered him to his feet. It was quite a sight to see this *weak* little woman control the movements of a gargantuan man with the strength to crush her with his bare hands, but the scene illustrated a timeless truth. Any woman with a man's pride in her palm is a woman who calls the shots.

Ivy was in complete control of the situation because they both knew one very simple yet indisputable fact; an NFL career is worthless with no dick. In a still, quiet voice, she reminded him of that reality. Beads of nervous perspiration quickly formed on his brow, the type that might be seen on a man pleading for his life at the hands of a terrorist or ransom demanding kidnapper.

The commotion startled the disappearing guests and they magically reappeared. The frat brothers made no moves toward Ivy, at the request of the honoree. When he yelled, they halted in their tracks. They had never seen him cry before, but this evening they were privy to quite a display of tenderness, albeit induced by the cheese knife in his crotch. They did their bests to stifle their tongues, although one of them could not keep from blurting out, "Damn, this bitch is crazy!"

Ivy was not fazed by the sudden outburst. She was focused now and directed her attacker's naked body to the bridge of the ship where she instructed the lone crewmember to immediately turn the vessel around and head for the marina. Without a moment's hesitation, the ship's course was reversed. She kept both hands locked in place as they powered back to shore. When they docked, Ivy deafened herself to the frat brother's orders to release the new recruit. She would not. Even Yavonne approached her to attempt to reason, but the piercing look that she received backed her away and silenced her completely. The other female guests stared at her as if she was an escaped mental patient, but they said nothing. She led him down the dock, to the parking structure and right to her car. She ordered the chase group that followed to stand away. They complied. Now holding the knife and his manhood in one hand as if she were preparing to slice a carrot, she activated her car alarm remote to unlock her door, and then pulled him close. Looking past his eyes and into his soul, she whispered, "Never do this to any woman ever again." And with that, she released him, dropping the knife as he again dropped to his knees. Then she left.

She raced away with the accelerator pinned to the floor, and had a difficult time believing what she had just done. She could barely feel her hands. They had become nearly frozen with the vice-like grip of a locked deadbolt. Ivy was amazed at the power of the adrenaline that raced through her veins, but it soon wore off and a mental recount of every detail of the night fell on her like a ton of bricks. A lone tear traced its way down her soft cheek as the whole scene replayed over and over in her mind, and when she finally entered her studio apartment, she bolted her front door, ran straight to her bathroom and began to violently throw up. Even with a master of emotional control, nerves are bound to kick in, sooner or later. She carried this secret experience, and many others, in the private pocket of her heart, the pocket in which no hand was allowed to reach.

CHAPTER 5

Ivy was truly something else. She had a history of making sure that she was in control of almost every situation in her life but there were new circumstances and outside issues that made things more complicated now, and that's what worried Gemma. And that was Ivy's flaw. She did all she could to control every aspect her life to a fault, often cheating herself out of happiness because of her intense desire to do things "correctly." It was not a matter of self-righteousness, but more an issue of creating barriers of what she believed were layers of protective security. In reality, what appeared to be the ability to control life around her and keep intruders at bay was simply a concerted effort to protect herself from herself.

"So what are you going to do, girl?" Gemma asked, her smile now fading.

"Nothing." Ivy replied, "There's nothing to do, Gem. It's really not that big a deal." There was a brief moment of sarcastic silence before Ivy put on her best Southern drawl and added, "But he sho' is fine!"

The two, again erupted in laughter. These conversations were not unusual, as they had learned each other over the years. Gemma had retained almost every event of Ivy's life that she had witnessed, as Ivy did Gemma's. They used the memories to help find their way through the muck and fog of the present, as everyone does, or at least, as everyone should.

Gemma knew that Ivy's interaction with Donavon Davis was, in some way a prelude to peril. Somewhere deep within, Ivy knew it too, but she convinced herself that it was harmless and meaningless, and nothing had happened and nothing would happen, unless she wanted it to. Besides, he was "all that" and anyone who is "all that" has got to have an

Achilles heel somewhere and if push came to shove, the fearless, fright less Ivy would find that weakness and bring Mr. Davis to his knees. That notion was to remain afar off and could only be brought into focus as a result of some unforeseen desperation. For now, it was what it was: a well contained rendezvous that began simply as a chance meeting. It led to drinks and conversation, then lunch and conversation. Nothing more, nothing less.

"That's enough about that, *Geronimo*! What's on your agenda today?" Ivy changed the subject knowing full well that her mind was still very much on the congenial, Mr. Davis. Her experience in courtroom litigation often gave her the advantageous ability to steer conversations. But that was not often the case with a worthy foe like *Geronimo*. Today however, she would let it rest, at least for now.

"I'm going to church today," Gemma replied. "You know, when I'm in town I have to go back and get myself grounded again."

"Girl please, you know you go just to look at that fine young pastor they have over there. What's his name, Rev. Hebert? Your Grand-Mamma told me all about him."

"No, no, no," Gemma said, her infectious smile and chuckle again bleeding through the receiver. "I go to get that good Word from the Lawd!" she said with a sarcastic loss of composure. They were both laughing again.

"Yeah right!" Ivy matched the sarcastic comedy.

"Seriously Ivy, sometimes the traveling and the shows and the cities really get to me, and in this business the S-I-N is on a rampage. Even I get caught up a time or two and I need something to get my focus back in line. Luckily the show is going to be in town for a few weeks and I'm planning to be somewhat stable in the fellowship. Sometimes when I'm on the road, I would gladly trade my place in front of five thousand critics to be seated in my little old church surrounded by the people who I know love me just for being me."

"Amen to that, Gem," Ivy, concurred.

Gemma was right. Life as a premiere singer and dancer was tough to say the least, and she had definitely paid her dues. She had always known what she wanted growing up, and she had willingly shared her dream with others. When she was five years old, she stood before a packed sanctuary and sang her first solo. The crowd fell in love with her, and she fell in love with the feeling and the emotion that the crowd's response had generated inside her. She knew from that day forward that she wanted to savor and hold to that feeling for the rest of her life. She was not one of those prodigy children whose immediately focused mind led them to know exactly how to do what they wanted and attain the distant goal. Instead, she simply knew what she wanted to feel, and at every performance and in every aspect of her life, she reached for that feeling.

There are interesting facts of life that people seldom face. One of the most intriguing is the fact that all human effort is based on attaining rewarded feeling. When really thought about sincerely, money, sex power, accomplishment in business and education, climbing mountains, swimming across large bodies of water, and everything else that requires some semblance of effort beyond comfort are all catalysts to acquiring and maintaining certain feelings. Humans are simple creatures who often engage in very complex means to achieve very simple ends.

In the constant search to gain that feeling, Gemma Kimbro had made some, expected mistakes and made some unfortunate decisions. The most major being her marriage to a European Casanova she had met in Barcelona, Spain. The romantic courtship was a whirlwind fairytale. It was a story-book filled with barefoot walks through the Tuscan country-side to casually sipping Chianti in a Madrid hideaway after cheering the premiere matador after a championship bull fight. It was dinner at *Alla Vecchia Bettola* after an afternoon of fine art discovery and very public displays of affection at the *Galleria degli Uffizi* in Florence.

Alfonse seemed as though his funds were unlimited just as his love for Gemma, as they would romp through London and gratify their cravings for Gucci, Prada, Fendi and Armani at Harrods. After that, it was on to Manzi's for the best fish 'n' chips. Alfonse was postcard pretty, tall and tan. His teeth were a dentist's example of perfection. They were beyond the result of brushing and flossing; they were a genetic masterpiece. This attribute, of course, was an assumed product of genetic mastery, as Gemma never met his parents, another red flag to which she turned her head. She loved those teeth, especially when they glittered with his trademark smile as his head bounced to the rhythm of jazz at *Capolinea* in Milan. They lived fast and loved even faster, and made the world their playground. Nothing was off limits or out of reach. It was all theirs for the taking.

She had worked hard to convince herself that the fantasy she lived was real, and although intuition and logic often rang the doorbell of her psyche, she forced them to adhere to the "do not disturb" sign hanging on her often locked door of mental reality. For the moment it was real, but the fantasy came to a screeching, realistic halt one evening in Monaco's Grand Casino. One night, one bet, one loss, and then chaos. There were three things that Alfonse loved: Gemma's legs, Bellini's made with Dom Perignon of course, and high stakes roulette. The problem, as she soon found out, was their order. Gemma was not as high on the list as she thought. From horse racing in Singapore to camel rallies in Qatar to private crap games with Chinese gangsters in the red light district of Hong Kong, her quick-fix husband supported a well-fed passion.

The Grand Casino is a unique sight. Perched high on the cliffs of Monaco's harbor, it can be spotted from a mile out to sea. The heart skips a beat at the harbor's entrance, as crews, who work seemingly oblivious to the gawking onlookers, service yachts of inconceivable luxury and opulence. Designer boutiques line the winding road that leads to the impeccably manicured grounds where the mega-rich traverse en route to quaint espresso bars covered with red and white awnings. Upon reaching the entrance, one might be overwhelmed by the gigantic, gold-plated doors that serve as the guarded gateway to Mecca for the international world of big game players. The gaming rooms are notably quiet as Arabian monarchs, Prince's, oil-tycoons and Hollywood master moguls enter in silence, greeted by the outer security with a simple nod. Those backroom private areas in Vegas casinos reserved for the super elite jetsetters pale in comparison to the main floor in the Grand Casino of Monaco. All stakes are high stakes and players gambling with $1,000,000 chips are as common as eyeglasses. But in this casino, you had better believe that anyone willing to gamble with a million could afford to lose a thousand times that without blinking. Although his tan, clothing, jewelry and the woman on his arm placed him graciously among such company, Alfonse was not in that league. He secretly knew that, and he was one bet away from Gemma knowing that as well. He had been living a fairytale life, financed by foolishness.

When they sat down at the roulette table, it was all smiles and quiet moments with giggles between sips of complimentary champagne. Alfonse saw impressive wins by the two gentlemen who flanked him and that was all he needed to see, and with that, he placed one colossal chip on 35 black to win. The worst thing for a gambler is to be seated between two winners. Alfonse lost. Unaware that this placed him a million dollars deeper in debt with international loan sharks, Gemma continued to smile, laugh and run her fingers through his well groomed hair. They had whimsically blown hundreds of thousands of dollars on fantasies without a second thought. What should be different now? Of course she had historically turned her head to his activities from the inception of their relationship, and had never questioned his income sources. Besides, when she was working she was focused on her career and he had never asked her for a dime.

This loss was the end of the line for Alfonse. It did not seem like anything out of the ordinary to Gemma, however. She had seen him win and lose before, but she was unaware of the gravity of this particular failure. This was the venerable, straw that broke the camels back. He slowly got up, noticeably pulling himself from the grasp of his spouse and headed for the exit. Another gambler might have played another round in hopes of winning the money back, but when you lose a million dollars you never had and you are in debt with international hoods for another ten, you get up and leave, and you do not look back. Gemma got up and ran behind him, and facing him on the street, she saw that the smile she fell in love with was replaced by an empty expression of despair. The relationship went down hill from that day. Alfonse made no attempt to settle his debt himself, he began to search for beautiful people to settle it for him, beautiful women and men. Numerous affairs and an unending series of heartless rendezvous' followed, quickly leaving Gemma hurting and lonely. It was a rude awakening from fairytale to reality. Even the French Riviera had lost its ambience and ability to stir of the no holes barred romantic passion inside her.

She auditioned and was chosen for a role in the states and finally after a month into a Broadway production of *Aida*, she received a large package in the mail followed by a legal sized envelope. The package contained designer clothes, jewelry and personal effects, most of the items she had left in her London flat, the last address she had shared with her husband. The envelope contained a letter from Alfonse informing her that he was not only suing her for divorce, but also, five million dollars in lump sum alimony, stating that she had feverishly and thoughtlessly spent all of *his* inherited money. She was floored, and so was her bank account, as she stayed tied up in court for nearly two years fighting a man who sought to own her financial future. The lesson she learned was expensive and painful, and she would have probably gone insane had it not been for the tenacious fight that resided in her best friend's heart.

Ivy was determined not to allow her friend to be taken to the cleaners by her leech of an ex-husband, and her legal maneuvers were masterful. After Alfonse realized that he could not win, he finally just went away having his attorney send a letter indicating in very stoic legal terminology that he basically surrendered and was not interested in fighting any longer. Gemma and Ivy were not sure if he had really given in, or if he had simply found another victim to sweep from his or her feet and finance his fantasy life. They agreed that it was most likely the latter, but none-the-less, he was out of Gemma's life for good, thanks largely to Ivy's legal blockade. She was eternally grateful for her dear friend as they now used similar experiences of the past to help navigate the present and define a future.

Gemma's relationship with her church was special. Although she was rarely in regular attendance anymore, she considered it a consistent and unwavering lighthouse on which she could always depend. She shared that common vein with other stars whose careers were inaugurated in the local congregation, before embarking on the life journey search for stardom. The church would always be "home." She had practically been born into the "family of Faith" now pastored by the great nephew of the late Rev. Mark Anthony Hebert. Her grandmother's prayers were that she would stay near the church and never forget the lessons learned there. Gemma remembered the lessons but had often strayed quite far from their application in her decision-making. When Grandma would point out the fact that she was needlessly headed for error, the ever quick-witted Gemma, would retort with that Bible scripture that says "...all we like sheep have gone astray." The truly inherited spitfire tongue of her grandmother always was prepared with a topper like, "Yeah baby, but sheep is dumb; they ain't got no good sense. What you're doing is just plain stupid" or "Why go the long way 'round?"

Gemma's grandmother had invested greatly in her faith. As one of the charter members of the church, there was a long-standing rumor that she was more than just a supportive parishioner to old pastor Mark Anthony. But that was then. Old holy church folks have always been holy, or at least, they have been holy longer than the present generation, to which they are generous with corrective advice. Many people did not understand her undying support of the church and the pastor, but she contended that there were few things in life that would play such an active role in ones life as church and faith. She always said that a preacher would be the first and last person to probably visit you in earthly life, so it was important to take good care of God's man. "A preacher's gonna bless you comin' in and he's gonna bless you goin' out," was her historic quote.

"Ivy, you should come with me! You know you need a little Holy Ghost," Gemma darted.

"You know, I would love to but we have been tied down to this case and I've got to prepare briefs for a war meeting tonight and be ready for court Monday morning."

"I know you've had a lot going on. I understand. How 'bout some late dessert tonight? You know, to really build cellulite on your butt and a fat stomach, eating sweets and then going to sleep is the thing to do! It's part of my 'Build-a-Booty' program." The *Geronimo* sarcasm had again arrived just on time to stir up a chuckle.

"You're on. Call me when you get finished with the praise party. Where are you going to be, your Granny's?"

"You know I am. I'm so sick of wheat grass and Slim Fast, I don't know what to do. I need some greens and corn bread, some black eyed peas and smothered pork chops!" Her voice began rising and falling like the ebb and flow of a good 'ole southern preacher.

She was on stage again and continued her comically rhyming sermon on fatty foods, ending with, "Grease at last, grease at last, thank God, Almighty I'll have grease at last!" She yelled into the receiver as if she were closing Dr. Martin Luther King, Jr.'s, 'I Have A Dream' speech. Gemma was a constant performer and she couldn't help it. Ivy loved it. She could take the darkest situation and suddenly turn it into the most remarkable episode of hilarity.

"Well girl, save me some peach cobbler, with your crazy self!" Ivy struggled to get the words out; she was laughing so hard.

"Okay Sweetie, I'll see you later," she paused, "and hey Ivy *'League'*, I love you."

"I love you too, *Geronimo*," Ivy replied, singing the 'O' as if she were fading away in a cavernous fall. They hung up, both unaware that this was probably the last conversation they would enjoy.

Gemma giggled to herself as she trotted to her bathroom for a quick shower. She would choose what to wear after she finished. Several years as a stage performer made her a master of putting together a well appreciated outfit in a short period of time. She had learned from the wardrobe and make-up professionals just how to add the perfect touch, and they had learned from Gemma how a star should wear her beauty. Her loveliness was undeniable and went far beyond physicality. She was the essence of beauty and her presence and personality had drawing power. When she was on stage, her voice filled a concert hall from front to back with attention commanding authority, and her ability never faded. Once starring in an off-Broadway production of *Chicago*, she was lead vocalist on twenty-four show tunes and her voice never faltered nor did her legs waver, as she sang and danced in almost every scene. She was an experienced professional, respected, loved and in some circles adored. But with all of her beauty and talent, she was still, a most insecure and vulnerable person. She was prey for a prowling predator.

Gemma got out of the shower and wrapped herself in a towel. While bathing, she had mentally assembled her clothing ensemble for the day, perfectly tasteful, and something that her Granny would not make too many comments about. Since childhood, Gemma had developed quite shapely legs. All of the dance and ballet classes had given her two long and shapely assets that had head turning effects on both men and women. The problem her Granny had with all of that was Gemma's love of showing those legs, even in church. There had been a constant battle of wills when it came to skirt length. Granny won inside the house, but Gemma made adjustments when she left the house. Instead of pulling things down, Gemma was often guilty of pulling things up. These days, Granny was so happy to see her when she came home that it did not matter what clothes she was wearing as long as she wore that Tony award-winning smile.

A black Prada dress cut comfortably above the knee with a "made-to-match" shoulder wrap, closed toe mules by Dolce & Gabbana that she picked up during her last visit to Venice, and platinum accessories were the choices for Sunday service. She was by no means over dressed, as the Calvary Baptist Church was becoming the Mecca for the young and affluent religious folk, or at least those who dressed the part. No breakfast for Gemma. She had worked hard on maintaining her perfect size four, and a major contribution to that actuality was an assortment of vitamins and supplements taken every morning in place of breakfast. At times that ritual was even followed in replacement of lunch and dinner.

After her eyes were lined and her lips were filled in, she was heading out the door. The phone began to ring and she momentarily stopped to answer it but decided to go ahead allowing her answering machine to pick up the call. She promised her Granny that she would pick her up this morning and being late was out of the question when it came to Miss Hattie Lee Ross.

CHAPTER 6

Reverend Hebert entered his church office after quickly greeting his secretary. Pushing the door closed behind him, he hoped that she knew not to bother him as he sat at his desk with his eyes closed. If someone did barge in they would probably suspect that he was praying or meditating, or possibly even focusing on the sermon that he would soon preach. Briefly opening his eyes, he made a phone call to which there was no answer. He was re-entering an all too familiar fight with himself, a fight that would challenge all he held dear. Under his right palm rested the note that he had prepared earlier that morning, and he wrestled with the thought of placing it in the hand of the object of his infatuation.

About a week ago, he and Angela had attended a Broadway production of *Chicago* featuring one of the most talented congregants he had really never truly met as an adult, Ms. Gemma Kimbro. They were aware of her success in the off-Broadway production and were excited to now see the star on such a prestigious stage. She was captivatingly magnificent and arrangements had been made for a backstage introduction. It was great all around, as a weekend in Manhattan was a much needed respite and a welcomed opportunity to meet the grand daughter of one of the long time members of the church. Furthermore, on a public relations note, celebrities are usually guilty givers. For some reason, they seem to feel that large donations are, in some way, atonement for their participation in life's unwholesome episodes.

The show was wonderful. As a lover of live music, he appreciated the orchestra and thought the conductor was simply phenomenal. When the final curtain fell, he and Angie were all smiles and cheers. The Minister was not prepared for what he saw back stage though. He met a woman with the most spirited and communicative eyes, eyes that made him blush and smile involuntarily. She was a ball of fire and it was the spark that he felt when he offered her his hand and she hugged him instead, that stirred something inside him. She was dangerous for him but like any man, only he could seal his fate.

Angie recognized it as well, but she was patient and was not going to douse a fire that was not yet burning. She was an intuitive woman who new her man very well. Angie saw the dance in Gemma's eyes when she looked at the Minister. That was normal. She knew how captivating he could be, but she also saw his eyes when he looked at her. Few people could draw such a reaction from him, and Ms. Gemma Kimbro had struck a chord that even fewer people knew existed.

The Minister sat at his desk trying more not to think than actually concentrating on what may be, but his mind's eye could not get the image out of his head, and then his door flew open.

"Shelby, what is it?" The Minister could not halt an oncoming smile. Shelby was the only one who could barge in and interrupt her father without any semblance of reprimand. She could charm the pants off the guards at the entrance of Fort Knox and they would gladly give her the gold inside. Although not needed in this instance, her skills were yet impressive.

"Hi, Dad," she said, plopping down in one of his office chairs, manipulating a mouth full of bubble gum. Everyone fought a losing battle with Shelby when it came to vying for the Minister's attention, and she knew that well. Like most fathers' daughters, she knew at five years old that she could wrap her father around her finger, make him turn back-flips for her and have him eating out of the palm of her hand. Angie knew that too, and she often used her little angel to break through her husband's distance when she could not. Shelby wasted no time and headed for the giant candy dish on her father's over-sized desk.

"Wait a minute young lady," he said. "You already have a big league pitcher's mouth full of bubble gum, and you want to get in Daddy's candy jar? Girl, your teeth are going to fall out of your head and your mother's going to blame it all on me."

"What's a big league pitcher?" She asked as if he were speaking a foreign language in which she had no interest. Then without even saying a word, she reached into the dish, grabbing a hand full of goodies and froze. With one hand still in the dish, she turned her face toward her father and placed her eyes on his heart with a well-rehearsed portrait pose that said, "Please Daddy, just this once; I love you."

"Alright, go on Baby, and give some to your brother."

She skipped out of his office without looking back, knowing from the moment she entered that he would concede to her request. The brief interruption momentarily broke his concentration, and that was a good thing. It is interesting how the smallest factors of correction can often realign focus. It was just another example of God's subtle way of encouraging righteousness in an otherwise corrupt mind. Even men of the cloth struggle between devilment and divinity at times.

The Minister, once again, pushed his door shut, but this time he walked to the window, closed his eyes and prayed. The time was right for praying. He prayed for focus and for those infirmed persons that he could remember, and for strength to deliver his sermon. He prayed for deliverance from the demon that sought to dissolve his focus. Although it may have seemed cliché or generic, he was sincere in his spiritual petition. He then completed his prayer by whispering a familiar scripture, *"Let the words of my mouth and the meditation of my heart be acceptable in Thy sight, O Lord my strength and my redeemer."* What he probably should have prayed about was the consuming situation that would soon have him flailing in the depths of his own deception. But in his mind, he wanted no help or spiritual intervention with that one. It would be handled his way.

He tried to prepare himself for the coming influx of people who felt they needed to see their pastor before service. There would be the common weekly reports that people found necessary to share with him; from births to deaths, from complaints about the church heating system to viewing their children's report cards. Some would be as outlandish as questions concerning the lack of a sign language interpreter during the service, when there was not one deaf person in the congregation, while others would be as simple as requests to do his dry cleaning and shine his shoes. He would field them all.

Angela was first to enter, and after spreading her usual rays of complimentary sunshine with the Minister's secretary, she walked into his inner office. The "sunshine" was essential overkill. As unthreatening as his secretary might be, it was still important that Angie spray a little territorial pee as a reminder of established dominance and possession. Men do it by trying to physically eliminate the competition in hopes that they will run away and never return, as seen on National Geographic or some other nature themed show. Women, on the other hand, choose to keep the competition close and under a watchful eye, like the CIA or some other intelligence gathering organization. If necessary, they will pounce on the situation with the information like the H-bomb on Hiroshima, completely annihilating the adversary for good. Her precautionary intuition was well founded, as India, the Minister's secretary, had kindled a low flame of obvious jealousy for years.

When the Minister was in the office or at the church, India felt that he belonged to her, as she made all who inquired clearly understand that they had to go through her to get to him. Additionally, she made discretionary decisions as to the value of the issue presented. But she could not deny giving the "First Lady" of Calvary Baptist Church the well-earned respect she deserved, and though Angie was aware of her subtly camouflaged feelings, she always made India feel good about herself. Perfectly designed surveillance camouflaged as "sunshine." She complimented her on what a fabulous job she did taking care of her husband, jokingly whispering that she depended on India to keep him in line. It almost made her feel guilty about the many times she had dreamed of sexing him in the choir room. *Did Angie know? Of course she knew.* Women know women, because they *are* women. Angela Hebert was a patient realist however, and though her husband was often a rat, he preached a universal Truth in which she believed.

The vicious circle of life offers its own reward, and when the time is right, truth invariably rises, clearly exposed for the entire world to see. Besides, when it was all said and done, the Minister fawned over his wife lavishly, and though some of it was fueled by guilt, Angie had learned to love every fur, every diamond, every expensive vacation, and every new car and complete access to all his accounts without question. And beyond that, she knew that he really loved her, and she would never love another, at least not like she loved the Minister.

Looking frightfully gorgeous, Angela entered the inner office with a special friend.

"Good morning, handsome!" she said as she lit up the room with her special flair and unforgettable smile.

As the Minister turned from the window, he faced two exquisitely attractive women, and an unrelenting, unrehearsed smile overcame his countenance.

"Ed, I'd like you to meet one of the newest members of the Links, Lydia Davis. She's married to line-backer extraordinaire, Donavan Davis." Angie grinned at Lydia who blushed modestly. *How could anyone not know who she was?* She had begun sharing the commercial endorsement spotlight with her husband, and her face was becoming almost as recognizable as his.

"Wonderful!" He carefully extended both hands to greet her. He had always been the most charming gentleman, always careful and respectful. He had seen the local papers and knew that there was some talk about Donavan Davis' free agent status and possible signing with the Giants.

"Lydia and Donavan are interested in settling down and I told her that she needed to come to the church and meet some good 'ole local, loving folks. And I'm sure you want to try to corral Donavan into the boys mentoring program; he'd be a great role model," Angela advertised.

There was no better PR professional than Angie. It did not matter what the business was, she was the ultimate spokesperson for the product. She had helped to make the church the new center for young urban professionals who were interested in some semblance of a spiritual life between corporate mergers and hostile takeovers. She was better than any hired agency could ever be, and she was quite the advertising tool, herself. Angie was not bashful when it came to approaching people and sharing a word about the church. She believed in her husband and his ministry, and was pleased when people found their way to the church and stayed. In some way, it validated her efforts.

"Yes, yes, yes," the Minister said rubbing his chin as he sat on the edge of his desk. "It's a pleasure to have you Lydia, and I look forward to meeting your husband when his schedule allows. Feel free to call my office anytime if you have any questions about anything concerning the church or community, or whatever. Angie will take good care of you; just make sure you two stay out of those malls and shopping centers." He flashed a jovial grin toward his blushing wife as they all chuckled.

"Well, thank you Reverend. It looks like we might be here a while with Don's new contract. We've both had enough of the "city-hopping" lifestyle and we're ready to put some roots in the ground somewhere. Your wife is a jewel and it's been a pleasure meeting you. I'm looking forward to the service." Lydia smiled a relaxed but confident smile. He liked that, and she liked his warmth.

"Call me Ed; the formalities are done," he said, gently touching her shoulder. "We try to be real people around here."

"Okay honey we'll see you a little later. Do you need me to get you anything before we go inside?" Angela took exemplary care of her husband. She also watched his eyes carefully and could see that it was time for her to interrupt his gaze.

"No, no baby. I'm fine; I'll see you guys inside."

As the ladies exited, the Minister noticed the well-manicured feet and lower legs of them both and shook his head. He loved the well taken care of look: soft hands and feet were a sure sign that a woman took time to be beautiful. But these two were not the corner shop manicure and pedicure patrons; they had the means to be ultimately pampered and were willing to pay top dollar for luxurious treatments. They were the women that men looked at longingly, and other women envied, and their men wanted them that way. Quite plainly, no man wants a woman who is not wanted by other men, and if other women desire her as well, her sex appeal is confirmed, case closed and victory sealed.

There were many who came to visit the Minister, as expected. A time of concentration and meditation would have to be forced and guarded, as the steady stream of concerned and inquisitive members continued to flow. The last visitor to the Minister's office was Miss Hattie Lee Ross. Dressed conservatively in a blue suit probably purchased at JC Penney or the like, her small matching hat sat cocked just enough to the side to give it that "church lady" look. There was always a rhythm and skip in Miss Hattie Lee's step. Maybe it was because she had been a member of the church usher board since Jesus himself had been passed a worship service program or offered a fan with some funeral home advertisement on the back. She was not merely a common "church lady." Every family has at least one of those. She might more appropriately be called a "church-worker lady," as she had been involved in several functional aspects of the church since it had been organized, and had probably changed the diapers, rocked to sleep, wiped the noses, tied the shoes, and quietly given hard candy in loud crinkly paper to half of the adult congregation.

Ms. Hattie had also taught them all the seriousness of a committed life and the value of prayer. She would often say, "Baby, every problem that I had, I prayed about it, and God fixed it; so whatever is goin' on in y'life, pray about it, 'cause God still answers prayer."

There was well-earned and deep respect for her within the congregation, and she enjoyed that attention. She had been as dependable as the sunrise in terms of her contribution to the life of the church because she truly believed that one day it would pay off, and deep within the recessed corners of her heart, she thought it just was right.

Ms. Hattie also believed that she had instilled that transcendental faith that she exemplified before the other youngsters, into her star grandchild, Gemma, who had veered off the path of "righteousness" more than a few times but always seemed to find a redemptive thread to navigate her way back to the church. For Ms. Hattie, that helped ratify her faith and conviction.

Prophetic and grandmotherly intuition had also led her to feel that little Edward Hebert would grow into someone special, although she never imagined that he would one day be her pastor. She had seen him over time growing from boyhood to adolescence, as he would often visit his uncle's church when his father allowed, which was rare. She would have loved for him and Gemma to get together as youngsters but it was not to be. Fate adheres to its own timeline. She was still very proud of her granddaughter and wanted to make the Minister aware of her talent and accomplishments. No matter how old or mature one feels they have become, a church going mother or grandmother will always boast to the pastor about great accomplishments, or request his prayers for a change from foolish ways. Either way, the pastor will be made aware of the activities of the children and grandchildren of his parishioners. *It's "Big Mama's" duty to see to that fact.*

"Ms. Hattie, how are you this morning? You look absolutely wonderful. Is that a new dress?" He greeted her with his arms wide open looking her up and down, and she could not conceal her blush.

"Good mornin' Pastor, and hush up all that fibbin'," she said chuckling.

"No, I'm serious Ms. Hattie, you did something different today. You got it together. What is it a new dress, or a new hat?"

"A new hat," she said quietly as she adjusted it slightly.

"I knew it was something! Oh, it's workin', Ms. Hattie; it's workin'!" He smiled that flattering smile that little old ladies love to see. "Now what can I do for you this morning, and by the way, Angie and I want to thank you so much for those theater tickets. We had a wonderful time and Gemma was fantastic!"

"Good, good," she said, "that's why I came by your office. I just wanted to make sure that y'all went and had a good time. Did you get a chance to go backstage and holla at her?"

"Oh yes ma'am. She's a charming jewel and I know you're very proud," the Minister said with a sincere sound. "Did she drive you in, this morning?"

"Oh yes, I think she's outside talking and socializing and going on. You know how it is with her being gone so long and everything. I guess she's tryin' to catch up on some of the things she's missed out on. You want me to go get her for you?" she asked eagerly.

"No, no, I'm sure I'll speak to her before the day is over. Thank you again Ms. Hattie for the tickets and we had a wonderful time. I'm sure my wife will thank you again when she sees you. Now I don't mean to rush you but I need to get myself together for service," he said apologetically as he ushered her out of his office.

That was true. He did have to close out the world of visitors and their requests in order to prepare for the imminent service, but he also could not evade an oncoming rush of excitement that he would prefer to enjoy alone. Miss Hattie Lee quickly obliged him and exited the office.

Another of Miss Hattie Lee's most exigent character traits was that she was unequivocally the biggest pastoral supporter in the congregation, and the Minister knew that. She had never worked a day in her life but her deceased husband made sure that their bank accounts were full while he was alive, and when he passed away, his multiple insurance policies placed her net wealth well into the seven figure range, and she shared that very generously with her church and especially with her pastor. She always had, and she had no plans to stop. Every pastor needed to have a member like Miss Hattie Lee in his congregation. She would almost unconditionally support the Minister, come hell or high water, and though she was quite unaware, the creek was rapidly beginning to rise.

The Minister was glad to know that Gemma was somewhere in the building, as her presence added tangible dimension to his fantasy. He glanced over at his desk, walked back, picked up the note he had penned earlier that morning and put it into the pocket of his suit coat. There would be time very soon for him to remove it and place it the hand of the one for whom it was intended. He had remarkable patience, for a man.

CHAPTER 7

On this Sunday morning, both the traditions and the stereotypes of Calvary Baptist Church were alive and well. It was time to testify, and people sprouted up all over the building telling stories of how they had been delivered from insurmountable circumstances and problems from which they could see no escape.

The testimonials ranged from tales of how God steered a vehicle out of the way of a deadly accident, to checks coming in the mail just in the knick of time, thereby preventing disconnection of utilities. Of course, these stories were supported by rousing applause and waving handkerchiefs. One lady even told a tale of how her uncle had a stroke, a heart attack, a seizure, and had fallen into a Snicker's candy bar induced diabetic coma while driving his car, which rolled and fell off a freeway overpass into a drainage ditch, and then floated three miles downstream before crashing to a halt against the base of an electrical power pole which sheered the car in half. Of course the uncle survived with no more than a scratch because he had his Bible in the backseat of the car. Sister Walker was known for drinking heavily at times, and sometimes her bizarre stories were an indication that the effects of the bargain basement bourbon from the night before had not yet worn off.

The deacons stood before a packed audience, clad in dark suits and dated ties, telling the congregation how good "Gawd" had been to them. The common catch phrase was, "He's been better to me than I been to m'self" and with that said, the old sister's rocked from side to side shouting "Amen!" and "Hallelujah!" and "Say it sir!" and "Pray on!" They sat with their arms folded atop bosoms that resembled extra large goose down pillows severely stuffed into pillow cases too small to handle the load. They hummed and moaned, fulfilling their stereotypical roles.

The normal church factions were all well represented, including the hat brigade, which was most notable, as usual. Hats that resembled a 7th grader's science project replication of the solar system; hats that must have left some wild bird freezing and featherless; hats that challenged the architectural design of the Empire State Building; hats that appeared to have wings and were designed to fly away whisking the person to safety in the event of an emergency; hat's that would probably float and surely came with a set of paddles or an outboard motor; hats with more flowers than a bridal bouquet; hats that appeared to be so hard and heavy that they must have provided earthquake protection and probably lit up in the dark; tall hat's, short hats, wide hats and thin hat's were all present and accounted for, especially in terms of their ability to block the view of the unfortunate parishioner seated behind them. If a person was intent on seeing the events that went on at the front of the church, they needed to arrive early enough to not be trapped behind the visual confines of the hat brigade.

The deacons led songs without the benefit of tempo or tonality, but the congregants brought the music to a roar with clapping hands and stomping feet, easily catching on to the recognizable lyrics and in time, taking control of the familiar tunes. It was not difficult, as the same songs had been sung for the last fifty years. They were generational, testimonial and powerful. And then that old deacon, the one with the big glasses and the thick tie, who had halted his fashion progress in about 1975 but still believed he was in style, the one who had a Bible in one hand and a rolled up church program in the other, fell to one knee and prayed his quotable and poetic prayer...

"Ouvah Fathah and ouvah Gawd, Fathah of Abraham, Isaac and Jacob,
Lawd, we come to ya the onliest way we know how,
We come as disobedient chirrun to a merciful parent,
We come because we have no other Gawd to go to,
Lawd, we come, first of all, to say thank ya,
Thank ya for last nights lying and down and this mo'nin's rising up,
We thank you oh Gawd that the bed we laid in was not ouvah coolin' bode and the sheets we slept in was not ouvah winding sheets,
We thank you because ouvah eyes were not sown shut and ouvah tongue glued to the roof of ouvah mouth,
We thank you because you let ouvah moment roll on a little while longer, and you just been so good,
Lawd ya been better to me than I been to m'self, and I wanna say thank you!"

By this point in his prayer, the stereotypical and patriarchal Deacon Earl Clovis had developed rhythmic inflection to his phraseology, and the other deacons who kneeled along side him chimed in behind him in the empty spaces of his speech, adding melody to his euphonic petition.

"Lawd, you been a mighty, mighty good Gawd, yes you have,
Thank ya for your mercy and your grace, oh Lawd,
Thank ya for your kindness and your love, thank you Fathah,
Bless the sick and the shut in, oh Lawd
Bless those that don't know you in the pardon of their sins,
'Hep 'em to understand, my Fathah, that if they confess with their mouth and believe in their heart that thou art the Son of Gawd, they will be saved, oh Lawd,
Bless ouvah pastor and first Lady,
'Hep him, as he tries to do your will, oh Lawd
Bless the deacon bode, the ushers and the choir, thank you Mastuh,
Bless every family represented in this church today,
Bless this church as a whole, thank ya Lawd,
Now Lawd! Now Lawd!
When we've done all that we can do down here on this earth, and we can study war no more,
When we've prayed ouvah last prayer and sung ouvah last song,
When ouvah eyes have been shut for the last time, never look on this side of glory no mo'
Please, oh Gawd, we wanna hear you say, "Well done, good and faithful servant; you've been faithful over a few things; come on up higher and I'll make you ruler over many."
Now Lawd! Now Lawd!
Now Lawd! Now Lawd!
Just give us a place in your Kingdom where we can praise your name fo' ever and ever,
These blessings we ask in Jesus' name,

> *Amen"*

A song broke out immediately following the prayer, and the communal emotions were stirred to a boil. There were those who worked themselves into such a frenzied state that their behavior beckoned the immediate attention of the ladies sporting full nurse's uniforms with hats and capes, armed only with fans, tissues and Dixie cups full of water for comfort. Fans, tissues and water are universally recognized medical protocol in Black church for those who become ill with over whelming cascades of emotion during the service. It is also appropriate medicine for those who just need some attention and had probably planned the scene they would make, the night before.

This portion of the service was usually done with no instrumental music nor the assistance of the choir, as they had not yet entered. They were still in the choir room warming up, making final adjustments to their robes and working themselves into their own emotional frenzy under the leadership of their flamboyant director, Crawford, whose name in another life was "Centipede." *No exclusive discussion at this point as that name and life warrant another novel all together.*

CHAPTER 8

The self-named, Moncell Crawford was quite a piece of work. As the devotional period neared its close, Crawford, adorned in black velvet pants, a ruffled tuxedo shirt buttoned to the neck, and a multi-colored sequined blazer, led the band into the sanctuary. He could not help but be conspicuous, as planned. The musicians settled into their respective instruments, and then Crawford blazed up the organ, picking up the last tune that the congregation sang under the deacon's musical leadership. It took things to a whole different level. As he writhed, rocked and contorted his body to the beat, his fingers danced across the keys with amazing dexterity and the crowd again went wild. The ladies in nurse's uniforms with the matching hats and capes, along with the assistance of several ushers, found multiple calls for their back-rubbing, eye-glass removal, and fanning services. And the Dixie cups filled with water and covered with napkins were not far behind.

Crawford could make a Hammond B-3 organ sweat under his command, and he knew the songs to play to cast a spell over the audience. Even the young "Buppies" or Black Urban Professionals, who were sophisticated in their worship and interested in empowerment and wealth stood to their feet and yelled, as if they were attending a sporting event and their team just scored when Crawford made the organ talk. They almost forgot about his openly gay life style that had caused his alleged contracting of the A.I.D.S. virus and his numerous brushes with death. And though he had denounced his active participation in the lifestyle, swearing that he had been "healed, delivered" and "set free," before the congregation of, so called, "saints", there were still those who secretly knew him as Centipede. His body had ridden a medical roller coaster and his recently rapid weight loss had been a billboard to his critics and those skeptics who just knew he was on his way out. But to others, his life was a testimony just like those heard earlier in the service, and he had the right to be healed by the same God who helped them avoid the deadly car accident and keep the utility bills paid.

Regardless of personal opinion, good or bad or otherwise, his gift was astounding, and when he and the other members of the band converged on the church, a praise party was on the way. The lethal balance between gift and vice is a most interesting phenomenon. The most uniquely talented have, historically, always been the most tempted or challenged. Moncell Crawford was textbook, and despite his confessions before the congregation, his prayers and his meditation, his counseling sessions with his pastor, and advice from his dying secret lover, his homosexuality was like crack to an addict, like alcohol to an alcoholic, and unfortunately, sometimes like milk to a starving child.

As the mass of choir members sashayed two by two with rhythmic strides down the center aisle, Crawford ordered the balance of those still seated in the audience to their feet. Most of them were already standing, swaying with a matching in-place strut. He led them all in songs of praise and from time to time he had to get off the organ to walk to the center of the church and engage in his own "praise strut." The band maintained the festive rhythm while Crawford did his holy dance before the congregation. He called it "holy" but any good 'ole southern, church grandma would have simply called it the "huck-a-buck" and said it belonged more in a juke joint than a church. Good or bad, it was exciting, and added a welcomed dimension of animation to the service.

Crawford was a figure of paradoxical melancholy. Many viewed his life as one of sadness and despair, wondering how he could be happy having been confined and stereotyped by his unclaimed illness and lifestyle. Others applauded him for the freedom he appeared to have and the confidence he seemed to enjoy by not living a life conformed by outside opinion. Although forgiveness, kindness, and understanding are often elusive in religious settings, he seemed to have found a place where he was not openly criticized and made to feel uncomfortable. In his heart however, Crawford knew that his talent was the only tangible expression that saved him from the convicting darts of the fundamentalists within the zealously religious mob, the crowd within the crowd. He also knew that the Minister stood as a buffer between him and the critics, often heading off the cruel comments before they reached him. Those often came from the "saved on Sunday" crowd amongst whom his behavior, lifestyle, clothing choices, and alliances were very much the topic of discussion behind closed doors. But Crawford could be depended upon to be what many could not, and that was simply being himself.

In a world of having to constantly analyze personal motive and angle, there was no need for assumption when it came to Moncell Crawford. He was who he was, and though judgmental onlookers may not have agreed, they could not help but respect his talent, and sympathetically appreciate the brutal honesty of his identity. He was loved and despised, often within the same heart. And then there were those simply predicted and awaited his end. It would come, but not yet.

The Minister had not yet entered. He listened in his chambers with a few of his associate ministers who would soon walk out with him. This had been his ritual since he had come to the church. He enjoyed listening to the, sometimes questionably spiritual, escapades at play outside the walls of his office. But his real reason for remaining behind closed doors during the early portions of the worship service was to build intrigue and excitement about his "fore-warning-less" entrance. Many speculated that he was still finalizing sermon points, or praying, or giving last minute instructions to his assistants. None of these were true. He was simply waiting for the right time in the service to enter. Just as Crawford's entrance took the flock to a new level of exhilaration, the Minister waited patiently for the appropriate time in the service when his appearance would further propel the crowd to an even higher plateau of frenzied excitement. He was a charismatic performer and he knew how to milk a crowd for all they were worth.

When the time had come, he signaled his cohorts with a simple nod and they gathered themselves up in neat arrangement around their leader. Their distracting entrance resulted in the planned effect without hesitation, as the crowd stood to their feet with an interruption of rousing applause. They filed in, surrounding him as if they were secret service agents protecting a high-level government official. He had entered during the announcement period, a rather mundane portion of the service, and instead of parishioners listening to the scheduled events for the upcoming weeks, their attention was suddenly focused on the ruckus caused by the Minister and his entourage being seated in the pulpit area. It was an effective plan as it often bridged a gap in the service and signaled to an expectant crowd that something was about to happen.

The clergy group came in and was seated in the peripheral pulpit chairs, but the center chair, hand-made of carved cedar and upholstered in crushed purple velvet, would stay vacant for a moment, as the Minister knelt on one knee in front of his chair and offered a quick and conspicuous prayer. Although he was sincere, it looked textbook cliché, and the old-school parishioners loved to see it. They loved textbook material, and he knew it. Adding himself to the picture was the Minister's assistant, Brown. He stood over him while he prayed, doing his best to look needed and important. But despite his efforts to draw attention to himself, all eyes and thoughts were on the man kneeling in prayer at the center chair of the pulpit. Ed Hebert was everything the congregants wanted him to be. He was their chosen one.

CHAPTER 9

There is an unparalleled concept of mystical love, admiration, respect and loyalty that surround the African-American preacher, especially around one who holds the pastoral position. They are historic figures whose presence has, in some way, impacted almost every aspect of life, and they are uniquely embraced. Although most are good men, many have lied, cheated, stolen, defamed, and just been plain weasels, and yet they are forgiven and taken back by the fold. Many cannot, and probably never will understand the unquestioned support and loyal protection of this man; this "God-man" to whom many would give their last dollar or even go hungry trying to feed. Those who envy his position, but fear his association, to both God and man, surround him and within the circumference of that circle, there is a freedom with which he operates. He knows that the people to whom he preaches are often like subjects to a loyal king. Most love unconditionally and those who do not are subject to having their voices silenced by the throng of supporters.

The Minister was careful in his kingdom. He knew of the loyalty and confidence offered to him by the membership, but he was also aware of the fragility of those who were fanatically faithful. He normally made every effort to steer clear of their often misguided affections. He had learned his lesson with one he still could not excommunicate, but the reality was that he really did not want to give up his addiction to readily available pleasure.

Preaching time was imminent and after Crawford stirred up the choir with one last soul rousing number, the Minister stepped forward to the podium. With his associates standing behind him, prematurely shouting "Amen!" and "Preach pastor!" he slowly scanned the audience appearing that he was so overwhelmed with the Spirit that he could not speak. This elicited additional shouts and calls from the audience as well. His brief display of vocal impotence was treated like confirmation of his spiritual connection with God. He appeared to have just stepped off the pages of GQ magazine in his black Hugo Boss suit, and finally without a Bible or any semblance of notes or manuscript, he began to recite scripture.

The Minister's preparation and ability as an orator was beyond impressive. Words to him were like handfuls of clay to a sculpture, color and texture to an artist, or free-floating notes to a jazz musician. In the moments to come, he would create a masterpiece of intelligent prose with passion that would have parishioners begging for more.

"Recently I read a very interesting article in Time Magazine about a gentleman by the name of Heinz Prechter," he said looking into the balcony seating.

"The article was in the obituary section of the magazine where they list, with a picture and brief biographical information, famous persons who died on the date that the copy was placed in news stands. The name 'Heinz Prechter' really didn't mean anything to me until I read what he was famous for and how he died. It was then that we are all very familiar with both."

The crowd listened intently, waiting anxiously for the Minister to bring relevance to the reference, as they knew he would. It was just another useful tool that he used to create intrigue and capture the interest of his listening audience. He almost never began a sermon the same way twice, and they loved that about him. The room was relatively silent as the old and the young, the rich and the poor, the simple and the complex, inclined their ears to the Minister's message.

"My brother's and sister's, Mr. Prechter is credited with the development and manufacturing of the first convertible automobile," he revealed, "and after what he had done to his own automobile caught the attention of car companies, they began to approach him for his design expertise. Soon his idea had grown into a business, and that business grew into a functional company, and that company which had gone from cognition to fruition was yielding financial fruits beyond description. You might say that, by way of his invention, Heinz Prechter hit the jackpot, and had it all!"

He paused to allow for the various responses from the crowd before continuing. It was also at this juncture that he took a moment to do an intensive visual scan of the audience. He liked what he saw, and he was not always looking at faces. There were other things in the pews that engaged his interest. He pressed on.

"My friends, Heinz Prechter committed suicide," he exclaimed, which evoked a gasp from the audience.

"He suffered such terrible bouts with depression that, one day, he decided to end his life. The business and the money did not matter. The home and the family did not matter. The means to do whatever he wanted whenever he wanted did not matter. The ability to engage in financial transactions at a moments notice without worry did not matter. One might wonder how this person with so much could feel so compelled to exit this life by choice. Heinz Prechter had scored great victories in business and finance but he lacked the essential benefit of a life sown together and held complete by the daily victories we all must have; victories that keep the soul buoyant; victories that keep us from throwing in the towel; victories that help us overcome crisis; victories that help us make it."

The volume of his delivery was steadily rising, bringing light to his point as he raced to his topic for the Sunday morning sermon.

"And that's what I want to talk to you about, today; 'Daily Victory in Jesus!'"

An appropriate and expected response filled the sanctuary. Even the aged and polished beams that stood as sentinels of tradition between the stained glass story-picture windows seemed to delight in his exposition. The crowd began to applaud again, looking forward to what the Minister was going to share. Angie smiled when she heard his topic, as she could see the development, study and research in his delivery. She glanced at her new friend, Lydia, in an attempt to catch the breeze of her opinion, and she saw that opinion very clearly in her eyes. Angie smiled slightly, dismissed what her intuitional radar had detected, and returned her attention to her husband; her Minister.

"I am not standing before you today offering my personal opinions on solving your problems with proof positive formulas and theories. I am not a gray-haired granddaddy who has lived life to the fullest and can guide you successfully around life's obstacles en route to a utopian existence. I cannot predict your next dilemma in hopes of steering you out of harms way. I wish I could, but I can't."

A plethora of "Amen's" and waving hands were heard and seen in the audience, especially from Miss Hattie Lee, who sat with her granddaughter. Gemma listened and looked intensely as the Minister continued. In her mind, she momentarily re-visited their brief backstage encounter, closing her eyes to study the memory of his chiseled face. There was a torment hidden within the smoothness of his brow that, for some reason, attracted her. The free-spirited side of her conscience was whispering as he continued his intriguing sermon, and she struggled to realign her focus on the spiritual attributes of his discourse and not her sexually suggestive thoughts of how fine he was. Soon, she resigned to the latter.

"I am a husband, a father, a man and above all, a child of God just like you, trying to make the right decisions and appropriate choices while treading the water of real life. My successes and failures are a constant ebb and flow of the tide of truth. And the truth is that we all must struggle in a daily battle that is absent of knives and guns and other sophisticated weaponry. The battlefield of life is in the mind and heart, and the fighting soldier is the soul! Saint Paul, in his letter to the new believers at the church of ancient Ephesus, said that 'we wrestle not against flesh and blood but against principalities, against powers, against the rulers of darkness of this world, against spiritual wickedness in high places.'"

Seemingly dismissing the reality of how applicable the scriptural quote was to his own life, he began to move about the pulpit area appearing to develop an essence of rhythm in his delivery, drawing an even more vocal response from the crowd. His delivery was poetic. Angie sat with a constant smile on her face; proud of her husband admiring her tasteful choices in clothing he wore. Lydia sat next to her seeming to be pleasantly surprised at the Minister's sermon and its easy application to some issues with which she was currently dealing. He had her undivided attention and she was poised to hear more. She noticed the glances and nods from those around her who recognized an unfamiliar guest of the Minister's wife, but her focus was on the man behind the acrylic podium.

"Our fight, my dear friends, is painfully internal but the evidence of the battle is clearly external!" The crowd responded appropriately, as church folks do.

"We push and pull, seeming to go no where but to fall into a pit of depression and spiritual poverty.

"I've found that the most important educational degrees are not those earned after four years of intellectual study at the most prestigious universities, and then after that, more study. Don't get me wrong, my friends; I have nothing against being educated or going to school, but I'm talking about a daily victory that can't be achieved from just any book."

The congregation applauded as many of them anxiously anticipated the next lyric of his sermon. He scanned the audience making eye contact with several people without really looking at them. He was a professional at this and they it.

"Oh yes, we're dealing with a different monster these days, and simply making it to tomorrow is a major accomplishment." As he continued, his voice began to take on qualities of a song: cadence, tone rhythm..

"Got up and went to work today, didn't kill anyone on the expressway, and no one killed me; degree awarded. I dealt with the abnormally normal stresses of a job that really doesn't fulfill my potential right now, but keeps food on my table so my family doesn't go hungry; degree awarded. On my way home from that job, I didn't retaliate at the person who cut me off and blew their horn at me as if I had done something wrong; degree awarded. Didn't throw in the towel and break down in tears when I opened my mail at home to find pink notices and " account over due" letters waiting for me; degree awarded. When my wife is too tired to cook, and I comment on how good the microwave dinner is and I say, 'we should have this more often'; degree awarded. Degree rescinded when she recognizes my sarcasm and says, '*you* will.'"

The crowd cheered and applauded, as they vocally agreed. As the Minister continued, he again scanned the audience to see who was watching him. Everyone was looking at him, but there were a few specific people who were watching his every move, and listening keenly to every word he said.

He moved gracefully about the pulpit area, continually adjusting his gestures. At times he carelessly placed his left hand in the pocket of his blazer, sometimes both hands in the pockets of his trousers, sometimes he grabbed the edges of the podium as if he was so moved by what he was saying that he had to hold on to a stable anchor. He was impressive even amongst preachers. His staff of associates, who were really more like opportunistic hyenas, tried their level best to mentally impound the Minister's style and movements. They would then present themselves in his persona to a distant congregation who would hopefully be impressed enough to adopt one of them as their own. Their most common fault was that they never went far enough away to establish themselves outside the Minister's recognizable reputation, and because of the richness of his delivery and the versatility of his style, they had to stay close, as students under the teachings of a great philosopher.

"Life is most definitely filled with victories and defeats," the Minister continued, "and I guess the successful person is the one who, not only recognizes this fact, but is able to manipulate the system in his or her favor by balancing the scales every now and then. Oh, yes, we often think that we're balancing the scales of economic hardship every time we play the state lottery or engage the one arm bandit's of Las Vegas or Atlantic City. But I want to talk to you, my brother's and sister's, about a continual victory; a real victory; a lasting victory; a complete victory;

an unwavering victory; an unending victory; a refreshing victory; a daily victory! I want to bring forward to you today, the fact that there is victory in Jesus Christ!"

The Minister's hands were raised high above his head and the excitement in his eyes was hypnotic. His conviction was energizing and charismatic, and movements about the pulpit were physical exclamation points to his speech. He walked, shook and contorted his face as if the faith within him was an explosive inferno on the verge of volcanic release.

The crowd went wild, standing and shouting, waving handkerchiefs and fans. Crawford snaked his way over to the organ, which seemed to excite the congregants even more. It was time to "have some church" in here. The Minister felt his element and the ensuing point in his sermon at which even he was becoming invigorated and excited. He and Crawford began a rhetorical ballet that was masterfully balanced, as every phrase the Minister uttered was now elegantly qualified by Crawford's hands at the organ. In some church circuits, it is called "whooping," and it takes the vocal skills of the most talented opera singer to be done correctly. The Minister had skills. Even the young, spiritually intellectual crowd who might have otherwise looked down on this historical aspect of Black preaching, absolutely loved to hear the Minister "whoop." Had he been an old-school

R & B singer like Teddy Pendergrass in a concert setting, singing a love song, instead of a preacher behind the pulpit, panties would have been seen flying through the air, en route to the stage. The line between "saved" and secular was thinner than many realized, as urges to participate in a lingerie launch were on more than a few minds of the female parishioners.

He continued with an in-depth biblical analysis of human defeat and triumph through Christian principals. His Biblical examples supported by real life experiences gave stellar illumination to his points, and drew people into a more logical and functional understanding of faith. He was not only a preacher; he was a well-trained psychologist who knew what to say to motivate people to action, and it was that power of suggestion and direction that would help orchestrate the moves of those around him sometimes without them having full cognition of their actions.

Ed Hebert was like a cartoon super-hero, whose power could be used to fight the evil that constantly threatened to shadow the free world. But unfortunately, he was a human being, vulnerable to common temptation, which jeopardized his super-human strength, and his "kryptonite" was not a green rock like the type that drained Superman of his might, nor was it like the many foes of Batman; not the Joker, the Riddler, the Penguin, or

Mr. Freeze. His weakness sat before him, and to his right, about six rows from the front, next to a feisty little old lady with a royal blue pocket book and a common church hat resting sassily on her head. His "kryptonite" wore a black Prada dress cut comfortably above the knee with a "made-to-match" shoulder wrap, closed toe mules by Dolce & Gabbana that she picked up during her last visit to Venice, and platinum accessories, all perfectly tasteful, perfect for Sunday service, and perfect to drain a "Super-preacher-man" of his power. The difference in this case, was that a unique shroud of passion and power had befallen the beautiful Ms. Gemma Kimbro, making her an adversary to them both. She did not want to want him, but she just could not help herself.

The Minister continued his sermon, moving swiftly toward an unannounced close, and when he got the crowd to its feet, screaming and jumping, he brought his eloquent discourse to an abrupt halt. This rehearsed move incited an excited frenzy in the congregation, and that was the goal. Always leave them wanting more. The worst thing in the world that a preacher could do was preach too much or too long. The same laws of supply and demand apply to fickle church folks and other religious fanatics. Too much truth at one time might become cancerous to a career in spiritual leadership, especially in an African-American Baptist church setting. But the Minister knew people very well and he used all he knew to his advantage.

Continuing with a display that sometimes seemed theatrical, the Minister fell into his pulpit chair, spent after the exhaling, of what appeared to be, all his energies. Immediately, his associates rushed to him, shaking his hands, rubbing his back and congratulating him on what an amazing job he had done. They unfastened the top button of his shirt and loosened the grip of his Versace tie, as if they were preparing to give him CPR, and handed him water in a crystal goblet. They fawned over him like he was royalty, and in the minds and hearts of some, maybe he was. He sat still for a moment, simply collecting himself. He was not ill or even hurting, just tired, and that would only last a little while. He even had a lovely woman dressed in a nurse's uniform to come into the pulpit area to check on him and deliver more water and a fresh handkerchief. She was his personal attendant and sat just outside the pulpit area each Sunday to do exactly what she did. Soon his energy would be restored, and his mind would be allowed to move to more interesting thoughts.

They all fawned and flattered him, except for one, Brown, who went straightaway to the podium upon the Minister's seating, having an agenda all his own. While the crowd was still in their joyous and frenzied state, Brown tore into a solo, sporting theatrics of his own. He squalled and screeched, sometimes standing on one leg and nearly swallowing the microphone. He had a faction within the congregation that supported his hi-jinks and he fed them with foolishness in an attempted camouflage operation, hoping to sway the entire crowd in his favor. It would never happen. There was too much love for the Minister in this room. Even Crawford, who normally made the organ talk when any soloist took center stage, kept his music down to a careless whisper while Brown was singing. His ploy was that obvious, and that common in the arena of church politics. Surely Jesus himself had to deal with a few jealous and over zealous disciples every now and then. But he never had to worry as his identity was always secured and qualified by his matchless abilities. Brown was in no way a threat. He was probably more trustworthy than he wanted to be, but un-erasable circumstances dictated his loyalty.

The Minister scanned the audience now with penetrating eyes, viewing the reactionary group. He chuckled lightly at Brown's efforts and paid little attention to his fruitless fishing. This was the Minister's crowd and he knew it. He looked away from Brown and allowed his gaze to rest on one. She smiled radiantly with an experienced innocence in her eyes. They were eyes that had good intentions but could easily fall in caution-less love. They were eyes that he would look into and see something he had planned since the evening he had seen her on stage in Manhattan. What he did not realize was that there were eyes on him; new eyes. This pair of eyes had not planned to find him as interesting and compelling as he was. They stared with intrigue and longing, seeking understanding and comfort and counseling. Eyes that would try to put him out of her mind in that other way, because these eyes had an image to uphold and a reputation that needed security. These new eyes would look away and close tightly attempting to pressure seal her mind and sterilize unhealthy thoughts. Her efforts were successful, for now.

The service came to a close and a familiar feeling of anxiety overcame the Minister as he was quickly ushered to his chambers to change clothes. He would not greet his parishioners in sweaty apparel, even if it was "designer" and could have placed him on the cover of a male fashion magazine. His congregation deserved to see their pastor at his best, and while he changed, this Sunday, he was planning, thinking, fantasizing. He grappled with the pain that attacks between right and wrong, and becoming his own patient if nothing more , might offer therapy to his conscience, quieting its warnings, confirming the fact that evil is a choice. It was time for a dismissal of righteousness, and the irony of his preaching would soon rest on his actions.

He quickly changed, exited his office and there she was. Being greeted by a small crowd who was happy to see her back, and briefly catch up on old times, she stood graceful and captivating. They would make room for him when he walked toward her, and allow him a moment to say, "*Welcome.*" He was the Minister, and the Red Sea of people would surely part to let him through. They did not. The ocean of people swallowed him up with their own greetings and accolades, and he was not able to get to her physically, but he managed to catch her eye. Between all of the questions and comments with which he dealt, he was able to mouth the words, 'Can I see you before you leave?' His grin was that of a Cheshire cat when she mouthed, 'Of course,' matter-of-factly.

This was that ever-exciting and fascinating moment in gender play that has existed since the fig leaf era of Adam and Eve. Here was the moment in time when men and women play dumb and only allude to their attractions knowing full well the depth of their desires and vividly dream of the fruition of their fantasy.

The Minister calmly turned his attention to the throng of members and guests before him. There was no need to worry now. He would have his chance to speak his mind, or at least offer a scripted thought that might tease her interest. But he had already done that, whether he knew it or not. She had been attracted but respectful, and besides, she was rarely ever there. It was easy to dismiss lustful feelings when the object was 10,000 miles away, in a different time zone, and different place. As he turned to walk back into his chambers to gather himself and meet his family, Gemma took the chance to watch what all women love to watch, a real man's walk.

CHAPTER 10

True confidence is carried in the shoulders and can be seen best when a man walks away. A real man does not need the army order, "chest out, stomach in, and shoulders back." Pride and confidence makes it simply happen, naturally. There was power in the Minister's gait and a rhythm in his step that called her name. And when he squatted to accept the hug of the little girl in light blue ruffled dress, lacy bobby socks and shiny shoes, she caught a glimpse of his rear end. It seemed to be just the way she liked it; firm and strong. She tried to arrest such thoughts. *Why was she thinking this way? What was wrong with her? This was not a man who should be thought of in such manner. This was a man of the cloth.*

Gemma questioned herself about a matter even though it had not yet developed, but that was also who she was. When her head was turned away from reality and sensibility, it was completely turned away, but when she questioned herself, or her motivations, she often went overboard. Maybe she would discuss it with her friend, Ivy later in the evening. Maybe she would not. Maybe she would just leave and not come back until she had properly placed whatever was going on inside her head. And that was what she had decided to do until her grandmother emerged from the crowd.

"Baby, did you get to go over and talk to the Pastor?" Miss Hattie said smiling from ear to ear. She had just caught up on a few tidbits of gossip herself, after a covert conversation with her best friend and head usher, Elnora Stubbfield.

"No, no Granny, I saw him and we spoke over the crowd. Are you ready to go? You know Ivy's coming by and I wanted to go and—"

"Nonsense. Come on here, girl!" Before Gemma could finish her statement, her grandmother had grabbed her by the arm and began plowing her way through the crowd toward the Minister's chambers. She was determined to have him see her star child face to face, a meeting that he was looking forward to, and now Gemma was not. They made their way to the outer office where India greeted them.

"Hey Miss Hattie!" Her smile was bright and genuine, and her hands full of papers of some sort. With the Minister's busy schedule, there was always something for her to do, which often including eavesdropping.

"Hey baby, is Pastor inside?"

"Sure, go right on in. He'd be happy to see you."

There he was, with his back to them, buttoning a fresh shirt as he looked out the window. Gemma felt a familiar weakness in her knees, but dismissed it like a good girl. Brown was in the office too, looking like an out-of-place fixture that belonged in another room.

"Hey Pastor, look whose here!" Miss Hattie said grinning from ear to ear. She was rightfully proud of her star child.

"Well hello there; how are you?" The Minister spoke with a slight rasp. A result of preaching that made his voice soft and seductive.

Gemma smiled coyly extending her hand, "Good to see you again Reverend." She was a great actress, but Gemma's curiosity and attraction bled through her generic greeting. To the average naïve onlooker, there was nothing recognizable, but the Minister was neither naïve nor average, and he easily detected the sparkle in her eye.

"And it's good to see you; very good. I was telling your grandmother how much we enjoyed your show and all. You were simply magnificent. Lady, you are in a league of your own. Simply magnificent."

As he spoke, he looked through her, in a way that only he could. His gaze was a penetrating survey that did not make her feel uncomfortable at all. She felt appreciated. It was strange, and not what Gemma expected. She had briefly over-reacted but planned to secure the myriad of feelings that now seemed venerably misappropriated. He was a master of kindness and sincerity and his eyes seemed to caress her rather than undress her.

"Well Ms. Kimbro, welcome back. Will you be in town a while?" he asked as Brown helped him put his coat on.

"Call me Gemma, Pastor, and no I won't be here too long but while I'm here I wanted to make sure I came and saw you, I mean came to church. I'll be leaving for Chicago in a couple days." She could not believe she had made such an embarrassing slip. But the Minister appreciated the Freudian faux pas. It spoke volumes in terms of what he needed to hear, but he acted as if he had heard nothing but what she meant to say. Gemma covertly motioned to her granny that she was ready to leave and the message was received.

"Well Pastor I just wanted to stop by and make sure I said hello and you got to see my baby girl before she left town again," said a smiling Miss Hattie as she made her way toward the door. Her interruption was a necessary quelling of the heat that was rising.

"Oh yes ma'am, I'm glad you stopped by and brought Gemma to see me. I didn't even know she was sitting out there in the audience this morning. Had I known, I would have had her stand up and share a few words with us," he said with his hand on Miss Hattie's left shoulder. He knew she was there. He had a most difficult time concentrating on anything *but* her being there. And then he turned to Gemma, looked into her eyes without a blink and took her right hand in his.

"And it was very good to see you again Gemma. My wife and I loved your show. You were absolutely awesome, and whenever you're performing, anywhere, please let me know because I would love to keep up with the career of one of my most talented members."

She smiled as he smiled, and as he spoke and squeezed her hand, Gemma could feel that he was transferring something from his hand to hers. Everyone else in the room was oblivious to the transaction. Miss Hattie Lee was simply glowing with the naïve radiance that proud grandmother's exhibit, and Brown was gawking at the beauty that was before him.

He was insignificant because his behavior was expected and ordinary. Exceptional women never pay attention to common men, because they do common things, like stare and wink and gawk and whistle. Brown was common.

There are moments in time that present themselves for human beings to display nobility and righteousness. The opportunities are fleeting and rare but always obvious and clear. As Gemma and the Minister released their grip, she could have immediately opened the note, read it aloud and put a stop to whatever sinful possibilities were imminently present. Instead she quickly placed the note into an easily accessible compartment on the outside of her purse, and retained her gratuitous smile. Brown *did* see that, and he would sort through the meaning of what he saw some other time. But he would say nothing. Not now; not ever.

The Minister viewed the move as compliance and acceptance of his advance. Few people had ever rejected him, and Gemma Kimbro would not be the first, if he could help it. He turned away after brief good byes and Brown caught his eyes. Their unspoken communication was brief but clear. 'Mine, mine, mine.'

Again the unwritten laws that dictate deceit and the opportunity for redemption thrust forward. Just as Gemma and Miss Hattie were leaving the Minister's office, Angie and her new friend Lydia were approaching.

Angie had been showing Lydia the facility and the final stop was the Minister's office.

"Well, hey there ladies," Angie greeted with her stellar smile. Gemma was caught off guard and appeared to be just a bit startled. Any other time she would not have been, but this time she had something in the side compartment of her purse that cast a little shadow on her nerves. She and Miss Hattie responded appropriately to the First Lady's niceties and the introduction of Lydia Davis, who immediately sized Gemma up with a quick look from head to toe.

Angie reiterated her husband's sentiment about how much they had enjoyed Gemma's show and their gratitude to Miss Hattie for giving them the tickets. Hugs, hand-shakes and farewells were shared all around as Angie and Lydia moved into the office. "You were really good, today, honey," Angie said as they walked inside.

"Yes, I really enjoyed the whole service," Lydia said.

"Well thank you ladies. Lydia you sound surprised. Were you expecting something other than what you saw?"

"No, no, I don't mean it like that," she paused, "well I guess I do mean it like that. It's been a long time since I've really enjoyed a service like this, and it feels good. You're really down to earth and understandable. I can see why the church is growing like it is."

"Well, I try to talk about the things that help people make it from day to day. You know there is still a life to live after you've been saved. That life can be tough, especially without a strong and workable faith."

He was always prepared with the right answer, and he would really make sure that this one heard and understood well. She was an unexpected treat.

"I appreciate your compliments, but I owe a lot of the success of this church to this lady right here." He moved over to Angie and placed his arms around his blushing wife. "Her support is unreal and I couldn't be what I am without her." Again Lydia found this man impressive: good-looking, spiritually committed, and complimentary to his wife. What more could any woman ask for?

As he released his wrap around is wife, the Minister introduced his associate, Brown who was then quickly ushered out of the office.

"Are you ready, sweetheart?" Angie asked.

"Oh yeah, I'm ready. Where are the kid's?" he responded as he grabbed his briefcase.

"I told Junior to get his sister and meet us at the car."

"Okay, you all go on down to the car. I'll meet you there in just a second. Lydia it was my pleasure meeting you and I hope you'll come back and bring that husband of yours with you." He gripped her hand with a unique strength and softness as he spoke. She liked the way that felt, and she would most definitely return.

Lydia reciprocated the smile he shared and exited the office. As the ladies walked down the hallway, Lydia stopped momentarily and returned to the Minister's office.

"Reverend?"

"Ed," he interjected.

"Ed," she blushed, "if you don't mind, I'd like to give you a call to talk about some things that are going on at home."

The Minister could see the difficulty that she had in making the statement and was genuinely concerned. It had obviously taken quite a bit of courage to release whatever she had been holding back, and her visit to church that day was more than coincidental. Maybe she had shared some things with Angie, maybe not.

"Of course. You're welcome to call me any time. I'd be more than happy to speak to you." There was a long list of parishioners, and friends and family members of parishioners for that matter, who had appointments to speak to the Minister about various personal issues, but Lydia Davis was now at the top of the list. He would field her call immediately, whenever it came.

"Everything okay?" Angie asked as Lydia rejoined her.

"I think so. I'm going to set an appointment to talk to your husband."

"Good, I'm sure he can help."

Angie knew that Lydia had troubling issues but she had not pried. She recognized that Lydia had been drawn to her, for some reason, and was okay with that because she really liked her too. They had so much in common that it felt like they were very old friends instead of relatively new acquaintances. Lydia had alluded to some issues in her personal life that needed attention, but had not appeared to be quite ready to open up. She had excitedly accepted the invitation to attend church, which Angie viewed as a step in the right direction.

The Minister took a brief moment to sit behind his desk just before leaving the office. He smiled to himself realizing that he had placed a well camouflaged invitation to pleasure in the hand of a new beauty and received a request for counseling from another. What next? With his eyes closed he imagined things that he knew he should not, but his actively creative mind was always in search of fantasy, sometimes to escape boredom, other times to combat complacency. It was not always his desire to fantasize and think of things in such ways, but he just could not help himself. Realistically, he needed therapy or counseling himself, but that would be frowned upon and seen as a sign of weakness or inadequacy in his eyes. *'Physician heal thyself'* was the standard by which he chose to live. He was everyone else's counselor and problem solver. They came to him for solutions to the most private issues plaguing their lives. He was the Minister, for God's sakes, and he should be able to manage his own demons. But the battle was constant and unending. Just as he was moving into a new realm of illusion, the door swung open, startling him.

"Angie's waiting for you, Pastor."

"Thank you, India. Thank you very much." His tone was a bit annoyed as he was not pleased with his nosy secretary's intrusion. He quickly gathered himself and walked out of the office. As he scurried down the hall, India yelled to him.

"Will you be needing me tomorrow?" She stuck her head out of the office. He could see the smirk on her face with the eyes in back of his head.

"No," he replied without looking back.

CHAPTER 11

Most pastors take Monday off, after a long hard day of soul saving. Normally the Minister would get up early before Angie and the kids, and make himself a pot of New Orleans French Market coffee and chicory which tasted even better with bit of cinnamon sprinkled in the coffee filter. When the kids made it to the kitchen he would scramble some of his famous rice and eggs for their breakfast, and help pack backpacks and sign things that all children need to have signed in the mornings. They loved his eggs. With any rice that may have been left from Sunday dinner, the Minister would make a stir-fry masterpiece. Placing it in a heavy miniature wok, he would add bits of onion, garlic and chicken breast pieces. Then raw eggs were scrambled separately and eventually added to the hot pan. The ingredients were briskly tossed and stirred over high heat, and a little soy sauce was added. The dish was always a hit, and the children loved to see their Dad in action. Shelby loved it especially, as the Minister always made it a theatrical production, tossing the ingredients of the wok high into the air, adding commentary in a hilarious voice, as if he were doing a televised cooking show.

When the children finished eating, gathered their things and Angie had finished the "hair war" with Shelby and helped Ed, Jr. find his other shoe that never seemed to be on his other foot, the Minister would salute the troops from the doorway as they marched off to the morning carpool. After she dropped the children off at school, Angie usually returned home for a power walk through the neighborhood with her husband, almost invariably ending up at a local soul food restaurant for breakfast. She would, some how, find something relatively healthy as she was determined to maintain her youthful figure, and she was greatly successful. Few women, after two children, two difficult births at that, had the drive and commitment to redevelop and maintain a body like hers. Following the last swallow of OJ, they would walk home, bathe together and almost always make love under the warm waterfall of the multi-jet shower. She would then dress and leave for shopping or meetings, or PR consulting, which she still did occasionally. He would return to his coffee and newspaper before getting lost in the comfort of their Italian leather sofa in the den.

Angie gave him Monday's to do what he pleased, to rest and relax in whatever level of solitude he desired. The routine had been the same for a long time now, with a few subtle changes along the way, but basic consistency was always reliable. This Monday, however, would be very different. It would start relatively normal, but it would certainly end very differently.

The Minister rose especially early this Monday, following portions of his routine, as usual. He made his pot of New Orleans French Market coffee and chicory, put a touch of cinnamon in the filter to give it that extra special kick as usual, walked outside in the early morning darkness to retrieve the newspaper after waving to a couple of early morning joggers as usual, but on this Monday he did not return to bed or enter the kitchen to start his special breakfast for the children.

He went straight to his study, and without turning on a single light he found his way to his desk and sat down. After taking a long sip of the hot coffee, like a chain smokers exaggerated drag of the day's first cigarette, he clasped his hands behind his head and thought. He thought about yesterday. In his mind he saw beautiful smiles and sensuous complexions. He revisited the fragrances he experienced as well, each distinct and identifiable. He liked that. He loved signatures; signature style; signature mannerisms; signature fragrances. And yesterday he met women of signature, and each had left indelible impressions. He knew how to recognize signature women very well. His wife was one. She had a style all her own, mannerisms that identified her and a fragrance that had drawn him to her from the moment they met. But yesterday did something to re-engage his psyche, deleting the boredom brought on by lack of challenge. These two women of signature had most definitely peaked his interest. One was an unexpected treat, to whom he would now have to respond. His predication was that their beauty forced his hand, or at least, his pen.

From the upper right-hand drawer of his polished desk he pulled two sheets of stationary. Although this parchment appeared innocuous in its anonymous, off-white simplicity, it too was signature. It was time to write again.

Thank you so much for coming this past Sunday. It was a pleasure having you there. I was charmed to make your acquaintance and appreciate your confidence in discussing whatever may be troubling you. Please know that my door is always wide open to you and I invite you to call me whenever you like. As a matter of fact, I will be in my office this morning if you would like to call or stop by. Thanks again, and remember, the pleasure of meeting you was all mine.

EAH

He sealed the note in an unmarked envelope and wrote Lydia's name on the front. The issue facing him now was how to get the message to her. It would not be that difficult at all. He knew exactly how to do it.

By the time the house began to stir, everyone dressing, packing backpacks and signing things that needed to be signed, the Minister was already fully dressed.

"Hey Dad," Ed, Jr. said nonchalantly as he passed his father en route to the pantry for cereal, "why are you all dressed, and stuff?"

"Well, I've got to go down to the church this morning to handle a couple of things," was his father's reply.

A simple "Oh" was his son's confirmation of understanding. He re-engaged himself in the normal morning activities: cereal, television and picking at his little sister. Ed, Jr. glanced again at his father as if there was something he could not figure out; something he wanted to say or some question he wanted to ask, but then turned back to his morning routine.

The boundaries of intuition are non-existent in children, but adherence to the sense usually comes much later in life. Children are simply in harmonious syncopation with the metronome of life, easily recognizing change or trouble when the familiar rhythms around them are somewhat off beat.

When Angie walked in carrying the weapons for the morning war with Shelby and her hair, she noticed that her husband was not in the Monday morning exercise attire that was commonly the uniform for the day.

"What's up honey, you have something going on this morning?"

"Yeah, I forgot that I promised Brown I'd come down to the church to go over his ordination questions and answers with him today. I remembered it early this morning, so I was in my office trying to pull up some of that old stuff from back when I went through it."

"Oh, okay. I was hoping we'd walk this morning but it's no big deal. Lydia said she'd like to get together and go to the gym today anyway, so I'll get my workout in when we get together," Angie replied without looking up from her task of brushing and braiding Shelby's thick hair.

This was working out better than he had planned. It was almost too perfect, and when something seems too perfect, or too right, or too easy, it is usually a warning sign for disaster.

"You know what?" He said thoughtfully. "Would you give her this 'Thank You' note? It's just a little something to say thanks for coming, and inviting her and her husband to come back to the church. You know I'd really like to get him involved with the mentoring program for the young men. He seems to be such a great role model, and everything. Don't you think it would be good to get them in? She seems to be a class act herself. That drug awareness commercial they do together is really powerful. I mean, it's really heart wrenching when she talks about her sister being addicted to prescription drugs and how she lost her to an overdose. I think it's the honesty that makes that campaign sink in. Today's kids really need to see that."

He went on and on about how the Davis' should be members of the church and what great people they appeared to be, and what a great impact their presence would have in the community. He was talking too much, a common mistake of a deceitful heart. But Angie was involved in what she was doing, and he was right in everything that he said. No red flags, yet.

"Oh sure, baby, they'd be great. Just put the envelope on the counter there. I'll pick it up on my way out and give it to her at the gym."

He glanced at Angie, another mistake. She was a vision of loveliness right then and there. In her short night gown which exposed her cheeks when she bent forward, her hair pinned up, several bobby pins in her mouth, and a comb and brush in each hand, wrestling with her daughter's hair. This was beauty. The elegance was in the consistency, the versatility and the adaptability of her countenance. Yesterday she was a church lady, classic and graceful. Her opulence placed her in the pages of the most popular fashion periodical. The suit she wore was chic and trendy evoking compliments from all who saw her. She was a beacon of admiration. This morning she was the perfect mother, impeccably balancing all the duties and scheduling challenges of the job. Even with delicately manicured hands, she handled hair and dishes and backpacks and sandwich and snack preparation. She spot cleaned dribbled Jell-O and quick pressed wrinkled collars. Later she would be hip and trendy, most likely having lunch at some in vogue bistro with her friend Lydia, and she would look like an actress in a Julia Roberts film. Throughout the venerable persona changes, the dignity of her style and the grace of her character would remain unchanged and unchallenged. She would be gorgeous from sun up to sun down, and she would be the same.

The Minister was only bothered briefly when considering the fact that he would begin the hunt for another while having such loveliness at home. His wife was one who went to intemperate lengths to fulfill his every need. But he would soon suppress and secure those feelings in order to move forward with his plans.

The myth that for some men it is not quality but quantity is not all together correct. Quality is reserved for the "queen bee." She is securely possessed, and then made safe and sound, her position ferociously protected, never to be challenged or threatened by any outside force. When she is safe and sound, it is the thrill of the hunt that draws a man to safari. He struggled momentarily with the mental composition of his plans, but overpowered his conscience as he looked away.

After kisses and hugs from the family, on their way out, the Minister retired again to his study where he busied himself for a while. It was still too early to go to the church. He was only going there to wait for possibilities, and sometimes excitement deflates patience, and that was not good for his chosen demeanor. Cool, calm and collected was who he was and he worked to maintain such posture.

CHAPTER 12

When he finally arrived at his church office he saw India's car in the parking area and was not happy. *"What was she doing here?"* He thought to himself, but the reality was that he knew exactly what she was doing here. She saw something yesterday that fostered her interest as well. The Minister was entertaining two beautiful women, and she had worked for him long enough to recognize the twinkle in his eyes. She recognized it because she had always wanted to see that in him when he looked at her, but she did not. She had done everything short of coming into the office completely naked to try to get his attention, but nothing had worked, so she thought. He did appreciate her short skirts and obvious leans over his desk while a loose fitting low-cut top revealed a bra-less bosom, but she was too common. She was predictable. She was simple.

It was not that India was terribly ugly or completely unattractive; the Minister felt that simple people always make simple choices, and simple choices are thoughtless choices, and thoughtless choices are dangerous. Beyond that, he would never engage in a tryst with such volatile possibilities. India was hazardous and the Minister treated her as such, negotiating her psyche with kid gloves sometimes. She was an excellent assistant but her private desires and her willingness to make inordinate attempts for his attention placed red flags all over her. The Minister had no desire to entertain such an individual. He already had one of those. The only thing she had going for her was her intuition, and that only came because of her years of studying him, and simply because she was female.

"Hey Pastor, what are you doing here today?" She was in full effect. A short jean skirt with a split in the back revealed her thick thighs. It would only take one reach down for a fallen object to completely reveal what was beneath, and it was not much. Her blatant efforts often caused a chuckle within him, but today he was not amused.

"No. What are you doing here? You know I don't usually come down here on Monday's." He continued working his way into his inner office; shuffling keys, coat and briefcase.

"Well for some reason I thought you might be in today. Call it intuition. Call it a hunch. But anyway, if you need me for anything I'll be right here."

After making the statement she casually went to her desk and sat down. Swiveling the chair around and facing him she again said, "Anything, okay?"

She made sure that he could see that her legs were parted just enough to reveal her panty-less crotch. It was attractive but not appealing. Her bi-polar tendencies would have him later consoling her for what she had done, as she would become very sullen and embarrassed after her offer was unaccepted. The other issue that was strangely unique about India was the fact that everyone else viewed her as a very conservative professional. To everyday eyes that were not perceptively trained to pay attention to detail, she looked like the venerably prudent church secretary, friendly, efficient, skillful and extremely protective of her employer. She carefully tried not to show her affections in the presence of those who might think negatively of her, but what she did not realize was that the rest of the world, who she believed she had fooled, clearly saw through her efforts to camouflage her passions. Like the Minister, they too often chuckled at her simplicity.

He remained in his office most of the day, not even coming out for lunch. He fielded a few calls, including one from his wife who was simply checking on him to see how things were going. She too was patient, knowing in the back of her mind that something deeper than ordination study was going on at the church office. But the last thing she wanted to do, however, is walk in on something that would compromise her dignity, so she would wait, and he would explain. She knew it was not India even if she was there today. Angie was well aware of what appealed to her husband. She knew what he liked, and more importantly in the case of his secretary, what he did not.

By about five o'clock, the Minister had not received the calls he was hoping for and decided to go home. India peeked in fifteen minutes prior and dismissed herself after resigning to the fact that there would be no intriguing issues on which to spy. The Minister was alone when the final call of the day came.

"Good evening?" He did not use a greeting including the church name because it was his private line that rang.

"Hi." The voice sounded vaguely familiar, like someone from a time not long ago, but far enough in his past to not be immediately recognizable.

"This is Pastor Ed Hebert. To whom am I speaking?" He asked, trying to place the voice.

"I know who you are, Ed and you know who I am. Where have you been?"

"Who is this!" He demanded this time, as if his nerves were being tested.

"It's me, Alexandra," the mystery lady said finally revealing herself.

Alexandra was no mystery to the Minister. The two of them had shared a steamy affair off and on for the last two years. She had cut off communication for the last six months because her feelings were becoming involved, and that was that last thing she wanted. She had fallen in love with him, and that was not a prudent thing to do with a man like the Minister. He had made it clear to her that he would never leave his wife for anyone or any reason. He never had a negative word to say about Angie. He did not do what he did because of issues of being unfulfilled at home. That was part of his mystery and draw. He was brutally honest with his outside conquests when it came to his family. He never lied about his marital status or where his heart was anchored. He allowed those ill-advised persons who fell in love with him to do so of their own free will, with full knowledge of the consequences. Alexandra had allowed herself to go too far and the only way to regain control of her emotions was to abstain completely from any contact with the Minister, until now. She could not hold it any longer.

"Well this is certainly a surprise. I didn't think I'd ever hear from you again. You simply vanished into the wood-work. What did you do, change your assignment or something?"

Detective Alexandra Heart was a striking police officer whose last assignment took her under cover in the world of high fashion to apprehend a rapist who preyed on young models. Her beauty and youthful look gave her unquestioned access to a world known by most only in magazines and tabloid television.

They had met several years ago when the Minister assisted the Police Department with the development of a psychological profile of a rapist. His work helped police anticipate the assailant's next move, leading to an arrest and conviction that made headlines. His contribution was priceless and Detective Heart did not simply show appreciation for his services on behalf of the Department. Her personal gratitude was sensually expressed.

There had been fire between her and the Minister from the time they met, and it did not take them long to realize that the heat was hot enough to consume them both. So they tried as best they could to keep their interaction on a generically professional level. That effort did not last long. Their times together were explosive and the sex was beyond passion, it was primal. It was dog howling wild, and then it was over. Both had agreed to keep it in its proper perspective, but it became difficult for Alexandra because she always went home alone. Her loneliness consumed her in volatile ways.

She began to look to the Minister for all the things he did not look to her for, and his lack of reciprocation angered her. He had a companion, a friend, a confidant, a consistent lover, a better half; he had Angie. Alexandra had no one, at least, no one like the Minister. He often chided himself for knowingly becoming involved with someone like Alexandra. Her life and character waved several red flags of warning, but he could not help himself. He could not deny the hunger inside him, especially when he discovered that Alexandra was more than ready to perform beyond his wildest fantasies.

"What are you doing in the next forty minutes?" She said matter-of-factly, the way a detective does.

"I don't know. What should I be doing?" He was alone in his office with his feet on his desk. He pushed back in his chair, closed his eyes and smiled. He thought about the last time he had been with her. He thought about her father's German heritage and her mother's Brazilian background, and how the two had come together to make an exquisite beauty. She had her father's eyes but her mother's hips and bottom, and what a time he had trying to quench her fire.

"Why don't you meet me at the old stomping ground. We'll have a few laughs and talk about some old times," she said.

"I'll see you in forty minutes." Without saying 'good-bye' he hung up the phone.

He swiveled in his chair a few moments to think, and then called his wife. She answered her cell phone on the third ring.

"Hey, where are you?" He spoke nonchalantly.

"On my way to the market. What's going on? Did you guys get a lot done today?"

"Oh, yeah, everything went fine. I think we're going to stop for a moment and grab some dinner. Is that okay, or did you have something planned?"

His fingers were crossed because he had not yet developed a plan 'B' if she actually did have something in mind for the evening.

"No, no. Go ahead, Junior has soccer practice tonight anyway and it's my turn to bring the snacks. So that works out fine. I'll pick up Shelby when we leave the field and then we'll run through a drive thru, or something. The kid's will love that. By the way, Lydia and I had a great work out at the gym and ran into some old friends at lunch. We really had a great time and she wants you to meet Donavan. I told her that we all should have dinner next week. What do you think?"

"I think you're great; that's what I think." The Minister could not contain his exuberance even though it was for all the wrong reasons. He was happy about the fact that his wife would be busy and that he would have a couple of hours of freedom to do what he wished. He had simply mastered the art of emotional direction, which meant that he could direct his emotions wherever he thought they should go, which did not necessarily have to be the source of his pain or pleasure. It often worked in Angie's favor, as she often did not know who or what exactly generated his pleasure, but she was certainly the beneficiary of the labor, whoever the worker was.

After a few more pleasantries and inquiries about the children, they hung up. This time the Minister spun around in his chair like a school kid does in the teacher's chair when no one else is in the classroom. He smiled and shuffled a few papers around, some of them genuinely having to do with Brown's ordination. He thought about calling him to place him on notice but it was not really necessary. Angie would never call him. She, like most, could not stand him. He would be the last person sought for information and he would never expose the Minister anyway.

First of all, Brown did not know that much and beyond that, he was indebted to the Minister for covering some mistakes that he had made in the past. If revealed, those mistakes would most definitely quell the possibilities of a pastoral appointment in the future. There were several, but one of the most severe was the time he had allowed his hormones to rage out of control with an under age debutante. The Minister had walked in on Brown as he groped and prodded a sixteen-year old girl in the stairwell that led to the administrative offices of the church. The scene was a mess that should never have happened, but it successfully exposed something about his associate that the Minister needed to know, and stored as on call ammunition.

CHAPTER 13

It had happened a long time ago but the memories were easily recounted. Some things are just like that, and the Minister had quite a few items locked in the "use when necessary" corners of his mind.

Brown had agreed to take her home after a practice for a Debutante Ball the church sponsored yearly. The girls were taught about rules of etiquette and other social graces and worked to secure outside funding sources for scholarships. It was a wonderful time in their lives; a time of discovery, a time when they were pampered and praised for their efforts, a time when they were to cross over into womanhood and be respected as such.

The girls were young and beautiful, innocent and playful. Brown and one of the debs decided to grab some fast food and eat it in the car and when the conversation moved into questions about sex, Brown found a way to convince her that she would be better off shown than told. He quietly entered the administration wing of the church, and without turning on any lights, he began teaching things the girl did not need to learn, at least not from him. Although it appeared that the young girl was consenting, everything about the situation was wrong. Fortunately for the young lady, the Minister walked in to retrieve a forgotten item and discovered the two before Brown regrettably entered her. Startled and embarrassed, she jumped up, half naked, and ran to the ladies room. Brown stood still and silent, stunned to immobility by the Minister's surprise visit. He had lost complete control of himself and the Minister did not have to vocalize his disgust with Brown's behavior. His face said it all. With no immediate words for him, the Minister headed toward the end of the hallway after the teen. It took nearly two hours for the Minister to persuade the girl to come out of the restroom and allow him to take her home.

He privately counseled both of them and allowed the girl to make the decision as to whether or not she would inform her parents. She decided not to, and Brown vehemently entreated the Minister to keep the whole ordeal a very personal secret. The Minister complied with the condition that the same extension of loyalty be reciprocated and that he never behave that way again. He agreed, and from that day, the Minister knew that Brown would never be a worry.

This incident became one of many steering tools the Minister used occasionally to bring Brown within compliance to his will. But what he truly held against him was a history of public disdain, based on Brown's historic involvement with underworld figures. He had apparently come out of a life that once had him indicted as a lead participant in a money-laundering scheme, as well as several other criminal activities. Though never convicted, it was believed that he struck a deal with federal investigators in trade for his freedom. The problem was that this all happened while he was supposedly committed to a life of ministry, and though the church going crowd after pledges to forgive and forget, the reality is that they do very little of either. Brown would never have a stronghold in the Calvary congregation, or any other. Knowledge of his past had him tied to his current station, and the Minister knew it. But Brown was a snake, not a very intelligent one, but a snake nonetheless, and one should never turn their back on a snake.

As the Minister approached his car, a late model white Range Rover with tinted windows pulled up beside him. When the window rolled down, he was extremely surprised to see the sullen face of Lydia Davis.

"Holy shit!" He mumbled to himself as the lowered window revealed her visage, and then immediately he looked to the heavens and asked forgiveness for his profane slip. He thought he might possibly get a call but he did not expect her to show up, especially after having spent the better part of her day with his wife.

"Hello Reverend, I mean Ed. I thought I'd swing by. Angie told me that I might still be able to catch you here." She looked like she needed to talk about something that was on her mind. She also looked like she just wanted to come by and see him, and he had no complaints about that.

"Do you have a moment?" she asked. Her naturally curly hair was loose and blowing slightly in the autumn brisk. It looked only partially dried as if she had just stepped out of the shower and dressed quickly. It had not been specifically styled or combed but seemed to naturally fall into place. She looked especially sexy when she brushed a few wild strands out of her face that had been arranged by the wind. The parting of her soft lips, as she spoke, revealed a perfectly arched set of pearly whites. He was drawn to her but also torn in a way. She was dangerous, in different ways than India and Alexandra, or even Gemma. He was threatened by his own desire and he knew there was definitely something between them.

"Well actually I don't, and I'm sorry. I was kind of expecting you to call. Did Angie give you the note I sent?" He was trying to maintain his composure but he had an appointment for which he did not want to be late, and time was of the essence.

"No, she didn't. We had lunch today after a workout but she didn't give me anything. Did you send me something special?" She joked lightly and her tone interested him.

"Oh no, no. It was just a little note thanking you for coming and inviting you back. Nothing special, but I would like to sit down and talk to you whenever you're ready." He was trying to move things along so he could head to his rendezvous.

"I think I'm ready now," she paused, "but it looks like you were on your way out. Maybe I'll come back some other time." The sullen look on her face got heavier.

Once again the choice of nobility and righteousness reared its unwelcome head. This time its alarm was sounded by a stiff gust of wind that startled the leaves of a lone maple tree planted in the church courtyard. The Minister thought for a moment about what was awaiting him. The familiar touch of one from a time long ago called out to him. He could only imagine what she would wear or in this case, what she would not. She would do things to him that other men only dreamed about, and others paid for. But this lover did them because that was who she was, at least, when she was with him. Satisfying his every desire was her pleasure and passion. When he arrived, she would definitely be ready, just like the old days. He would see her car in the private parking area and she would write a number on a piece of scrap paper and place it on her dashboard. To anyone else, it would simply look like meaningless debris to be discarded at the next carwash, but to the Minister it would be instructions as to where to find her and what hotel door would serve as the aperture to a few hours of unbridled passion. To some, that time would be considerably absent of value or meaning, but to the parties involved, it would be significantly expensive and an essential ingredient to the concupiscence of the inextinguishable flame of their relationship.

Now Lydia was in his face, a real woman with a real problem, needing real help. There may be future possibilities with her but a major aspect of the danger of personal interaction with her was her budding relationship with Angie. He had always managed to keep things far from home. But now this diamond before him was beginning to spend too much intimate time with his diamond at home, and that could be a problem.

He thought about things for just a moment longer, looking to the ground and rubbing his chin. He thought of his higher calling and briefly prayed for assistance in successfully displacing those inappropriate thoughts that loomed in his psyche. He needed to concentrate on helping the soul before him. *She had come for help, hadn't she?* Right now, he was going to help her, and then later with Alexandra, he would help himself.

"Come on in, Lydia. My appointment can wait. Let's see what's on your mind."

They both locked their cars and headed back inside the building, down the hall, and into the Minister's chambers. As they walked, the Minister complimented Lydia on her attire, stone washed Levi's, high-end leather boots, a crisp white blouse revealing just enough cleavage to dispel rumors of being completely conservative, and a lambskin jacket. He was really beginning to like her style.

"Lydia would you give me a second to make a couple of important calls before we begin?"

"Sure, no problem," she replied as he seated her in the outer parlor near India's desk.

He thought quickly and first called Angie. He would have to play it safe, and safety meant honesty. He told her that Lydia stopped by and wanted to discuss some personal issues. She was fine with that and advised him to do all he could for her. He did not ask her about the note she had not delivered. It could mean nothing; she could have just forgotten. But it could be much more significant. Angie was not witless and her intuition was keen. He figured it best to simply steer clear of the issue. He quickly wrapped up the conversation by telling her that he might be home a bit later than expected. The second call he made was to Alexandra's pager. It was sheer luck that he even located the number. Although he had a mental file cabinet that was pretty reliable, he had written her pager number down after their last encounter knowing that one day he might call on her, and by that time his memory might have failed. Hopefully she would call back quickly and they could reschedule their tryst. He *did* have a cell phone number for her that he chose not to try. She might answer, and he had no interest in trying to explain his absence. Avoidance was much more practical in this instance.

He invited Lydia into his office after completing his calls. Because he was a trained psychologist, he knew what to do to get to the heart of the problem. He simply sat quietly and let her talk. She talked about several issues that were plaguing her: the desire to start a family, the need to find a place to call home, the lack of quality time she was able to spend with her husband, her loneliness, her image. These were all things that were serious and important but they were not what troubled her most, and the Minister knew that. These issues camouflaged her deepest concerns. As he listened, he began to consider the time. This might not take as long as he thought, and there may be a slim chance he could still make his way to Alexandra. And then Lydia began to weep, and his attention was refocused on the wilting flower before him.

"Something is just not right," she said repeatedly as her eyes welled and then gently overflowed. He still sat quietly, directly across from her on the edge of his desk.

"I don't know what I'm doing wrong. I try to do everything right but something just isn't right with us." She buried her face in her hands and her sobbing increased. She was talking about her relationship with her husband, and the Minister knew that, but it was not unusual for couples to have problems.

"All relationships have challenges," he said to her. But he knew something was different in this situation. There was a serious unspoken issue, an unsolved puzzle that was sticking out like an ugly mark on a masterpiece. Realizing that he would not get to the bottom of it at that moment, he simply extended his arms. Sometimes a hug is the most appropriate therapy and a warm touch can be more consoling than words. He was genuine and there was nothing covert about his gesture.

Without wiping her eyes, Lydia looked at him, took hold of his outstretched hands and found her way to the comfort of his chest. She released a mighty cry and the Minister simply held her. He held her sincerely without an unpropitious thought, and then she whispered 'thank you' in his ear. The moment seemed to last longer than it should have. She kissed his cheek, then his neck, and then his earlobe. He knew that he should probably back away but maybe she was simply caught up in a losing bout with repressed emotion. As he tried to feebly consider academic theories for her actions, she methodically put both of her hands on the back of his head, running her fingers through his hair, and then made her way to his mouth. It was almost as if she were operating outside herself.

She tasted like sweet lavender and her mouth was warm and inviting. When he answered her kiss with his own, he rested his hands on her shoulders. She wriggled out of her jacket without releasing his lips and his hands searched her body, finding their way to her buttocks. He kneaded the area like taut bread dough being prepared for baking. There was something special about the way she felt, and as much as he tried to force himself to release her, he could not. Her draw to him was absolutely magnetic.

The Minister silenced his conscience as Lydia turned her back to him, offering the nape of her neck and grinding her backside into his crotch. He wanted her to say, "*Stop!*" because he knew the word would not come out of his mouth. Instead, she guided his hands through the, gladly obliged, task of unbuttoning her blouse and removing her bra. *Jesus, was this what she needed?* Her breathing increased as she continued to rhythmically grind herself against him. Her button fly jeans were unbuttoned now and she was navigating his hands into the opening of her pants. He was so ready that his hardness could have cut glass. "*Please stop me!*" He shouted within himself as they checked caution at the door and allowed passion to overtake them. And then the phone rang. It startled them both, but Lydia especially, forcefully knocking her back to reality. He had to answer it, especially if it was Angie. He reluctantly pulled himself away from her. As he quietly spoke into the receiver, Lydia quickly and silently ran to the outer parlor where she had been waiting when they first entered the office.

The Minister was torn in the heat of the moment. He thought about the girl whom he startled on the steps with Brown who ran and locked herself in the ladies room. He wondered why that event that happened so many years ago was now suddenly fresh in his mind. Although the situation before him was between consenting adults, he did not want Lydia to panic in her embarrassment and do something detrimental to herself, or to him for that matter.

The call was from Alexandra, and she was not pleased with the fact that she had been stood up. She could, furthermore, hear the rushed tone of his voice and the increased breathing pace of his breathing.

"Where are you?" She asked dryly.

"I'm still at the church. I had something unexpected to come up that I had to deal with."

"I bet you did. Good bye Ed."

"Wait Alex! Wait just a minute. Don't hang up the--," He tried to catch her but it was too late. She was volatile and that was part of her charm and why their encounters were so electrifying, but it was also one of the many reasons why they could not spend much time together. The Minister put the receiver back on the cradle, took a deep breath and called Lydia's name. There was no answer. He scurried to the outer office hoping she would be where he wanted her to be, but she was gone.

CHAPTER 14

By Friday, Ivy had not spoken to Gemma personally. They had left each other several messages, which was not unusual. Ivy left the first one last Sunday when she apologized to Miss Hattie and asked her to inform Gemma that she would be unable to come by that evening for a big serving of her delicious peach cobbler. Miss Hattie explained to Ivy that Gemma had an impromptu meeting with her agent anyway and that she would be sure to give her the message. She also promised to make Ivy a peach cobbler of her own.

Ivy could almost hear the smile on the other end of the phone coming from her surrogate grandmother. She had a grandmother she never really knew because she passed away when Ivy was very young, but when the opportunity presented itself, fate paved the way for Miss Hattie to step right in and assume the role. She too was proud of Ivy, having met her during her college years and falling in love with her just like Gemma. She called Ivy her other baby-girl and boasted about her accomplishments just as if she were her own child. She was proud of the fight in Ivy and had appreciated the times she had helped Gemma navigate her way through difficult circumstances, especially those trying times with Alfonse.

Miss Hattie loved the relationship Gemma and Ivy shared, and did her best to look out for "her girls." Ivy was a great friend, but she too was getting caught up in something larger than herself. Miss Hattie could not see it and neither could Ivy. They both would simply have to wait.

Ivy was knee deep in an extremely capacious case that had her working exhausting hours both at the office and at home. She had managed however, to find time to see Donovan every day since their lunch encounter. He was becoming an unusually welcomed presence in her hectic but private world. Sometimes it was a brief lunch or a very late supper, or maybe a latte at the coffee stand by the law library. He always seemed to make time to see her, and Ivy like any other woman, loved the attention. It began with the delivery of a massive exotic bouquet of flowers to her office and a note that expressed his pleasure of having met such a captivating woman. When she walked into her office and saw the flowers centered amidst the sea of legal documents piled in stacks half way to the ceiling, she was astounded. Not only were they outrageously beautiful, they brought vibrant color to an office that was suffering a dismal and colorless death by suffocation beneath an over abundant and unforgiving work-load. The timing of his thoughtfulness could not have been more perfect. She had a million things to do but she unloaded her file laden arms, and immediately called his cell phone to express her gratitude.

He had been a gentleman since the evening they met, always seeming to know what to do to make her laugh or smile. He was truly a superstar on and off the field, and she could see why he was such a sought after commodity. Donovan was an impeccable advertisement for manhood, representing the product well. She was beginning to expect to hear from him daily and he was always timely with something unpretentious and unsolicited, but always special.

There were questions and concerns that she had never addressed with him mainly because she was just not looking to engage in that sort of conversation. Her aunt always said that if you looked for trouble, you would find it. She was not looking. When questionable thoughts or feelings arose, she quickly rationalized their relationship with a swift dose of mental litigation against her better judgment. Yes, she did always call him on his cell phone, but he had offered her his home number, which she declined to accept. Yes, he did have more free time than one would expect from someone in the middle of finalizing negotiations of a major NFL contract, but the season had not officially started and he was a celebrity and a veteran athlete, which in control of his time and career. And yes, he was rarely with his wife, unlike all the photos illustrated. Ivy had not seen them together since the night they had met, and even then, she left early.

Ivy was a lawyer and lawyers are known for picking evidence apart to create and develop cases, but she already had a case, one that consumed her lawyer energies, so when it came to spending time with Donavan, she released her grip on logic and gave her emotions a turn to play. Donovan was *recess*.

She arrived at her office early, like usual and although Ivy was preparing for the climactic court appearance that would culminate her efforts, her first intention before rehearsing her closing argument was to call her friend Gemma. She was anxious to tell her friend about the latest developments with the case and receive her well wishes. But she also knew that Gemma would be more interested in the situational developments with her new secret lover, and Ivy really wanted to talk about that as well. Although she was a super intelligent, corporate legal eagle, she was still a woman who loved to trade secrets with her best friend. She was shocked when she walked in and saw Donovan seated in *her* chair behind *her* desk.

"Good morning," he said in his tenor voice, smiling slyly.

He was dressed in a dark Armani suit with a royal blue dress shirt opened to the third button. His size would not allow him to put his legs under the desk so he sat back with his legs crossed, exposing his muscular thighs. He was clean shaven, hair neatly trimmed to a close fade, and his teeth glistened. His ears were absent of the common trademark piercing expected of a modern African-American athlete. He was a cut above in all ways, but especially etiquette and maturity. He had been a star at the Naval Academy during his collegiate years, and the officer training bled through every aspect of his gentlemanly character. On his left hand, a simple platinum wedding band dressed his fourth finger. The same finger of his right hand boasted an NFL Super Bowl Championship ring. Together they appeared as symbols of security and undeniable respect, and he wore both of them well.

"Good morning to you," Ivy replied with a pleased but bewildered look on her face. She was happy to see him but not pleased that her assistant allowed him in her office without her authorization. She would deal with that later. He knew he should not have been there either, but he took advantage of his celebrity and physical attributes, just as women take advantage of theirs to gain access to prohibited areas. Ivy's assistant had probably been hypnotized by his overwhelming presence, and she could not blame her for that.

"Hey, I know you're busy and I probably shouldn't even be in here, but I just wanted to see what your plans were tonight. I thought maybe I could come over to your place and make dinner for you to celebrate after you win this case today."

"Well, I don't have any specific plans," she said smiling as she unloaded her arms, "and I appreciate your confidence, but I don't know—"

"Just say, *yes*." He came over to her and put his finger on her lips and his hand on her shoulder. She did not have any plans, and she knew that she would be ready to celebrate being finished with this monster case, win or lose. But she was not sure if she wanted to celebrate with him. It might get physical and she knew she did not want to get involved with a married man, even though he never seemed to spend time with his wife, or even mention her for that matter. But again, she mentally litigated herself into agreement.

"Well, okay. I guess that would be nice. Let me give you my address," she said turning to her desk to reach for a pad and paper.

"No need, I'll just follow the scent of a beautiful woman," he said kissing her hand. He then smiled at her with his eyes and then left her office.

Ivy was concerned for a moment about the whole thing; him being in her office and having her address, but she had more serious issues to deal with at present. She got behind her desk and immediately her phone started ringing. She fielded several work related calls until she finally informed her assistant to hold all of her calls because she needed to focus on final preparations for the case. The first call that came in, just after her edict, was from Gemma, and Ivy's assistant would not put the call through. She apologized profusely but had already received a stiff reprimand from her boss about allowing Donovan in her office without authorization, and she was not about to incite Ivy's wrath again for not following directions. She explained to Gemma that she would be sure to relay the message and make sure that her call was returned.

Ivy returned her attention to her legal documents and story-boards that she had set up in the office. They were all valuable pieces to a closing argument that would be a brilliant display of legal expertise, impeccable preparation and a polished delivery. It was time for her to call Uncle Henry's boxing ring training into play. It was time to be fierce. It was time to put the opposition on the ropes. It was time for a knock out punch.

She arrived at the courthouse ready to deliver the closing argument of her career, and she did just that. She was so good that the gallery fought back an outburst of applause after she said those famous last words, "*Your honor, I rest my case.*" Her eloquent dissertation was completed before lunch, and the jury deliberated for less than an hour before returning with a verdict in her client's favor. After that she was asked to the judge's chambers and received unprecedented accolades from him on what a fine job she had done. Ivy had argued cases before him previously and though he had been impressed with her all along, he rarely ever broke away from his "poker face" gaze, giving no indication of such feelings. This time was no different while court was in session, but after everything was wrapped up, he could not help but say a few words of praise behind closed doors. It was completely unorthodox but the judge thought it was more than justified. Even opposing counsel congratulated her in a personal side bar, informing her that the next time they were in court, he hoped that they were on the same side. It capped off the day quite nicely, and would definitely improve her position at the firm.

When she finally got home after a few mandatory congratulatory drinks with a few of the partners, she could see by the blinking light, that her answering machine had messages. One of them was probably from Donovan. Her emotions were mixed. It would be great to see him tonight. He would probably have great conversation and the company would be welcomed. But she also thought about the limits of their sharing. Her courtroom victory was an incredible career milestone, a major feather in her cap, something to be shared with someone special; someone who would be around for other special occasions and victories. Donovan could not be that person, and no matter how hard she tried to dismiss reason, she knew that she would only end up hurting if she pursued any semblance of an emotionally intimate relationship with him. Beyond that, she was just drained after surviving a tremendous day.

She plopped down on her comfortable sofa. It was soothing and familiar; her first piece of furniture after graduating law school. Uncle Henry had bought it for her and it could always be depended upon for restful sleep. The décor of her condo had changed many times but that sofa stayed. Its style was dated and the color scheme did not really match her current interior design, but the pillows were still fluffy and there was something warm that seemed to embrace her when she rested her weary body on its soft frame.

Finally she decided on a glass of Pinot Noir and then a shower, and then maybe a call to Donovan to request a rain check on dinner. She would check the messages later. It was probably just a few more colleagues offering well wishes on her successful day in court, anyway.

Ivy pressed herself into the cushioned sofa after finishing about half of the wine, and before she knew it, she was dozing. She had been fueled by adrenaline for the last three weeks and her body had finally given in. Long days and sleepless nights had become par for the course, and it was just a matter of time before Ivy crashed. She felt herself drifting into a deep sleep, but was startled by the continued ringing of her doorbell. It was Donovan.

Groggy from the wine but more so because she was just dead tired, Ivy opened the door to a handsome hulk bearing grocery bags, a smile, and a bouquet of lavender tulips. There was a strange pleasure about the sight before her. She was extremely tired and had it been anyone else, a wrathful tongue lashing would have been their recompense for disturbing her rest, but she was honestly glad to see him. The always evaluative jurist in her however, could not help but subtly analyze the situation.

"Hey, I wasn't expecting you," she said as she attempted to straighten her mussed hair.

"What do you mean? I stopped by your office this morning and told you that we were having dinner tonight. Am I that forgettable now?" He laughed a cool casual laugh, one that she had heard before and liked. From the time she had met him, she was mesmerized by the confidence of his expression.

"No, no, I mean I thought you would have called when you were on your way or something." She stood in the doorway fighting back an oncoming yawn.

"So are you going to let me in or should I go back to the pier and release these two live Australian lobster's back to the wild? I don't think they'd be able to find their way home. Now, you wouldn't want to do that to these little guys would you?" Again he laughed.

"Oh, I'm sorry. Come in Donovan. It's just that I'm so beat. It has been a hell of a day, a hell of a week, a hell of a month for that matter. I just got home," she paused to look at her watch, "a while ago, I see." She had not realized that she had been dozing on her sofa for more than an hour. She was still trying to collect herself and grasp reality. Her mind had been trained for alertness and attention to detail, but her mind could not compete with a body that had been abused by the lack of rest.

"I tell you what," Donovan interjected, "how about you go take a shower and take your time getting dressed and I'll find my way to your kitchen and whip up a little magic?" He seemed to know just what to say.

"That sounds good. That sounds real good," Ivy replied with a smile. "The rarely visited *show place* of a kitchen is right in there." They both chuckled.

Showers are amazing places. They are the optimal transcendent think tanks of humanity. Answers to life's most puzzling riddles seem to come forth in the shower. Platinum songs are written and produced, including the lead and background vocals. The plots to best selling novels often spew forth in this place of steam and clouded vision. With closed eyes, an artist's canvas is seen in the shower, and vibrant color choices are inspired for masterpieces. Lawyers develop brilliant closing arguments and detectives solve mysterious crimes, all in the shower. Maybe it is the steam. Maybe the warm water stimulates a sleeping enzyme in the analytical area of the brain. Maybe it is the nakedness of the body that frees the mind to concentrate on subjects beyond self. It is a mystery to be solved upon the next shower visit.

As the warm water gently massaged her fair skin, Ivy leaned forward with both hands on the shower wall, allowing herself to be completely drenched. The cascading flow raced through the locks of her curly, sandy-brown hair and onto her shoulders, down her back and channeled its way down the midway of her taut buttocks. She thought about the man in her kitchen making the gourmet meal. She thought about how she was so attracted to him and how he was so perfect; a gentlemen and scholar. Her thoughts drifted to the enjoyable conversations they had shared and how she so enjoyed being with him. It had been a long time since she had felt this way about a man.

Ivy had several romantic opportunities, as she had suitors who proclaimed their devotion for her on a regular basis, but she had not felt for any of them what they felt for her, and she felt about no one the way she was beginning to feel about Donovan. But then she wondered about his home life, his picture perfect and very public marriage. This was an issue that she had decided not to deal with, but was unable to keep herself away completely. He was always available and seemed to pop up just at the right time. *Why was he here? Where was his wife? Why had there never been an opportunity to, officially or even casually meet her?* Then Ivy began to question her own motivations and the fact that she really did not want to meet his wife or ask why he was in her kitchen, or why he was always available. She decided to just enjoy him. She decided to deal with more important and pressing questions like what she should wear after the shower.

The shower is also a war zone; a place where the corners of the conscience release their soldiers to fight on a common battlefield. But almost always, one towels off before a victor is declared. The soldiers are instructed to return to their respective corners and be available for combat another day.

Ivy slipped on her button fly jeans and Columbia University Law School sweatshirt to a heavenly aroma, unfamiliar to her sterile kitchen. The new oven, stove and microwave in her kitchen, did more for decoration than use, as her coffee maker was the only true cooking device that regularly drew her attention. Donovan had done something magnificent as he worked a culinary masterpiece on the virgin appliances. He had concocted a Jamaican marinade in which he bathed two prime cuts of filet mignon, broiling them perfectly to medium rare. He plated them beside Australian whole lobsters that had been steamed, Japanese style, over water spiced with laurel leaves, green and black pepper corns, coriander seed and sea salt. On a bed of baby spinach leaves and diced Roma tomatoes, he had mounded symmetrical servings of saffron rice.

"*Who is this man?*" Ivy thought as she walked into the kitchen.

"Hello beautiful," he said as he pulled out her chair. In the time it had taken her to shower and dress, he had prepared an amazing table with wine and candlelight. She chuckled to herself because she did not know she even had half the items she saw on the table.

"Donovan, this is amazing. How did you do all of this? Why did you do all of this? Where did you find all this stuff?"

"You're an amazing woman Ivy, and I thought it the proper way to celebrate a well deserved courtroom victory. All I want you to do is sit down and enjoy."

His eyes were radiant when he looked at her, and she could see something in them that was different. He was different. He was uncommonly genuine and his efforts did not appear simply part of an elaborate scheme to impress her. It was a real time facet of his character, and she found it irresistibly fascinating. She dismissed all of the questions brought forward in the think tank. There would be new ones, but for now she would follow the instructions of her cavalier gentleman. As they ate and talked, they lost themselves in each other, just like the day Gemma had spied them in the Italian bistro. They did not engage in much conversation concerning careers, but focused more deeply on issues of personal and romantic concern. He was great, and when they finished it seemed natural that they would retire to the den and enjoy a night cap on the sofa.

"Come here Ivy." He brought her close to him and began massaging her shoulders as they sat. It felt amazingly wonderful and she was drifting away within his touch. He moved gracefully to her neck and then ran his fingers through her hair finding the spot that made her purr. She threw timing out the window, reminding herself that she was a grown woman and the time to kiss or touch or even make love, was her decision implicitly. She kissed him deeply, and he reciprocated. It was strange though, because he did not pursue her further. She expected that he would attempt a classic move to remove her shirt or unbutton her jeans. He was a professional athlete, for God's sake. His skills should be keen and impressive. He did neither. She did it herself, and then turned to begin unbuttoning his shirt, and then he pulled away. His move was subtle but clear.

"Oh Ivy," he said as he brushed his hands over his face, "I've got to slow down."

"What's wrong, Donovan?" She was puzzled. He had pursued her with calls, flowers, lunches and dinners, and now when it appeared that he was nearing pay dirt for all his efforts, he halted.

"Well, nothing." He paused as if thinking of something to say. "I just don't think it's the right time. You know I'm a married man." He stood up straightening his clothes.

Had he left his last statement off of the entire comment, he might have had a chance, but that sent Ivy to another place.

"Yes, I know very well you're a married man. The question here is whether or not you know you're a married man, because from the moment I met you, you sure seemed to behave as if you were single." She stood now, looking up at him and buttoning the top button of her jeans. Her shower meditation was beginning to bear fruit.

"You know Donovan, you're real funny. I meet you at a fundraiser, you're great, we talk and have drinks, and I think you're really impressive. At that moment, I really don't wonder about your wife or your career or anything like that. But I see you almost everyday after that. I hear from you at least twice a day. My office is a flower mart courtesy of your kindness, and now you come over, cook this romantic meal and start in on what I think might be a prelude to something special, and then it stops with you feeling like you have to remind me that you're a married man. Do you have the '*guilt's*'? Is that it? Because if it is, let me give you some advice; don't lead someone on. Don't pursue me just for the fun of it, because that's not okay. If you haven't noticed, I'm not one of the road trip groupies. You should know that. I didn't ask for all this attention, remember. The calls, the lunches, the dinners, were all at your lead."

"Ivy, Ivy, Ivy." He stopped her. "It's not what you think." He stood back, looking at the floor and shaking his head, repeating that statement.

"Then what is it, Donavan?"

"I can't go into it right now, and I'm sorry that I can't because I need to tell someone." She could see tears welling up in his eyes, and she was confused and sorry, in a way. Whatever he was going through was obviously quite serious, and she did not mean for her red-hot reaction to send him over the edge. She was hot, but seeing his reaction to hers scaled down her anger.

"Hey, I'm sorry. I didn't mean to over react. I guess I'm just on edge. Do you want to talk about whatever's bothering you? I guess you can see I'm a good 'talker' but I'm also a good listener." She smiled at him and tried to look through his eyes to see what was going on in his soul. But whatever was there was hidden and not meant for her to see. It was probably well hidden from everyone else, as well. If there would be no revelation, Donovan Davis would have to deal with his own demons, like every one else.

"I'm sorry too, Ivy," he said pulling on his extra large leather coat. "It's probably best that I leave now. I'll give you a call."

She walked him to the door without saying a word. There were several things she wanted to say and many questions she wanted to ask, but she bit her tongue, thinking it best to let this one go. She knew there were things about him that she liked, things about him that she could even love, but he was not hers to love. And maybe it was best that way. *Why torture herself into believing there could really ever be anything binding and special between them?* He was right. He was a married man, one whose relationship was extremely public.

Maybe when he walked out of her apartment, he would walk out of her life, and his issues would walk out with him. She closed the door behind him without saying a word, and then she locked it.

CHAPTER 15

Ivy leaned back against the door after Donovan left and tried not to think. She tried not to figure things out, or be concerned. She tried not to wonder if she had over reacted and if her fiery personality had caused her to jump too soon, and ruin something that might have been worth her patience. But then she stopped because she knew there would be another time; another time, with another man, with another problem. That was the story of every man she had ever met.

They all had issues. Some were full of promises, others full of money but void of promise. Some had plans and potential but felt they had been given a raw deal from life and would never succeed because the cards were ultimately stacked against them. The reality was that, very often, they were consumed by resentment, stifling their own possibilities but levying blame on an imaginary system of oppression. Some were brilliant but had no idea what to do with their knowledge. And some were just plain stupid. She had seen them all, but Donovan was special. He was different. What had just happened was different, despite the hidden issue. She decided to be patient. If he chose to share, she would try to be there for him. If not, life would go on.

Now feeling somewhat energized, she decided to check her answering machine and return the calls that could be addressed at this late hour, and that was just one. Before even pressing the playback button to listen, she dialed. When there was no answer at Gemma's apartment, she called her grandmother, figuring that she might have spent a couple nights with her. Her Granny was always so happy to have her around.

"Miss Hattie," she said quietly, "I'm sorry to call you so late, but I was looking for Gemma. She's not at home so I just figured she came over there to eat up the rest of my peach cobbler." They both chuckled.

"Oh baby don't worry about no time. Sleep ain't all that special to me anymore; I can do that any time, and you know you can call Miss Hattie any time you want. And speak up, child. You know you're calling a senior citizen, and all that whispering don't sound like nothin' but static on the line. But no baby; Gemma isn't here. She left for Chicago this morning. She's doing a show or something out there. I'm surprised she didn't tell you." They both chuckled. Miss Hattie was as full of life even at 2 a.m. Ivy spoke up.

"She probably did. I haven't checked my messages in a few days. I've been kind of swamped this whole week."

Ivy was right. There was a message from Gemma, not about a trip to Chicago or a stage play, but something about the Minister. She needed some advice, but unfortunately her friend was unable to oblige her. Realistically, she was more unavailable than unable, and for that she was sorry. Ivy apologized again to Miss Hattie for calling so late, and told her that she was sure that she would talk to Gemma soon. She knew she would call. She also knew Gemma's style and the life she lived. Leaving town at an impulse was not unusual. They would be together again soon, so she thought, and they would once again, help each other navigate the circumstances of their lives.

"You okay, baby?" Miss Hattie asked in a very concerned tone, moving away from her normal joviality.

"Oh yeah, I'm fine," Ivy quickly replied.

"No you ain't. But that's all right, 'cause you'll tell Miss Hattie when you're good and ready. Ya'll always do." Miss Hattie's intuition went far beyond female and way past feeling. It had reached a level only attainable through the trials and tribulations of experience and faith. Her advice was sage and cautiously sought, as her observations were almost always right.

"No, really Miss Hattie; I'm fine. I just wanted to try to catch up with Gemma since we seem to keep missing each other." Ivy tried to perk up her tone but she knew that Miss Hattie could feel her spirit and tell that something was bothering her. She was right; eventually she would talk to her surrogate grandma about what was troubling her, but not now, not tonight.

"Okay sweetheart, I'll leave you alone. But if you need me, you call me. You hear?"

"Yes ma'am. Goodnight."

For a moment Ivy fell into logic and practicality, which manifested itself as avoidance, cleaning up the dishes and straightening up the kitchen. She had to chuckle at herself as she searched for the proper cabinets to place the practically new dishes and utensils. Because they were so rarely used, she really had no idea where they belonged. *"Where did he even find these things?"* She thought to herself as she looked around the room. Finally she stopped. She would deal with this life-sized puzzle in the morning. She reminded herself that she was tired and it was time to go to bed. As she went into her bedroom and removed her clothes, she thought about Donovan and the issue that stifled their evening. She did not want to worry about it because in her opinion, worry was reserved for those you love, and only sometimes those you want to love. She liked Donovan very much but did not want to be in love with him, at least not now.

A quick shower was prelude to sliding her slim nude body between the soft sheets. She smiled to herself. Despite the evening's weirdness, it had been a good day. It had been a very good day, for that matter. She remembered Aunt Cindy often telling her to count her blessings, and as she curled into a comforting and secure fetal position around a large down pillow, she did just that. Though truly grateful for all her blessings, Ivy still missed having someone beside her, someone with whom she could share her victories. She wanted to feel a strong but gentle arm over her shoulder, pulling her tightly into a manly chest that signified security and passion. She needed to feel that that loving man's anticipation pressing at her from behind, prepared for the very intimate and personal celebration of not only her courtroom victory, but every other triumph life. She needed to turn to a face that slept soundly after mutual satisfaction; a face that made her happy; a face that she could love.

Ivy rolled over on that thought and once again against her better judgment, picked up her phone and called Donovan's cell phone.

CHAPTER 16

Saturday, in most households, is a good day to practice personal avoidance by being essentially consumed in organized mayhem. Shopping, soccer, ballet, gymnastics, basketball, beauty shop appointments, team meetings, unscheduled visits, unsolicited calls, and the general management of an active family, made it easy to become so caught up in the events of the day that real heart to heart issues, between adults, were almost never brought forward. That was just how the Minister wanted it, this Saturday. The things that happened this week were better left undisclosed, or at least un-discussed, and he knew that his intuitive wife recognized some of his abnormal behavior. To the untrained eye, there was nothing unusual, nothing strange. But to a heart that had been tuned to for well over a decade, something was developing, and he knew she knew. So instead of challenging her instinct, he conveniently avoided her as inconspicuously as he could.

Their normal routine was well in place as they split the Saturday child taxiing responsibilities. Angie took Shelby to ballet and gymnastics and the Minister shuttled Junior to Soccer and Basketball. Normally they would catch up with one another by late afternoon or early evening and have dinner together after delivering the children to Grandma's. But this evening, the activities would be a bit different, and they would challenge the Minister, his psychology, his spirituality, and his nerve.

He was well within his routine, sitting on the sidelines at the recreation center gymnasium watching his son run up and down the court. Ed, Jr. was an amazing little basketball player. He had not yet grown into himself but he made up for his lack of height with speed and agility. He was a little speedster with the heart of a lion, and he played with an unbelievable zeal to win. This would be a highly valued commodity in later years. Watching his son always stirred childhood memories. The Minister listened to the sneakers chirp against the gym floor as the boys moved with near geometric precision, and thought about his days on the court, which were absent of one very special spectator.

His father had taken care of him well, in terms of providing a stable home and financial access to a good education, but he had never actually seen the Minister play in one game, ever. He had never taken him to one practice or even shared a back yard tip or two. He had never brought drinks for the team or applauded wildly when his son received one of the numerous cheesy trophies with the plastic figurine on top. He had never shared a Kodak moment, comforting his son after a loss while he sat on his knee, telling him that there would be another day, another chance; another game. He had been to busy with the church. He was always there, always preaching, always teaching, always counseling; always doing whatever he did down at the church. He remembered his father kissing his mother on her forehead on his way out the door saying in his husky, gruff voice, "*If you need me, I'll be down at the church.*"

The parishioners loved him. He was their hero. But his family did not know him, at least, not like a family should. When he was a child, the Minister often wondered what was so mysteriously compelling down at the church, and why his father always had to be there. He knew what happened on Sunday's; he was always there for that. But in his young mind he often questioned the importance of his father's daily visits. In his teenage years, his wonder grew into resentment and disenchantment with a church that few understood, not even he. It would take many years of introspective thought before he would properly grasp the depth of his feelings toward both his father and the church that had removed him from being a fixture in so many consequential aspects of his life.

Ed Jr. shot from the outside making a three-pointer and the Minister broke his train of thought momentarily and cheered. When he returned to his thoughts of his father and childhood, and all of the missed programs, recitals, sporting events, award ceremonies, and momentous occasions, he considered what bothered him most, and it was not that his father had missed these events. It was that he had not missed his father. He had become so used to him not being around him for those special moments in his life, that he stopped expecting him. If nothing else, he was determined to make sure that his children would miss him if he was not actively present in their lives. So as difficult as it was with his active schedule of the preaching, teaching, counseling, and whatever else he did on the road or at the church, he made sure that he was at the gym to see Junior hit that three-pointer. When his son looked directly into his father's eyes for validation and congratulations that only his father could give, the Minister was going to be there. He, likewise, made sure that he was in the auditorium when Shelby twirled and twisted, leaped and tumbled her way across the stage, and then searched the darkness of the audience to find her father's adoring smile. It did not matter if he had to fly in and was dead tired from travel and jet lag. He would be there. He never wanted his children to think of him as he did his own father, or more accurately, not think of him, as he did his own father.

He and Junior had worked out some hand signals during their home practices, and although Junior listened to the coach for instructions, throughout the game, he glanced at his father for guidance and quick tips. The Minister would communicate where the next open shot might be, or what the defensive weaknesses were, or where the open pass was. He was the same sideline coach that every father cannot deny being.

It was in the midst of a moment of hand signaling that the Minister fielded a cell phone call. It was Angie calling to inform him that there was a dinner arrangement for the evening that she had conveniently forgotten to mention. They were to meet Lydia and Donovan at an upscale steak house in the city. The ladies had made the date at their last spa visit.

This would definitely make for an interesting evening, and the Minister thought, for a moment about his brief encounter with Lydia in his office. He was almost positive that she had not shared that with anyone. *Why would she incriminate herself?* She came on to him and he just responded, and besides there was obviously something much deeper about her actions. She was not searching for a tryst in the office with a man she hardly knew. Any man would jump at the chance to bed a prize like Lydia Davis. But something was going on inside her that she wanted to release to someone she trusted. The Minister was just confused about her method of selecting a confidante and her process of disclosure.

He tried not to think about how awkward the dinner might be, and the looming feelings of embarrassment that might have to be suppressed. He also tried not to think about the fact that his wife had been what seemed purposely slothful, about informing him about the engagement. *Did she know something? Was she trying to catch him off guard?* That was not her style. She was a patient sleuth. And if he was going to hang himself based on the revelation of some impropriety, he would do so with no help from Angie. That was her style, and it always worked. She would wait patiently for the story to unfold.

They hung up after exchanging updates on the children's activities. Shelby was twirling, leaping and dancing beautifully, and Junior was sinking jump shots nicely. The Minister put the thoughts of Lydia, Angie, the dinner and the office encounter in the hidden compartment of his mind and refocused his attention on the game. There would be time for that later, and no decisions were necessary at this point, anyway. He was, however, surprised that he had not heard from Lydia, especially since they would be seeing each other at dinner. But maybe that was her message to him. Maybe her silence was her security and her way of alerting him to behave reciprocally.

On the way home from the basketball game, the Minister and his sweaty little son stopped at a convenience store for a sport drink. When Junior was sent into the store to purchase the items, the Minister's cell phone rang again. He figured it would be Lydia, but was surprised to hear the voice of Detective Alexandra Heart on the other end.

"I waited nearly all night long for you," was her response to his 'hello.' The Minister was caught off guard but did his best not to show it. He did not think she even had his cell phone number, and he hoped that she was not using her professional privileges to track him down.

"Hey Alex," he said slowly, keeping his eye on his son through the store windows. He did not want to be found engaged in a heated conversation with Alex upon Junior's return. "I'm sorry I missed you. I tried to page you again but I figured you were already gone."

He was actually glad that he had not gotten in touch with her. She was like a drug for him, and it took formidable will power and circumstantial luck to keep him from her. He knew she was detrimental to any of his moral efforts and if he got too close, he might be unable to save himself. He could feel the knot in his stomach beginning to writhe.

"What's on your plate tonight Eddie?" She said dryly.

"Having dinner with Angie and some friends," he quickly and quietly responded, trying to rush the conversation along.

."Where are you right now, Eddie?"

He knew what that question meant. It meant that she knew exactly where he was and wanted him to know it. He paused as long as he could before answering. He began looking around the parking lot and spied an unmarked police vehicle with darkly tinted windows.

"You know exactly where I am, Alex."

She hung up and did exactly what he hoped she would not. Within seconds she was at the car window. She was strikingly beautiful yet menacing at the same time. She had an intriguing South American beauty that was compelling, but behind her eyes was a look of volatility that could spook a man. She graphically explained to him, in quite literal detail, what he had missed the night he was held up in his office by his encounter with Lydia. She took her time with the description because she knew how his mind worked, and how he loved to create pictures based on words, and what he saw behind her words made his mouth water. He abruptly halted his mental picture painting because he had his son to focus on, and when his children were present, his attention was to belong to them, or at least, that was to be his concerted effort. But as she walked away, he watched what had driven him crazy on many an encounter over the years, Brazilian booty. They made no plans. They never had before, and they would not today. But his interest was peaked and he would have to have her soon, and she knew that. That was her plan, although if she had had her way, she would have had him right then, right there in the parking lot, in broad daylight.

"Who was that lady you were talking to, Dad?" Junior said nonchalantly as he plopped down in the car.

"Nobody, son; just an old friend I worked with a few years ago." The Minister was so caught up in his thoughts that he had not noticed the giant sized frosted drink and candy bar that Junior had purchased, instead of the healthy sports beverage and protein bar he was supposed to have gotten. He glanced at his father, waiting briefly for his reprimand, smiled and then slurped away.

CHAPTER 17

Jonathan's Steakhouse was a chic eatery that catered to a mostly exclusive clientele. Though presumably pretentious, it was not stoic and cold, like most trendy and posh locales. The character was actually warm and inviting, especially to the touchable and modern elite. It was not unusual to see celebrities and behind the scenes movers and shakers dining there. The lighting was dim and intimate, and the booths were designed with circular smoked glass wall enclosures that made every party semi-private. The proprietors had done a fabulous job in terms of the artistry and design. It was the unique fusion of several types of wood and glass that made the interior a place of memorable beauty. They had successfully blended the traditionalism of beef with the modern, and always avant-garde, attitudes of fine dining, and the décor brought forth the ideal exquisitely.

When the couples arrived, the ladies greeted each other like old friends with sincere hugs and genuine air kisses, and then introduced their husband's. The men greeted each other warmly with their normal male apprehension well subdued, but still very much on alert. They were both warm and expressive, possessing similar character traits. There would not be an issue of territory tonight, as each stood handsomely with their most valued possessions beside them.

The women were equally beautiful in their own definitive ways. The picture was portrait material, as Lydia and Angela stood in the entryway with the most attractive male specimens in the building. Heads turned toward all of them and the men seemed pleased with both their women and themselves.

The Minister raised his antennae to maintain his awareness, especially because he had not heard from Lydia concerning their encounter.

He did not want to relax just yet, as he was unsure about what had been discussed, if anything at all. Although there had been no indication that she had said a word, he knew the nature of human beings and the often uncontrollable desire to talk about instances or events that are, in some way, special or exciting or simply outside of ones normal routine.

He covertly observed her carefully. He clearly noticed that Lydia was conspicuously focusing most of her attention to Angie and him, and almost avoiding engaging Donovan in any of the conversation. Donovan on the other hand seemed to focus his attention completely on the Minister. There were two, and sometimes three different conversations going on between the four of them. All the while however, Lydia and Donovan were nearly mute toward each other. Despite these idiosyncrasies, which could be meaningless, Donovan and Lydia were seemingly as charming a couple as they were made to be in the media. He was kind and generous, and seemed willing to be a part of anything positive for the community. He was also smart, not just for a football player, but as a man in general. He was familiar with popular novels, current events, and issues behind sports, and was willing to share very educated opinions on each. *He was special*, the Minister thought. He was not like most athletes and celebrities that were beginning to frequent the church. He would be a great asset to the mentoring program and he was sure the boys would love him. Most of them already did, and they would be ecstatic when they met him in person.

The Minister was very careful when it came to placing role models in front of his boys group at the church, especially when it came to professional athletes. Many of them were starting to visit the church regularly and deposit large sums of money in the offering plates, but for many of them, it was more like penance or guilt motivated confession in hopes of cleansing their consciences of the depraved lives that they lived. He did not want the boys to look up to just anyone. The Minister liked Donovan however, and genuinely enjoyed their conversation. He was exactly the kind of role model the boys needed.

Lydia was the same; warm, kind and charming. He had not seen her in this setting before. As a matter of fact, she had seemed rather reserved at the time of their initial introduction. It was almost as if the woman who had entered his office and thrown herself into his arms did not exist. She appeared confident and witty; knowing exactly what to say and how to say it. He watched her interact with Angie and could see that they shared something deeper than most friends. There was an obvious connection that had drawn them to each other and would probably keep them together. They giggled and whispered, pointing out people and things in the restaurant about which they shared common thoughts.

Everyone needed a friend like Angie. She was a glistening star that brightened any relationship. Lydia was just like every other person, including the Minister, who was drawn to her light. Lydia was a star as well. It was evident on screen and in the media, but now her light was viewed first hand, and the two of them created a brightness that filled the room.

The laughter, conversation and two bottles of Pierre Jouet coaxed the Minister to genuinely let his guard down and relax. He was enjoying Donovan and Lydia, and Donovan, especially seemed to want to connect with him. He dismissed the thought of having to try to send Lydia a subliminal message of some sort, and just enjoyed the evening. If she was okay, he was okay. By the time the dessert carriage arrived, the group was talking and laughing so loud that heads turned not only to view this group of gorgeous people, but also to try to hear the funny stories they were sharing, in hopes of joining in on the fun. After they ordered, the ladies excused themselves to freshen up, giving the Minister and Donovan a moment alone. Normally this might be a problem, with the blot in history that had been made with Lydia, but the evening had been so unpretentious and relaxing that the Minister almost felt safe and secure. This moment was also potentially awkward because the two had just met. But these two were diplomats, gentlemen and masters of poker face, probably knowing each other better than either would admit.

"So Ed; Lydia tells me that you were a psychologist before you became a minister."

"Actually, I still am. I think it gives me an added dimension of understanding when it comes to counseling the members," the Minister responded after taking a sip of his decaf.

"So do you only counsel your members or do you accept outside clients as well?"

The Minister looked over the rim of his cup directly into Donovan's eyes, sensing that there was something to this line of questioning a bit deeper than small talk while the girls were in the ladies room. This was the time to talk about sports or cars, not about counseling and psychology. This was the time to discuss the details of how Donovan picked up the fumble of an end zone sacked quarterback ran the longest defensive touchdown in NFL history. But then the Minister remembered that he was not just talking to an average guy. Earlier conversation had made that very clear.

"No, I do still have clients outside the membership that I see on a regular basis," he said. "Why, is there someone who needs my services?" He smiled unassumingly.

"Yes there is. I have a ball player friend who is dealing with some really tough issues and I think he needs to speak to someone soon before he does something he might regret."

The Minister placed his cup back on the saucer and folded his hands, preparing to listen, but just as Donovan was beginning to describe the problem that plagued his friend, the ladies returned, prompting him to abruptly change the subject. Because of his quick switch, the Minister gathered that the "friend" in question was probably really Donovan, and the subject matter was not something to be discussed in front of his wife. He smiled within himself at the normalcy of Donovan's quick attempt at private conversation and thought simply, *secrets. We all have secrets.*

Just after they sat down, the waiter delivered the desserts. In front of Lydia, he placed three dense and rich, chocolate marble fudge brownies topped with a dollop of cream cheese, a sprinkling of raspberries, covered generously with chocolate sauce, which ran down the arrangement like lava oozing down the jagged cliff-sides of an active volcano. Before Angie he placed her favorite; warm chocolate-hazelnut bread pudding, laced with hazelnuts and accented with a liquid chocolate center. The plate was decorated with an abundant sprinkling of bitter chocolate truffles and almonds. Before the Minister was a hot apple and walnut cobbler served steaming hot, crowned with a scoop of homemade vanilla ice cream. Donovan did not see anything on the dessert carriage that interested him. He jokingly expressed the fact that his tastes were a lot less sophisticated. With that said he had the server ask the chef to prepare him a huge banana split with a healthy side of whipped cream, nuts and cherries. He was obliged without hesitation. *Jonathan*'s was that kind of restaurant. They all "oohed" and "aahed" at the sight of their delectable desserts, wondering how they would eat them after such a filling meal.

"So tell me, Ed," Donovan said as began to laugh, "What are the psychological implications of what we ordered tonight. I know all this chocolate has to mean something."

They all waited impatiently with a laugh and tuned their ears to him like extras on the old E.F. Hutton brokerage commercials.

"Well, if you really want to know," the Minister said laughing as well and then settling into a tone of educational lecture, "the chocolate is supposed to be an aphrodisiac."

"Is that right?" Lydia chimed in with a response.

"That's right," he said, looking into her light eyes. "Aztec king Montezuma so believed in the aphrodisiac powers of chocolate that he supposedly drank fifty golden goblets of it every day. What more can be said? For those who love it, chocolate can be a religious experience, so if I was to analyze your plate, Lydia, I'd say you had something pretty wild planned for your husband tonight, or maybe I should say, something very spiritual."

"And I'm no psychologist, but I would say the same for you by looking at Angie's plate."

"Well let the church say, Amen!" The Minister's exclamation again sent the group to an outburst of unbridled laughter.

"I always tell him he's full of useless information, and maybe he should take that knowledge on *Jeopardy* and win a few bucks," Angie said laughing and holding her husband's chin in a sarcastic but adoring way. When she did that, it appeared that she inadvertently, but quite conspicuously used her left hand, displaying her significantly brilliant wedding ring. Lydia had not made a pass or even a questionable gesture, but women are known for establishing territorial rules early.

"I don't know, girl. Sounds to me like he's going to use that useless knowledge to his advantage tonight, with all this talk about chocolate and aphrodisiacs," Lydia said, laughing.

They all applauded and laughed when Angie simply said, "Well bring it on!"

"What about mine?" Donovan interjected. "What do you read into my dessert, Doc?" The mood was still light and comical.

"Well, maybe you should tell me. I don't know if I should touch the psychological significance of banana's and whipped cream." Once again the group laughed. But there was plenty of psychological significance to the dessert Donovan enjoyed, but there was no need to deal with it now. Its private ramifications would make a public appearance much later down the road.

As they waited for the valet to bring their cars around, Angie saw a former business associate and went over to say hello. Donovan went inside to use the men's room and Lydia was finally alone with the Minister for a brief moment. They said nothing to each other, and then Lydia slipped a note into the Minister's overcoat. Her gesture re-ignited his engines.

When the group reassembled, everyone shared pleasant farewells and promised to meet again soon. Lydia had turned back on like a light switch. Just a minute ago she was silent when he thought she should have said something, and now she returned to being the charming, public, smiling, entertaining wife. There was a new level of understanding beginning to develop in the Minister's mind. Some of the pieces of Lydia's puzzle were at least, visible now, and he took her slipping the note in his pocket as a desire for him to start putting them together. He was anxious to read her note, and when he and Angie came home and bedded the children, he headed for his study. He could always go there without question. Angie was not naïve, by any means, but she knew that the Minister's home office was his private domain, at least when he was at home to rule it. The note from Lydia read:

> *Thank you for your time. I'm sorry I had to run. I hope we can get together again because there really is something I need to tell you.*
> *L*

The Minister folded the note and placed it in his upper right hand drawer, the place that he thought no one ever looked. He folded his hands behind his head and leaned back in his chair, evaluating the whole scenario of Lydia and Donovan. There was definitely something going on there. The dynamic of the whole interaction was curious, but the Minister really did not want to think about it at the moment. He truly searched for spiritual focus. It was difficult though, because his mind continued to wander. He knew there was little room for righteousness in a sinful mind, so he slipped out of his chair and onto the floor. Laying face down and completely prostrate, he prayed aloud to combat his troubled mind. His biggest struggle was with himself, and he was entering dangerous territory.

He also took extra time in his study hoping that when he went into the bedroom he would find his wife sleeping soundly. That was his sign that everything was okay, and that there were no burning questions or suspicions that needed to be immediately addressed. He knew from experience that when a woman was suspicious about the activities of her mate, she could take on the virtues of an insomniac, staying awake for days waiting for him to come home to be interrogated.

When the Minister walked into the bedroom, Angie appeared to be sleeping soundly. He walked over to her, looking at her beautiful black hair and studying her face. There were no flaws. She was a natural beauty, one of a select class of women who never had to wear a stitch of make up to enhance her features. If and when she did, she did so by choice, not necessity. He kissed her cheek gently, and when he did, she smiled. Angie was not asleep. She never slept until he came home and she never rested until he was in her arms.

CHAPTER 18

Sunday morning was business as usual. The Minister had Brown pick him up early so that he could get to his church office before things got too busy. Several developing projects needed his attention. The Minister did all he could to delegate responsibilities to others in an effort to concentrate on spiritual leadership. He knew the danger of a pastor involved in too many of the intra-workings of the church and how it could tax his efforts toward sound spiritual guidance.

His plan was to meet with the various project leaders and discuss fiscal plans for the upcoming year. But when he arrived, he found several interesting messages waiting for him. One was from Gemma, which he was anxious to address; one was from Alex, who had him a bit concerned; and the other was from Donovan, about which he was very curious. *What could Donovan want?* They had just seen each other last night.

While the group assembled in the outer office under Brown's direction, the Minister went inside and closed his door after cheerfully shouting, good morning, and informing them that he would be out momentarily. He knew how to pacify Brown and keep him out of his hair. Put him in charge of something, if nothing more than stirring coffee. Brown was the type that needed to feel like he was in some way, more powerful or knowledgeable than someone else. The Minister's psychology always worked on Brown. As badly as he wanted to be separated and recognized outside the Minister's circle, Brown knew that his greatest avenue toward gaining the respect of the people was to be as loyal to the Minister as he could. The reality was that Brown's lack of intellect and often lagging intuition was his greatest asset, as far as the Minister's activities were concerned.

The Minister sat behind his desk and viewed his messages. Gemma had called the office before she left town, and left a number in Chicago at which she could be reached. She had also left a note.

Dear Pastor Hebert,

It was great seeing you and your family at church. I wish I could be there more often but as you know, my career forces me to travel. I remember you saying that you wanted to keep up with my career and to let you know where I was performing. Well, if you have any business in Chicago any time soon, I'll be performing at the Court Theater on the South Side of Chicago. It would be nice to see you, very nice. I left a number with your secretary before I left. Feel free to call.

Gemma

The Minister was energized and clearly read between the lines of Gemma's note. He had successfully communicated with her by way of his meaningful glances, and the tone of her note indicated some appreciable reciprocation. But his countenance faded when he read the note from Alexandra. It was written on her official precinct stationary.

Hello Eddie,

You should have the chef butterfly your filet mignon. That way you can make sure it's medium rare all the way through, just like you like it. I know you don't care for a bloody center. By the way, Angie looks great, and was that the new one that held you up the other night?

Alex

The Minister covered his face with his hands after he read the message, and sighed. He knew that he would have to see Alex now, because she was watching him, and the only way to dispatch her was to oblige her. He really wanted to see her just as much as she did him. He fought within himself because he knew that any encounter would most likely lead to trouble.

Alex had a problem with the Minister because he would never completely acquiesce to her desired conditional ideas of a relationship. There were things that she wanted from him that he could have done but was always unwilling. He had the same issues with her. There was no friendship for them to salvage. They had stopped being friend's long time ago. What they had now was a faceless, formless but terribly magnetic entity between them that linked them like distant Siamese twins joined at the genitals. As hard as either might try, they could not get away from each other. The success of their relationship was based solely on its non-existence, and the Minister knew that he would have to reach within himself to find the right psychology to properly deal with Alex. At that very moment, he thought about the day they had first met, and he wished he had never left that first note.

During a meeting concerning psychological issues surrounding a case on which he had been asked by the police department to assist, the Minister could not help but send and receive a few, very powerful, subliminal messages to the exotic looking officer across from him. There was a heat that emanated from her body and reached across the table and grabbed him, and he wanted nothing more than to burn with her. He knew that beauty was not relegated to profession but he just never expected such exquisite elegance in the police precinct. Overwhelmed by his inability to secure his lust, he left a note with the office manager, and asked her to make sure that Detective Heart received it. She was the most exquisite detective he had ever seen, and he felt that he had to say something to her. The note invited Alex to call him, which she did that very night, explaining that she too felt an overwhelming attraction.

The events that followed were the catalyst to two years of sexual insanity that the Minister thought he finally had under control. But he did not, not then and certainly not now. He should have never written that note, because Alex seemed to never go away. He thought that he could be satisfied with a single encounter, a moment of passion filled insanity, a rendezvous of animalistic madness. The real problem was that he never truly wanted her to go away. Not until now.

The voice mail message from Donovan had come in early that morning. Judging by the time record and an estimation of how far they had to drive after dinner, it seemed to have come in just after he and Lydia came home. His message expressed gratitude for the evening and the desire to get together again, and a promise to visit the church and assist with the mentoring program. But he closed by inviting the Minister to come out to the house they were renting, while waiting on their new purchase to close escrow, to shoot pool, alone. In and of itself, the message was harmless and meaningless, but it was the emphasis on the Minister visiting him alone that made him think. It sparked memories from last night's dinner. The Minister recalled how Donovan seemed to focus his own interaction with him and Angie, and how Lydia seemed to conspicuously avoid him, engaging in conversations of her own. It was not the avoidance of a battered wife attempting to maintain a façade of normalcy. It was deeper than that. It was almost as if their relationship was planned and professional, void of mutual attraction. But the Minister had to prioritize and deal with what was most intriguing to him. He had to find a reason to go to Chicago.

The Minister's moment of thoughtful planning was cut short when Brown peeked in the door informing him that the group was ready to begin the meeting. His secretary, India, joined the group to take notes. Although she had her faults, she was a valuable asset to the Minister's work at the church. He could depend on her to think about and remember things that he would probably let slip by. That was probably because his mind was often in places it should not have been, and India knew that. She was a stickler for detail, and when it was time for her to work, she did just that. She was able to get over herself momentarily and get the job done.

India sat conservatively dressed in a dark suit, her hair pulled back into a tight bun, with two legal pads that had almost every word of the meeting recorded, verbatim. The Minister had to chuckle to himself when he saw her because he knew that she took every word he said to heart. He had once paid her a compliment on her hairstyle saying that he was a 'sucker for a girl with her hair pulled back', and since that day, she had worn her hair pulled back and made every effort to listen closely for hints of his preferences. Maybe that might lead the way to his heart.

The meeting adjourned and it was time to get ready for another service. As the Minister retired to his office for a few moments of solitude, he expected visitors any moment. He wanted to drop everything and call Gemma in Chicago, but he purposely pushed that desire aside. It was time to focus on the task at hand. It was time to preach to the people.

When Angie finally came in, she was accompanied by her new attachment, Lydia. For some reason he did not expect her, but there she was, and she was beautiful. It was strange because there was something inside him that wanted her to change, and not be so attractive to him any more. He struggled to change her in his mind, in hopes of better stowing own desire. But her striking countenance still claimed the Minister's attention. Angie went through her normal routine of checking on him and making sure that he had everything he needed before she went inside the sanctuary. He was fine. All he needed was a bit of privacy, and after a brief moment of small talk, she granted him that. The Minister asked about Donovan, though he really did not expect him to be there. Lydia relayed his apologies and informed the Minister that he had some pressing business meetings that were scheduled for Sunday morning, and that he would, most definitely, be in attendance next week. The Minister thanked Lydia for filling him in, but he said nothing of the message he had received from her husband early that morning. He did not think that message was meant to be shared, and if that were the case, he would let Donovan do that. There had been indications of Donovan's desire for private conversation at dinner the night before.

The Minister sat with his chair facing the window, and with his door pushed shut, he prayed. He prayed about everything but the issues before him, and that was because he was not ready to be delivered from his dilemma. But he did ask God to help him to at least, shut out the developing situations that were circulating around him and help him to focus on his immediate assignment.

The last person to enter his office was Crawford, who was always good for a laugh. One of the reasons the Minister could tolerate Crawford's antics, and kept him on as head of the music staff, was because of their common sense of humor. Crawford was also one of the most intelligent people the Minister knew. His eclectic style and theatrical behavior was a smoke screen through which very few could see. With it, he camouflaged his brightness in exchange for acceptance by the masses. There often seems to be no place for the brilliant amongst the mediocre. Either they assimilate in some way or suffer, suffocate, and die.

The Minister and Crawford were in that select number of brilliantly bright who had actually found the ability to function within the masses. To the common individual, they had nothing in common but to those who could see behind their eyes, they were two peas in a pod. Few people knew that Crawford had scored a perfect 1600 on his SAT, or that he had once contributed valuable information to a stem cell research project as a laboratory assistant to a university professor. He also provided that professor with in home fringe benefits that helped establish his name, Centipede, in "the life" and a reputation that preceded him. The Minister appreciated Crawford's sharp wit and the fact that he was almost always dead on when it came to his observations about life and people. He and the Minister could always find something good to talk about, or at least laugh about.

Crawford entered this time only to inform the Minister of a performance project that he was participating in that might take him away for a few days, and possibly the following Sunday. He assured the Minister that the music at the church would not suffer and that the band would still be prepared as always. When asked where he was going, the Minister was surprised at his answer. Chicago. Crawford was conducting a workshop on Music Ministry for a group of Chicago area churches.

The Minister could not believe how easily an excuse to get to Chicago had fallen into his hands. He congratulated Crawford with a handshake and pat on the back, and told him that he might find his way to the "windy city." Crawford exclaimed that he thought that his visit would be great, and officially invited him to address the group at one of the sessions. He told the Minister that he would not inform the group that he was coming because he knew it would be a special treat and the workshop participants would be ecstatic to hear him. They would all be pleasantly surprised at his presence, and that would add a few feathers in Crawford's hat. Not only would he be seen as a skilled and knowledgeable musician, but also one who had enough pull to get a renowned "spiritual dignitary" there.

Crawford was beaming at the Minister's willingness to come to his event, and honestly could not believe that with his busy schedule, he could get away with such short notice. Beyond that, he was surprised that the Minister showed such interest, as Crawford had done similar events in the past and the Minister had never come before. But he just chalked it up to coincidence and timing.

The Minister closed the conversation, ushering Crawford out the door and said, "I've been looking for a reason to get to Chicago."

CHAPTER 19

The church service went as usual. The deacons, the mother's, the ushers, nurses, and venerable hat brigade all played their normal roles like members cast in a "made-for-television" movie. The vocal worshipers, the stoic and impassive ones, the sophisticated and the country were all poised in praise, and ready for their weekly dose of religion.

Crawford worked the crowd to a frenzied state with the music, and everyone sat prepared for the entrance of the Minister and to hear what pearls of wisdom he might share. He entered and after his salient prayer on one knee behind the podium, he sat down and scanned the audience to see where certain people were seated. He was only really concerned about two, and they were just where they should be.

Lydia's smile looked almost seductive this morning, even though that may not have been her intent. She had opened a door to the Minister that would not be easy to close. His thoughts would drift far beyond counseling now. When he looked at her, he saw someone who he wanted to help in a very different way now. He wanted to give her what she wanted even though that was most definitely, not what she needed. And then there was his jewel, Angie, who sat and looked as she had for many years; tastefully gorgeous. The Minister always knew he could look to her for the support that he needed, and for the bulk of their relationship, she had been an ever-yielding spring of reliable encouragement.

There were numerous similarities between Angie and his mother. Both of them had often pointed out that fact to him, but he had always dispelled the theory that men seek mates that are duplicates of their mother's. Though it was often true in most cases, he believed it did not apply to him. It did, as it does to almost every man. Be that as it may;

his thoughts about his beautiful wife were an interesting lead into his sermon.

The Minister preached a charismatically gratifying sermon basing his points on the 23rd Psalm, but he illuminated his thoughts from a very different perspective. After reading the biblical text, he closed the Bible and put his hands in his pockets. Everyone knew he was preparing to deliver a unique message from an unparalleled approach. The crowd waited patiently for him to begin.

"I thought my mother was great," he said as he stood behind the podium. "I still think she's great." He briefly glanced at the floor. "But as a young boy, she was larger than life. With her mere presence or voice, she could change the way I felt."

The deacons on the front row followed him with their eyes. Even though some of them sat steeped in tradition with their pant legs pulled high, exposing shiny white nylon socks and vintage Stacy Adams' biscuits, they were still eager to hear what their young pastor had to say. They were proud of their pastor, to such a point that he was often a topic at their traditional barber shop town hall meetings. It was there that they discussed the most important issues of the day.

"I can remember a particular time when I was about seven years old, and I was suffering from a nasty cold, and Mama had to leave me to go to the market for a little while. She really didn't want to leave and she asked me if I'd be all right staying home with Daddy for about an hour. She'll never know how much I appreciated her asking about my thoughts and feelings. My friends, a child's world can often be made or broken over some very simple issues."

The crowd echoed sentiments of agreement, in church crowd fashion.

"I told her that I thought I'd be okay but to hurry back. And she did. But while she was gone, I was in absolute misery. Everything that hurt seemed to hurt worse. Everything that ached seemed to ache even more. Every aspect of my illness, however simple it may have been, was worse. My nose ran more. My head ached more. My throat hurt more. Everything just seemed worse. My father was there and he asked me every now and again if I was okay and I would nod a simple 'yes', but deep down inside I knew that my medicine was at the market and that the aches would not cease and the runny nose would not get better, and my throat, and my stomach, and my head and everything else that was hurting would not get better, until Mama came back.

"You see, Mama was better than aspirin. She was better than Tylenol or Cold Eaze or Nyquil or BC powder. Mama's presence was all

I needed. I just needed her to be there. Oh yes, she gave me some over-the-counter medication that I'm sure helped my condition, but the virtues of comfort and the divinity of healing that God grants his people was made clear to me that day, as His love for me was manifested in the presence of my caring mother. There were things that Mama could do that just couldn't be done by anyone else."

The inflections of his voice were already bringing excited responses from the crowd. Some of them thought they knew where he was going, and in Black church when one thinks they know where the preacher is going or want to signify their agreement, they are encouraged to shout, 'Amen!' He moved to the side of the podium, grabbing it with his right hand.

"And when she came back, both my physical and my mental condition changed. When I saw her familiar face and her compassionate smile, things didn't seem to hurt so badly. When I felt her soft touch on my forehead and sank into her outstretched arms, things just didn't seem to be as miserable. I didn't cling to her leg for the rest of the evening. I didn't have to do that because it was enough just knowing that she was there. Just knowing that if I needed her, and she was there. And being there was enough. Her being there gave me confidence! Her being there gave me hope! Her being there was my deliverance!"

The Minister allowed the congregation time to applaud his intro and then moved into his scriptural exegesis, sharing that David writes this 23rd Psalm about a God who is always there and willing to attend to the needs of His children. He discussed the parental aspects of the nature of God and how everyone deserves His care. He powerfully exclaimed the faithfulness and divine concern shown in God's relationship with David, the author of this often quoted scripture. He brought forth the issue of mankind's familiarity with this particular Psalm and how it is often called on in times of stress and fear. He focused momentarily on verse four, where David wrote: "Yea though I walk through the valley of the shadow of death, I will fear no evil: for Thou art with me; Thy rod and Thy staff, they comfort me." He made the congregants understand that David trusted God even in the worst and most trying circumstances, and felt protected and confident just knowing that God was there. The crowd went wild when he detailed God's constant presence, and the same confidence he had in his Mama was the confidence he now had in God.

"Whenever I need Him, He's there," he sang, his voice rising and falling again, as if scooping up the next phrase with rhythmic precision.

"Whenever I call Him, He's there! Whenever I'm lonely, He's there! Whenever I'm sad, He's there! Whenever I'm lost, He's there!

Whenever I'm hurt, He's there! Whatever my condition, whatever my circumstance, even with all my flaws and all my shortcomings, God is there! Even with my unreliability, and even though I'm not all I should always be, He's there! He's there! He's there! He's there!" He fell into his seat, seemingly spent after the energetic discourse, and the congregation went wild.

His sermon was beautiful and right on time. Once again it pricked Lydia as she thought about the absent attributes of true love in her life. There was something or someone on which she sought to depend. Lydia knew that she was reaching out to the man who stood before her preaching, but she was not sure how he saw her, or if he was willing to accept her in that vein. She had presented an aspect of her psyche that she knew should not have been brought forward, at least not yet. But she could not help herself. She had been overwhelmed by personal issues that the Minister knew nothing about, and he had been on the receiving end of behavior that was inevitable, especially after his inviting expressions of warmth and underlying pulse of detectable passion.

Angie glanced at Lydia and could see in her eyes that there was more than just a spiritual understanding of the sermon in her gaze. Women know women by more than just the virtue of gender. They are trained to recognize and listen to their own intuition. While women are encouraged to act based on feelings, men are often taught to act in spite of them. Angie was not sure, but she could see that there was something in Lydia's heart that needed attention, but she was not willing to have that attention come from her husband.

The service continued and drew to a close well within the tradition of normalcy. Even in the excited state of the congregation, there were no immediately recognizable surprises. Brown came forward and forced his solo, as usual, after the Minister had finished his sermon completely. The Minister had a few outbursts from his seat that signified his being caught up in the Spirit, which drew the crowd in even more. Crawford gave Brown half-hearted musical support, as usual, and there was a small contingency of the crowd that applauded Brown, while the majority could not wait for him to sit down. He had a forum and it was his natural character to take full advantage of his fleeting opportunity. It was business as usual. But no one and nothing could take away from the power of the Minister's message. People all over the church were still standing and shouting as a result of his sermonic eloquence.

Angie leaned over and nudged Lydia, who seemed to still be focused on the Minister. There was a new intensity with which she watched and listened, and though Angie recognized it, she said nothing about it. There was no need to read into something that might be nothing, but she was a wife who had seen this look before, and she knew what it could mean. In the very recent past, she had seen certain women leave the church after their subtle advances were intercepted and thwarted by those who, not only, protected the Minister, but also the First Lady.

Angela Hebert had quite a multitude of fans and supporters, as well. Lydia was at a complete disadvantage if she ever thought that she could successfully disrupt the sanctity of the picture of perfection that the church membership adored. And because Angie knew that, she was almost never worried about the miscellaneous attractions to her husband. She also did not believe that Lydia had cruel intentions of any sort. She had issues that needed attention from a counselor, and as far as she was concerned, there was none better for the job than the Minister. He really was a gifted psychologist who had even helped his lovely wife get through very tough times in her life. That was another aspect of his complexity. Angie had a difficult time clinging to anger at his improprieties when they were scaled against his proven abilities and genuine love for her and the children. Maybe she was wrong for feeling the way she did, but she was secure in her beliefs and opinions.

One of many church traditions is that the minister, who has preached that particular day, offers the benediction prayer after his or her final comments. It is the privilege of having the last word. Normally this was the Minister, but today Brown said the prayer. After preaching this time, the Minister was escorted out of the pulpit by two of his associates. This was common. Someone usually accompanied him to his office to assist him with hurriedly changing clothes and returning to the service to give the closing prayer. But this time, upon reaching a safe distance in the hall, he told them to return to the sanctuary, as he would make his way to his office on his own, change his clothes and then return to pray the benediction prayer. Just for a bit of insurance he told them if he was a little late returning to inform Brown that he was to handle the task. The Minister had no intention of returning to the service. There was something that he felt needed his immediate attention, and he was going to oblige the urge. He also knew that his office would soon be flooded with visitors and his moments of privacy were fleeting.

When he entered the office, he moved quickly past India's outer area and headed for his desk. He was glad that she was not in place yet. It was not unusual for her to make her way to the office before the close of service, being there to greet him upon his arrival. But this time he beat her. He opened his drawer and found the note from Gemma. Placing it on his desk before him, he dialed the number that she had left for him.

When the hotel operator answered, he asked to be connected to the suite of Gemma Kimbro. He had no intentions of talking to her just yet; he just wanted to make sure she was there, and she was. Her voice was sultry, but boasted the innocence of a diva whose life was not lived on stage; one who still searched for excitement and yielded to impulse. After she answered, he simply hung up the phone. There was no need to become impatient. His reservations would soon be secured, and he would be on his way to Chicago. He would not speak to her until he saw her face to face. That would make his presence more impacting, he thought. He had no idea whether Gemma would be there alone but something instinctive told him that she would.

More people seemed to recognize Lydia, this Sunday. They knew she was someone special because she was a guest of the Minister's wife but now they were matching her face to the face they had seen in magazines and on a numerous television Public Service Announcements. Several members came up to her and thanked her for coming and made sure that they asked her to return and bring her husband. That was the request of most of the young female worshipers, of course. She was perfect when it came to public interaction. Even Angie, a pubic relations master, admired her style. Just as they were preparing to make their way to the Minister's office, Shelby ran down the aisle and jumped into her mother's arms.

"Girl, are you trying to knock me down," Angie said smiling at her daughter. Shelby could not hold back her radiant, toothless smile that always generated a laugh. She was precious, and everyone at the church fawned over and spoiled her rotten.

"Who is this lady, Mommy? Is she your new friend?" Shelby whispered into her mother's ear, as she had both arms draped around her neck.

"This is Miss Lydia, Shelby. And yes she is Mommy's friend. Turn around and say hello."

"Hi," Shelby said, studying Lydia from head to toe.

The shamelessness of children can be trying, and it is important to make sure that exposure of personal flaws will not be heartbreaking, as they will, most definitely bring them to light. But even after Shelby's examination, Lydia had no flaws. At least none that were immediately detectable.

"I like your earrings," Shelby exclaimed, as her gaze rested on Lydia's medium sized diamond covered hoops.

"Why thank you, Shelby. I think yours are really pretty too. I think I'm going to try to find some just like that, and wear them next Sunday. Where did you get them?"

Shelby looked at her mother and shrugged her shoulders, breaking into that unforgettable smile.

"I don't know," she said, "Mommy got 'em for me."

"Well I'll talk to Mommy about it, okay."

"Okay." Shelby released her grip around Angie's neck and skipped away.

"I guess I passed?" Lydia looked at Angie with a big smile.

"I think you passed," Angie replied, "but I'll keep you informed if she comes to me later and asks why your shoes were the wrong color or why your lipstick was so bright."

They both laughed hard. Shelby was good for being expressive that way, but there were no external flaws to be exposed on Lydia Davis. The inside was a whole different story, however.

The Minister got through Angie and Lydia's visit to his office. He was very careful to make sure that they did not run into Miss Hattie because she might spill the beans about Gemma being in Chicago, although normally, she was more vocal about Gemma's returns that her departures. He told Lydia that he was looking forward to seeing Donovan at church very soon, and then told Angie to go ahead without him to dinner. He would catch up in about fifteen minutes; Brown would see that he was safely delivered. He sent word by India for Crawford to make his way to his office. Upon his arrival, he asked Crawford a few questions about the Chicago event. He had to get a few details without letting on too much about his own plans. The Minister navigated the conversation in such a way that Crawford eventually found a reason that he should, again, ask him to come and be a part of the meeting. That was just what the Minister wanted.

He was piecing together the cosmetics of his of his deception. That was another one of the talents he had perfected over the years. It was like the time he wanted a new baseball glove when he was a child. It cost eight dollars, of which he had none, but there had to be a way to make it happen. He had a glove but had seen another one in a sporting goods store that he wanted more. It was, in some way to him, better than the one he had, and he had convinced himself, not only that he needed it, but also that the risk of consequence was worth his deceitful efforts. That had been the story of his life.

The Minister knew his parents would not buy another glove just because he wanted another one, especially when the one that he had was in good condition. So and before even approaching them with the inquiry, he put his glove out in the yard knowing full well that after the family dog got hold of it, it would be virtually destroyed. That part of the plan worked capably. The dog destroyed the unsolicited gift completely, and the glove was useless. He endured a little flak about being more responsible with his items, but he knew that his parents would view what happened as a mistake, and be angrier at the dog than him.

The next day he took a ten dollar bill out of his father's wallet while he sat on the toilet, one of the few times he was at home and did not have his meticulously organized money with him. The Minister then went outside and threw the bill into the wind and watched it float down the street. After about a fifteen second head start, he darted behind it. When he caught and secured it in his pocket, he ran into the house exclaiming that he had found ten dollars and what a blessing it was seeing that he needed to purchase a new baseball glove. He further bent the story in his favor by saying that he was so responsible and conscientious that he would not ask his parents to make the purchase; instead he would use his new-found wealth, his bogus blessing from the heavenly skies, to make the purchase himself.

His actions gave credence to the theory that it is not a lie if the teller believes it. Unfortunately, he was not yet smarter than his father, who easily dissected the story, and then lashed into him like a freight train after fully unmasking the truth. That was the other thing on which his father prided himself: swift, harsh, unchallenged and unquestioned discipline. Though often more severe than necessary, there were times such as this when the Minister needed a strong hand.

This episode set a foundational precedent in the Minister's life in many ways. He walked a dynamic parallel of choice at that time. He had to choose between favorable behavior that insured the avoidance of his father's swift hand, and improving the weaving in the fabric of his lies. He chose the latter. And though he eventually learned his lesson about taking material things that did not belong to him, his desires simply morphed from things to people.

Now, the Minister was a master of illusory manipulation, and he was able to bring people into carrying out his wishes, not by way of intimidation or threat, but by feeding on their genuine desire to please him. Crawford was his friend, but as one who also admired the Minister as a member of the congregation as well, he felt honored that he was so interested in his event, and was coming to participate on his behalf. The Minister knew that Crawford would broadcast his appearance at this event to only the right people. In this case, the only person he needed to know was Angie. He would simply mention it with the added underscoring of the invitation that was offered to the Minister. That was all that was needed to provide decent cover. The Minister would have to make another rare

Monday morning visit to his office. Hopefully India would not feel the need to come down again to spy on him, but if she did, he would not allow her presence to be restrictive. He had travel plans to make, and nothing was going to stop him.

CHAPTER 20

When Ivy arrived at her office on Monday morning, members of the staff greeted her with hearty congratulations on her recent victory. News of her valiant efforts and success had spread. It evoked a special feeling of accomplishment and confidence that would be helpful later in the day. She had worked hard on a case that was consuming and exhaustive, and she had proven herself far beyond the events in the courtroom. She had shown tenacity, perseverance and sound legal knowledge, impressive qualities about which the partners of her firm were proud. They had high expectations for her when she came aboard, but Ivy knew that there was a glass ceiling, especially being an African-American female, that she would have to break through to receive the respect she knew she deserved. She always wanted to feel that she was not hired because she was a double score in the quota game of corporate political correctness. To a certain extent, her intuitive thoughts were accurate, but this case put her in an even more favorable perspective in the eyes of the legal leaders of her firm.

Ivy was a great attorney and they knew it, and though she was a definite asset in the corporate world of unspoken quotas and other politically correct illusions in the work place, she could truly hold her own. Her superiors were very well aware of that fact. As she walked confidently to her office, she received numerous high-fives from some of the white male associates, and several whispers of *"You go girl!"* from the Black females. However, many of the African-American male lawyers said very little or simply gave a nod in her direction. But today Ivy had no time to be bothered by the ignominy and insecurity of those who offered no accolades. She simply shook her head as she passed wondering when the *brotha's* would understand the fact that she was not a threat, but an asset. When she scored, they scored, and vice versa. Unfortunately, many of them viewed her success as a personal attack on their pride, when in fact, it was quite the contrary. She opened the door to three elaborate bouquets on her desk, each of them unique in their exotic design. She was speechless and wondered when the special treatment would end, but at the insistence of her secretary, decided to stop wondering and just enjoy it for however long it lasted.

"Your office has been the flower mart, this morning, "Miss Popular", and you well deserve it," her assistant said as she looked up from her computer.

"No, we deserve it," Ivy replied. "You know I could not have made it happen without you. I mean, all the late nights and all those visits to the law library; you know you were just phenomenal, and I can't thank you enough."

"It was my pleasure, and my job. You know I'm only as good as I make my boss look. And if it'll make you feel any better, you can thank me today by taking me to lunch. How's that?"

"You're on!" Ivy retorted quickly with a huge smile.

"Okay, now that we've got that all out of the way, you better hurry and get down to the war room for the morning assembly. I'm sure that they have a few congrats to share with their big winner this morning."

Ivy's assistant was right. There would be quite a few complimentary words delivered from the company brass. But before Ivy headed down the hall, she wanted to take a peek at the cards that accompanied all of the flowers that now inspired her office décor. She could guess who one of them was from and she was right. Donovan, who had not contacted her all weekend, even after the late night cell phone message she had left, was back on his duties of flattery. She really did not know what to think about his revival of efflorescent romance, but it did not matter at the moment. She was on her way down the hall for a little corporate stroking, and she was ready for it. The other two bouquets were from the managing partner of the firm and a very thankful client.

Ivy Page entered the dark wood paneled war room as humbly as her inner excitement would allow her. On the outside, she was an elegant, professional woman with shoulder length sandy brown curls slicked down and pulled neatly into a bun, dressed in a black Tahari pants suit, tastefully accented with ethnic jewelry. But on the inside she was a seven year old in pig-tails who had just won first place in the first grade spelling bee. Her inner smile was ear to ear and she did her level best to hold the jubilant scream within her. After the legal team and firm partners stood and offered her rousing applause, she finally broke and could not contain her smile. The managing partner offered his congratulatory remarks, and the sentiment of his speech was echoed by all of the other partners in the room. But no real time was to be wasted on further felicitations. There was work to be done. This was the time when the status of cases in process was discussed, and new ones were brought forward and assigned.

The firm was doing very well financially, and that was due to the driving work ethic of the leaders; and that ethic was expected within the ranks. When Ivy first joined the team, it was not unusual for her to work eighty or more hours in a week. It was a mystery how her sleepless eyes managed to look bright everyday, but that too was expected by the powers that be. Now she was more senior, and though she was not required to put in the hours expected of the freshman associates, her ongoing personal work ethic coupled with that bred by the managing partners, was proving incredibly successful in making her an integral part of the company. They were handling some very tough cases that called for extreme efforts, especially since these tough cases meant big payoffs if victories were secured. They were making a name for themselves as the type of firm to handle higher risk, higher profile cases that were often surrounded by a wealth of the major players. And that called for a standard well above the norm.

Ivy was told that she was being considered for handling another engrossing case that would demand the same tenacious attitude and attention to detail that she displayed on the last. Within herself she shouted, "*Yes!*" because she knew that she would not have been considered had she not done such a good job previously. She had secured victory for her client, which also meant victory for the firm. The fees that she billed on that case alone were staggering, but she was working for a big money client, and that was just how the firm wanted it. Now she would possibly have the same opportunity with another big money client whose lucrative payoff possibilities could only improve Ivy's rising position in the firm. She could not wait to sink her teeth into the process. Again, the fighter in Uncle Henry's basement gymnasium rose within her spirit.

The managing partner explained to the group that a celebrated sports figure was being sued by a popular tabloid magazine for not allowing them to print a story he claimed was false, even though the reporter claimed to have pictures and a scandalous video that proved the story's authenticity. Apparently, according to the reporter, he divulged the information himself but now is trying to keep the magazine from printing it, and he has won a court injunction that has held up the process of releasing the story to the public. This was a celebrity who was, obviously, embraced by the public and whose image alone was quite influential in the "who's who" of luminary social circles. The partner further said that the whole issue was bordering legal mayhem and that the representing counsel would have to work diligently to get to the bottom of it all.

The firm had been substantially retained, and would represent the magazine and the reporter, which was unusual, in terms of the normal list of clients. In the firm's youth, the directing partners had steered clear of volatile cases involving entertainment and celebrity issues, unless it involved the representation of major movie studios, or the like, but no more. That was where the money was, and that was where the firm was supposed to be, according to the brass. But the real interest in this particular case was due to the fact that several of the athlete's endorsement companies were considering suing him for breech of contract issues based on personal misrepresentation, and some other deep dark secret that had not yet been fully disclosed. That information that was tightly held but apparently the reporter had the goods.

The firm's success with the tabloid case could be parlayed into a plethora of companies standing in line to secure representation. That meant an abundance of billable hours, win, lose or draw. But the precedent had to be set with a win, and Ivy was the firm's most recent big winner. Sometimes what matters most is not the number of victories but the one most fresh in the hearts of the gallery.

"Miss Page," the managing partner said in his business-like voice, "this case is yours. I expect the same effort you displayed in the Creed Pharmaceuticals case."

Then looking over his reading glasses, pushed almost to the end of his nose, Armand A. Blum passed Ivy a file containing several investigative documents relevant to the case. And with a grin that displayed both confidence and expectation he said, "And, Miss Page, I expect the same result."

After a few final formalities, the meeting adjourned and Ivy headed back to her office. Though she was still tired from the events last week and the weirdness of her weekend, she was ready to sink her teeth into the challenge. But when she got back to her office and checked her messages, her assistant informed her that Mr. Blum had just called and needed his message addressed immediately. *"Already?"* she thought to herself, but she knew that that was the way he did business. She was surprised however, when she listened to his message and heard him say that he really needed her sharp on this case, and to take a couple of days off to recuperate from the culminated madness of last week. He did remind her to take the file home, or wherever she was going, and to begin developing a plan of action.

That was fine with Ivy. She could stand a couple days of forced rest, but she was not completely ready yet. She still needed to look over some things on her calendar and then take her assistant out for a great lunch. It would be a great time to inform her that another big case had just been dropped in her lap, and that she would need the same quality of work and effort that was displayed in the last couple of months. Unfortunately, Ivy had no intention of giving her assistant a couple of days to rest. She needed her to begin the leg work right away, so that when she returned to the office, she could hit the ground running.

The last statement of Mr. Blum's message instructed Ivy to open a sealed envelope on her desk that had her name typed neatly on the front. When she did, she surprisingly found two tickets, orchestra level seating, to the ballet and a note that gave her an evening of carte blanche access to one of the areas finest restaurants and limo service for that night, all compliments of Mr. Blum. She was elated about her boss' unusual gesture of kindness, and immediately began thinking of whom she would ask to join her. Only one name came to mind.

Just before she left for lunch, Ivy's phone rang, and without even looking at the caller I.D., she knew who it was. The call bypassed her assistant, who was away from her desk gathering her things, and would have gone into voice mail, as planned, had Ivy not picked it up. She knew it was just a matter of time before Donovan called, but she had honestly forgotten all about him today. She was on a fierce roll and when it was time to focus, she could easily block out everything else.

"Hey, how 'bout lunch today?" He said after Ivy answered the line in her pseudo professional and purposely generic voice, knowing full well it was him but acting as though he were some unknown, distant caller.

"Oh, I'm sorry; I would have loved to, but I can't do it today. I got the flowers and they're beautiful. Thanks."

After a few more noticeably short and transparent answers to his questions, it was clear that Ivy was rushing Donovan off the phone and he did not know if she was just busy or really not interested in hearing from him. The reality was that she was very much interested in hearing from him and appreciated the flowers, and would have loved to have seen him for lunch, but none of these were feelings that she wanted to have any longer.

At some point between then and now, between roses and tulips, between Kobe beef and Australian lobster, she had decided that she did not want to engage her feelings for Donovan. Maybe it was because he had not returned her late night call, or maybe it was because she had evaluated the circumstances of their relationship and found them insurmountable, or maybe she had remembered some of Aunt Cindy's sage wisdom concerning men and women, and what they should and should not do, or maybe she had simply decided to catch herself and go no deeper with him, in an effort to protect a heart that she knew would eventually be broken. Whatever the case, she decided it best to get him off of the phone to avoid giving in to him.

"So how 'bout dinner? Why don't we go back to that little Bistro? You know, the one where we had our first lunch. I hear they serve a delicious lobster ravioli in white wine sauce." He was trying to get her attention with his charm and it was working, but as difficult as it was, she would not to give in.

"I'm sorry, Donovan. I would love to but I can't. I just took a really big case and it's going to really tie me up, tonight."

"Ooh, I wish I could tie you up tonight," he replied with conspicuous sexual overtones.

Ivy rolled her eyes and looked at the ceiling. She thought to herself that she recognized this pattern, again. He would make sexual innuendos and stir her up with anticipation and then decide to remind her that he was moral when it came time to make love. She did not want to hear it. She did not want to take herself there. So she acted like most women do when they are trying to send a man a subliminal *get lost* message; she simply acted as if she had not even heard him. But Donovan was smarter than that, and Ivy knew it. She hated that she had revealed so much of herself to him in such a short period of time. But she could not help it. His personality and charismatic demeanor had been so inviting to her that she would have had to anchor herself to the Rock of Gibraltar to not be drawn to him. He knew what buttons to push. It was almost as if he had made it his job to learn her; and he was a stellar pupil.

"Okay Ivy," he said chuckling, "I can see I've lost this round, and I probably have some explaining to do about the weekend. But you know I'll be back for round two."

"You don't have any explaining to do. Everything is absolutely fine. I'm just really busy, and when I get time, I'll—"

Before she could finish her series of statements, ineffectually trying to show that his behavior and his existence for that matter, was of no concern, Donovan had hung up the phone. When she hung up, she froze for a moment, wondering why she felt so flustered and unbalanced, and when she looked up, her assistant was staring right at her. Ivy gave her that *you know you shouldn't be looking at me* look, but she knew that her tone obviously deserved, at the very least, a turned head. Her assistant said nothing even though she knew much. How could she not? She had received most of Donovan's calls and placed all of the floral arrangements. Though she did not eavesdrop, it did not take a genius to sit along the sidelines of the dynamics between Ivy and Donovan and know what was going on. But her assistant was still relatively new on the job and thought it best to keep her thoughts to herself; and besides, Ivy made it very clear that she was not ready to entertain new friends in the intimacy of her personal life. She needed her friend Gemma. Even though it seemed that Ivy had bailed her out of more tumultuous situations than vice versa, she was still the best person that Ivy could think of to talk to. Even if she did nothing more than make her laugh, the therapy was far reaching and definitely helpful. But Gemma was away doing what she does and Ivy had a full plate as well, with the new case and all. The conversation would just have to wait.

At lunch, Ivy did all she could not to make it a working lunch, but she could not help it. It was a time to celebrate and show some gratitude to her assistant for all of her hard work over the last couple of months, but she also dictated new assignments and expected that the process should begin upon her assistant's return to the office. That was just who she was. All of those boxing lessons with Uncle Henry had done more than just teach her to defend herself. The individualized intensity of the boxing ring had been often ushered into the courtroom. The difference now was that she pulled others onto her winning team, in hopes that they would share in her attitude of ferocity, a condition of mind that some feared and others admired.

Ivy was a master of the *courtroom counter punch*. She always seemed to anticipate the next move of the opposition and was prepared to deliver a staggering blow to an area they might have left unprotected. She and her lunch mate concentrated on the subject matter before them, and her assistant did not mind Ivy's drive. As a matter of fact, she admired it and often thought of her boss and her fierce will when addressing issues in her own life, so she welcomed Ivy's instructions about who to contact and what leads to research. It also was a great case to be nosy about. *Who was this famous sports personality, and what had he or she divulged that was so taboo that even the tabloids could not print it?* The "gossip-ability" factor was beyond intriguing. It was compelling.

It was easy for Ivy to get consumed by her work. It sometimes seemed that she retreated from life and hid herself within it. She had a work load heavy enough for two attorneys to be exhausted. But even in the midst of her mind flush preparation of the case before her, she could not help thinking about Donovan. She just could not clear him out of her head now. Some way, by more than just a charming smile and flattering conversation, he had etched his way onto the surface of her heart. It was not love, but more, a feeling of anticipating and desiring his presence. There was something in her that almost expected him to show up just before the final course of the meal. He had such a record of being at the right place at the right time. But this was neither the right place nor the right time, and she knew it.

Ivy was very serious when it came to keeping her career and her personal life very separate. That was probably one of the reasons she did not receive the cheers of her African-American male colleagues earlier. There were probably more than a few quality suitors at the firm but Ivy held to her strict policy concerning workplace romances. As far as she was concerned, they just did not work, and could only cause more trouble than they were worth. Most of the men did not agree, which was expected, and felt that she was simply arrogant and aloof when she turned down their advances. She simply remembered one of her Uncle's sage pieces of crude wisdom, *"Don't shit where you eat."* Uncle Henry also taught Ivy to cuss.

She tried to apply that policy of separatism to her romantic thoughts as well. Clear thinking on the job had always been one of her most valued assets, and her associates considered her one of the most focused individuals at the firm. They never knew what was going on in her personal life because Ivy placed considerable effort into closing the door to her private life the minute she stepped off the street and broke the threshold of her office doors. That included all of her outside thoughts, dreams and desires. They were always kept as private privilege to the few chosen to exist within Ivy's circle of personal intimacy. But now she was troubled because, for some reason, her thoughts, dreams and desires were, not only, becoming centered on a man she should not have, but also trickling into the forbidden area of her world. She could not manage to displace her thoughts of Donovan. He seemed to be with her wherever she went.

After lunch, Ivy and her assistant browsed around the area boutiques and found their way into a quaint little jewelry store. It was more planned than by chance, and Ivy took the opportunity to purchase a hand-crafted necklace for her assistant that she had expressed a particular interest in the last time they were in the area. She explained to her that it was not only to say *"thanks for a job well done,"* but also an anticipatory gift for the great job that she would do with the upcoming tabloid magazine case.

While they shopped, Ivy noticed a couple holding hands, laughing, and dipping in and out of several art stores in the area. She stopped for a moment and her thoughts drifted to the events a couple nights ago, after Donovan left. The catalyst to her calling his cell phone that night was her overwhelming desire to share her victory with someone special. She was not lonely, by any means, nor was she in search of a *booty call*. There was plenty to keep her busy, but that was all she was, *busy*. She was ready to open a door in her life that had been closed too long. She was ready to make love with a man in whom she found reciprocal desire, respect and passion.

Ivy could hear Gemma's contention in her head. She never felt that Ivy went after the men she really wanted because she paid too much attention to the circumstances surrounding the romance. Gemma's advice was always to throw caution to the wind and live, and for her, living by that advice had been exciting but costly. They had connected because they lived vicariously through each other. Gemma was spontaneous and often flew by the seat of her pants, and Ivy could always depend on her to bring something daring and interesting to her life. Ivy, on the other hand, could be depended on like clock-work. She was beautiful, hard working and responsible, and was the essence of stability. Gemma knew that if she ever got in a bind, her best friend would always be there to get her out.

Ivy continued to look at the couple, admiring what they appeared to share, but soon snapped back to reality. There was work to be done, but beyond that, she thought about the few days of freedom and relaxation she had ahead of her. She needed it terribly, and she knew it. So after a few more minutes of window shopping, she and her assistant headed back to the office.

Ivy gathered several files and stuffed them into her slim line briefcase that was not so slim looking anymore.

"I thought you were ordered to take a few days of R & R," her assistant said as she leaned in the doorway.

"Oh, I will. I just want to look over a few things," Ivy replied without looking up.

"Get some rest, boss," her assistant said after walking into the office and putting her hand on Ivy's shoulder. "I'll have everything ready for you when you come back; trust me."

Ivy looked up and they both smiled. She picked her briefcase removing a few documents that she figured she could deal with upon her return, and headed for the door. After thinking about it, she realized that she did not really have to work that hard. It truly was time for a breather.

"You know I can't help it. Thanks," she said as she exited. She left the office trying to manage the exhilaration of the day.

When she got home, Ivy decided to expel some of her nervous energy by jogging, something she had done since college. When she was in law school, she ran at all times of day or night, and her slim, physically fit body was a much appreciated by-product by those who were privileged to see her naked. She used the time unlike most who thought that the activity helped them to focus. Instead she used it to try to stop thinking, and offer her mind some relief from being overloaded with process, concept and rationale. After she returned, showered, checked her email, read snippets of news and ate a bowl of yogurt with sliced peaches, she sat on the sofa and battled an overwhelming feeling of anxiety. The early evening run did not have the desired effect. She had done everything she could to avoid the thing she most wanted to do, and at that very moment her phone rang. Once again she wondered how this man was so able to read her, and knew just the right moment to call. She looked at the phone as it rang four times and then went into voice mail. She listened as Donavan tried to get her attention, "Ivy, I know you're there, will you please pick up?" He said it three times and then he hung up. *"How did he know she was there,"* she thought to herself. *Was he a stalker now? Was he watching her every move?*

As much as she wanted to respond, she fought all urges to pick up the phone. It rang again, but this time Ivy removed the plug and turned her attention to the legal documents she had spread on her coffee table. She avoided the call. It was not Donovan.

CHAPTER 21

The Minister arrived at his office later than he had planned. His goal was to get there early to make plans for Chicago and then make a few phone calls. One would probably be to Alex. Even though his over active mind enjoyed the thrill of the hunt for his mistress of the stage, his loins were intuitively inclined toward a sure thing. He really did have work to do, and this unscheduled trip could cause his, already busy schedule, to become even more chaotic. But he was willing to take the risk. That was what sometimes drove him.

The life of ministry was becoming somewhat uneventful and boring by the standards of one whose psyche craved stimulation, and although he did not think so, Angie knew that better than he. She knew that he required much more than the average man, in all facets of his life. Some men are like that. Their intentions are not to be harmful or injurious to anyone, but their personal requirements are far beyond common. What he did not know, was that his wife was willing to give him some of the things he wanted, but like most men, he made assumptions, instead of petitions. In some ways he was like the old school Italian gangsters from the movies who commonly had women outside their marriages who did the things they thought their wives would not, or should not. The reality was that they would not allow their wives to do such things. They were held as prized possessions and treated with a level of respect reserved specifically for them. What they failed to understand was that their wives should have been their other woman, mistress, wife and everything in between.

The Minister had once counseled a prominent businessman who was having an affair with his secretary, with such mentality. The man told the Minister all the things that his outside lover would do and when he was asked why he could not request the same treatment from his wife, he indicated that his wife's mouth was the same mouth that kissed his children goodnight and could not be defiled in such ways.

The Minister loved Angie with all his heart, and mentally justified himself by saying that it was not his heart that lusted after other women. His heart belonged to her completely; it was just the other parts of his anatomy that he shared with others. Men inherently desire that their wives be better than they. That does not mean that they do not enjoy a woman with similar perversions and freakish rapaciousness, it is just never appropriate to marry such a woman.

He sat behind his desk, the sun having set early as autumn approached the end of its reign. Though it fought to stay in power, winter had tapped fall's shoulder with a few bitterly cold nights to signal its arrival. If India had come in that day, she missed him, and he appreciated the solitude. Normally she made all of his travel plans and had relationships with several travel vendors often securing discounts and other perks, but she was not clued in on the Chicago excursion. It was not that she would have said anything to Angie. She would have loved for the Minister to confide some important secret in her, but he was careful not to give her anything that could someday be used against him.

India had a longing heart, and longing hearts often cloud rational thinking with irresponsible choices. And such feelings have striking similarities to the concept of celebrity stalking by over-zealous fans. The Minister was very careful with his interactions with India, and even though he did not think she would go as far as some, he still thought it best to play it safe.

Before he picked up the phone to make the first call of the night, the Minister swiveled in his chair and looked out the window. He could see the lone tree in the church courtyard and noticed the wind teasing its branches. He focused on the trunk and thought about all of the years that it had survived efforts to destroy it, some willfully, some simply by the coincidence of nature. It had been climbed on, kicked, chopped, scratched, cut and leaned on, but it was changeless. It had seen people come and go; survived beating rain, heaping snow, and winds that laughed as it uprooted or broke lesser opponents. He remembered his own boyhood afternoons in the Summer when he and his cousin, Franklin, spent hours climbing in the tree, waiting for his uncle, the former pastor, to complete whatever he was doing in the church.

That tree had been the venerable Saturday playground for the boys. It had been the center point of every game they imagined. It was an aircraft carrier on the high seas, as they launched themselves as fighter jets from its thick lower branches; it had been a fortress as they fired imaginary rifles at the approaching enemy; it had been a hide out for the Lone Ranger and Tonto as they faded into the foliage before pouncing on the bad guys; it had been a protective giant as its huge branches seemed like mighty arms, kindly supporting the romping weight of two formative imaginations.

That tree held a wealth of fond childhood memories. It had seen a lifetime of change around it, but the old oak tree had never moved. As the wind rustled its leaves, it seemed that there was a mutual respect in the air between the two. The tree stood as if its arms were crossed and its weary eyes grinned as the wind abstained from taunting. The breezes that whispered through the branches were more like a tender hand stroking the gray hair atop the head of a wise old man. It was as if the evil winds had given up attempts to destroy the righteous old tree. It had stood its ground through the years, and by simply being firm and constant, it had won enough battles to now be respected and left alone.

Deep inside, the Minister longed to be that tree, unmovable, always abounding, steadfast, weathering the storms of his desires. One of the qualities he most respected was consistency. He was intrigued by anything or anyone who was willing to establish a path of constancy. He once preached a sermon on the dependability of the devil. He was careful not to pay tribute to the devil or his devilish workers, but he did illuminate the point that the devil is consistent. His works are constant and unending, and the myth of his trickery should be dispelled as it is far outweighed by his predictability. He admonished parishioners to always consider the devil a worthy adversary, who could be depended on to show up at the most inopportune times. There was, again, the focus on a quote from the Apostle Paul: "…when I would do good, evil is always present…" It was as true in the Minister's life as it was in Saint Paul's. The only difference was the living cloud of witnesses that the Minister tried to constantly hoodwink with his deception. But the tree he watched with analytical eyes represented nothing devilish or evil, but virtuous and good. It demanded respect based on its record of righteous stability. It was consistent, unvarying, unswerving, unyielding, faithful, and true to the purpose of its design. The Minister respected the tree.

The noise of his silence broke abruptly. For some strange reason, he did not expect the phone to ring so loudly. It was Lydia Davis.

"Hello Reverend." She spoke dryly with a disturbingly seductive, but recognizably nervous tone. He could sense that something was wrong.

"Lydia," the Minister paused, "I had almost given up on hearing from you. Is everything all right?" The Minister had not really given up on hearing from her as much as he had momentarily lost interest. His focus had moved to Chicago. But her unexpected call brought him back to her.

"Everything is fine. I just wanted to tell you how much I was helped by your sermon yesterday. I mean, you are really talking about things that are hitting home with me. Did you get a chance to read my note?" She sounded shaky and a bit fragile but the Minister did not acknowledge her emotion, immediately.

"Well, I thank you for that compliment and I'm glad that the Word is touching your life in a meaningful way. And yes I did—"

"That was awful generic, Ed." She sarcastically interrupted him before he could finish his statement. His answer *was* generic and he knew it, but it was also true and there was a sense of sincerity in his tone, at least to some degree.

"Excuse me?" The Minister was taken aback by her tone. It was a bit left of ordinary, for Lydia. "I really *do* hope that you were helped by the sermon. That is my intention when I preach. My hope is that a life would be touched and inspired by the Word."

"Is it really? I expected something a bit different this week especially since my visit to your office."

"Well why? What does the meaning of my preaching have to do with your visit? Lydia, I am a preacher behind that pulpit. When I'm there, I'm doing God's will, and I'm doing my level best to shut out everything that might hinder me from doing so. So, if you're questioning how I was able to preach and not focus on you or whatever that was that happened in my office, I'm sorry that I can't flatter you this time because I was not."

He was not being completely honest. An accomplished liar's skills are keen. Lydia had no way of knowing, at least not yet. Her thoughts were not really about what the Minister was thinking about or how he preached or his motivations, or anything of the sort. She was a lonely woman who lived a life of fantasy created by people other than her and her husband, and she seemed like she was reaching out for any kind of physical affection that she could find. The real problem was that Lydia Davis was a fan in search of a hero; that was why she had married Donovan in the first place, and now for some weird reason, yet some seemingly very specific reason, she had chosen the Minister. After responding to her remark, there was a brief moment of silence, and then the Minister could hear her sobbing.

"I'm sorry, Reverend," she said softly, "I didn't mean to offend you in any way. I was just teasing you. You really have helped me and I'm so sorry about what happened in your office last week. I don't know what came over me. It's just that things at home with Donovan have been so stressed." She was really beginning to weep uncontrollably, like the time in the office.

The Minister listened to her go on and on for a while and then decided to see if he could help. Though he was an accomplished and skilled liar, and had his faults, when it came to preaching and counseling, he was truly sincere.

"No one knows what I'm going through and I just can't take it all by myself. What you see is not always what you get, and I just won't deal with it any longer!"

"Lydia, calm down," he said kindly yet purposefully. "Things can't be that bad. We all just had a lovely dinner together, and your husband seemed great. Maybe it has something to do with the contract issues that he's dealing with." He glanced at his watch.

"No, it has nothing to do with that." Her voice was getting noticeably louder and her crying was becoming more intense.

"Then what is it? What had you come to see me about?" She did not respond to his question, acting almost like she did not even hear him.

"He doesn't think I know, but I do. I've always known. I've known since I met him, but he just thinks I'm supposed to smile and go on and as if it doesn't exist, but I know all about it, and I can't deal with it. I just can't!" She was screaming now.

"What, Lydia? What are you talking about?" The Minister's voice was raised now as well. He was genuinely concerned, and had lost his focus on making his Chicago plans. Gemma would have to wait. Lydia had his full attention.

"I just can't!" she yelled again. The Minister leaned forward in his chair and picked up the receiver. She had been on speaker all this time, a dangerous move when surrounded by walls that might have ears. He wanted to hang up and call someone but he honestly did not know whom to call. *Who was the one to care for this distressed soul?* She had already implicated her mate as the source of her suffering, and their only common acquaintance was Angie, and in his mind, that was not an option.

"Lydia where are you? Are you anywhere near the church? Why don't come by my office and we can talk this thing out." He spoke calmly and directly, trying to help her to regain her composure. He could hear her breathing slowly as he spoke, as if she were doing some Zen focusing exercise. That was good. Had she been in his office, he would have encouraged her to do exactly that. *Had she been in counseling before, or under psychiatric care?*

He thought for a moment about the common stresses and issues many spouses of celebrities or athletes had to deal with. Her husband had been in the lime-light, and so had she for that matter. And although the adjustment to such life can be difficult and stressful, she should know how to handle it by now, he thought. It was a lie to assume that the attention celebrities receive was unsolicited. The choice of pursuing their craft or gift was a knowledgeable request for all the attention that came with their ultimate success. It too was payment for their skills. *Why such anguish and pain?* He could hear the muffled sound of tissue wiping through the receiver. She was hopefully moving toward regaining equanimity.

"Lydia," he said in almost a whisper now. "Are you all right?"

"I think I'm okay," she responded sniffling. "I'm sorry, Reverend. I'm really sorry."

"No, no, no. And what have I told you about that 'Reverend stuff'?"

"Okay," she said with a slight giggle. "I'm sorry, Ed."

"Lydia, are you nearby? Would you like to come by the church and talk a little bit?"

"Yes, I'm nearby. I'll be right there."

Lydia hung up immediately, and the Minister rubbed his face with his hands in relief. Within about thirty seconds he heard footsteps tapping rhythmically down the long hallway that led to his office. He thought to himself, *that damn India has come down here to spy on me! She just couldn't stay away!* But he was surprised to see Lydia turn the corner and enter the outer office. She had been sitting in her car, in the parking lot the whole time. In the early afternoon, she had called Angie to see if the Minister would be available. Angie explained to her that he usually did not work on Monday but he had been going to the church for the last couple of weeks, and that she could probably reach him there. Lydia had been driving by the church all afternoon, into the early evening, and when she finally saw his car, she made the call.

CHAPTER 22

When the Minister looked up, he was clearly startled by her presence but did not ask how she had arrived so quickly. It was obvious, and because his mind, to some remaining degree, was still on his Chicago plans, he did not wish to delve into the peripheral issues surrounding her unusual behavior. Her curly hair bounced on her shoulders, and her makeup-less face was still enchantingly beautiful. It was clear that she had been crying, as swollen, red corneas surrounded the light gray irises of her eyes. She wore a long lambskin, ankle length maxi coat and black leather gloves. Her outer attire was appropriate for the season, but he thought it strange that she wore sandal type shoes that revealed most of her bare feet. He also could not see a dress beneath her coat and hoped that this was not a prelude to the activities of the her last office visit, but then dismissed it all giving the entire scenario the benefit of the doubt, thinking that she was on her way some place where her attire was apropos.

She smiled when she saw him and then rushed immediately to his arms. He held her tightly but was careful not to show passion in his grasp, as he consciously kept his hands well centered on her upper back. The Minister was determined to control the situation, which simply meant controlling himself. She was terribly beautiful and enticing, even in her distressed state.

She was special and he recognized that from the moment they had met. She was what he and his teenage buddies had called a "red bone." These were the untouchable girls, who boasted fair skin, straight or naturally curly hair, signifying most likely, a white parent or one of some fair skinned descendant other than African-American. But they had enough African-American genes influencing their physical structure to also have a knock out body with features especially unique to Black women. The face, hair and skin belonged to Barbie, but "Jameeka" made the body.

He knew that when he released their embrace he might have a difficult time concentrating on whatever she had to say, and that he must choose his words conscientiously. It was his composure that would be difficult to maintain. Realistically, he did all he could to fool himself, often longing for the redemptive honesty that he prayed still dwelled somewhere within his soul.

"Let me take your coat," he said after she freed him from her hold. That was his first mistake. Underneath her long coat was a simple, but sheer, black silk dress. Its hem rested well above her knees, revealing legs that had been tanned by God with divine strokes of delicately applied white chocolate pigmentation. When he looked at her, he could only imagine that she was the divine cognition from which Eve must have been created: no clearly definable nationality to be confined or categorized into race, but the best features of every ethnicity from which all women would eventually be blessed. The difference was that most women were blessed with some special attribute, and in rare cases, maybe two. But Lydia had them all. Perfect breasts were outlined like silhouettes of perfection as they pushed their way through the applause of her approving dress, flawless nipples were erect just enough to be acknowledged and appreciated, and her hips and buttocks made the soft garment smile.

Her hands and feet were delicate and unblemished, details of a lifestyle of privilege that supported a softness with which she could have only been born. Her draw was outrageous as she, like the Minister's wife, was a trophy wife, an untouchable entity reserved only for the very special man who had labored intelligently to earn her interest. Lydia's essence spoke to him personally, and he struggled against himself as he examined her patiently. The Minister had an arduous task before him as he tried to stay focused. *Why had she come?* It was a question that would soon be answered, as all questions are, in time.

Contrary to some popular beliefs, truth is the most dependable constant in the universe. It is often elusive, hidden, smeared, buried, confined, and guarded impeccably by the best liars, but it is pure and its most significant comrade is time. The Lydia Davis question would soon be answered, truthfully, but not tonight in the Minister's office. Illusion would prove much more interesting and definitely more enticing.

"Lydia, sit down and make yourself comfortable. Can I get you a glass of water or something to drink?"

That was his second mistake because when she sat down her short dress rose and her legs slightly parted to reveal what he should not have seen. The Minister massaged his brow with his fingers as she sat, and looked at the floor. Looking away was almost as bad as looking directly at her, as his active imagination began run away, in just a split second. His mind put her in such seductive places that it would have been difficult for the most religious zealot to maintain his vow. She seemed unaware and still a bit distraught, and the Minister knew that there was something wrong with the picture before him. As sensual and enticing as she was, her fragility was more than obvious.

"As a matter of fact I could use a glass of something," she said as she crossed her legs and shook her hair.

"Water?"

"What else do you have?"

"I'm afraid all I have is water," the Minister said, knowing full well that there was a plethora of beverage choices in the cabinet in his office. There were several juices and soft drinks that India kept stocked. She made sure that his favorites, Mango Madness Snapple and Nesbitt's cream soda were always available. The Minister was not like some of his associate clergy who had their offices stocked with spirits and other hidden treats that only certain congregants were aware of. But then alcohol was not his weakness. He was not trying to be inconsiderate by not offering her something other than water; he just did not think she really wanted anything. She had not come there to quench a dry throat. She was thirsty but a beverage from his cabinet would not suffice.

She looked around, examining her surroundings almost as if she had not been there before. The Minister never took his eyes off of her. He could not get away from her expressive look. Though he had previously dismissed it, he was genuinely concerned that she had not only sought him out, but had also been sitting in the parking lot while she was doing all of her sobbing and hysterics. It was not that he doubted her sincerity, but he was somewhat worried about her safety, especially in her distressed state. He sat down in a chair directly in front of her. When he counseled individuals who came to his office, he never sat behind his desk when speaking to them because he thought it was impersonal and might make the person psychologically visualize the desk as an imposing barrier, hindering the free flow of meaningful dialogue. He also sat in front of Lydia because he enjoyed looking at her. There was no denying her radiance, and whether she knew it or not, she was exactly what the Minister preferred in his women, a natural beauty. He tried to focus.

"So tell me what's going on, Lydia. You know I'm willing to help you in any way I can." The Minister leaned forward, looking directly in her eyes. "I know you mentioned that things at home were not what you wanted them to be. Is there something I can do to help?" His question was not completely loaded; there was some sincerity to his request, but he did want her to subtly but clearly understand that his door was open to more than marriage counseling. As hard as he tried, he just could not help it. That was just who he was, and deep inside himself he almost hoped that she would not acknowledge that side of him. Maybe the fog of her crisis was so thick that she would not be able to see his camouflaged lust.

"I don't think anyone can help," she replied looking away. "It's too late to help. I should have been gone years ago." She stood and moved toward the window. "I should have never let him do this to me. I knew and I didn't do anything; I didn't say anything!"

"Tell me, Lydia. Tell me what you knew, and didn't do anything about." The Minister was trying to help her get to the bottom of her issue by, at least, talking about it. He knew that it might not get solved right then and there, but despite his sexually stimulating internal thoughts, he was trying to be a helpful psychologist and concerned pastor. She was beginning to sob again but she was talking.

"I knew all along and I thought we could live this lie forever. I didn't think I would need what I need now, and I know he can't give it to me."

"Give you what?"

Lydia put her face in her hands and began to cry uncontrollably. The Minister's first intention was to immediately go to her and offer his chest and arms for comfort, but then he remembered what happened the last time he offered his counseling services. He remained in his chair and looked at her. It was probably the wrong thing to do, aesthetically, but he could not be concerned about pictures at that moment. He had to do what he knew was right. He could not be motivated by the design of his primal urges.

"Lydia, I'll be right back," the Minister said as he rose from his seat. He went into his inner office and thought for a moment, and then decided to quickly call his wife. He needed a quick breather from what he was witnessing before him, and it would be a good move for multiple reasons, he thought. He could attempt to gain some insight on the wreck of a woman seated in the next room, and then also cover himself if anything happened. There would be no questions about coming home late after he explained to Angie that her hysterical friend stopped by as a result of her advice. He called and briefly explained the current scenario to Angie, who said that she knew that Lydia was dealing with some tough issues but she had not completely divulged any personal or private information to her.

After hanging up, his desire was to call Chicago to, at least secure his accommodations. He needed something to divert his attention, briefly. But instead, he got some bottled water and a crystal glass, and walked back into the area where Lydia sat. She was the kind of woman whose beauty demanded that you change your immediate plans, and focus on her. She had the Minister's undivided attention. He wanted more time to consider what was going on in Lydia's mind, and possibly consult some reference materials in relation to her condition, but there was something in her that created an insurmountable feeling of impatience in him. He wanted to move toward some level of understanding with her. When he entered the room with water in hand, she turned to face him. Her expression was different now and she seemed as though her mind had gone other places.

"Lydia," the Minister said softly as he sat directly in front of her on the edge of his desk, "you know I'm ready to listen to you when you're ready to talk. There are obviously some pretty serious things going on with you, and I want you to know that I'm here to help."

There was a long, silent pause. He expected her to say something. He expected her to go ahead and spill the facts about Donovan, and then he would use one of his many anecdotes, analogies and parables about relationships and marriage to help her understand her problems, and then send her on her way. There was a solution; he just needed a hint of what the issue was, and then he could set in motion one of his many healing theories that had always worked with the other parishioners who came to see him concerning their mates. The door was open and she spoke, but she said nothing related to her behavior.

"I want to talk about you, Ed," she said as she twisted in her chair to face him directly. Her countenance had clearly changed and as she sniffed, he could see her eyes clearing up.

"What about me? I don't think this about me, is it? This seems to be about you and Donovan, from what I gather." He tried to keep the conversation and the suggestive thoughts in his mind under control. It was important that he not make an obvious move toward her, even though what he saw in her eyes stirred the inevitable possibilities of some type if sensuous physical contact. He did his best to keep his cool but he could see that there was something extraordinary going on in Lydia's mind.

"I've seen you looking at me, Ed. I saw you the first day I walked into your office with your wife. I saw you struggling to keep your eyes in a place that didn't offend me. Maybe I should correct myself; I saw you trying not to look at me."

"Oh; really?" He tried to make sense of what was going on, and even tried to think of impassive responses to her questions and comments that would keep their interaction at a harmless station. But he could see that she was not steering her remarks toward harmless conversation. What she did not know was that the more she talked about her memories of their initial introduction and the events thereafter, the more he was sexually turned on. He loved when women made him aware of their awareness of his interest, and beyond that, he loved an intelligent woman. At that very moment, the fight within him intensified. This was supposed to be about Lydia and Donovan, not him. But his interests were peeking and he was holding on by a thread.

"Yes really," she said as she looked directly into his eyes. "You're a leg man, but pretty legs are not enough for you, are they?"

She continued to stare directly at him, but the Minister did not respond. He tried to quickly assess her comments. She had not yet smiled which might signify a possible welcoming of his advances, nor had she frowned or scowled in some way to show that she was not interested. She was a puzzle but he was a master at deciphering even the most complex puzzles when it came to lascivious matters.

"You're a very beautiful woman, Lydia. What man wouldn't recognize that? I'm sorry if I made you feel uncomfortable in any way. Did I?" He raised an eyebrow as he awaited her response, which she viewed as a rather sarcastic gesture.

"Did I appear to be uncomfortable when you scanned the audience during the church service and your eyes always seemed to find their way to me? Did I appear to be uncomfortable when you tried to play "footsie" with me under the table when we were all having dinner the other night? Did I appear to be uncomfortable when you stuck your hand in my pants the night I showed up at your office? You don't make me uncomfortable; you make me horny, just like I make you."

For the first time in a very long time, the Minister did not have the words available to immediately respond to her. She was going in a direction that he knew that he should not go with her, and now he was re-evaluating his actions. He was covert, but always obvious enough that his intended target would get the message concerning his interest. But now he wondered if he had been too obvious with this one, and more importantly, he wondered if he was dealing with a woman who was a bit off her rocker. He was aware of her stress and fragility in regards to her marriage. Though she had not yet given details, and it did not seem like she would tonight, it was clear that whatever was going on at home had a lot to do with what was going on in the Minister's office. Again he attempted to choose his words carefully. *Was he to be angry that she so bluntly told him about himself? Should he have been embarrassed and apologetic for making subtle passes at her?* He was completely off balance, but only for a moment. It would not take him long to gather himself.

"Yes Lydia, you're right. I love legs. I love well-manicured feet and shapely calves that are perfectly balanced and show that a woman works out just enough to keep them tight. Oh yes, I love legs, legs that are supporting shapely thighs that are so soft they're like dripping milk out of a baby's bottle that has been warmed to just the right temperature."

As he spoke he returned the intensity of her gaze and never blinked. He knew that he was fighting a losing battle in terms of self-control and it was just a matter of time before caution was thrown to the wind. But if she wanted to talk, he was going to talk, and if she was not careful, he was going to talk her right out of her little black dress.

"Lydia," he said as he crossed his legs, "why did you come here tonight? Did you come here to scold me for flirting with you? Did you come to tell me off and warn me to keep my eyes to myself? Did you come because you really are having some serious issues with your husband and you want to discuss them with me? You seemed extremely distraught when you first called and I have stopped what I was doing to take time out for you, this evening. I'm not trying to appear rude in any way but I really would like to know what I can do to help you tonight?"

The Minister was getting a bit impatient and after taking inventory of the multitude of factors and emotions surrounding her visit, he needed to move forward, if not for her, for himself. He was an engine, and either he needed to be driven at top speed or shut off.

Without saying another word, she stood up and moved toward him. The Minister did not move. She stood directly in front of him and then slowly made a 180 degree turn placing her back to him. Silently reaching back she bowed her head and moved her hair to the side. The gesture was clear and it was at this time that the Minister clearly recognized another opportunity to choose between nobility and naughtiness. He looked at her sensuous shape for a split second that seemed to go on forever, and keeping one hand on his desk to steady himself like an anchor, he used his free hand to reach for her zipper and did the honor of peeling her silk shell. Her dress hit the floor and she did not turn around immediately, and he did not touch her. Somehow, she comprehended that he was a man who enjoyed pictures, so she allowed him to visually ingest her without the clutter of speech. He drank what he saw and swallowed hard.

"You strike me as a man who appreciates both words and pictures, Reverend, so I'll let you look at the picture for a while," she said without turning around.

CHAPTER 23

The Minister could feel his juices flowing. He knew that he was getting excited because his tongue felt hot and his toes were cold. He always taught other preachers who had stage fright or trouble addressing crowds to recognize the things that happened to them physically when they became nervous or anxious, and then deal with them directly, like cold symptoms. He had learned, early in his public speaking career that a hot tongue and cold toes were his telltale signs of over-active nerves, but he had never had those things happen when he dealt with the opposite sex. These feelings were new to these circumstances, but in some way he enjoyed their presence. The charge that he felt was electric and fresh.

Finally Lydia turned around and put her hands on both sides of his face, pulling him toward her, and began kissing him passionately. He tried rather effortlessly to release himself from her grip but he could not deny what he had in his arms. She was perfect and she was more than ready. He reached around the small of her back and allowed his hands to roam freely on the surface of her bottom. She was supple and her skin felt like satin. He kneaded her buttocks as if they were made of velvet bread dough. As he sat on the edge of his desk, her body fit between his legs like a hand inside a fitted glove, and he tasted her neck and shoulders with his tongue. She leaned back and her body jerked with passion as if she had been depraved of sensual touch for far too long. She was hungry and seemed to have decided to feed on the Minister. Still fully clothed, she began unbuttoning his shirt. He did not help her nor did he stop her. As her fingers worked rhythmically unbuttoning his shirt, he took the opportunity to hold her by the shoulders and move her back from him just enough to take a captivating look at her naked body. His eyes expressed his passion.

She was all that he had imagined beneath her clothes. Her breasts were full and her pink nipples were erotically saluting his gaze. It was definitely not cold in the room so he was sure their erection was for him. Her thin waist gave way to hips that must have been the blueprints for the curves of Route 66, and guarding her flower was a meticulously manicured thatch of golden hair that seemed to have been dipped in refined honey for color. Her legs were long and unending and though they were slim, they were thick in all the right places.

As he watched her work, he noticed her lips, full and shiny. There was something inside him that wanted to stop her, wanted to be Christian and holy, noble and righteous, wanted to show her that there was another way to deal with the problems that were motivating her actions. But there was a selfish man inside him also, and that man wanted to make love to her the moment he saw her. That man had waited patiently for the chance to touch her the way he was touching her at that very moment.

He ignored whatever sparks of divinity that resided within him and pulled her close to him. He held her by her curly hair and massaged his hands deep into her scalp. She purred like a cat. He brought her mouth to his and searched its interior with his tongue as she did his. She began kissing his neck and shoulders as she carefully removed his shirt, consistently working her way down. With his hands still holding the back of her head, she moved across his chest with her tongue and lips, resting with powerful slurps on his nipples. She could taste his stimulation and see his rise preparing to burst through his pants. With his left nipple between her teeth and his hands exploring her most private orifices, she unbuckled his belt and unzipped his pants to release his aching tool, and when she did, he vocally exhaled his approval.

The Minister rarely ever lost control and he was determined not to be swept away by the moment. He was the one usually doing the sweeping and the person who fell beneath his spell was out of control. But he was going places that he had never been with Lydia. The locks and chains that normally gripped the private places of his mind were being loosed, and the woman who knelt before him had the keys.

There were some places that remained sacred even to him. One was his church office. Though he had been propositioned there, many times, and even made some proposals himself, he never engaged in any semblance of sexual behavior in his church office. That was something that India did not understand and he purposefully never took the time to explain to her. It was not just the fact that he had no real interest in her advances, but the venue was "all wrong" for such activity. Even he had some redeeming mores opposite his iniquitous behavior. But he was on a pathway to ecstasy with the woman he held in his arms, and his mores had gone out the window, for the time being.

After Lydia released the machine below his belt and took him into her hands, she had to look at what she was feeling, and before she could restrain herself the words, "Oh my God," came from her parted lips. He was massive, not painfully so, but perfectly pleasing. In her mind she thought of how blessed her dear friend Angie was to be able to ride this mechanical bull whenever she pleased. And she was sure he pleased. With nothing left to say, she did what she came to do, and took as much of him as she could into her mouth. The Minister's head jerked back as he closed his eyes and gripped the edge of his desk so tightly that his fingers made permanent indentations in the mahogany wood. He closed his eyelids as his eyes rolled back into his head and found places void of inhibition and restraint. He was losing himself within himself, and the rhythmic thoroughfare to his ecstasy was rapidly intensifying. Finally he spoke.

"Lydia, wait a minute," he said as he attempted to catch his escaping breath. "I can't make love to you, not here. It just wouldn't be right. I just—"

"Don't worry Reverend, this is between you and me. Just let me do what I came to do, and I'll go." She released him only long enough to make her statement, looking into his eyes from her squatted position.

Again kissing him deeply, she stood him up without stopping and moved him away from his desk. He had no idea what she had in mind but the brief interruption gave him a moment to think almost reasonably. That would not last long. Without even taking a millisecond to examine the cluttered papers on his desk, she swept it clean, toppling everything, including his framed family photos, onto the floor. She then motioned him back to the desk and when he sat on the edge, she swung his feet around its perimeter, making him lay flat on his back. The Minister did not protest. He enjoyed watching her work. He just enjoyed watching her. With him on his back she wriggled his pants to his ankles and made sure that his shirt was wide open. Again she took as much of him as she could into her mouth. The Minister's body contorted with pleasure as she rhythmically devoured him.

"Lydia, wait!" He again tried to speak between breaths to tell her that the place was wrong for this type of behavior, and that he had never had sex in his church office, and that he loved his wife and his children and his dog, and every other thing that men try to say when they try to use words of conscience to stop a freight train that they gave license to race down the tracks of irresponsible passion. But this time when he spoke, Lydia climbed atop the desk herself and straddled him in an ungodly position that put her privacy in his face as she continued to massage his stiffness with her hands and mouth. He could not resist her and she tasted as sweet as he had expected. She was Eve. And in minutes that seemed more like seconds there was a reciprocally eruptive climax that had them both quivering and twitching with orgasmic jolts. Lydia screamed almost at the top of her lungs when he gripped her buttocks hard and pulled her down on him, sending his tongue deeper inside her than any tongue had gone before. She, again, jerked and twisted as her lower body rhythmically contorted.

After about thirty seconds, Lydia peeled herself from the Minister, found one if his handkerchiefs on the floor and wiped her mouth. She picked her dress up off the floor and slipped back into it. She put her ankle length over coat back on and then pulled a small compact out of her purse and looked quickly in the mirror. She looked at the Minister, still flat on his back on his desk with his head turned away from her, and then she left. She had never taken her shoes off.

The Minister finally opened his eyes after he was sure that she was gone. He looked blankly at the ceiling, his body frozen, cold and unmovable. Several thoughts raced through his head and he waited patiently until their transit was complete. When his mind was again void of thought, tears pooled in his eyes, overflowed their borders and ran down either side of his face. For more than two hours he laid there, his pants around his ankles, his shirt wide open, the articles from his desk on the floor, the tool below his belt now soft with regret, and tears flowing down the sides of his face making small saline pools on his grand desk.

He was startled by a sound outside his window, but after he found no sign of trouble, he got dressed and went home.

CHAPTER 24

The myth that the world and all its inhabitants sleep during the night, waiting for morning to engage the activities of the day is not all together true. The greatest plans are laid, the most mind-boggling mysteries solved, the most puzzling riddles answered, and the most effective surveillance are all done under the illuminating cover of darkness. More seems to happen after the sun has hidden itself than during the brightness of day. Such was the case with the purposeful rattle at the window of the Minister's office. It was he who was being accounted for, his movements recorded for some future disclosure, his struggles, his triumphs, his defeats, and in this particular case, his surrender. The darkness was the avenue by which the *Watcher* worked. There was a job to be done and the evening shade would not halt its progress. An intuitive engine had been started and was now running, and because of its sheer will to know the absolute truth; it would not stop, at least not any time soon.

Night still reserves its right to a mysterious appearance despite lights efforts to destroy it, especially to those who simply choose not to unravel it's loosely wound secrets. The darkness is not judgmental; it is simply misunderstood, and an often abused privilege. Truth is truth however, in darkness or day, and there was a burning desire for the revelation of fact amongst the fiction of the Minister's life. On the heels of that premise, a very interesting conversation took place between two unlikely cohorts, the night Lydia paid her visit to the office of the Minister.

One of the hardest lessons related to divinity in humanity has yet to be learned. *There is always someone watching.*

"Was he there?" The *Caller* said quietly, showing almost no emotion.

"Yes."

"Was she there?" Again, the question seemed cold and glassy.

"Yes."

"What did you see?"

"Nothing."

"You mean you sat there all that time and saw nothing?" The *Caller's* voice was slightly raised, as if there was something being withheld. "I thought you said they both were there."

"I did."

"And nothing happened?"

"I didn't say that; I said I saw nothing."

The *Caller* now a bit frustrated, began to think that maybe this was not such a good idea, or maybe the wrong individual had been retained to track the actions of the Minister, but then there was some reassurance.

"Listen," the *Voice* said, "I'm on your side and I'll stay with this thing all the way. Don't worry about a thing because I'm sure I'll have something solid for you soon. He's quite a man, you know. I almost hate to see him fall."

There was a momentary pause while the caller thought about the involved actions. The truth that now cam to mind was simple, yet powerful. *Look for trouble and you will surely find it.* There was no question that trouble was on the horizon of this undertaking.

"I understand," said the *Caller*. "Just keep me informed; that's what I'm paying you to do. Just keep me informed. I'll contact you soon."

"I know you will," the voice said softly, and then the line went dead.

The *Voice* in fact, had seen a great deal and all that was observed was recorded. It simply remained undisclosed to the *Caller*. It almost seemed as though the events of the evening were now a personal possession, and to some degree, an obsession.

The flawless naked body of Lydia Davis in devilishly erogenous attachment to the Minister's had all been discretely captured on video tape, and would join a growing file of information on the whereabouts and thereabouts of one Reverend Doctor Edward Alan Hebert. He had become a very special subject in the hearts and minds of several interested parties, but on this night, his reputation would remain protected by the very one who had been hired to aid in its destruction.

After hanging up, the *Voice* removed the tape from the camera and placed it in the VCR. Seated in a leather chair covered in a satin sheet, and with every stitch of clothing removed, the remote in one hand and a

Nesbitt's cream soda in the other, the tape was watched and rewound, over and over again.

CHAPTER 25

When the Minister arrived home, Angie was waiting for him, and he knew there might be some suspicion or uncertainty in her mind. He hated the fact that he could not stop thinking about the events that had just transpired, and he did all he could to clear his mind. He came into the house and placed his keys on the key rack just as he always did, and then walked directly to the bedroom. It was her silence that bothered him most, and she knew that, so she used it to her advantage. She was dressed in a lounging negligee that was more suggestive symbolism than simply a sexy nightgown. It was a personal message sent directly and matter-of-factly to his psyche and also to whatever guilt worthy behavior he engaged.

Angie had learned a lot from her husband. Without another word, the Minister answered the subliminal call before him. He simply moved gracefully toward his wife, scooped her in his arms, and made passionate love to her. Neither said a word. That was her way of keeping things in check, on this particular night. At this stage in the game, she did not have to search for satisfaction. The Minister rose to the occasion without hesitation, another tool she used to her advantage.

When he was sure she was asleep and his house was still, the Minister headed for his study in search of calm for his restless mind. The events and thoughts of late had been mentally taxing and sleep escaped him. He clasped his hands before him and closed his eyes. *Was prayer the order of midnight meditation?* He opened his drawer and removed his personal journal. It was the one in which he placed entries that held hidden truths that only he and God could decipher, just in case it was ever found. He needed it, just as everyone human psyche calls for an avenue to release the truths that hide beneath layers of privacy, fear and fallacy. Scanning his bookshelf, his eyes fell on a particular book authored by

Thomas Moore entitled *Soulmates*, and from it, he entered the following quotes into his journal.

The only thing as challenging as getting tangled in the underbrush of a relationship is trying to write about it. My own experiences with relationships, the good and the bad, weigh heavy as I try to write for others. And so I write in faith, focusing on the soul, without many judgments and without prescription for success. I present relationship here not as a psychological problem or issue, but as a mystery in the religious and theological sense, knowing that it is always a mistake to talk authoritatively about mysteries.

The heart has its own reasons. When we try to understand why relationships come into being and fall apart, why some families are nurturing and others devastating, why some friendships endure long absences and bitter arguments while others fade, we come face to face with the unknown core of the human heart. Of course we spend a great deal of time coming up with all kinds of explanations for unexpected turns in emotion and feeling, but these "reasons" are more rationalizations and simplifications than understanding. We are left with Plato's solution, that relationship is based on a form of madness, erotic madness. Rather than finding solutions for understanding and controlling this heart, we may have no recourse but to honor its mysteries.[1]

Thomas Moore

The Minister closed the book and leaned back in his chair. When he thought of the woman to whom he had just made love, and the roaming desires of his heart that would lead him to Chicago early the next morning, he opened his Bible to the 51st Psalm and closed his journal entry, copying the following passage of scripture...

Have mercy upon me, O God, according to thy loving kindness: according to thy tender mercies blot out my transgressions.
Wash me thoroughly from mine iniquity, and cleanse me from my sin.
For I acknowledge my transgressions: and my sin is ever before me.
Against thee, thee only, have I sinned, and done this evil in thy sight: that thou mightest be justified when thou speakest, and be clear when thou judgest.
Behold, I was shapen in iniquity; and in sin did my mother conceive me.

Behold, thou desirest truth in the inward parts: and in the hidden part thou shalt make me to know wisdom.
Purge me with hyssop, and I shall be made clean: wash me, and I shall be whiter than snow.
Make me hear joy and gladness; that the bones which thou hast broken may rejoice.
Hide my face from my sins, and blot out all mine iniquities.
Create in me a clean heart, O God; and renew a right spirit within me.
Cast me not away from thy presence; and take not thy holy spirit from me.

There were several Biblical characters with whom the Minister personally related: Samuel, as his extraordinary call of God is chronicled in the early books of the Old Testament, Solomon, who most theologians agree was also a Proverbial king named Lemuel, noted for his acknowledgment of his mother's guidance and his expressively literal sensuality, Saint Paul, a brilliantly persuasive orator, well educated, well traveled and committed to spreading the Gospel, and David, a blemished Old Testament king who still found ultimate favor in the eyes of God. For this instance, a passage written by the young king would sooth his troubled conscience.

The Minister closed his journal, placed it back in the drawer and then shut his eyes. He would rest now, but true peace remained elusive as he struggled to suppress deceptive thoughts that took him to Chicago. He did all he could to concentrate and focus on his chosen task, rest. But he could not help but feel the downward spiral of his passions. There was a war within and he was no different than any other fighter. There would be bruises before the final bell would ring.

CHAPTER 26

The rousing applause of the opening night audience was Gemma's drug. She always received a matchless high yet never a completely satisfying fill. She would have to return for more. Gemma could imagine no other life for herself. The undying romance between she and every crowd she encountered had begun when she was a small child singing solos in community churches. She was a performer in the truest sense of the word, and she knew that she had nailed her debut performance in the Chicago theater stage play. It was a rare feeling to be savored to the utmost, and she could not wait to read what the critics had to say in the Trades. *How could they be otherwise?* There were no missed notes or cues. Every step was mastered perfectly, as if she had written the role herself and been allowed to ad lib her own lifestyle to music. But it really did not matter what they said. She was so high that even the worst review could not bring her down.

Gemma Kimbro was simply brilliant on opening night, and that was one of her personal secrets to success in the profession. *"Always knock them dead on opening night, and then make every night even better than the first."* That was her goal, and she had done that masterfully this evening with a performance that would not be soon forgotten.

Gemma was charged when the curtain rose again and she was beckoned to center stage by an ovation that seemed to call her name. The other cast members were great, but Gemma was clearly the diva of the evening, and it felt way beyond great. The cast had recognized early on that she would make them all shine, so they supported her all the way. They loved her and the crowd loved her, and that was a good thing in the world of live entertainment, where fickle audiences could severely damage a career.

She was superbly distinguished at her craft yet still faced struggles when it came to securing roles as an African-American female in the United States. Her agent often had to force auditions with directors and producers because of their predetermination that an African-American was wrong for whatever the role might be, without even seeing anyone. But once they saw Gemma and heard her vocal mastery, they were almost always overcome by the enormity of her talent and charisma of her personality. Their prejudiced opinions were soon laid aside. Now things were finally turning around, and the offers were coming to her even without solicitation by her agent and management team, and her opening night performance in this play seemed to be a promising catalyst in terms of opening even more doors in her career.

Finally retiring to her dressing room after basking in the glow of the audience's adulation, Gemma took her time getting dressed, mainly because the director and producer continually interrupted her, bringing "important people" back to meet the star of the show. There were no complaints from the venerable diva as she maintained superstar composure greeting her admirers. She also took the time to relish the moment. Having lived in the world of live entertainment for many years, she knew that notable moments like these were fleeting at best, and should be tenaciously gripped by the mind and heart. Wrapped in a royal blue silk kimono she had been given by an admirer during her last visit to Singapore, she greeted the well-wishers in style and grace, realizing that every meeting was a potential future connection that held unknown benefits. As far as she was concerned, she may have been shaking hands with a multi-million dollar star maker, so she treated everyone she embraced as if they were special and their name worth remembering.

Gemma never minded meeting people, for that reason specifically, and loved the attention she received from the public. Her dream was to receive the attention in the States that she received on the streets of Europe, which was the same goal of many performers who had taken their talent over seas to fans who were more loyal and less critical. There, she was well already known, admired and respected. She signed autographs daily and it was rare that she ever completed a public meal without being recognized by a patron or someone walking the street who inadvertently glanced through the window, seeing her striking face.

Tonight a major steppingstone toward the fruition of her dream had been born into reality as she enjoyed the stateside honors she deserved. At the opening night party for the cast and crew, she was the worthy focal point, and the room seemed to light more brightly when she entered.

The night was magical; full and complete, and Gemma feasted on every congratulatory remark and accolade served her way. Once again, the producer and this time, the owner of the ballet company that performed with the featured cast, brought a myriad of decision-making entertainment moguls to meet her. It was a brilliant "win-win" exchange, as Gemma was a glorious drawing card and advertisement for the play and production team, thus helping to secure a bright future in the theater, which in turn, elated the "company brass." She, on the other hand, would soon reap the personal and financial rewards for her efforts. The music blasted and the champagne corks flew into the air to rousing cheers. There were no complaints; everyone was having a glorious time. By the time her limo pulled forward, her lips and cheek muscles were sore, having blown a multitude of diva kisses rehearsed since childhood. The crowd wished her well and looked forward to her upcoming performances.

She sank into the backseat and watched the Chicago skyline race by, sometimes falling into a restless doze as her exhausted body struggled against her vivacious mind. She did all she could to force her dashing psyche into slow motion, attempting to more slowly absorb the enchanting details of the night. She could not help drifting to various points of sensuality and passion: the colors, the sounds, and the music. She was extremely tired but there was an undercurrent of electricity that would not allow her to rest. After everything that seemed relatively meaningful made its way through the corridors of her mind, something, or rather someone unexpected appeared in her thoughts. It was almost as if he appeared by way of telepathy, and thoughts of him brought a smile that could not be restrained.

She thought of his eyes, remembering when he looked at her and how he said that he wanted to know where she was performing. He wanted to keep track of her career, he said. She thought of the unusual warmth of his hands when he shook hers, and how there was something unexplainably special about him. She thought of the conflictive inner explosion she felt when she saw him and how her female intuition informed her that the feeling was some how mutual. It was strange, as if something dormant had been awakened by a simple glance. And then without thinking, she placed her hand into the pocket of her overcoat and was surprised to find the note that he had given her.

The pleasure of meeting you yesterday was mine. You are a song that just keeps playing over and over in my head, and judging by the dream I had last night I must play your tune again. I am now caught in the rhythm of your enchantment, and the beat goes on.

Gemma re-read it, crumbled it, and then tried to throw it in the trash can at her feet. But something would not allow her to let it go. Again looking out the window as if trying to avoid the magnetic draw of the note in her hand, she crumbled it and placed it back into her pocket. Maybe she could crumble him up and put him out of her mind, but like the note in the pocket of her coat, the Minister was now in the pocket of her consciousness, and removal was difficult, if not impossible.

When she finally arrived at her hotel, Gemma sauntered slowly through the lobby, allowing herself to be romanced by her eclectic surroundings. That was the way she was, especially on a special night like this one, where everything that could have gone right was better than perfect. There was an aroma of excitement and electricity in the air, and Gemma inhaled deeply with every stride, being energized to a point of pleasurable restlessness. Upon entering her well-appointed suite, she smiled after viewing the myriad of bouquets that had been delivered. She had given the hotel staff permission to enter and make the deliveries while she was away so that she could come home to her botanically enchanted garden of compliments and well wishes.

There were roses everywhere, even an arrangement from her best friend, Ivy who had never missed delivering an opening night gift to her talented friend. The gesture had become a consistent expectation that always brought a smile to Gemma's face, no matter where she was, or how the performance had gone. It had started in college when Ivy gave Gemma a gold locket after her first lead role in a campus production of "*A Streetcar Named Desire.*" It was then that Ivy knew that Gemma had been created for stage and screen, and pledged undying support to her friend. And tonight Ivy's flowers were a perfectly apropos salute to the talent and tenacity of a true diva. Gemma looked around and decided that she would not sit up all night and read each individual card but that she would take the time later to acknowledge as many as she could.

As she walked down her short hallway en route to her powder room, she noticed an exceptionally large basket of lavender tulips that stood out amongst the roses. They were beautiful and unusual, and there must have been 100 of them. She could not resist reaching for the card that identified the sender. The envelope simply said, *Gemma…*

Beautiful flowers for a beautiful flower… These blossoms honor you with their loveliness and applaud the fragrance of your talent. Please accept them as a symbol of my anticipation of inhaling your sweet aroma the next time you blossom on stage, blessing my heart like you did in Manhattan. Looking forward to your dance...

Ciao Bella

Gemma's heart skipped a beat after she read the card because she knew exactly who it was from. She did not really want to believe it, but deep within her, she was ecstatic to know that the Minister was thinking about her, and that he remembered the captivating moments of their backstage introduction in New York. There was nothing absolutely conclusive to indicate the basket was from him, but she knew without question. She had only received one other note like this one, in her life from a man, and that one had come from the Minister.

His style was clear and concise. He was not crudely forward, but he wasted no time with guessing games and was clear with his intention. That was how he reeled in his prey. He was not a spider that captured its kill by placing a transparent snare in the path of an unsuspecting victim, nor was he a wild cat, hunting on the plains of the Serengeti stalking its meal and then forcefully pouncing on it at the right moment to ensure the kill. He was a killer whose victims fell willingly as he calculatingly poisoned them with his romantic concoctions, and Gemma Kimbro, a neophyte of romantic impulse, was preparing to gulp down the *Kool-Aid*.

The note stopped her in her tracks, and instead of continuing with her plans for the powder room, she went to her closet and reached into the pocket of her overcoat. Pulling out the note from him that she had been reading in the car brought forth an unstoppable grin. Gemma was smart, and she knew herself well. Her mind drifted to Alfonse and how she had allowed herself to be swept away in romance, and how there had been more than a few trysts fueled by impulsive passion, over the years. There was something pleasurably hypnotic about that aspect of her life, and she could not deny that she enjoyed it immensely. She loved to feel, and loved, even more, the men who made her feel. Things probably never turned out like they should have, and of course, there were some major regrets, but she was a rather hopeless romantic, specifically making allowance available for the next encounter.

She thought for a moment more, allowing her face to settle, and then she inhaled deeply, shrugged her shoulders and headed to her desk to power up her laptop computer. She searched her computerized address book and found the Minister's contact information. He had given her one of his personal cards that had his email address and direct dial phone number on it. Gemma looked at the screen for a moment and was hesitant, thinking briefly of the consequences of her actions. Something inside her knew that the first key-stroke that she made was the most dangerous, but she had been a master of talking herself out of reason, and it was true that that character trait had often led to problems, but it had also been the very factor that had opened numerous doors. That aspect of her character made her most successful at her craft and a magnet to all who encountered her sometimes recklessly aggressive spirit.

It was time for her to classically convince herself that it was okay to send the Minister an email. *There was nothing wrong with it*, she thought to herself. After all, it would be rude for her to not express some form of gratitude for the basket of flowers he had sent. It was harmless and there was nothing between them. Oh sure, there were a few sparks when they met back stage but she was an adult, as was he and they both could be relied on to put any romantic feelings into proper perspective and treat each other cordially and professionally. He was her pastor for God's sake, and she was just another member of the church. He supported everyone who endeavored something great and creative. There was nothing special or covert about his gesture.

As hard as she tried, Gemma knew in her heart that none of her persuasive thoughts held any gravity against the desires of her heart.

> *Dear Pastor Hebert,*
> *I must thank you for the bouquet and card. They were lovely. I'm honored that you remembered my opening night and I must say that the night was simply magical. Everything went exactly as it should have. I believe you would have enjoyed the show immensely, and if you're in the Chicago area any time soon, please let me know; I would be happy to reserve a ticket for you. I have a special dance that I'm sure you'd enjoy.*
>
> *Always,*
> *Gemma Kimbro*
>
> *P.S. Please say hello to your lovely wife for me.*

Gemma read the note several times before activating the "send" option. She wanted to make sure that she was as generic as she could be without allowing her true feelings to bleed through. But she could not help herself. She thought maybe the post-script line that sent regards to his wife would keep him at bay, or more importantly, cover her if there were to be any unforeseen repercussions. But she *did* want him to know that she was interested and had received his message loud and clear. With that done, she closed her computer and headed for the bathroom. She did not wait on a response. *Who would be awake at this hour?* She thought. But the Freudian truth was that she was afraid of her response to his. Had he responded quickly, an email conversation would have ensued that would have put a steamy Harlequin romance novel to shame.

Gemma knew where her mind was and that there was definitely meaning to the fact that since Manhattan, the Minister rarely escaped her thoughts. Finally she stopped asking why he was there and simply enjoyed his presence. In the oversized Jacuzzi tub, she drew a luxuriously relaxing bubble bath and sank into the suds. With her hair wrapped and her eyes closed, she fell into a dream that carried her right into the arms of the Minister.

CHAPTER 27

By Wednesday morning, Ivy just could not take it anymore. She had gotten so used to Donovan's smile, conversation and warmth that she just had to speak to him. She reasoned with herself the way any good attorney should, presenting arguments from both sides of the issue, and finally she was convinced that she had nothing to fear but fear itself. It was cliché but it worked for now.

She sat in her bed trying to prepare the appropriate words for the call but nothing special came to mind. The woman of a thousand words had nothing specifically prepared for the hopeful exchange. But finally, she released her grip on verbal needs and revitalized her paralyzed fingers, allowing them, at least to dial.

"Good morning," he said in his usual sexy voice.

Ivy was still apprehensive about calling him even though he had said that she could call his cell anytime, day or night. It still felt strange knowing that he was married. *What kind of relationship did they really have?* But she moved forward, fueled by his suggestion and her growing desire to be with him.

"Hi, Donovan," she said with a sigh. "You know, I just want to apologize for my behavior lately. I was under a great deal of stress with the last case I was working on, and I'm really sorry but I just didn't really understand what was going on with you and I know I probably jumped to the wrong conclusion and," she paused, "I miss you."

He laughed quietly as if he knew she was going to call. His patience, like the Minister's, was enduring. It was not a chuckle of conceit but one of relief that the one in whom he was infatuated finally responded.

"Ivy, listen. You don't have to apologize. I've been under quite a great deal of stress myself, and I've probably been a little weird too. And

I miss you too." He paused for a moment of thought. "Hey what are you doing today?"

"Nothing special, just going to work. I've got a new case in my lap. Why?"

"Don't go in today. Let's spend the day together! What do you think?"

Ivy thought for a moment about her workload and the new case that she was eagerly waiting to sink her teeth into. Days of leisure would soon be a distant memory. Then she thought about Gemma, and how she always commented on her grinding work schedule and how she had often advised her to take a chance, and more importantly, to take some time, and some risks, and enjoy the benefits life has to offer. Ivy also remembered that her boss had given her a few days off to re-energize and prepare for a taxing case that would require her full attention and focus. One more day could only make things better, and a day with Donovan could only make things great.

"Let me call my office and see what my day is looking like and I'll give you a call back," she said, trying to hide any remnants of excitement that might be recognized in her voice. She did not want him to know that she had already made up her mind and was looking forward, with extraordinary anticipation, to seeing him. As far as he was concerned, she still wanted him to think that she really was not interested in pursuing a relationship with him, but Ivy had missed him terribly, and after a few days of introspection and solitude she decided that it was useless and unreasonable to deny herself the pleasure and possibilities of romance. She would simply keep things in proper perspective, and keep her expectations at a minimum. Whatever happened from here on out would be a treat, sort of like an unexpected tax refund.

"Okay, 'Miss Corporate Star'," Donovan replied jovially. "I'll wait to hear from you. But don't keep me on hold all day; I might decide to share all this fun and romance with someone else."

"I'll call you back in a minute; I promise," Ivy said as she laughed.

Ivy took her time before returning Donovan's call. She phoned her office and checked in with her assistant, who told her that adjusting her schedule would not be a problem, and to enjoy her day. She did, however, inform her that she had received a call from the reporter involved in the new tabloid magazine case, but she could not remember her name off the top of her head. It had been written down and placed on the growing stack of messages on Ivy's desk.

The call was mentioned because the reporter said that she and Ivy were old friends from school. Her assistant offered to go get the message so that she could give the correct name but Ivy told her not to bother. Though it might be interesting to know, Ivy spent little time on the issue. Her focus was on spending the day with Donovan. Her passion was there now.

Briefly reminiscing, there were a few people she remembered from school who majored in broadcast journalism but she had lost regular contact with them. It was not unusual however, for their professional paths to cross periodically, so Ivy rather looked forward to seeing the old comrade, who ever it was. She instructed her assistant to arrange a meeting for the end of the week, and by that time she would be ready to roll. Ivy reeled off a list of additional last minute directives, enough to keep three assistants busy for a week, and then hung up the phone.

Looking through her meticulously organized closet, the task at hand was simply to decide what to wear. Should she be sexy or practical, or practically sexy? It really did not matter, she thought.

Ivy went to the phone to make the call and agree to spend the day Donovan, and see what was on the activities agenda. Maybe then she could make sure that her clothing choice was apropos. But she decided, instead, to just play it by ear, clothing wise, and to make him wait a little while longer on her call. She did not want to seem too eager. Ivy stepped into the shower and allowed anticipation to run wild like the water rushing down her naked body. The day could only be filled with pleasant surprises.

CHAPTER 28

Donovan had not seen or heard from Lydia in three days, but that was not unusual, especially under these circumstances. He knew that the stress level was high and challenging but he also knew they had been living lives that would eventually lead to days like these. She would call soon, and when she did he was ready for her call.

"Hi 'D'," she said quietly. Her voice was genuine and the heart felt emotion that only she could show was clear and present.

"Hey baby. You okay? When are you coming home? Everything all right? You know I miss you." His concern was genuine and sincere, as well.

"I'll be home soon," she replied sighing. "You know I've just got to try to sort this whole thing out."

"I know." He did not want her to feel pressured in any way. His eyes were closed as he held the receiver, briefly, away from his ear.

"What are you doing today?"

"Oh nothing, just running around and taking care of some business."

"Just running around and taking care of some business?" She retorted in an alerted tone.

"Don't worry baby. I have a meeting with the lawyer that I think can make some sense of this thing and make it right."

Lydia sighed loudly; it was more frustration than anger. And then she started to quietly sob.

"This is just so hard, Donovan. You promised it wouldn't happen again. I thought you were finished with that, and look where we are. Our lives are about to be ruined." She was getting frantic and the desperation in her voice was clear.

"Shhh, I know baby, but I'm gonna work it all out, okay. Just give me a chance. I think I have someone who can help us out, really. Just give me some time." He changed the subject abruptly. "Have you been taking care of yourself, relaxing and taking your meds?"

"Yeah, I'm okay," she said.

"I know you've been hanging out with that Minister's wife. She seems real cool, like a good friend, and her husband is quite a man."

"Yeah, they're really great people," she said, without any semblance of guilt in her voice. "I promised him that you would come to the church soon."

"I will." Once again he steered the conversation. "Have you told them anything about us?"

"Of course not; why would I do something like that? Do you think this is a topic to be discussed over brunch, Donovan? God-dammit, this is serious!"

"Okay, okay, okay," he buffeted. And then quietly asked, "When are you coming home, baby. You know I miss you."

"No you don't 'Donnie', not completely. But I guess there is a part of you that does, and I miss that part of you, as well. I'll be home tomorrow afternoon. I love you 'Donnie.' I love you so much."

He did not contest her statement because he knew she was right. She was honest now and was not afraid to be truthful about her feelings concerning the sorted facts surrounding their life together. It had been a roller coaster ride of deception and camouflage, but it would soon be coming to a screeching halt, probably sooner than they both thought.

"I love you too baby." He paused. "All of me. I'll see you tomorrow. Be safe."

The couple exchanged "tele-smooches" and then hung up. Lydia rolled over and pulled the elaborate goose down comforter over her shoulder. She would try to rest but her brain would not stop racing through the myriad of scenarios that she had experienced of late. For the last few days she had been occupying a stylish suite in an exclusive, but very private, hotel about twenty minutes outside the city. Though her activities had brought her into the city for a couple of unscheduled counseling sessions, she had taken up residence away from home at the advice of her doctor and her husband. She and Donovan had agreed that it was the best way to deal with her recently increasing stress level. But being away did not rewrite the history of incidents that had brought her there. Her life was in trouble and she knew it. Everything that she had ignored was coming to violent climax and a major part of her psychosis was the fact that she continued to kick herself for what she felt she had allowed to happen.

After he hung up, Donovan immediately got dressed and headed out to spend the day with his lawyer, the one he would try to retain by the end of the day, the one who had no idea what she was dealing with or the depraved fallacies to which she was opening her door. He did not allow himself to think. He was on a mission, one that would hopefully be completed by the end of the day.

CHAPTER 29

Ivy first put on a pair of jeans, tennis shoes and a turtleneck under a sweatshirt. She looked in the mirror, disapproved and then put on a jean skirt with splits in front and back and a cashmere pullover. Again after a quick evaluation in the mirror, she took that off. Finally settling on a dark tan leather pants suit and blouse that accentuated her athletic figure, she picked up the phone to call Donovan to say "yes." She was interrupted by the doorbell and hung up the phone. When she opened the door, he was there.

"I knew you'd say yes, so I hustled my butt on over here before you exercised your female privilege and changed your mind."

His smile was like a glaring suspension of stars and he held it long enough to let it penetrate its way through the crust of her doubt and apprehension. In her mind, she could only think of the *Crest* toothpaste commercial he had recently done, and was amazed that his teeth were even more white and brighter in person than even the television showed.

At first Ivy was disturbed by his unannounced arrival, but then she remembered his style and how he always seemed to have great timing. This was no different. She fell into his arms without a word and they kissed like reminiscent lovers reliving passionate memories. Ivy searched herself for the source of such expressive feelings. There were emotions that had been suppressed for quite a while by her own design, but standing before Donovan, her control was gone. Chuckles ensued as the couple relinquished their embrace. Ivy used her thumb to wipe away the traces of lipstick still on Donovan's mouth, another personally intimate gesture that surprised her.

"Come in," she said holding his hand and leading the way.

"These are for you," he replied as he stepped through the doorway, and from behind his back he produced a striking bouquet of exotic flowers.

"Oh Donovan, you didn't have to do that."

"Yes I did," he said matter-of-factly. "I was not going to take a chance on losing a very special friend; especially one who I know loves exotic flowers. I've missed you Ivy. I really have." He was studying her face and body as he stood before her holding both her hands. She paused momentarily before responding and then looked into his eyes.

"I've missed you too, Donovan."

There was something needful in her eyes that he recognized, and that was good. Maybe she would be receptive to the request he was going to make later in the day.

"Let's not waste anymore time," he said. "Let's enjoy this beautiful day. I've got all morning and most of he afternoon reserved just for you."

"Really," Ivy replied smirking and smiling with her eyes. "And who is the night reserved for?"

"Well counselor, did you have something planned for the night that we can't do during the day?" Their eyes locked momentarily and they both shared devilish smiles, and then they broke out in laughter, probably for very different reasons.

When Ivy stepped out the door, she took a deep breath of the fresh air, as if she were inhaling a new lease on life, or at least a new perspective. She had decided to be open to whatever a relationship with Donovan would bring. This would be the first day of life without fear of consequence. Without even speaking to her friend Gemma, she had heeded her philosophy on enjoying life. Even work would take a backseat to the pleasure of the day. She had placed the information and all of the documents she had brought home completely out of her mind. It was time to concentrate her energies elsewhere. *Hell, I'll even turn my cell phone off*, she thought to herself. She was wide open to whatever Donovan had in store for her, and that was just how he wanted her. He knew how tough it was to get inside Ivy's guarded zone. He had been working at it for over a month now, and he hoped that he had found his way in.

Their day began at a little hole in the wall soul food restaurant located in the heart of the city. The delicious smell of bacon and homemade sausage could be detected more than a block away. It was almost as if the savory aroma guided patrons to the eatery like the bat signal guided Batman to the scene of a crime. Ivy's stomach unleashed an unladylike growl as they approached the entrance that sent them both into uncontrollable laughter.

"Looks like you've moved to the city but your stomach still lives in the hood," Donovan said as he rubbed his own stomach and laughed.

Ivy was a little embarrassed at the statement her stomach made but it could not be helped. It had been treated unfairly for quite a while now, and it had to state its jealous opinion on what a privilege the nostrils had, inhaling the blessed aroma.

Ivy ordered old fashioned, thick cut maple bacon, eggs, grits and biscuits with gravy. It was like being home again and it stirred up memories of pleasant times with her aunt and uncle. It brought a warm smile to her face that Donovan quickly noticed. For a moment she was eight years old again, swinging her feet, above the floor, at her aunt's table, smiling as her uncle sipped hot black coffee out of a little bowl and her aunt hummed a hymn over the sink while she dried and put away the breakfast dishes.

"I haven't had grits like these since I was a kid," she said after taking her first bite. "I remembered how I looked forward to going home for semester break when I was in college, just to get some of my Aunt Cindy's good home cooking. Everybody else was heading for some place sunny and 'beachy' to get drunk and act wild, but I had to make a stop at home first."

"Ah, so you too were getting drunk and wild. You just had to stop off and grab some soul food on the way." He looked at her with a jovially examining grin.

"You didn't hear me say that. I was a good girl."

"I bet you were very good."

They both laughed and then focused on the incredible meals before them. Everything was going well, and Ivy felt completely relaxed, comfortable being with Donovan and feeling as though their relationship had turned a corner and reached a new plateau. She was not sure what that plateau was but there was some new feeling that electrified her, and she did not question it. She just enjoyed it. All was well until an old friend walked into the restaurant, recognized Donovan, and then immediately made his way over to the table.

The men spoke briefly and Ivy noticed the fact that Donovan did not immediately introduce her, and it was also clear that the man knew Lydia. When he finally did introduce Ivy, she was title-less. She was just "Ivy." The old acquaintance also skirted around asking questions about Lydia. It was a red flag that she suppressed. She had litigated herself into the pursuit of a question free and pressure free relationship with Donovan.

Men are so stupid, she thought to herself as they exchanged closing salutations. She thought about the protective network that men appear to have. They never rat each other out, unless they have something to gain, and the fact that Donovan was a sports celebrity made him special in these terms. Maybe the friend thought that Ivy was just another notch in Donovan's bedpost. What was funny was that, at this point with Ivy's "new" perspective, she would not have minded if that were the case. There were no designs on a future with him and if that was what they wanted to do, so be it. She wanted to question him as to why he brought her to a place where he knew they might run into his friends and cause an uncomfortable situation, but she kept her questions to herself.

"You okay?" He reached for her arm in some sort of comforting way.

"Of course; why wouldn't I be?" She took in another fork full of steaming hot grits.

Ivy had a feeling that Donovan expected her to react negatively to the scene but she was holding fast to her new outlook. Besides, she thought, there was nothing conspicuously salacious with the scene and nothing public had really happened that might justify any negative perception.

Ivy was amazed at the small portions of food that Donovan ordered for himself. She would have expected a man of his size and weight to consume enormous amounts at every sitting. But what she found even more interesting were the numerous vitamins and supplements that he took out of a small pouch and placed on the table. There were at least twenty-five pills varying in size, shape and color. Some of them were so large that she thought they were more suited for a horse. She figured their next stop had to be a stable because she could not imagine any thoughtful human being ingesting such a large pill.

"Good lord, Donovan; are you going to take all those?" She stopped her fork midway to her mouth.

"Well, something has to keep me competitive, pretty lady," he replied with a smile.

"Yeah, but that's a bit excessive, don't you think?"

"Well Mother," he said sarcastically, "they don't pay me to think. They're interested in me running and crashing into running backs and quarter backs, and half backs and any other kind of back they tell me to, and they'll do whatever it takes to make my body do just that."

"And you're okay with that?"

"No, I actually hate it, and would rather not be doing it."

"So why are you doing something you don't want to do?"

"Because that's been the story of my life, Ivy." He looked away momentarily and then glanced at the floor.

Ivy could see that this was a topic that he was uncomfortable discussing, and frankly she was too. She had no intentions of going this route in the relationship. Although she had convinced herself to be open to whatever with Donovan, she could not help considering boundaries and limitations to set for herself. But of course, her mind went south and her heart went north leaving her wide open to be drawn in by his innocence and charm. There was something in her that wanted to care for him in a deeper way. Maybe it was his complexity. Maybe it was her biological clock alerting her maternal instincts. Who knew?

"I'm sorry; I wasn't trying to pry or tell you what to do, or anything. I was just making an observation," she said in a back pedaling manner that hopefully offered sincerity. She really did not want him to get the wrong idea.

"No, no, no Ivy. I'm just kidding calling you mother. It's just that I've heard it before."

"Where, from your mother?"

"You got it, from my mother."

They both laughed as they continued their meal. Ivy was still amazed when Donovan poured glass after glass of a large carafe of orange juice and swallowed the pills three and four at a time. As an athlete herself, she knew the value and necessity of supplements and vitamins, but she also was aware of the danger involved. She knew first hand of the numerous stories of both amateur and professional athletes whose internal organs were damaged after several years of consuming dietary additives and performance enhancing supplements. She tried to hold her peace when it came to discussing the issue with Donovan. *That's not why I'm here.*

"So, are you thinking of retiring from football, or something?" She could not help herself. She probably should have been talking about the weather or something, but he opened the door to this topic.

"Oh no, that's not it at all. I love the game; I'm just tired of all the crap that goes with it. I mean, it's just not pure any more, you know. Image-makers and body sculptors surround me all the time. The Donovan the public sees is the Donovan they want you to see. People don't know the reality with the endorsement thing either. I don't believe in a quarter of the stuff they have me selling because basically the mess just doesn't work, but there I am smiling and cheesing like I love it and you just *have* to buy it. Hell Ivy, I'm a slave just like 'Kunta Kente.' They just pay me fifteen million dollars a year to pick their cotton." Ivy could clearly hear the bitterness and dissatisfaction in his tone.

"So why do you do it?"

"Well, initially you take what you can get and you're on such a high by just being in the league you think your invincible and you've been held down in college by amateur status, for what seems like an eternity, and then they tease you with the opportunity to make some real money, and then some agent takes advantage of that rush and lays a guilt trip on you about how hard he's working to secure your future to solidify his cut, and family you've never heard of starts showing up out of the wood work and claim they helped raise you, and it just goes round and round."

Ivy noticed in Donovan's little dissertation that he did not mention the thoughts and feelings of his wife, and though she was interested in some way, she did not ask. He continued to talk about his feelings and observations on his personal life and the intra-workings of the league, agents and endorsements, which Ivy thought was absolutely fascinating. She wondered if he spoke to anyone else like this. *Who else was privy to the disclosure of his soul? Lydia?* Then suddenly Donovan stopped.

"Damn Ivy," he said looking at her with a demeanor of puzzled joy, "you are the first person I've really opened up to like that. I don't know where it came from and why it even came out but you must have cast some kind of spell on me." He reached toward her, grabbed her hand and looked deeply into her eyes and said, "Thank you."

"For what, I didn't do anything but listen." Her eyes were still locked on his, like the time Gemma had seen them having lunch.

"Exactly," he said with a smile that should have been on a hallmark greeting card. "For the first time in a long time, someone just listened to me and didn't tell me what to do." It was planned, professional and effective.

"You're very welcomed," she replied innocently.

"Let's get out of here. There's a whole day waiting for you and I want you to get every second of it." They stood up and put their coats on and as they did, Donovan nonchalantly glanced at Ivy. There was one more thing to say.

"By the way, remind me that I want to talk to you about something later, okay."

"Sure, I won't let you forget."

CHAPTER 30

The long green grass bent gently in the breeze and every few miles there was a simple farmhouse that stood as a reminder of tranquility and uninterrupted calm. The rolling countryside was therapeutically beautiful and Ivy engaged in a visual conversation with nature at its very best. Ivy needed every moment of whatever was happening to her by simply looking out the window. Donovan seemed to know that. He said nothing for almost an hour and allowed her to simply absorb all that the view had to offer. It was rare to find someone with whom the precious commodity of silence can be shared and enjoyed. He was so, so right. The further they drove, the easier it was to free her mind from weighty cognition.

Finally they turned off the main highway and onto a single lane road that wound its way up to an exquisite ranch style hide away. Donovan's customized black on black Range Rover absorbed every bump and knoll with ease. By now, Ivy was so relaxed that she did not have a thought in her head or a care in the world, and that was just how Donovan wanted her.

"How ya doing over there, gorgeous?" he asked as he shut down the motor.

"I don't know if I could be any better," she exclaimed. "This place is absolutely beautiful. Is it yours?" She got out of the vehicle, stretching her arms and legs, taking a 360-degree survey of her surroundings.

"I call it *La Ventana de Bonita*," he said as he came around to her side of the car with a smile. "Come on in; I'll show you around."

The house was tastefully appointed with numerous paintings and sculptures, some of which were still unfinished and under tarps, and the general décor was stunning. High vaulted ceilings gave the feeling of grandeur and majesty, while the rich smell of forest pine was a greeting that felt personal and inviting. As she looked around, Ivy noticed a plethora of autographed pictures on the walls, all of very recognizably famous athletes and entertainment industry personalities. She tried not to be overtaken by the innate desire to look at every one closely like an adoring fan, and focused her attention on the abundance of art all over the main floor of the house. There were paintings of flowers, birds, trees, landscapes, street scenes, faces, bodies, and body parts, which she found very interesting. The sculptures, on the other hand, were all human body sculptures and they were all male. Everything in the house was very much up to date and appeared to be lived in regularly, which did not surprise Ivy because she figured Donovan had someone else probably use the place while he was away. She did, however, wonder who the occupant was. "Who's the artist?" she asked as she studied one of the paintings.

"You're looking at 'em."

"What, you're an artist too? You're kidding. I had no idea." She turned to him briefly and then continued to examine the pieces.

"Yeah, it's just something that has always been in me. I guess it's just another part of the 'Donovan' that the world doesn't know." He smiled, this time, with a newly recognized boyish grin, and looked down at the floor. Ivy came over to him and found his eyes.

"Just who are you, Donovan? My God, who are you?"

"I promise I'll tell you, probably sooner than you think," he said returning her gaze with intensity. "Follow me, for now."

He grabbed Ivy by the hand and guided her out the back door where she could see two horses saddled and loosely tied at the barn, about fifty yards from the main house. It had been years since Ivy had been on a horse and she was like an excited child. She was fearless and could not wait to climb aboard her mount. The two departed and headed up a trail into the hills with Donovan leading the way. About half an hour later, they arrived at their obvious destination.

Donovan helped her down and spread a blanket he had in his saddle-bag. Once again, Ivy could not help but admire the beautiful and serene surroundings. They had set up right near a brook that ran calmly over the rocks. Donovan gathered a few pieces of wood and quickly built a small fire to help alleviate the effects of the daytime chill. The air was crisp and cloudless, divinely clean and pure. It was a scene right out of a movie or a romance novel. He then uncorked a bottle French wine and pulled out an assortment of fruits and cheeses. Ivy watched him closely as he spread everything before her. He worked meticulously, not like anything one would have expected from a burly lineman, but there was a novel softness in his face that she could clearly see, a sensitivity that gave definition to his character.

They ate and drank, giggled and laughed. Ivy was losing herself in his chivalry and he knew it. He constantly complimented her and told her how he had never seen anyone so beautiful, and how he was intoxicated by the way that the sunlight bounced off the curls of her sandy-brown hair. His comments were as flattering as they were true. Ivy was truly gorgeous and the sun reflected the hypnotic intensity of her piercing gray eyes. Though Donovan had planned for Ivy to lose herself in him, he was actually the victim of her spell, losing himself in her. The purity of her beauty was undeniable, and though he had other intentions in terms of his own attractions, there was just no way around the enchanted vision before him.

There was a side of Ivy that wanted to inquire about his feelings for Lydia; there was a portion of her that wanted to slap him for the disrespect of his wife; but there was a greater and more overwhelming part of her that sank into his flattery and dismissed reason. And it was at that very moment that he leaned over to her and kissed her. Their tongues danced an oral waltz and when it was over, they both seemed to know that it was time for more. Ivy dismissed thoughts of their previous encounter that sent her into a tailspin. This time she knew it had to be right. She took visual inventory of her surroundings one last time and her mate concluded that the day was perfect. With no further delay, they stood and he helped her onto her mount.

"What about the blanket and food?" Ivy asked.

"Leave it there," he said without taking his eyes off her.

They rode back to the house talking lightly and romantically. He continued to compliment her on how her beauty fell in harmony with the nature around them, and she continued to fall deeper within the grasp of his magic. He was charming, like a prince trotting through Sherwood Forest. When they arrived he tied the horses and they made their way inside.

"Donovan, that was absolutely great. I really wasn't expecting any of this," she said as she removed her jacket. Ivy felt that it was important to share her gratitude before things moved any further. She was sincere and his plans were truly medicine for a weary mind.

"The pleasure was mine. I'm just glad you decided to let me back into your life."

"I'm sorry I shut you out in the first place. I should have given you more of a fighting chance, and been more understanding," she said shaking her head.

"Don't worry about it now, sweetheart. We're here now, and before anything happens that changes the magic of the day, I want to take full advantage of you."

Ivy smiled a relaxing and sensual smile. Donovan responded appropriately.

"Let's go take a shower," he said grabbing her by the hand. He whisked her up the stairs to the elaborate bathroom across the hall from the master bedroom. It was as immaculate as would be expected in the vacation home of a professional athlete. Wood, stone, and gold plated fixtures were beautifully supporting the rustic theme. The shower seemed large enough for four people and had eight locations that forcefully sprayed water all over the body. It was something to be seen on a television specialty channel.

"Donovan this is absolutely gorgeous. Your decorator is something else."

"Why thank you, I think I did pretty well too," he said as pulled two fluffy towels from the closet.

"You did it yourself?" Her surprise was clearly evident in her tone.

"From every stone to every fixture," he responded modestly and then paused. "Well me and a friend."

"Oh, Lydia," she said laughing as if she had discovered his secret. "That's great that you still refer to her as your friend. More couples should be friends these days." She was, in no being sarcastic as she spoke almost nonchalantly as she looked around the room.

"No, not Lydia," he said rather dryly and short, as if the door to investigation of that mate was tightly closed. Ivy got the hint and just let it pass. Her new outlook would not allow her to go into dangerous or hurtful territory. That was not to be her concern.

"Well you are truly amazing," she said as she began to disrobe. "I don't know a whole lot of professional football players with the time or the talents to do half the things you do." She was so comfortable with him that she almost forgot that she was undressing in his presence, and he did not remind her.

"Let me turn on the water for you," he said.

"Aren't you getting in?"

"Of course; I can't wait, but I need to make a quick call to my agent. You go ahead and I'll be right in."

"Don't make me wait too long," Ivy said as she unzipped her leather pants. Donovan looked down at her curves, taking special notice of her lace panties. He gently caressed her face and kissed her gently.

"I won't."

Donovan exited the bathroom and went into the bedroom. His cell phone had been on vibrate mode and knew that he had not answered a couple of calls while he and Ivy were out riding. He knew he had to return one of the calls, and that call did not come from his agent. He dialed and the phone was answered on the first ring.

"Hey baby, how are you?" His voice was calm and suave.

"Where are you and when are you coming home?" Lydia said without responding to his question. Her voice was needy and pleading.

"I'm in a meeting with the lawyer. I told you I was going to take care of this thing, didn't I?"

"Yes you did, and I'm trusting that you'll do that because I just can't take this any more and— " She was beginning to go on and on.

"Lydia, I said I would take care of it. Everything's going to be all right. Just let me work things out, please."

"So when do I get to meet this savior of a lawyer?" She willed herself into regained composure.

"Hopefully tonight; I'll see what her schedule is. I've got to go babe; they're waiting for me in the meeting." He hung up the phone without saying goodbye, placed the cell phone back into his pocket, and headed back to Ivy.

He swallowed hard as he viewed her silhouette through the steamy glass. She was more than beautiful and he was surprised at how much he wanted her. There were so many things going on in his mind that he had a difficult time focusing, but he knew what he had to do. He removed his clothes and entered the shower. Ivy started to turn around but with his hands, Donovan instructed her not to. He wanted to see her from behind, just as she was. She tilted her head back and allowed the water to rush through her hair. She soaped herself repeatedly until he finally asked if he could wash her. She agreed, only if he would allow her to return the favor.

The combination of Donovan's large hands and the water pulsating from several directions was enough to send Ivy into orgasmic convulsions several times without penetration. He started at the base of her neck and moved his thumbs up into her hairline. Then he moved to her shoulders and traced the path of the river of shower water as it cascaded its way down the small of her back. He knew the human anatomy very well and commented on the tautness of her muscles, scientifically naming them as he kissed and touched them. He gripped her waist and when he reached around and moved up to her chest, he could feel that her nipples were erect and ready. She pushed her buttocks against his manhood but he did not enter her. He did not have to, for again, the sensuality of the moment sent her into orgasm.

Finally he turned her around and their tongues ravaged each other like hungry animals. Without another word, she picked up the soap and began lathering Donovan's pristine body. It was a work of art itself, and she studied it thoroughly. She started with his back and shoulders, but when she got to his waist, she could not help but reach around and grab his manhood. It was thick and meaty but it was not hard. Slowly she began stroking it with one hand and rubbing his backside with the other. The moment was taking charge of itself and there was no guidance as to what might happen next. Ivy continued this movement and could feel the phallus coming to life in her hand. She was not sure if it was her rhythmic stroking with her left hand or the deep massage of his backside with her right. Whatever it was, they were caught in passionate rhythm that was not going to stop. Then, without really thinking, she stuck two of her fingers deep into his anus. He suddenly became as hard as a rock releasing unexpected sounds of pleasure. Though caught in the moment, Ivy was weirdly startled. The linebacker fell to his knees and Ivy moved right with him. It was almost as if he were assuming a position. She continued her backdoor treatment for a while longer. He seemed to enjoy it greatly. And then he stood up. Ivy faced him, ready to mount him, but with his eyes closed tightly and a grimace of pleasure on his face, he instructed her to turn around and assume a doggy-style position. He entered her from behind. It did not last long, but it was explosive. He lifted and pressed her against the wall as they both panted with relief.

"I think I love you," Ivy whispered without turning her head or opening her eyes.

"I think you love me too," Donovan said quietly with a drifting smile. He held her in place with his massive body and kissed her sweetly on the back of her neck. Finally he took a step away from her and turned her around, and again he kissed her deeply.

"I'm going to get dressed," he said. "I left something for you to change into when you get out. Take your time."

"Okay," Ivy said quietly.

Donovan grabbed a towel and exited the shower. He went into his bedroom with the towel wrapped around his waist and got a box from his closet. Walking quietly back into the bathroom and again admiring Ivy's silhouette through the foggy glass, he placed the box on the counter and walked out. Ivy washed herself again quickly and allowed her mind to race uncontrollably. She thought about the scene that had just taken place and dismissed any strangeness and focused on the passion. Her mind was not allowed to wander and think about what had just happened and why he seemed to enjoy the things he did, and why his erection came to life only when she entered him, and why he closed his eyes when it was time to actually have intercourse, and why he had taken her from behind, and why it only seemed to last a minute. Those were not the questions that should consume her, she thought. She had not felt with anyone the way she felt with Donovan, in a long time and she would not allow cognitive riddles to quell her chance at romance. She reasoned herself into enjoying life for the moment, a character trait that was normally not her style.

When she got out of the shower, Ivy noticed a box from The GAP clothing store on the counter. She smiled at Donovan's thoughtfulness and marveled at his ability to plan ahead, another score in his favor. Around every corner was another indication of how different he was from other men. In the box she found jeans and a sweatshirt, both in correct sizes, but it was what was at the bottom of the box that startled her. In an unmarked envelope she found a check made out to her in the amount of $50,000. She gasped, dropping her towel to the floor, and at that very moment, a fully dressed Donovan appeared in the doorway. It was not that she had not seen that kind of money before, as she had worked on some big money cases and her bonuses had been quite substantial. But she had never been personally approached in such a way with such a figure.

"What is this?" She asked, completely confused.

"It's a retainer, counselor," he responded nonchalantly.

"A retainer for what?"

"A retainer for your services. Ivy I want you to represent me."

She looked at him strangely and honestly wondered what was going on. She was trying not to raise her suspicious and intuitive antennae, but she probably should have had them raised long time ago.

"Donovan I don't quite understand this. You know I work for a firm and yes I do some outside work on a relatively small basis, but with a retainer like this, there is no way that you're interested in small issues. Besides, what do you need me to represent you for? You have a lawyer, don't you?"

"I want you Ivy."

"You want me for what?" The composition of the scene was interesting in and of itself. Ivy stood completely nude and questioning Donovan as if she were deposing a potential witness, and he, standing fully dressed speaking quietly, in a very controlled tone.

"Donovan, I can't take you on as a client without running it through the firm brass. You know that, and I'm sure they would welcome you as a client."

"I don't want the firm; I want you. As a matter of fact, leave the firm, and don't go back. I'll double your salary."

"What?" Ivy was completely taken aback by his suggestion. "This is crazy! What's going on?"

"Will you just think about it later?" There was a dramatic pause. "Please?"

Ivy tried to re-ignite the questioning but Donovan quieted her and would not engage the exchange. He insisted that there was nothing strange going on and pleaded with her to consider his offer. Finally she agreed to think about it and promised that she would get back to him with an answer within the next couple of days. He encouraged her to come down to the kitchen with him and assist in preparing dinner. It was exquisite, as expected and once again, Ivy dismissed the thoughts of what had happened upstairs, and concentrated on the man standing across from her. There would be time to think of all of this later. She continued to convince herself that she was supposed to enjoy the evening.

When they returned to Ivy's town house, they exchanged well wishes and expressions of gratitude, but before he pulled away, Donovan made Ivy promise that she would address his offer within the next 24 hours. As much as she questioned the whole thing in her mind, her heart forced agreement, and with that promise, he was on his way.

Home was his final destination but he would not go there directly. *What man ever really does?* He would stop to pay a visit to an old friend from another life, a secret life. Then he would go home, and deal with the woman he called his wife.

CHAPTER 31

Angela Hebert noticed that her husband did not have much to say on the morning he left for Chicago. She did her best not to take such special notice of his behavior but just could not help herself. Angie had become a near master of discerning his demeanor. As special as he was, he could be counted upon for some categorically predictable male traits to help tell the untold story of his newest motivation. Angie was patient; she would simply wait and see. There was no need to corner him or push him into explanation. She would not make him a suspect just yet. She did not have to because she knew in time; he like any man would try, deliberate and convict himself all on his own. *"Patience is a virtue,"* she told herself. *And then maybe he really was going to assist Crawford at his workshop.* There had not been anything visible that was immediately condemning.

The Minister *was* very supportive to his staff, one of the many reasons they were so supportive of him. When he had the time, which was very rare, he treated many of the support staff like his children, in that he tried to at least, make cameo appearances at their events. If it was important to them, he made sure that they felt that it was important to him. Even Brown could not deny the Minister's support, and he knew that if he were really in a bind, he could call on the Minister for help, and he would be there for him. It was not just because he had what could be considered blackmail information; it was because the Minister had always presented himself in a way that made everyone around him trust, love and respect him.

"Call me the minute you touch down," Angie said as she kissed him in the doorway.

"You know I will, baby," he replied.

There was a brief moment when their eyes met, in a different way, and it was those looks; that glance, of Angie's that the Minister always attempted to avoid. It was the brief moment in time when the desires of the heart were visible through the window of the eyes. Only a select few had the ability to peer inside and understand what they saw. Angie had the key, but unlike any other with the privilege, she sometimes chose not to investigate. There was something, however, about the Minister that made it almost seem like he wanted her to know the truths locked away in his soul, an innocence that was only available for her recognition and touch.

Brown did not come to the door when he drove into the half circle driveway. He simply got out of his old Mercedes sedan and came around and opened the passenger door for the Minister. A wave and a smile is all that Angie got from Brown, but she knew she could get more if she wanted, and he knew to keep his distance form the Minister's wife. There was a clear line that he knew not to cross.

"Bye, sweetheart." The Minister kissed his wife gently on the forehead.

"Bye, Ed. I love you."

"I love you too, babe," he said as he made his way down the stairs.

She watched them drive away, and did her best to clear her mind and create some focus on the many things that needed doing. Whatever her husband was up to was not something that she would deal with right now. It was best to find something better to worry about. She leaned against the doorway for a while before walking back into the house, looking at the flowers in the turn style of the driveway. Instead of seeking some great insight of monumentally metaphoric proportions about the significance of the flowers or their beauty, or the definition of their radiant color, or how they stand gloriously in praise to God, or how they grow and bloom, and then shrivel and die, she tried to think about nothing at all, and she looked beyond the flowers into an empty space that she struggled to create in her mind. She then decided to go in and give her friend Lydia a call.

The Minister struggled to contain his excitement, and Brown tried his best to closely observe the demeanor of his Pastor. He had made it his priority to take the Minister to the airport whenever he was traveling, even if it meant taking off from work or getting out of his warm bed at one or two in the morning. It was almost as if he coveted this position of closeness to the Minister. In Brown's mind, no one was as close as he, and no one would ever be allowed the opportunity, if he had any say in the matter. He had been positioning himself for years to breach the inner circle and become the Minister's number one confidant. He had even tried on occasion to insinuate that he and the Minister were so close that they shared things that Angie did not even know about, but he was put back in his place when the Minister purposely allowed Brown to over hear a conversation between him and Angie in which they discussed some of Brown's undisclosed history. From that point on, Brown never tried to squeeze between the Minister and his wife. He found out the hard way that he had no place being there and that there was a bond between the Minister and his wife that no one could breach. He concentrated on simply getting closer to the Minister and he was successful, in some ways. Beyond that, what Brown failed to realize was that the Minister had no confidants, and that was by his own design.

The Minister made sure that anything that Brown saw was made to look clearly coincidental, and all that he heard was unconfirmed hearsay. He knew that Brown had seen some things that might have been misconstrued or misinterpreted, but he had never allowed Brown to catch him red handed. The Minister handled Brown the way he thought he should be handled, always subliminally directing him with subtle suggestions. He made him talk about things he liked, women, money, power, success, but especially women, and the Minister simply listened and agreed. Before he knew it, Brown would spill his guts about some impropriety he had been involved in, and because the conversation was full of laughter and fun, he did not think about his admissions until the Minister was long gone. That was always the Minister's intention. He knew Brown would bite his tongue in humility and kick himself in frustration later, for having shared self-incriminating information, all the while wondering how and why he had said what he did.

"You have everything you need, Pastor?" Brown said as he weaved through traffic.

"Oh yeah, Henry. I'm fine," he replied as he looked at his itinerary. "You know what, I do need to stop at the bank, though, if we have time."

"Okay, no problem Reverend, I know where an ATM is just a couple of blocks from here."

"No, no, I need to go to my bank so I can go inside. I don't need 'twenties'; I need some real money, 'Doc'," he said with a mischievous grin.

"Okay, not a problem. We should have plenty time." Brown was always on time and he made sure that whenever he picked up the Minister for an airport drop, he left with time to spare in case there was traffic or some other circumstance that might impede swift progress. He also wanted to please the Minister, just like everyone else.

Brown caught the Minister's quick grin and thought that maybe he might be privy to the details of this trip. This stop at the bank en route to the airport was kind of unusual.

"So you're on your way to Chicago, Pastor? I'm sure it's already getting cold there." Brown knew where the Minister was going.

"Yeah, I brought my long johns," the Minister replied with a chuckle. There was a moment of silence as Brown took time to formulate the next question in his ape like head. The Minister knew that Brown simply wanted to be nosy but he never indulged people like that; he forced them to ask what they wanted and then he would decide whether or not he should answer.

"Crawford said he was going to be doing something in Chicago this week, a workshop or something," Brown said, still fishing gingerly for information.

"Yeah, that's why I'm going out there. He asked me to come and speak at one of the sessions. You know I'm always down to help Crawford."

The Minister could see the poorly camouflaged disappointment on Brown's face. He was hoping for something a little more revealing than that. Had he known the truth, he would not have been able to handle it. Brown was not one who could be trusted with information like that and he would never be given the chance. There were several people who believed they were in the inner circle of fellowship with the Minister, but the reality was that he was alone in his sinister quests, and he trusted no one.

"Okay, I remember him mentioning that thing to me. He asked me to come and sing a while back but I guess I forgot about it." In another quest to seem involved and important, Brown lied. In a million years, Crawford would never ask Brown to sing at an event in which he was involved, and Brown knew it; so did the Minister. Brown was one of Crawford's biggest critics and his criticism was fueled solely by jealousy. He could not deal with the fact that Crawford appeared to have a special relationship with the Minister and that they often communicated with simple glances during the service and always seemed to share humorous moments that clearly flew over everyone else's heads.

The problem Crawford had with Brown was his weasel like attitude when it came to confrontation. He would have no beef with Brown if he were ever man enough to share his opinions to his face. Instead he gossiped with the renegade coalition of Pharisees that exist in every church. They are the "holier than thou" group that finds some false strength in their ability to highlight fault in others. Crawford neither gave Brown or the

Pharisees any energy. Instead he ignored them all and treated them as though they did not exist, which irritated Brown even more.

As they continued their drive to the airport, the Minister took control of the conversation and brought Brown to where he wanted him to be, for the moment. The Minister had no problem feeding into Brown's needs; it helped keep him loyal.

"I don't think it's that big a deal, Henry," the Minister said nonchalantly as he looked carelessly out the window, "and I just needed a couple days to myself, if you know what I mean."

"Oh I know what you mean, Pastor. I'm going to get away for a few days myself." Brown could never be outdone, even with the simplest things.

"Oh yeah? I didn't know you ere planning a vacation. I've got to see about that, man. I'm so used to you helping me; I don't know if I can get along without you. You know you're my right hand, 'B'." The Minister was flowing freely with the juice that fueled Brown's ego, making him chuckle securely.

"Oh, I'm not going anytime soon, especially if my Pastor needs me," Brown gratified himself in the minister's comments as he eyed the traffic.

"Well tell me, which lovely lady are you going to be taking on your trip? I see you surveying every Sunday." They both laughed. Here was a subject that the Minister knew Brown would appreciate.

"Well as a matter of fact," Brown said as he scratched his chin, "I did notice a certain football player's wife in the audience for the last couple of weeks. Maybe I need to throw some charm her way."

"Man, you're crazy," the Minister said as he began to laugh uncontrollably. They both knew that Brown was only kidding, as he knowingly had no chance with a woman like Lydia, but the Minister found it interesting that he even went there. That was not usually his style and he definitely found it strange that he would comment on a woman who was obviously a friend of the Minister's wife; definitely dangerous territory. He almost never mentioned any of the Minister's guests, especially those who appeared to be close to Angie. But this was not the time to analyze Brown's thoughts or motives, but to simply manage the conversation and divert attention from questions surrounding Chicago.

"Yeah she is fine isn't she?" the Minister said as his laugh settled. "But I wouldn't touch her with a ten foot pole. I wouldn't want her linebacker husband after me." They both laughed as Brown nodded his head in agreement.

They exited the expressway, preparing to enter the airport, when the Minister's cell phone rang about three minutes too early. It was Alex.

"Hey Reverend, how are you today?" Her voice was purposefully sultry, as always.

"I'm fine; how are you?" the Minister responded rather dryly, glancing at Brown who became conspicuously quiet all of a sudden. This was not a conversation that he needed to over hear, and the Minister knew that Brown's ears had suddenly become inclined to surveillance. His attentiveness was keen when it came to information that was none of his business.

"Where are you Eddie?"

"I'm in the car on my way to the airport." His answer was curt and she immediately ascertained that there must have been someone else in the car.

"What can I do for you?" The Minister was careful not to mention Alex's name.

"Well I want to read you something."

"Okay, go ahead. I'm listening."

Brown could see that there was something going on with the Minister's cell phone conversation and he almost hated the fact that he was pulling up to the terminal. Whatever it was would soon be a secret to him. He, searched for traffic to justify his suddenly slow pace. The Minister waited impatiently for Alex to read whatever she had for him to listen to.

She was a unique person and sometimes her eclectic ways worried him. He knew that she had amazingly deep feelings for him and would probably never purposefully hurt him, but she was still dangerous, and whatever she wanted him to hear was probably dangerous too. But it was better that he just listen and not upset her, and that is exactly what he did.

"Does this sound familiar to you, Eddie?"

Hi there,
Long time, no see… It seems like forever since the last time I saw you. I wish it could be more often, but I guess, the times we have will have to do. I was really looking forward to seeing you this weekend. I went to sleep Friday, Saturday and Sunday nights with the same thought running though my mind, having you inside me. Yes… I've been playing that over and over in my head. Our last engagement was quite memorable and I enjoyed every stroke.

CHAPTER 32

The Minister ran his hand through the top of his head while he listened to Alex without saying a word. Through the corner of his eye, he could see that Brown was engaged in evaluative listening, with his eyes and ears. He looked to the Minister's face for expressions he could not hear. Maybe he could decipher what was being talked about by the changing frowns and wayward glances. Even though the Minister had the face of the best poker player, some people could still cause a rise, and Alex was one of them. They pulled to the curb, finally arriving at the terminal. The Minister quickly exited the car, waiting for Brown to pop the trunk and get his bags. He did not interrupt Alex as she continued to read slowly, deliberately. As much as he did not want to admit it, hearing the words that he inspired caused an element of electricity and excitement to flow through his body.

I must admit that you are an incredible lover. Every time you touch me, I feel a tingle go through me, from the top of my head to the bottom of my feet. Whenever I see you I want to grab and kiss you, and that's what I'm doing mentally right now. I do that all day, everyday. I am constantly kissing you, holding you and making love to you in my mind. You suggested to me the other day that I was in lust with you, not love, but I must say no. I possess more than just an intense and excessive sexual desire for you. I enjoy everything about you. I am fascinated by your way with words, even though sometimes they seem so deep that they appear to be full of crap. At least you take the time to make them sound good. You are so, so good.

"Can you hold a moment, please," the Minister said coldly interrupting the reading.

Alex stopped momentarily. She knew that he was in an uncomfortable position of some sort, but that was how she liked things, just a little off center. The call had caught the Minister off guard but he had learned to expect the unexpected when it came to dealing with Alex.

Brown approached the Minister after he had placed his bags in front of him. His smile was that of laughing hyena. He did all he could not to ask the Minister about his phone call because he could see that there was something deeper than normal being discussed. It was really the lack of discussion that intrigued Brown, as he noticed that the Minister had almost nothing to say; he just listened, and Brown would have given his left arm to hear what his Pastor heard, but that was out of the question.

"Well Pastor, you're all set. I'm sorry to interrupt your call there. It seems like it's something important."

"Oh no, don't worry about it; just some old business I need to take care of," the Minister replied as he reached in his pocket for a few dollars to give Brown. He always offered him some money for chauffeuring him all over town, and Brown always refused the first two attempts and then always accepted on the third. It was a ritual. But this time the Minister seemed a bit distracted and rushed by his call and peeled off two crisp, new one hundred dollar bills from the wad of cash he had picked from the bank and held them out to Brown. Without any semblance of hesitation this time, he took them and put them into his pocket. With his cell phone to his side, the Minister thanked Brown for the lift, picked up his luggage and walked away. Brown watched him closely as he headed inside the terminal.

"Alex?"

"Yes, Eddie. I'm still here. Tell Henry I said hello, and can I finish reading now?" She knew Brown and everyone else in the Minister's tight circle. But no one knew her. At least that was what the Minister thought.

"Alex, what is going on? Is there something wrong? Did I forget something that was supposed to remember? Can you please help me here?"

The Minister was somewhat irritated, mainly because he had been caught off guard by the call and then Alex's sudden desire to reminisce. He wondered if there was some anniversary that he should have remembered. His sorted life was full of forgotten anniversaries but he knew with Alex that really did not matter.

"Nothing is going on, sweetheart. I just miss you. You stood me up, and then when I saw you in the parking lot, you didn't have time for me. Absolutely nothing is going on, so I thought I'd take a trip down memory lane. You know I still have every letter that you ever wrote to me, and copies of every one I ever wrote to you."

"Why?"

"Can I finish reading please?"

"Sure," the Minister replied as he rode the escalator to the gate.

I love your company, even if it's mainly in the bedroom, and I can't say that for too many people. You make me laugh. You make me smile. You make me happy. My life right now is not in the best of shape but whenever I'm with you, I'm in another world. I often ask, "Who are you?" because you seem too good to be true. I just hope that this is the real you and not some superficial person. I would rather find out now before I fall any deeper. I like you more than I planned and I really don't know why I'm allowing you in, especially when I know that this could be detrimental to my well-being. But I guess it's too late; you're already here, so we'll just see what you do with my heart. Love has been rather cruel to me in the past, but nothing ventured, nothing gained.

Well Love, I am looking forward to many secret smiles, secret laughs, walks, talks, gateways to pleasure, and private moments with you. Please don't disappoint me… I know I won't disappoint you…

Love,

Me

"Are you finished now?" the Minister asked, rubbing his weary.

"Now I want to read one you wrote to me," Alex said.

"You don't have one that I wrote to you," he said sighing, as if she were trying his patience.

"I know but I wrote one to myself, and made it from you. I put down the words I knew you would say; just listen." She started reading to his almost immediate interruption.

My Dearest Alex,

How I have always wanted to tell you how much I love you; you mean the world to me and I—

"Alex, I don't have time for this. I'm about to get on a plane."

"Where are you going, Eddie?" She stopped abruptly knowing that it was pointless to continue.

"Do I really need to tell you, Detective?" The sarcasm was clear.

"I guess you really don't," she said, knowing exactly what he meant. She was a cop with a face and badge that gave her an all access pass to information.

"Oh, Eddie, I was hoping that we could get together. I watched you watch me the other day in the parking lot, so I know you want me as bad as I want you."

"Listen, Alex, now is just not a good time for me, but I promise when I get back I'll call you and we can revisit the old stomping grounds, okay."

"Do you promise?"

"Of course I promise. Have I ever let you down before?" He was beginning to work his magic on her, and though deep in his loins he lusted after her and was eager to sexually engage her, right then, he just wanted her off his phone and out of his hair. He had another rendezvous to initiate, and he wanted to stay focused.

"You better not let me down, Eddie. You know you want what I have for you," she said seductively, almost as if she was naked, and knowing her, she probably was.

"Alex, please," the Minister said in a covertly pacifying manner. "You're driving me crazy here in the airport and they're calling my flight. You know I'll call you when I get back. Now, let me go before I come over to your place and miss this flight." He thought that playing into her might cause her to release him, and it did.

"Bye Reverend," she said impassively, and hung up the phone.

The Minister had some common feelings about almost all police officers he had ever met. They all seemed to function with some untreated form of psychosis. His theory was that it was a necessity to be able to stomach the job, and Detective Heart helped to qualify the theory. She was uniquely beautiful, almost to a point of fault, and no one would ever place her in the profession she chose by simply looking at her. At a glance, one probably would have assumed she was a dancer, or model, or music video diva, but never a police detective. But the Minister was one of a select few aware of the undisclosed aggression that resided just below the surface of her character and manifested itself outrageously when it came to both her career choice, and her sexuality.

Alex had a history of tumultuous relationships with both men and women. She often opened the door to passion filled encounters with her looks and then panicked and acted extremely intolerant when her suitors tried to exit the relationship, usually after tiring of her instability. Most she did not care about, but there was something about the Minister that she just could not let go, and the real psychosis in the picture was that he would not let her. It was the insanity that attracted him. She was what he called a "lemon drop," a candy with a sweet outer shell that was wildly sour on the inside. Alex was classic; righteously beautiful on the outside and devilishly chaotic within. He would have her, as she was therapy for his own untreated psychosis.

CHAPTER 33

The Minister carried two pieces of designer carry-on luggage. He always flew first class and other passengers always thought he was a high-powered entertainment business executive, or the like. They were always surprised when he told them he was a preacher, and when they finished engaging him in conversation, they always concluded that he was like no preacher they had ever met. It was then that he sometimes told them that he was a psychologist as well and the response was always the same, *"Oh that's why you talk the way you do."* Many people had problems uniting an expression of faith in a higher power with science or logic, but the Minister had such a way with words that those with whom he spoke could often, clearly digest the correlation. It was this parabolic approach to both ministry and life in general that was a major part of his success. *"Meet people where they are and they will soon go with you to wherever you want them to be,"* was his philosophy, and he had proven the theory again and again.

He settled into his seat and surveyed his surroundings. The plane was relatively empty and he noticed a female flight attendant eyeing him on the sly. He figured it was only a matter of time before she came over and drummed up the venerable, *"Aren't you...?"* conversation. He was used to that. But this thin, white flight attendant, who had hopefully gotten a "multi- procedure discount" on her plethora of cosmetic surgery, simply sauntered over to him and asked if she could get him anything. She seemed however, to ask in such a way that sent him the message that she meant "anything" in a much more literal way than, coffee, tea or milk. The Minister declined the offer but asked her to check with him later. She was more than willing to oblige. He knew what she was up to. She was the same as every Hollywood restaurant waitress who hoped that a big time producer was seated at her table. There was an unwritten rule that was always broken amongst flight attendants who serviced the first class passengers, which instructed them to never inquire about personal issues with passengers because it may appear as an attempt to solicit attention for personal gain. But the rule was never an obstacle to those parties who were professionals at both, in-flight services and "after-flight" company. The young woman servicing the Minister had her eye on the latter. He was not concerned, however; his interests were elsewhere.

As many times as he had been on a plane, the Minister was still fascinated by flight, and for him, the take off and landing were the most exhilarating parts of the trip. He admired the skill and dexterous control that it took to maneuver the massive vehicle on the ground, and then the coordination of forces that it took to get the aircraft into the air. After that, it was boring and monotonous, and that he could not stand. He looked out the window as the plane ascended after takeoff and watched the city minimize before his eyes. He thought about the things that he was leaving behind and tried to minimize them as well.

He tried to clear his mind of the last encounter with Lydia and thought about his last journal entry. Someway he felt purged by his recognition of his transgression but the reality was that he was in no way cleansed of his iniquity. He had preached to various congregations throughout the nation about healing and forgiveness, and though he felt forgiven for what had happened, he was not healed. The scars of his passion and desire for Lydia were undressed wounds, wide open and poised for infection. He thought about calling her from the air-phone but then changed his mind when he could honestly think of no reason to call. He had nothing to say, nothing helpful, and nothing insightful. His mind was beginning to whirl around and he sensed an oncoming headache. He was saved by the interruption of the flight attendant.

"I told you I'd be back to check on you, handsome," the flight attendant said as she steadied herself holding the back of his seat and leaning in a few inches from his face. "Now, what can I get you?" She tried a bit too hard to be seductive and all he could think about was her similarity to India.

He came to himself with a chuckle when he looked at her. She was probably one of those party girls who was nearing the end of her prime and was looking to continually secure her self-esteem by choosing a passenger to hit on. The Minister was the lucky one, this flight. She had chosen wisely but the interest just was not there.

"You know what? I'd just like some coffee, please," the Minister responded smiling.

"Cream?" she asked suggestively.

"Black, all black. Thank you."

The Minister laughed out loud as she walked away. The flight attendant had gotten the message. He laughed even harder when she sent someone else with his coffee and he watched her run the same game on a man seated on the other side of the plane. *"Well at least I was first choice,"* he thought to himself, as he continued to chuckle within.

He asked for coffee because he could never sleep on airplanes. It did not matter how long the flight was; he could never rest comfortably enough to fall asleep, so he always brought his laptop computer onboard with him. He figured, if he was going to be awake that he should do something productive with his time. Usually, he worked on sermon notes or looked over case notes of current patients, but this time he decided to "surf the net" and check his email, and he was pleasantly surprised when he scrolled through them and found the one he was not looking for, from Gemma. He noticed the time it had been sent and found it interesting that she did not wait until morning to send it. She had received his gift and addressed it almost immediately. He liked that. The Minister read the email several times while he contemplated responding. He wanted to make sure that what he said was poignant and direct because she had obviously bitten at the bait of his gesture. He also was not sure if he wanted to tell her that he was coming yet. He knew the power of surprise and advantage of spontaneity.

Gemma,

I'm glad you enjoyed the tulips. I fell in love with tulips the last time I was in London on Oxford Street. There's just something about the beauty of a lavender tulip that I can't get over. Please enjoy.

You told me that I should contact you if was in the Chicago area and you'd reserve a ticket for me. Well I might be in the Chicago area in the very near future and I would like very much to come to the show of one of my most talented members, only if she would allow me to show my gratitude for the ticket by accepting an invitation to dinner after the performance. I'll look forward to hearing from you. Enjoy your day.

EAH

The Minister thought before he activated the send option and decided that he should in some way offer Gemma a hint, alerting her to his impending arrival. Although he did enjoy spontaneity, he preferred a sure thing, and he did not know Gemma's status in Chicago. For all he knew, she might have another man there, which did not bother him. In his mind, he held no rights to any woman, except his own, but he did want her to prepare for his arrival and if that meant telling another man to disappear for a while, that was what needed to happen. He had to be number one for the moment.

The Minister took a sip of his coffee and nodded to the flight attendant whose earlier advances he thwarted. He smiled as she turned her nose up, looking in the opposite direction. As he looked out the window, he was surprised to hear his computer make a sound that informed him that new email had arrived. He sat and grinned at the screen. Gemma Kimbro was online.

> *Pastor Hebert,*
> *It's so good to hear from you, and yes, I loved the flowers. It's funny that you should mention London and Oxford Street. The thoughts bring back many pleasant memories. Thank you for mentally taking me there. I'm glad to hear that you will be in the area and just let me know when you're coming and I'll be glad to reserve some tickets for you. How many do you need and what day will you be coming?*
> *Gemma*

"*This was getting better and better*," the Minister thought to himself. He loved words and he could see that Gemma was interested in engaging him. His morning was suddenly brighter, and the dreaded monotony of the flight was now broken. He called the flight attendant over for a fresh cup of coffee. He purposely called the one who had turned him off, and when she came he commented on how beautiful her smile was, and as she placed the china cup on his tray, how soft and delicate her hands were. And this time when she asked him if he wanted cream in his coffee, he looked at her with the same seductive eyes that she originally laid on him and said, "Plenty." She was his best friend for the rest of the flight. He took a long drag of the fresh cup and then settled in for an engaging email conversation with his "*Chicago Tulip*."

Gemma,
I only need one ticket, for tonight's performance, and you did not address one very important question I asked in my previous email. Will you have dinner with me tonight, after the show?
EAH

There was quite a pause before the response came in, this time. Technology is sometimes slowed by conscience, and Gemma mentally paced before sending the response she knew might be a prelude to peril, but she could not help herself. She was a passion driven being and she knew herself well. She had been in trouble before and would be in trouble again. There had been electricity between them when they spoke briefly backstage in Manhattan, and she wanted to see him as much as he wanted to see her.

I would love to have dinner with my Pastor. Tell me where you are staying and I will have a messenger deliver the ticket.
Gemma

The Minister assumed by the delay that there was some contemplative time taken, and that was good. He did not want his conquest to be unsure about her desires. That would only make things more uncomfortable.

Gemma,
I'm on vacation for a couple of days this week so please, let's drop the "pastor" and just have dinner with a very impressed admirer of your work. I have a suite at the Drake.

The Minister reclined his seat back after activating the send option and this time, did not necessarily expect an immediate response from Gemma. He did not need one. He had all the information he needed, and she had opened the door to him as he hoped she would. Everything was going according to plan and there was no unexpected turbulence. He closed his eyes for the duration of the flight, not to sleep, but to think, plan and fantasize. There was a lot to look forward to in the next few hours, and he was charged about the possibilities. A multitude of unpredictable pleasantries awaited him. That much he knew. He stretched his long legs and smiled as he crossed them. He was satisfied with his focus. He had learned to find contentment there. As he could never completely clear his mind, he now found what he needed to aid in the displacement of unwanted thoughts.

When the aircraft pulled to a stop in the Chicago terminal gate, the Minister stretched and reorganized his belongings. Just before he stood up, the flight attendant came over to his seat and introduced herself. Before he was able to respond, she had already written her phone number on a napkin and placed it in the inside pocket of his suit coat that had been stowed in the courtesy closet. He simply smiled and thanked her. And with a simple nod, he disembarked and threw the number away at the first waste receptacle he saw in the terminal.

The Minister had quite a "to do" list now. This was not the time to think about an over-zealous flight attendant who would probably be shocked to find out he was a minister and not a music producer. He knew that he promised Angie that he would call as soon as he touched down, but he did not want to do that just yet. She was the last person he wanted to speak to when his conscience was filled with deceit. She might say something that would cause cascading guilt to influence his choices, and he needed his free flowing energies to float toward his evening with Gemma. As he walked through the terminal, headed for his ground transportation, he noticed a Michael Jordan memorabilia store, and knew that he should go in and purchase something for his son. He knew that he should not come back empty handed. That policy had been instituted by his children. He purchased a ball and jersey for Junior and then noticed a fine jewelry kiosk across the way. He bought matching platinum pendant cross and necklace sets for Shelby and Angie, and then he called. He was relieved when she did not answer the phone and gladly left a message stating that he had arrived safely and was on the way to his hotel.

When he got there, he checked in and was given the envelope that had been delivered earlier that day. The Minister waited until he was in the security of his suite to open his package. He hoped that there was something extra to read, and he was right. In the envelope he found a single orchestra level ticket and backstage access pass, along with a little note from Gemma.

I can't tell you how glad I am that you're here. I've been looking forward to performing for you again. I hope you enjoy the evening and I look forward to many, many more. I also plan to be very hungry after the show.

G

The Minister smiled and placed the items on the desk, as his phone began to ring. It was Angie.

"Hey honey, I see you made it in safely," she said after his greeting.

"Yeah, you got my message, huh? Everything went well, and I already have something special for Junior and Shelby so tell them not to bug you about it." They both laughed. She too was aware of the edict placed in effect by the children.

"Already? That's not like you. You usually wait until the last minute and buy something in our airport just before you get picked up. What's gotten into you?"

"Well I guess I'm trying to get a little more organized," he said as they both continued to laugh. "And I have something special for my number one girl too."

"Oh honey, you didn't have to get me anything and you know that," she paused "but what is it?"

"Now, it wouldn't be a surprise if I told you, and yes I did have to get you something, and you know that. Tell Shelby she won't have to be jealous. Now, let me get changed so I can catch up with Crawford."

The Minister needed to change all right, but it had nothing to do with a meeting with Crawford.

"Okay dear, you be safe and tell Crawford I said 'hello'," Angie said as her laugh quieted.

"I will, baby. I will. I love you sweetheart," the Minister said.

"I know you do, Ed. I love you too."

CHAPTER 34

The Minister could feel the intuition of his perceptive wife muscling in on his psyche and he needed to move away from that power. He did not want to feel rushed so, although he still had time to spare, he headed for the shower, the place of mind clearing contemplation. He was interrupted when the phone rang again. This time it was the hotel operator informing him that he had a pending fax, and if he liked, she would route it to his suite. He instructed her to do just that, and decided that he would go ahead and shower and then have a look at the fax when he came out. It was probably Crawford sending the information about the workshop and letting him know how to get in touch with him. That could wait.

The Minister looked at himself in the mirror when he got into the bathroom. He noticed that his eyes looked glassy, almost transparent. They were tired because he rarely gave them time to rest. He always made them search and scan for new conquests, and over time, they had grown weary of his directives. If his eyes were the windows to his soul, they were showing a soul clouded and heavy with unattended distress. This was not the time to focus inwardly though, as the evening that he had been waiting for was drawing closer to fruition.

He groomed himself impeccably and put on a perfectly tailored black Armani tuxedo with all the accents. He looked great, and he knew it. Angie had always complimented him on the things his well-toned body did to a suit, and how he made everything he wore look better than it did in the display window. He walked back into the bedroom area and noticed that the fax was waiting on the desk. He was shocked when he picked it up, realizing that it had not come from Crawford at all. The words he read were his own.

I'm taking a big chance by writing this to you, but I am a risk taker and a go-getter, as you might imagine.

Life is funny. At times, it's down right hilarious. I often wondered about the cliché, "absence makes the heart grow fonder," but now my suspicion of its validity is confirmed and I know it's true. I miss you terribly! Hearing your voice, alone does unimaginable things to me, above and below my waist. I know you know what I mean.

I realize that there is much about you that I don't know, but my trust is in the belief that a matchless inner-beauty is in perfect equilibrium with an unerring outer beauty. Dare I say that the look of love is in my eyes when my gaze finds your flawless face. There is a passion in me that transcends reality when you're in the room, and my overwhelming desire is to peel your garments away, slowly, but deliberately, then massage scented oils into your tense muscles with artistic rhythm, and then kiss you passionately, sensuously and deeply.

Please don't be put off or alarmed, for I am in the uttermost control of my emotions and feelings. I am patiently waiting for the time and place that avails us both to lose control, fully and completely. I don't live in a fantasy world, but I pleasure in a visit every now and again. There are many "firsts" that await us. Are you as anxious as I am to experience them one by one?

I have completely cleared my day tomorrow. I realize that you have obligations, but let's try to find some time to spend together. It will be well worth your while.

Ciao Bella

The fax had obviously come from Alex, and when the Minister read it, he was furious. He would have never expected her to send a copy of the first letter he had written her, but she was not the only one who had received letters from the Minister, and she would not be the last. That was his trademark style, and every woman he had ever desired had received a note from him to initiate the passion. He understood, and fed from the romantic nature of women, and he preyed on the most beautiful and the most hungry he could find. Though they had agreed early on to deny him ever penning anything to her, this communiqué was real. With rage in his eyes, he picked up the phone and called Alex's cell phone. She picked up on the first ring.

"Alex, what is your problem? I said I would call you the minute I returned. I am not even going to ask how you found me." His voice was slow and deliberate, showing clearly that he was irate.

"Jesus Eddie; don't be such a sour puss," she whined. "I just wanted to have a little psychotic fun. Is that so wrong? I thought it might turn you on."

"Turn me on? Is that what you're trying to do, Alex. You want to turn me on? You think faxing me a letter that I wrote to you years ago would turn me on. What makes you think I'm in the mood for this crap? What makes you think that's a good method to get me hot? We had agreed to never relive certain aspects of our past!" He was going overboard, but it was the culmination of the various stresses that were falling down on him.

"My God, Eddie, we used to play like this all the time. Don't you remember the games we used to play and the fun we used to have? What's wrong, don't you want to play anymore?" She paused briefly like she had suddenly come upon a new discovery. "Oh I get it, you've got a new playmate. That's it, isn't it, Eddie?"

"No, that's not it, at all," he said trying to down play the comment and cool his angry head. Alex was nuts but she was also a very intelligent and perceptive woman.

"Yes it is!" she yelled.

"No it isn't," he said, rubbing his head. "What if Angie or the kids were here and happened to read that fax. It was just not a very thoughtful thing to do, Alex."

"Angie's not there and neither are the kids," she said distinctly.

"You don't know that."

"Are they there, Ed?"

"No," he said quietly. "Alex, I will call you when I get back. I'm here on church business and I promise I will call you when I get back." The Minister spoke very slowly as if his nerves were being tested.

"Ed, have fun with whoever you're banging in Chicago because you won't be banging me when you get back." And with that, she hung up the phone.

The Minister slammed the phone down on the cradle and headed for the door. He tried to put the encounter with Alex out of his mind, as it was just another reminder of why they could have no real relationship. There was nothing positive in their future and it was becoming more and more dangerous for him to interact with her, but she was like a drug. He could not help himself. By the time he got to the lobby, his mind was already floating back to the days he wrote the letter to Alex. The memory was like an erotic fragrance that tickled his lungs as he inhaled the lustful aroma.

Alex knew exactly what she was doing, and what she was doing was waving raw meat before a hungry dog. There were several truths about the nature of their relationship with which they honestly dealt. As disturbing as it was, they both knew very well that this was just another episode of the volatile interaction on which their affinity had been established, and that what happened today was just another catalyst to the lustful emotions that would bring them together again. They both knew that the friction between them would only increase their desire to be together and cause that encounter to happen sooner than later. It was an enigmatic version of the Chinese yin and yang mystery of balance that seemed to describe the misgivings of the two of them. The problem was that the two were never simultaneously balanced, as the ancient philosophy suggested. With Alex, one day was all "yin" and then three days of "yang" followed. She was intolerable sometimes but as irritating as she was, the Minister was left salivating with anticipation as he grinned with the thought of lust-filled memories and the assurance that the day would come very soon when they would rip through each other like animals. He had almost lost track of his anticipatory thoughts of Gemma when he was startled back into the present by the opening of the elevator doors.

CHAPTER 35

The Minister was surprised when he entered the hotel lobby and asked the concierge to hail a cab for him and was told that a private car and driver had been reserved for him. It was Gemma. He was beginning to like her style even more. It was not unusual for people to do impressive things for him, but her gesture was an unexpected surprise, and he could not wait to thank her in person, in his own special way. His interest was being acknowledged and reciprocated, and the evening that he imagined was developing quite nicely in her mind as well.

The car moved swiftly toward the theater and the Minister took time to concentrate on the difficult task of clearing his mind. As he watched the Chicago skyline race by, he considered the innumerable assumptions about what actually went on behind the varied structural facades. Some looked stoic and majestic with their Neolithic design, polished stones and gaunt doorway figurines, while others were modern, with stealthy reflective windows. They were all powerful portraits of character, yet they were empty and lifeless. From the distance, the skyline appeared to be a meticulously painted picture, and the Minister knew quite a bit about pictures.

He knew that pictures were revealing yet they did not always reveal the true depth of the story. They did not always express the true heart of the painter or photographer. Behind the walls of each building was the uncensored story of individual humanity, all with equal parts of glory and shame. The buildings were nothing more than mortar, steel and glass; pieces of a picturesque skyline, meaningless. They were the external shields to a human pulse that used them daily for cover and protection.

Lights dimly flickered as sleeping machines waited for their masters drive them to failure. But what he thought about most was the fact that there were millions of stories hidden behind those fragile walls that looked so strong; stories that were representative of every aspect of emotional humanity, simply because real people were behind those walls.

It was a dead and meaningless skyline without the people who brought those buildings to life and established their purpose. He thought about the walls that surrounded his own psyche and how so many assumed the best about him, but behind his facade was a pulse that defined him in a very different way; in a way that he would express later that evening. He was both painter and picture, and he had been creating and erasing the masterpiece of his life for many years now.

The Minister had fallen into a contemplative trance when his ringing cell phone startled him back into consciousness. He had already decided that it was Alex, and he was prepared to go ballistic when he answered. Enough was enough, and she would reap his verbal wrath for interrupting his moment, especially after he had worked so hard to escort her out of his thoughts. After his less than friendly greeting, he was surprised to hear the frail, soft voice of Lydia Davis.

"Lydia, how are you?" He was sincere, but showed clearly that he did not expect or desire her call.

"I'm sorry to bother you, but where have you been? I've called your office and couldn't find you and I really needed to speak to you." She spoke so quietly that he could barely hear her.

"Lydia? I can hardly hear you," he said, leaning forward and pushing the phone closer to his ear.

"I hadn't heard from you and I really needed to speak to you. Things are getting worse at home. Where are you? Can I come by your office?"

"Well Lydia, I'm sorry but I'm unavailable due some pressing church business." He was trying to keep his answers short to discourage further questions from her.

"Oh, I didn't realize you were away," she said.

"Well I was actually preparing to leave town the night you came by my office and as a matter of fact, I'm in Chicago right now." He could sense that there was something wrong even though she gave no details.

"Oh, I see," she said quietly, almost as if in a drug-induced lethargy.

"Lydia, are you all right? Where's Donovan?"

"No, I'm not. I need to speak with you. I need to see you, now. Things are not all right and I don't know where Donovan is, but I know

I need to see you." The desperation in her tone was intensifying, but the Minister tried not going to emotionally budge.

"Well, as I said I'm in Chicago right now but I'll be back in a few days. Maybe we could get together then. Would that be okay?"

The Minister did not inquire further about Donovan. He really did not want her to know where he was and why he was without his wife. The call was becoming more stressful than it was worth, and he was not going to allow it to go any further. This was not her time; it was Gemma's and he wanted to devote all of his energies toward the object of his attraction. But Lydia was not going to let that happen, at least, not easily. He did then what he knew might be a mistake, but his desire to focus on his own lust outweighed his caution.

"Why don't you call Angie?" His tone was almost careless. "I know you guys have been getting pretty close, these days." There was a five second pause that seemed like five minutes.

"Do you really want me to call Angie, Ed? Is that what you want? I'm reaching out to you! She doesn't have what I need. I need you, right now." Her volume was increasing.

"Okay Lydia, I'm sorry. I'll be back in a few days and I promise you we can get together and talk. I'm sure everything will be fine." He tried to withdraw his thoughtless suggestion and console her at the same time. He feared that she might see beyond his facade and notice his purposeful distance. That was the last thing that she needed to feel at this time in her life, but he had already moved away from her.

"Where are you staying?" she asked quietly.

"What?"

"Where are you staying?" She repeated, this time louder.

"I'm at the Drake, why?" He had slipped.

"I'll be there tomorrow."

"No! Lydia, don't do that! We can talk when I get back. Lydia? Lydia!"

The Minister yelled into a line that had gone dead. She hung up after acquiring the information she sought and now masterfully complicated things. He could tell that she had either been drinking heavily or had taken some type of depressant, probably Valium or Xanax. It was evident in her quiet tone and slowed responses. *"What was going on with her?"* he thought to himself. And more importantly, *"What had he gotten himself into?"* He was not sure if she would really come. He knew that she had the resources and she obviously had the kind of adjustable schedule that would allow her the time. *But what about Donovan?* He wondered if her spur of the moment decision to leave town would raise a question in her husband's mind. Maybe she was as devious as he and could quickly concoct a reason to be in Chicago. *What kind of game were they playing? What kind of relationship did they really have?*

There was obviously a myriad of emotionally overwhelming issues between them but after his last encounter with Lydia, the Minister decided it best to withdraw from whatever form of intimacy had seemingly developed. He could feel a monstrous explosion coming on and he did not want to be anywhere near the epicenter of that catastrophe. His abrupt decision to, physically separate himself from Lydia had been foolishly fueled by nothing more than his overwhelming desire to romance and seduce Gemma, and he was making the same mistakes made by all practitioners of deceit. He played with a universal element over which he had no control, time.

Fate, destiny and time have partnered since the infancy of the universe, and since Adam's first bite of the forbidden fruit, man has tempted and gambled with all three. The Minister was operating like most men who live within the thoughtless belief that time is on their side, but what he did not realize was that time had run out, and was now working against him. Soon he would be required to answer the calls of fate and destiny with undeniable honesty.

The stress was building but the Minister was a professional when it came to stress management. He would enjoy this evening and put tomorrow out of his mind. He thought about the essence of a biblical scripture that instructed people to be concerned about today, as tomorrow is not promised. Once again, he fooled himself into believing he had time and that the floating elements that plagued him were under his command. Just as he squeezed his eyes shut and turned off his cell phone in another attempt to quiet the adversaries of his psyche, the limo pulled up to the theater's side entrance.

"Excuse me Sir, Ms. Kimbro left instructions for me to escort you to the side entrance so you wouldn't have to deal with the crowds at the front," the driver said as spoke into his rear view mirror without turning around.

"Oh. Okay, thank you very much," the Minister responded, looking through the tinted windows as the guests watched the car roll by.

They probably thought that he was some special celebrity who was using the back entrance to avoid being mobbed by the crowd that might recognize him. He sat back and enjoyed the attention, watching the heads turn as the car moved slowly. *If they knew the reality of his purpose, would they still be intrigued by his presence?* The Minister fought to quiet his thoughts and engage the moment. It was time to re-address his appetite and with a mental lick of his lips, he gathered himself as he prepared to have his dessert before his dinner.

Inside, he expected that Gemma would find a way to greet him at the door, take him by the hand and guide him through the maze of backstage corridors. It would be there that the game of their seductive romance would begin. But it did not work that way at all.

Gemma was busily engaged in last minute preparations for the evening's performance and a major part of that was a moment to quietly focus on efforts toward remembrance. As seasoned as she was, she was just like any other stage performer, and human being for that matter, who still had to place maximum effort in keeping lines and steps in the forefront of her mind. She usually found that solace while her makeup was being applied. As she closed her eyes while the makeup artist worked, she made sure that there were no unnecessary interruptions and unauthorized noises. She was deep within that moment when the wiry little production coordinator barged in with a clipboard and headset and informed her that the Minister had arrived. The makeup artist shot him a look that scolded him for the interruption but Gemma informed her that he was following instructions.

He went back and met the Minister where he had left him, just inside the theater's rear entrance and then led him to his seat.

"Okay, sir, I did inform Ms. Kimbro that you were here, so just have a seat here, relax and enjoy the show," he said as he looked the Minister up and down.

The Production Coordinator was conceitedly gay and wanted to make sure that it was well recognized. His over emphasis of the instructions and stereotypical vocal inflections helped to define his pompous character. It was also obvious that he was much less important that he believed. The Minister chuckled as he switched away, constantly speaking in the microphone of his headset and checking off items on his clipboard. He gathered that the task just completed had just been checked off when the young man turned around and headed back toward him.

"Excuse me sir, I almost forgot. Is there anything I can get for you? The general public has not yet been allowed in so would you like something to snack on while you're waiting?" Although he was sincere, he also shot the Minister one of those "read between the lines" looks that expressed his availability for more than just fetching coffee and doughnuts.

"No thank you. I'm fine," he responded with a smile.

"Well I can see that, but do you want something to eat?"

"Oh no, no, no. But thanks again." They both laughed as he walked away.

The Minister thought about Angie and how she always used to kid with him, saying that he was a gay man's dream, with his tight buns and huge member. He was in no way homophobic so it was easy to laugh off the young man's pass. As long as he was respected as a heterosexual, he was able to respect others who chose alternative lifestyles. He may not have agreed with them, but he certainly did respect them.

As he waited for the show to begin, he noticed that there were other special guests entering from the theater's rear entrance and being seated by the same man with the clipboard and headset. Every time he seated someone, he checked something off on his clipboard, said something in his headset, and found a way to catch the Minister's eye mouthing, "Do you need anything?" The Minister's response was always the same, "No thanks" with a sincere smile.

The general public was finally being allowed in and in no time, the theater was full. As he looked around, the Minister thought great thoughts about Gemma and was completely impressed at the response of so many people coming to the performance. It could only do wonders for her career, he thought, and he found her powerful draw absolutely fascinating.

The Minister sat quietly and patiently as those seated near him wondered who he was. *Was he a critic, a journalist, another actor, or producer?* He could imagine the questions in their minds and he enjoyed the fact that he did not have to formulate and deliver a response. But soon they would not question or even be interested in him, and that was part of the beauty of his presence. He was able to hide behind the fact that the spotlight shined elsewhere, unlike his days at home and at church, and on the road evangelizing when all eyes were on his every move, and waiting congregations hung on his every word. He needed to answer to no one, except himself. The lights were dimmed, and before the curtain could rise, the applause had already begun.

The bulk of the cast was now on stage doing the opening number, but the star had not yet appeared. The anticipation of seeing and hearing her had the hairs on the back of his neck standing on end, and he was not alone.

When she appeared, another ovation rose from the crowded theater. The Minister clasped his hands in front of him and allowed his smile to develop without restraint. She was stunning. Her costume called for her beautiful jet-black hair to be pulled back into a very neat bun, and of course, the Minister loved it. He was a sucker for a girl with her hair pulled back, and some, like India, tried to force their way into his attraction. But Gemma represented a unique innocence and naivety because her beauty was an unintentional by-product of her character. As she sang and danced, the Minister could only imagine that the angels were seated around a transcendental screen watching one of their own perform on the other side of the heavens.

He watched every move she made. It was almost as if the rest of the show operated in haze or fog, or not at all. He only saw Gemma, and was completely enthralled. The show moved forward to Gemma's solo number and dance. This must have been what she referred to in her email. As soon as she started, he remembered her saying that she had a special dance that she was sure that he would enjoy. This was it. All night, she had been the ultimate professional, looking over the crowd and softening them like clay in her hands, and this number was no less captivating, except that this time she seemed to somehow find the Minister's eyes, in the dim lighting over the audience, and it was as if she sang and danced to him, exclusively. It was not seductive or necessarily suggestive, but it was communicative. It clearly and simply stated, "*I know you're here and I'm glad you came, and I'll do my best to make your visit worthwhile,*" and that was enough for the Minister. He was not looking for her to throw herself at him, or come out of character just to please him. Those things would have turned him off. He was engaged by her natural beauty, her commitment to her craft, and her willingness to share her gift with him on a very personal level.

The show went forward and the Minister went with it, more specifically, he went with Gemma. At the intermission, most people seated in the general public seating made their way to the lobby for light snacks to be. The Minister looked around for the man with the clipboard because he really could use some coffee now, and if he was willing to get it, he would allow him. It was not long before he appeared quickly pushing a dessert cart with several decanters of coffee and a variety of pastries. It was his job to serve the special guests, and he made his way directly toward the Minister, passing other guests, to serve him first.

"How 'bout a little coffee and Danish while you wait for the show?" he said looking into the Minister's face with a smirk.

"Don't mind if I do, my friend."

"How do you take your coffee? I bet you like it black," he said as he poured.

"No, I like a little cream and sugar in mine," the Minister responded. The man could not see that the Minister was toying with him, and that was fine because there was no need to be insulting.

"Are you enjoying the show?"

"It is absolutely unbelievable. There just aren't words." The Minister stood shaking his head after taking a swig of the coffee.

"So did you come by yourself? I don't really see a lot of people coming in solo."

"Well, I was in town on other business and was a special guest of Ms. Kimbro's, but I guess you knew that because I was on your list there. Right?"

"Oh yeah, you were on my list, all right," he said looking at the Minister's broad shoulders. "How do you know Ms. Kimbro? Are you a personal friend of hers?"

The Minister had been looking forward during the brief conversation but the man's intrusive interrogation caused him to look him directly in the eye.

"Isn't the intermission only about fifteen minutes?" The Minister responded. The man nodded. "Well there are a few other folks who might like some coffee and pastries before the lights go down and the curtain goes up. 'Don'tcha' think?"

The man turned around and saw that there were a few people looking his way and probably wondering why that cart had not been rolled their way. He also got the message that the Minister was not interested and was not answering any more questions.

"Oh, I'm sorry, sir. Enjoy the rest of the show. I'll come back and get you after the final curtain and take you back to meet Ms. Kimbro," he said in a very professional voice. With that, he pushed his cart toward he other guests and did not look back.

The Minister was in a position of readiness when the curtain rose again, signaling the beginning of the second half of the show. In many cases, the best is saved for last, and the Minister was in agreement with those around him who had high expectations for the completion of the performance. No one was disappointed. Gemma continued her stellar display of talent and won the crowd easily. She was absolutely amazing, and it was impressive to listen to her voice, as it only seemed to get stronger as the show progressed. When the curtains closed after the final number, the Minister joined the crowd that jumped immediately to its feet and offered an adoring ovation.

Gemma was simply magnificent, and the applause continued until she returned to the stage to take another bow and receive several bouquets handed to her by the stage manager. The Minister focused on her smile. It was one of complete satisfaction and endless energy. To him, she looked like she was ready to do it all over again, and she probably was. This was what she lived for. This was the fluid that her heart pumped through her veins, and she could not wait for more. She fed on what the crowd gave her, and they fed on what she had given them. It was a perfectly balanced and complimentary exchange.

When the lights rose and the crowd began to disburse, the Minister waited for the wiry little man with the clipboard and the headset to re-appear, and it was not long before he did. But this time he did not walk right over to the Minister; he greeted several of the other special guests first, and invited them backstage to meet the cast and congratulate the star. The Minister found it strange, but then figured that he was probably just sore because he had quelled his advances. To some degree he was right; the man had no reason to flirt with a man who was not interested, but he had also been instructed by Gemma to make sure that the Minister was her last visitor.

"I'll be right with you," he mouthed to the Minister as he directed a small group of people to follow the corridor ahead to the backstage area.

The Minister waved his hand and nodded as if to say, "*No problem,*" and then sat down in his seat. As he waited, he reflected on the performance. He had heard about Gemma and how talented she was, and even seen her in Manhattan at the show that Miss Hattie Lee had sent him and Angie to, but there was something special about tonight. There was a new light that seemed to shine through the darkness of his desires generated by the multifarious lumens of her talent. Maybe it was the intimate setting of the small theater, or the royal and unexpected treatment that he had received from the limo ride to the backdoor entrance of the theater. He was not sure but he knew that something was different.

CHAPTER 36

Gemma was an African violet that bloomed every time she was in the presence of the sun, and the sun for her was any place she was allowed to shine. She was radiant, and the Minister was now even more captivated by her beauty and talent. His usually cluttered mind seemed clear as he was focused totally on Gemma. It was strange considering the catastrophic possibilities that surrounded his trip. He probably should have been worried because there were upcoming curves on the roller coaster ride of his life that he could have never anticipated. The man with the clipboard interrupted his thoughts.

"Okay sir, I'm sorry to keep you waiting. Would you like to come back now and meet the cast of our show? Ms. Kimbro says she's ready for you."

The Minister snapped out of his introspective dream and returned to himself. "I'm ready," he said as he stood and grabbed his overcoat. Before making his way to Gemma's dressing room, he was introduced to several of the cast members as they also greeted guests who had been specially invited. He congratulated them on an excellent performance and spewed forth a multitude of sincere compliments. He could see by the myriad of people backstage that more than just the cast members should have been congratulated. There were so many people that had so much to do with the success of the production that it was mind-boggling. Gemma was the hub of a well-oiled machine that operated in intricate syncopation, and though she was clearly the most important part and hub of the turning wheel, she graciously shared her accolades with those around her, as she should have. The Minister thought to himself that everyone should have the opportunity to go behind the scenes of a major production to better appreciate all that went into the final presentation. It was an educationally gratifying experience. They finally made their way to her door after a few more handshakes and brief conversations.

"Excuse me Ms. Kimbro, it's Jason. I have Mr. Hebert here for you," the man with the clipboard said after rapping gingerly on the door. He had no idea who the Minister was, or that he was even a man of the cloth, for that matter. He knew him only by the last name on his clipboard, which he clung to like a bible.

Gemma was the star of the show and she greeted guests in her dressing room, unlike the other cast members who circulated the hallways and gathered in small rooms that had been setup with small assortments of hors d'oeuvres. Her dressing room, on the other hand, was usually filled with flowers, champagne and several large trays of exotic fruits and specialty hors d'oeuvres, as she would soon be flooded with guests of the producers and director of the play. They loved showing off their prize performer in style, and she loved being surrounded by fans and admirers. It was just another well-deserved fringe benefit of Gemma's years of hard work that sometimes went inadequately recognized and under-appreciated. She also understood that what happened after the show was almost as much of a production as the onstage performance, and this was the time that the show's director, writer and producers shared the spotlight and were complimented on the star's presentation of their work.

When the door was opened she appeared from behind a quick-change barrier that was made of hand painted silk panels, decorated with Chinese characters. Her smile was enchanting and he melted, as she stood wrapped in her kimono with her hair resting on her shoulders, freed from the confinement of the bun, bouncing thankfully for its emancipation. He stared at her for a while before he spoke, as if his thirst was being quenched by her beauty.

"You were absolutely brilliant, tonight," he said as he looked directly in her eyes.

"Why, thank you Reverend. I was more than shocked that you came, but for some reason, I kind of expected you." Her smile was still beaming and it was clear that she was as enthralled with him as he with her.

"Reverend?" A voice interrupted their gaze. Jason, the man with the biblical clipboard and headset who seemed to be more of a growth than an attachment, was still in the room. They both turned around and looked at him simultaneously, as they had been so caught up in staring at each other that they had forgotten that he was even there.

"Thank you, Jason. Would you give me about ten minutes before you let the world in, and close the door on your way out?" Gemma was not stern, but specifically direct. She knew Jason's type very well. There was one in every production company.

"Sure," he said as he grinned. "Hmm, a minister, huh? That would be new," he mumbled to himself as he closed the door.

"Thank you, sweetheart," Gemma sang as he left. She laughed to herself as her eyes found their way back to the Minister. "He's nosy as heck but he's harmless."

"Yeah, I think I found that out earlier tonight," he said, continuing to ingest her with his eyes.

"I can't tell you how happy I am that you came, Reverend," she said again, clasping her hands in front of her.

"Now what did I tell you about that "Reverend" stuff? Can I just be 'Ed' this weekend, or better yet, you can use my middle name if you like, and I'll be someone whom only you will know personally. How 'bout that?"

"That would be fine, Alan."

The Minister was surprised that she readily knew his middle name and that the instruction had not initialized a whole new conversation. There were no questions asked, just speedy acceptance of his request. She was pleasing him more and more, and she did not even know it, which made it even better. In a very smooth move, almost choreographed or staged, he cupped one of the blossoms of the myriad of rose bouquets, leaned over to sniff it and told her that he would not have missed her performance for the world. His gesture was effective as she watched him closely and seemed to hang on his every word. Gemma was intelligent and sophisticated but she had a track record that exposed her as a sucker for cliché romance, and though he was sincere, his movements could have been scripted by Spielberg. They were just that perfect.

The moment was still somewhat awkward despite the magnitude of their mutual attraction. Neither made much of a physical move toward the other. This was one of the most talented members of the Minister's church and she came from a family that had been historically associated with his for decades. He knew Gemma relatively well and though they rarely saw each other growing up, as he was a few years older than she, they could still be considered long time acquaintances. This was territory that was not only uncharted, it was taboo, and the problem was that they had both mentally pursued each other, at some time or another, and now they were overwhelmed by their mutual infatuation.

The Minister was hesitant because his intuition told him that the attraction was not just cerebral or physical but that a heart might become involved, his heart, and that could be dangerously destructive. After a moment of silence but very communicative smiles, Gemma moved first, which was well within her character. She took both of his large, soft hands in hers and pulled him close.

"My dressing room is going to be swamped in a minute and I don't want to be rude so I really want to again say, thank you so much for coming, Alan. You have no idea what it means to me to know you were out there watching."

She reached up and kissed him gently, but deliberately. She was soft, warm and inviting, and the Minister responded as expected. He could hear the throng of people marching their way to Gemma's dressing room, a place that had now become significant on the list of "firsts." As they released their embrace she reminded him that she still wanted the dinner he had promised after the show if he was not too tired. She had no idea what her lips had done to him, nor the passionate details of the evening he had planned.

"Tired? Are you kidding? Right now, I'd take you out for a cheese burger on the moon, if that's what you wanted and where you wanted to go," he said with seductive innocence, as if his heart was being stolen. "Take your time and greet your guests, and when you're done, I'll be right here waiting for you. You deserve every compliment they give so don't rush them; let them fawn all over you. Besides, I love watching you smile."

She smiled as her hands slid out of his and she rhythmically turned around just in time to greet those whom Jason introduced. The Minister positioned himself in a nondescript area of the room and watched her work. She was as captivating backstage as she was on stage, graciously thanking everyone individually and honored every autograph request with a sense of style and grace that he had seen only from one other woman in his life. Occasionally, Gemma would glance over at him and smile, giggling probably, because there were some who questioned her about the handsome gentleman who quietly stood in the corner watching her like one admiring a work of art. But for the most part, no one really acknowledged the Minister's presence, which was fine as far as the he was concerned. It was Gemma's night and Gemma's crowd, and he was simply enjoying what he saw.

When the fanfare settled, she introduced the Minister to the director and producers of the show. After light conversation, the team was quite impressed that her pastor would travel such distance to see the show but were even further impressed by his knowledge of the arts and theater, particularly. He explained to them that his appreciation bred a need for education and that he took several theater courses in college. They left, thanked him for coming and invited him back. He had made an unforgettable impression, as he always did.

"I'll just be a second changing," she said as she went behind the dressing panels.

"Shall I grab a cab while you do that?" the Minister asked. He really did not want to leave her presence.

"Not necessary. The limo is ours for the evening if we still want it."

"Really?"

"Yeah, the company rents it out for me, not so much out of the generosity of their hearts, but mainly, to make sure that I show up at whatever the 'after show' event is, and then after I make an appearance, it's mine for the rest of the night. I know you mentioned dinner, and I can't wait because I'm starved, but do you mind stopping by the director's party for just a moment, on the way?" She was still talking from behind the divider.

"I don't mind at all. As a matter of fact, I'm looking forward to it," he replied as he glanced at her silhouette, enjoying what he saw. Finally, she emerged.

"I'm ready," she announced with a beaming smile.

"So am I," he said, and then repeated his words with a tonal decrescendo as she walked past him and out the door. "What about your flowers?" He halted her before she completely exited.

"Don't worry about them. Jason will take care of them and have them sent to my hotel. Knowing '*Mr. Efficiency*', he'll probably have them in my suite and perfectly arranged before we get there."

The Minister mentally acknowledged the fact that she used the words *hotel, suite* and *we* in the same sentence, and he liked that. He knew that it did not mean that she had intended sexual overtones in her statement, but he simply took it as her feeling some amount of comfort and anticipation about his presence. The last comment before they left was his observation about the Chinese characters on the panels of her dressing room. In large print were the symbols for *Prosperity* and *Passion* and Gemma found it most interesting that he even knew what they meant. She was becoming more and more fascinated with him and discovering her desire to know him more intimately. What she did not know was that he only knew the meaning of those characters because his wife brought him a pair of hand made cufflinks she had picked up during a business trip to Hong Kong years ago.

229

As they drove to the director's party, the Minister could not tell Gemma enough times how great her performance was, and he was truly sincere. He was good at manipulating verbiage to achieve his goals but that was not the case with Gemma's talent. Something inside her pulled at the most honest portions of his heart. She continued to thank him for coming and showing an interest in her work. She knew that he was extremely busy and how little time he had with such a popular and growing ministry. But there was something that told her, the last time she was at church, that she would see him again soon, something beyond his words. At the time, she was frightened by the prospect, but her fear was soon overwhelmed by desire, and it was that volatile mix of feelings and the desire that she could see in him, that stirred inside her yet still somewhat cautioned her. Now she was tossing herself back into her natural character and living by the advice that she so often gave, moving swiftly toward throwing caution to the wind. She was not like her friend Ivy who reasoned herself into action and counseled herself into movement. Gemma normally went with the flow of the river's current and in the case of the man with whom she sat trading compliments and suggestive conversation, the current was moving swiftly toward dangerous rapids.

When they pulled up to the after-party, Gemma leaned over and said, "We only have to stay for a second." She could see that the Minister looked around and hesitated when the limo stopped. It was important to her that he felt comfortable and there was something in his eyes that prompted her statement. He had come to see her, and although he was a cordial gentleman who could fit comfortably in any situation, this was not necessarily the place for him. Though his vice had brought him to Chicago in pursuit of satisfying his lust, he had a higher calling to which he knew he must answer, and so his preference was to keep himself clear from at least, public engagement in sinful activity. His private sins were a different matter.

"Well, if it's just going to be a second, why don't I just wait for you here in the limo?" He looked at her with eyes that made her only want to spend less time inside and more time with him. His look was magnetic.

"I'll be right back," Gemma said as she exited.

Every first date has a moment of awkward silence, and the Minister was glad that he would experience that time alone. He could be silent in the quiet car while she was away, and she could find intimate silence while caught up in the noise inside, he thought. He was on the prowl, the hunter methodically stalking its prey, but even within that vein, there was still the brutal honesty of being human, and that is what usually caused the moments of awkward silence; humans just being human.

The Minister clasped his hands before him but, as much as it should have been, it was not time to pray. *What would he pray for, success of his mission?* Truly, it was not the man upstairs who was guiding and anointing his cravings. He had given in to the quests of his loins many times over. It had become rather routine, which only energized his pursuit for more satisfying conquests.

Tonight he quietly thought of conscience and consequence, which was something that he often tried not to do. It was too early for that; too early for repentance. He strategically planned, which was something he always did, especially in times of sinful deed. He developed the picture he desired, and imagined the radiant beauty he had witnessed on stage as the star of his personal show. He looked forward to every piece of the passionate puzzle: her overwhelming pleasure in seeing him, her unending gratitude, and the special treatment that she had extended to him, his own uncontrollable proclivity, and the fact that there was not another man seated in the "special guest" section of the theater who was there at her invitation. She only wanted him, or at least, made him feel that way.

That was something else that made him different. He never minded if his conquests had other men; he actually encouraged it, as long as he was made to feel that only he existed when he was in the women's presence. Gemma had clearly done that, but in her case, there really was no other man in the picture, and though it was not a problem now, it would be soon.

He closed his eyes and slowly began to relive her performance, but in his mind, he silenced her, simply desiring to watch her move without the pollution of scripted words. He watched her mouth silently form words and focused on her lips that glistened under the stage lights. He watched her neck as she belted out ballads without the grotesque protrusion of her veins, unlike those who often tore up church solos and in some way felt that it necessary to contort and twist their faces into ugliness in order to squeeze out notes. She was smooth and sultry, sensual. He watched her slim upper torso rhythmically gyrate to the calculating beat of the music while her legs danced with elegant precision and grace. He could watch her legs all night. They were legs that did not deny heritage, especially seen when his eyes moved from bottom to top. As he mentally traveled to the place where they joined and began to move her from the stage to other places in his mind, the door opened and she was back inside.

"That wasn't long at all. Are you sure you fulfilled your obligation to the fans?" The Minister honestly had no idea how long she had been gone. He had been so comfortably entranced in his thoughts that he had not noticed the time.

"I did everything I needed to do: smiles and princess waves for the masses," she said with a chuckle. "But now I'm ready to eat."

"Well I'm ready to feed you," he said crossing his legs. "What's your pleasure? Your wish is my command."

"Oh, you're trying to spoil me."

"Of course I am. What more does a star deserve?" He was a master at his craft.

"Well, let me think about it while we swing by my hotel so I can change. Do you mind?"

She wanted him to see her in something else, and that just charged the Minister even more. If he had not been special, the current outfit would have sufficed, but her peaking interest was the catalyst to new and improved costuming. He loved a woman who made presentation a priority, especially when he was the lone audience member and object of affection.

"That would be fine. It's up to you. I know you're hungry and I want to make sure you get fed tonight, in a very satisfying fashion. But my time is your time, so whatever you want to do is fine with me."

Silence crept into the backseat of the limo and sat between them like a third passenger, but it was, in no way, awkward. It was electric. It was contemplative and devising. There was a fire burning within the two of them and they both knew that a combined inferno was imminent. Gemma had made the first physical move back in her dressing room and the ball was now in the Minister's court. Without repositioning himself to face her directly, he seductively turned his head toward her and looked into her eyes.

"Celebrity agrees with you, Ms. Kimbro," he said looking her up and down.

"And flattery will get you everywhere, Reverend." Her quick wit and fast response turned him on even more. He smiled as their eyes locked momentarily and then he looked away, continuing his gaze out the window.

CHAPTER 37

Strolling through the hotel lobby, the Minister watched Gemma bubble over with elation generated by the events of the evening. He watched and learned. Seeing her in action was an education that he welcomed, and he would use that knowledge to his advantage in the very near future.

"Oh, I see that Jason has made his floral delivery," the Minister said as they walked into her suite noticing the vast botanical display.

"I told you he'd take care of it," she said smiling as she headed for the powder room.

"Yes, I see. The star is well taken care of, as she should be."

The Minister took a visual survey of his surroundings, as he always did in unfamiliar territory. It was not that he was afraid but more an issue of distrust, knowing that he was in a situation in which he could only depend on himself if things went sour. He also used her absence to learn more about her. He wanted to see if clues of her character and her desire might have been left lying around the suite, but then he remembered that maid service usually kept things sanitized and generic. But he did notice her desk, where her laptop computer was open, and the numerous scented candles that were near it. He was stimulated by the thought of her sitting there in the wee hours of the morning sending him emails that accepted his advances and acknowledged her own interest. *What was she wearing when she gave in to her wishes? Had she bathed and sat with only her open robe exposing her naked beauty as she contemplated her words? Which of the candles burned and lit the way to her romance as her manicured nails clicked lightly on the keys, or were they all on fire?*

She interrupted his thoughtful whirlwind speaking loudly from her walk in closet.

"Can you just give me a couple of minutes? I want to take a quick shower and put on something a little more comfortable. Make yourself at home and I'll be right out." She peaked out from behind the wall. "Help your self to something to drink. There's plenty in the little fridge there."

"Take your time; I'm fine. Call me if you need me to wash your back, or any other parts you can't reach."

"I'll keep that in mind," she said as they both chuckled and she disappeared.

The Minister had no intention of going into the shower with her, at least not yet. That would spoil his anticipation. He was looking forward to peeling her slowly, and every aspect of their evening was another layer to be removed. He thought of the unfolding events like the numerous leaves of an artichoke, and it was still too early, even for him, to take a bite of the heart. He rested his muscular frame on the sofa and laid his overcoat beside him. The fragrant aroma of the flowers around him was overwhelming, almost nauseating, but the circulating air helped calm his stomach. It was probably good that he had not eaten yet because his dinner might have been in the toilet. He closed his eyes and turned his thinking off to allow room for the picture of loveliness he would soon behold. And then she appeared like a flower in full bloom, and it seemed that every rose on the room turned her way and wilted a little, out of respect of her beauty.

"I'm ready," she said coyly, causing his head to turn her way.

"Good God from Zion!" he said. "'Ready' is not the term that does you justice. You are absolutely stunning, Gemma."

"Why thank you," she paused, "Alan."

"Good, good. That's what I wanted to hear. Let's check the 'reverend stuff' at the door. Tonight Gemma and Alan are having dinner, and hopefully, dessert a little later."

Gemma was dressed in a tastefully seductive, lavender chiffon two piece set that beautifully accentuated her figure. The skirt was cut high, but not too high to leave nothing to the anticipatory imagination, and was made of a sheer material that allowed the eyes to peer through to an effervescent inner lining that covered her fully. She wore no stockings and her amply oiled legs looked like trophies balanced on heels that were display platforms. The Minister had a hard time taking his eyes off of her, like most men, but unlike others who often looked away after stealing a glance, he kept his eyes glued to her every move.

"Now I know your closet is full of choices, so I just have to ask what made you choose that particular ensemble. You don't know what it's doing to me." He shook his head, holding his chin with his right hand while his left arm was across his chest. Gemma moved very close to him and looked up into his eyes.

"Well, I was surprised by a basket full of lavender tulips from a very welcomed, but unexpected admirer on opening night, and something just told me that I should be in that color tonight."

"I like your style Ms. Kimbro. I like your style."

"And I'm liking yours more and more." She paused for a moment and then moved from the subject rather abruptly. "So are you going to feed me, Alan, or are we going to stand here and get full from compliments and 'goo-goo' eyes all night?"

"So what is your pleasure m'lady?" he asked, bowing slightly.

"Well, it's so late and we have no reservations anywhere so it's probably impossible to get to any of the top restaurants."

"I didn't ask you to analyze and evaluate the impossibilities of our situation, gorgeous. I said, 'what is your pleasure?'" He smiled and bowed again. "You have reservations at all the top restaurants in the city."

"You're kidding, right?" she said as she smiled and shook her head in disbelief.

Charlie Trotter's, Everest, Tru, Season's, 302 West, MK, Carlos', and the Ritz-Carlton Dining Room, all stand ready and waiting for you to honor them with your choice and presence."

The Minister had made late evening reservations at each restaurant before leaving his hotel. That was his style, especially when weaving a secure web of passionate entrapment.

Gemma was flabbergasted and shocked at his uncanny ability to plan. He was not like other men, even Alfonse who fed on her love for romance and flattered her often. His differences and superiority in comparison to other men was becoming more and more evident. Again her mind drifted momentarily away from her physical hunger and found its way to another part of her psyche that sought satisfaction as she looked into his eyes.

"You're not like other men, are you," she said with a starry look in her eyes.

"Never have been, and hopefully will never be," he responded. "So what," he said slowly, "is my lady's pleasure?"

"I think the Ritz-Carlton would be perfect," she said.

"I couldn't agree more."

As they walked out, the Minister could not take his eyes off of the rear portions of Gemma's body, and she knew it. It was perfect. She was perfect. It was very rare that he found a woman who's looked pleased him completely. Some had bodies made by Venus or Aphrodite, and faces made by Dalmatian, while others had faces conceived by the great Michelangelo but bodies that were either made by Peterbilt Trucks or looked as if they had been hit by one. Gemma's package was complete. She was physically beautiful, and he was even beginning to enjoy her mind as well, which was dangerous for him because that was what was always most captivating and personally destructive.

She was intelligent and her wit targeted the part of him that searched for that spark in every one with whom he dealt. Some who lacked that aspect of their character were tolerated, while those who did were embraced. However, he could not help to think of how easily she had played into his hand. In his opinion she appeared smart enough to know better, so *in his hand* must have been where she wanted to be. She would find out later that he had done more than make dinner reservations at the Ritz. He had made dessert reservations as well, and if all went as planned, he would soon have her *a la mode*, with nuts, whipped cream and a cherry on top.

The limo ride to the restaurant, made him mentally salivate, as he looked at her slightly parted legs. They glistened as the city lights bounced off of them creating brief periods of hypnotic illumination. It was sensual. Silent smiles were shared, as this probably should have been the time for questions to be asked by both parties. This was, in essence, a first date, but they knew all they needed to know about each other, for the time being. She wanted him and he wanted her, and that was clear in the camouflaged language of their bodies.

"You have beautiful hands, Gemma" the Minister said as he glanced his way up her thigh and decided it would be more polite to comment on her hands than her thighs.

"Thank you. So do you."

Gemma took his large hand in hers and examined it. She was not just being rhetorical with her comment. The Minister really did have unique hands. They were memorable and she went back in her mind when she had first touched them and could not believe how soft they were. Even then there was something inside her that longed to feel them in other places on her body, but she hid herself from those feelings, knowing that they were dangerous. She continued to hold his hand and rub it gently, and he did not pull away. He was enjoying her subtle touch as she rested his hand on her lap. By this time, they were screaming to one another with silent looks of suggestive passion. Had the limo not pulled up to the destination within the next few seconds, a kiss would have been the next.

The restaurant was relatively empty, as even the late diners had already gone home. Just a few couples in distant and secluded areas of the dining room remained. This was better than the Minister thought it would be; he would have her all to himself and she could comfortably focus all her attention on him. There would be no distractions.

The décor in the restaurant was traditionally fabulous. Tables were covered with white tablecloths and presented with fine china and a fresh bouquet of flowers was the centerpiece. Colorful tapestries and other fine paintings brought the walls to life and warranted second looks, but not tonight. The Minister sat across from the only work of art he was interested in viewing and she appeared to feel the same way. The waiter stood patiently at their side waiting for them to make a wine selection.

"Alan, are you a wine drinker?" she asked with a look on her face that conveyed to him her desire not to offend his calling, but also a nonchalant dismissal of his possible knowledge regarding the matter of choice. "We don't have to have wine if you don't want; it's okay." She sounded almost sorrowful, but really gave no room for a positive response.

"Well normally I don't. But tonight is a special occasion so I think it would be appropriate."

The Minister did periodically have a glass of wine but he made it a policy to never drink in public, and especially not to indulge with any of his church members. But tonight he had already told Gemma to check the "reverend stuff" at the door and that he would simply be *Alan*, and whatever went with that private character was allowed and accepted.

"Well, let's see," she said as she eyed the extensive wine list. She never passed it over to him assuming that because he was not a drinker, he was not a connoisseur. She made her first mistake but he would not hold that against her.

"What do you like, beautiful?" He inquired.

"Well, I like Pinot Noir's and sometimes Merlot's," she said without looking up.

"May I make a suggestion?" The Minister spoke quietly. "Try the *Estancia Meritage* by Ken Shyner. It's a perfectly blended mix of pinot noir, merlot, and chardonnay. I'm sure it's on the list and if it's the 1998 vintage, it should be delicious. That was a very good year for California wines."

Gemma's eye's crept slowly over the menu and went straight to his. "I'll have that," she said dryly to the waiter without taking her eyes off the Minister.

"Make that two. Better yet, we'll have a bottle," he instructed.

"Very good, sir, excellent choice," the waiter said and then hustled away.

"I'm sorry," Gemma interjected. "How did you—"

"You didn't ask. You just assumed, but its okay. I won't hold it against you. Let's just enjoy our evening."

She continued to look at him trying to figure things out that she did not understand. He was an amazing man and she was falling deeper and deeper into his hands.

"Who are you?" she said shaking her head.

"Tonight I'm *Alan*, and *Alan* just happens to know a little bit about wine," he said laughing at her visible mixture of embarrassment and astonishment.

They slowly enjoyed every course of their meal, and as the wine took hold of them, their conversation became more suggestive and revealing, especially Gemma's. She told him that she had felt something electric when he hugged her backstage in Manhattan and how she became frightful of her feelings when she saw him at the church. She spoke of how she had no intention of dealing with him on that level and that she was surprising herself even at that very moment because she did not expect him to be who or where he was.

The Minister had gone far beyond her expectations and he liked that. It was all part of his plan. He listened patiently and was pleased with everything he heard yet he was very careful about the comments that he made. He simply continued to flatter her with compliments on her talent and beauty. That seemed to be enough to keep her from asking him to be specific about his feelings for her. He was still very protective, as far as that was concerned, as he always wanted the upper hand when it came to matters of the heart. It was not that he did not have feelings for her, or that he had not felt the electricity between them at that backstage meeting in Manhattan, it was just a matter of simple self-protection, preservation and control. The wine helped keep undesired questions at bay.

The Minister studied her, as they ate. He watched her laugh and smile. He watched her pick up her fork and gracefully toy with her food. He looked at how she sat with perfect dancer's posture. He was a perfectionist and he looked for signs of physical imperfection that might turn him off. There were none. Her earlobes were not too fat. Her top lip did not sit out too far and was not larger than her bottom lip. Her nostrils did not flare out wildly. Her eyes were not too close together, possibly indicating a primate in her family tree, nor were they too far apart, indicating failed attempts at cosmetic surgery. She was perfect. She had dimples when she smiled that could melt a block of ice and her eyes sparkled with laughter and energy even as the clock approached midnight. Her teeth had been made for a winning smile and her lips were painted tapestries that longed to be kissed and sucked on. Her nose was proportionately perfect for her face, with a straight ridge that could have only been genetically engineered.

Gemma knew that he was examining her, but she did not mind. She had nothing to hide. That was the kind of person she was. Even if there was something that other women would have hidden, she would not. She was an open book and that was her style, and she had been blessed with a face and body that made it easy for her to operate that way. But she was looking at him as well. She evaluated his complex eyes, knowing that there were deep secrets behind them. She liked what she knew about him but she could tell that there was so much more she did not. This was the time she was supposed to question herself, or even more importantly, question him. This was the time that she was supposed to evaluate the big picture and run like the wind.

She remembered sitting in a small restaurant in London, across the table from Alfonse and being captivated by his flattery and not asking questions that probably would have saved her several months of heartache and pain, but she said nothing. She remembered the conversation she had with her friend, Ivy, after it was all over when she asked, *"When did you know that you were in trouble?"* *"I knew I was in trouble the first time we had dinner at Dino's,"* she responded and vowed to never fall into that situation again. But here she was again. He was quite different from Alfonse though, and every other man she had been with, for that matter, but she still knew she was in the danger zone.

The Minister interrupted her thoughts, as he saw that her plate was nearing completion and she had taken, what appeared to be, her final taste of the wine.

"How was everything?" he asked.

"Simply scrumptious; I enjoyed every bit of everything."

"So are we ready?"

"For?"

"Dessert," he said seductively.

"I'm really full but I guess it won't hurt to take a look at the dessert carriage."

"Well, I kind of had something else in mind. You appear to be a woman who likes surprises. Why don't you come with me?"

Gemma's heart began to race with anticipation. She did like surprises, especially from a man who was already amazing. She could only imagine what he had planned.

"What about the check?" She inquired as he came over to help her from her seat.

"Don't worry about it; it's all been taken care of."

They walked out of the restaurant, through the hotel lobby and to the elevator. The Minister took a key from his pocket and inserted into a special slot for guests who had suites on the executive floors, and depressed the button for the 35th floor. While the elevator rose, he placed both his hands on Gemma's shoulders and massaged them gently. Standing behind her, he was unable to see her face but he would have been pleased to know that she smiled and closed her eyes as his hands worked rhythmically and magically. He caressed her in a way that made her feel comfortable and secure which was something that she felt was rather surprising. She was preparing to enter a hotel suite with the married pastor of her church. All kinds of lights, sirens and warning bells should have been sounding but they were not. A seductive silence overpowered them.

When they entered the suite, Gemma was amazed at what she saw. There were more that fifty bouquets of lavender tulips all over the room. She was speechless. The Minister smiled and then kissed her lightly on the cheek as he walked passed her, striking a match to light a few of the scented candles.

"Now, it's my turn to shower. I'll be right out," he said, leaving her standing in the middle of the room with her mouth still hanging wide opened.

Gemma could not believe what she was seeing. She was amazed that he would go to such trouble to please her, especially at a time like this. She had had several men come into her life and spoil her with material things in hopes that she would give in to them, and there were a few who were successful, but this man was approaching her from an unfamiliar avenue. What was happening was definitely a first, and her stomach knotted a bit, as she was unsure of her feelings. She had always been one to go with the flow of the river, and most times she brought her own paddle and pushed even faster than the current, but in this instance, she felt like the paddle, and all other controls, had been removed from her hands and she was being subliminally guided by some other force.

Confusion was now being fostered by the multitude of feelings that were simultaneously befalling her. There was an element of fear but it was dispelled by the fact that she knew him. She had no reason to feel threatened or that he would hurt her in any way but she was sure about the presence of that emotion. She felt unbalanced, but not in a way that left her insecure. It was really more pleasurable in some way, as she was filled with nervous excitement about what he would do next. She also could not deny her overwhelming anticipation as she waited to see him come out of the shower.

The Minister had worked his plan magnificently. His goal was that she would be completely satisfied and relatively content in the suite, and she was. All prior events that night had played roles toward a perfect culmination. She had had a victorious evening on stage, followed by a wonderful dinner and conversation with a familiar attraction with whom she shared reciprocal desire and now she wanted for nothing, so she simply moved to the sofa, sat down and waited.

Gemma considered calling Ivy, and she probably should have, but immediately dismissed the thought, as she had so many times before. She was a big girl and she could handle this on her own. Besides, she was not interested in being talked out of her passion by the mind and comments of reason that she knew Ivy would give. Her logical friend would sound the alarms, ring the bells and blow the whistle, for sure.

When the Minister came out, Gemma could not help but release the smile she held within. He was gorgeous, and the white hospitality robe with the Ritz-Carlton logo on it complimented the rich brown color of his skin. He assumed quite a bit, walking out half naked before a woman he barely knew, but he knew her well enough to know that she wanted to be right where she was, and that she was not leaving. Gemma's initial inclination was to stand and go to him, press into his embrace and kiss him passionately, but she knew that that was not how he wanted her. She could tell that he was a man who liked to watch and evaluate, critique and review, so she decided to do things his way. She decided to stay exactly where she was and look him over since he had no shame in allowing her to do just that.

"Have you enjoyed your evening, or should I say morning, so far?" he asked looking at the wall clock and plucking a grape from a bunch that was a part of an assortment of fruit that had been delivered earlier.

"How could I not? You've wined me and dined me, and now it looks like you're ready for dessert."

She did her best to control her emotions and her hormones; both were going wild. She slowly and deliberately began to take visual inventory of what she saw and could not find anything that turned her off. With his hair still somewhat wet, she watched a bead of water trace its way down the side of his face and recognized the power in his jaw-line, as well as the absence of razor bumps and stubble. His face was soft and his eyes were unassuming. From the dimple in his chin, she traveled along his neck and down the opened portion of the robe that exposed the curly hair on his chest. It was not so much that he looked like something fit for a National Geographic exposé on the missing link; it was just enough to run her hands through and not get stuck in her teeth when she attacked his nipples. She continued down past the knot of his sash, she stopped momentarily at his mid-section and then his crotch. She could not help it; it was what women did, but the robe flowed too loosely there to get an indication of what rested beneath. Sooner or later it would be revealed though. She could feel it. His thighs were covered but as her eyes moved to the floor she noticed his feet. They should have been twisted with corns and bunions seeing that she vaguely remembered that he played sports as a teen, but they were smooth and well manicured. Everything about him was unusual, but pleasing in every way.

For all intents and purposes, he was perfect, but like every man who appeared that way, his appearance of perfection was his most conspicuous imperfection. The night had Gemma in its grasp and the Minister had her caught willingly in his web. He moved toward her and kneeled on one knee directly in front of her, tenderly forcing her to slightly part her legs to make room for him. His movements were smooth and stolid.

"You seem like you want to say something," he said as he chewed another grape just a few inches from her face.

"I don't think its words you want at a time like this," she responded, looking him dead in the mouth.

"What do you want, Gemma?"

"If you have to ask, maybe I should go downstairs and try to catch the limo."

He took another grape from his pocket, placed it between his teeth, and pressed his lips onto hers, keeping his hands on either side of her to balance himself. As sexual as he was, there was still something very chivalrous and gentlemanly about him. He had gone through hoops to put this evening together and he obviously had a goal in mind, yet he was noticeably respectful with his hands.

Gemma took it all in and tried to evaluate the sinful pleasure she was enjoying. That was not her style; regrets were for some other occasion. Not only was he a gambler willing to take high risks for high payoffs, he was a winner, she thought, and his efforts were coming to fruition. She caressed the back of his head and neck, opening her mouth and allowing her tongue to dance with his, after devouring the grape he had in his mouth.

He moved slowly, as they kissed bringing his hands to her outer thighs, making his delicately sensitive touch his examining eyes. He massaged her, rhythmically moving down the sides of her legs to her feet, and removed her shoes, taking each of her feet into his hands and rubbing hem from heel to toe. She could not help but shiver with anticipation. As a dancer, her feet were sensitive and after a performance, the pleasure of a foot massage was probably the most relaxing and erotic movement anyone could do. He moved as if he knew that, and his consideration stirred her deeply.

She did not want to move from the sofa, and he was not going to make her. He brought his hands all the way up the sides of her body and found her face with his soft palms. Momentarily pulling away from their kiss, he smiled at her again as he ingested the beauty of her countenance, allowing her to hear his silent compliment. And as if an alarm clock had signaled him into action, he scooped her into his arms and carried her into the bedroom. Placing her on the king-sized bed, he peeled her clothing away like petals of a rose, first exposing her excited bosom that made its wishes clearly known through her decorative lace bra. He released her taut breasts from the confines of the bra but he was not yet ready to satisfy their craving for his tongue. Slowly he removed her lavender chiffon skirt to view his fetish, the most complimentary piece of lingerie known to man, the lace thong panty. He pulled back for a moment to again ingest her absolutely magnificent body. She was a masterpiece and he could not take his eyes off of her as her hips gyrated slightly in anticipation of coming gratification.

Gemma could hear the increased pace of his breathing, but she was so engrossed in the sensuality of his touch that she kept her eyes closed, bordering on a very welcomed orgasm. With skill and precision, he lowered himself again to one knee and grabbed hold to the top of her panties with his teeth, removing them without hitch or incident. Then he gently parted and lifted her legs, with his hands behind her knee joints and vigorously indulged in the sweetest of desserts. After twice bringing her to an orgasmic frenzy, he pulled her to a seated position at the edge of the bed. The look on her face showed that, for all intents and purposes, she was spent, but anticipation for more overwhelmed her and she found new energy when he stood before her and placed her hand on the sash of the robe and nodded the instruction to pull.

The Minister was all she expected and more. Lust replaced passion as she filled her mouth with his manhood and eagerly indulged on her dessert. He stroked his large hands through her flowing hair as he allowed her to feed on him for a while and then removed himself with a smile. She had seen that smile just a few moments ago and knew that it meant that it was time for a change. With that, he moved onto the bed with her and turned her over on her stomach, kissing her back, shoulders and neck. He pulled a condom from the pocket of his robe, readied himself, and then entered her from behind with a genteel power she had never felt before. Within moments she was on her hands and knees, howling like a coyote in the light of a full moon. He was magnificently majestic and they made love wildly, all night long. She was amazed at his stamina as they tried every position imaginable and invented a few new ones. By the time they entered the third round, all inhibitions were cast away and the screams of pleasure echoed down the hallway. He took advantage of her flexibility and willingness to be twisted into erotic knots around his efforts, and they both knew that a primal craving had awakened in them and that satisfaction was lustfully reciprocal. They fell asleep joined in an ungodly knot, wrapped in sweat-drenched sheets, both of them dreaming of far away places.

CHAPTER 38

The bright light of the sun could not wake Gemma until well past one o'clock in the afternoon. She rolled over and thought that she was reading the clock incorrectly. She had not awakened this late in years but she also had not experienced a night like the one that had just taken place, in her life. She eased out of bed and made her way to the bathroom. As she stood there completely nude, she thought about the events of the previous evening and then splashed handfuls of water on her face. Looking back into the bedroom area she noticed that something, or better yet someone, was missing. The Minister was nowhere to be found. She ran back into the bedroom only to find a folded note on the side of the bed.

Dearest you,

My night was spectacular. I watched you in the moonlight and then watched the sun bring light to your face, and in both instances, you were more than beautiful. Your talent is without compare and your company is matchless. I could not bear to wake my sleeping beauty, but I'm sure you understand the necessity of my departure. I cannot wait to see you again, mi Bella.

Alan

She expected to simply wake up in his arms; at least that was what she wanted. She looked around the room and wanted to question herself about what she had done, as there was some calling toward maturity that told her to address her somewhat troubled conscience. But self-analysis was interrupted by the alerting sound of her cell phone.

"Where are you?" the panicked voice said on the other end.

"Huh? What? Who is this?"

"It's Jason, Ms. Kimbro. We have *Press* today at one o'clock. Did you forget?"

The man with the clipboard was on his job, keeping things organized for a press photo and interview session, but he was missing one thing, the star of the show.

"They're all gathering here and looking for you. I thought you'd be here by now. Where are you? I can send a car right over!" His voice was getting higher and higher as he spoke quickly. Gemma could hear the voices in the background.

Calm down, Jason. It was a really long night," she said as she rubbed her head. "Yeah, send a car over to the Ritz-Carlton and I'll be downstairs and ready, okay?"

"Oh, the Ritz. Is that where the sermon was last night?" He said sarcastically.

"Jason!"

"Okay, okay; the car will be right there. I'll stall things a little. Go get pretty and we'll see you in a few."

"Thank you," she said with a sigh. She could hear him chuckling as she hung up the phone. His chuckle exposed his nosiness and his assuming notions. Jason was like that and Gemma had a God granted ability to read people. His chuckle also expressed a hint of his jealousy, and his desire to have been an observant fly on the wall, if not a participant in the night's escapades.

Gemma hustled into the shower. She could not believe that she had forgotten about the press conference. This was the big break that she had been waiting for and as she quickly washed, she kicked herself mentally for not being more conscientious. She had gotten caught up in a moment of passion that infringed on her career, and that was not supposed to be allowed. That at least, had been her decision since her fiasco with Alfonse. But in her heart she knew that her behavior represented a part of herself that she could not deny. She loved to love, and enjoyed every part of the romance that went with it.

She dressed and grabbed an apple out of the fruit arrangement as she ran out the door vowing that she would not let a moment like this happen again. As she rode in the limo, she tried to concentrate on her preconceived responses to the press questions and her loosely concocted explanation for being tardy, but thoughts of the Minister infiltrated her mind, disallowing concentration on any other subject. He had been successful in his quest and deep in her heart she knew that if she continued on this path, things would get a lot worse before they got better. He had made a powerful and lasting impression that had launched deep into her vulnerability, attaching an unbreakable nexus of desire. She wondered how she could ever turn back, even if she wanted to.

While Gemma smiled before flashing camera's and inquisitive reporters looking as if she had just come from a full glamour makeover, the Minister sauntered into the Drake hotel in a daze. He was just plain tired. Having been wake for nearly thirty-six hours, he did not even notice the very significant people he passed in the lobby, nor did they notice him, but it would not be long before coincidence and circumstance would fall right into his unsuspecting lap.

He went to the elevator and almost fell asleep standing against the wall. Making his way down a hallway that seemed almost unending, he finally arrived at his suite. He had never felt more welcomed by the sight of a bed, and without removing his clothes, he fell into the softness of the down comforter and pillows that covered it. He was usually one who meticulously undressed and hung his clothes neatly in the closet before bedding, but today his body was spent. There was no energy for neatness. He had amazed his lover with his stamina but his efforts had taken an amazing toll on a body that was not as young and strong as it used to be. It was at times like this that he discovered the fact that he could not deny the natural progression of time.

Rolling over just before closing his eyes, he noticed that the message indicator light on the hotel phone was illuminated but he did not bother to check it. Not now. He might say something that he should not or maybe forget what the caller was saying. He decided that even though there were calls that he should probably return, calls with catastrophic possibilities from Alex or Lydia, he was in no shape to address them now. His door was locked and his room was nice and warm, and whatever was happening or going to happen outside the walls of purchased solitude would have to wait.

While the Minister slumbered, the factors of coincidence moved closer to positions of chaos and calamity. He slept hard and did not dream, at least not to his knowledge. There were no spiritual convictions or revelations that would lead to repentance when his eyes opened. He was past that, still in a zone of fantasy where everything was working as he planned. As far as he was concerned, he would wake up to a world that would invite him with lustful arms without question or consequence, a world that would appreciate his passion and long for his presence, a world that he had faithlessly created but loyally continued to piece together. The guarantees were all there, every unpredictable piece: Angie, Gemma, Alex, Lydia, Donovan and a host of collateral entities all poised for closure. His task was simple; he needed only to wake up.

The blinking light on the phone that indicated waiting messages, silently exercised patience as he slept, signaling the Minister that it would hold all it knew until he addressed it, and would tell no other soul. It would serve as the sentinel of circumstance, rhythmically alerting, *there is something I must tell you.*

CHAPTER 39

Lydia and Donovan checked into the Drake Hotel almost unnoticed. It was not long however, before the woman at the front desk recognized the football star and his wife. Trying to remain professional and not create a scene, she continued the check-in process, attempting to hold a nervous smile that she could not contain. There were plenty of celebrities that stayed there and some of them created scenes and hysteria of their own volition but there was something uniquely impressive about Donovan, especially when it came to women. The young lady behind the counter was no different. She did her best to keep her eyes from screaming and melting as she watched him sign the registration card and flash his diamond smile. Lydia was familiar with his effect on women and was in no way threatened by their reactions, as her beauty often quelled any inappropriate moves in her presence.

Fate, and a very controlled episode of synchronized coincidence, had brought them to Chicago. The one who really controlled the chessboard of the Minister's life, Angie, had pretty much sent them there. Lydia had done exactly what the Minister had hoped she would not; call his wife, and Angie had done exactly what Lydia did not expect, told her exactly where the Minister was.

When Donovan had come home after making the offer to Ivy, he got in touch with Lydia at the spa and informed her that he was going to get away for a few days to play in a golf tournament in Chicago with some of his celebrity friends, and without another word she said that she was going with him. The timing could not have been more perfect, and though Donovan had no idea why she was so responsive, especially after her visible mood swings in previous conversations, he gave in to her company. He had done what he needed to do with Ivy and the ball was in her court. It was his turn to escape for a while and force her to think. A golf tournament was just what he needed while he waited on the response he was so sure he would get. Like the Minister had done with Gemma, Donovan had laid considerable ground work with Ivy, and in his mind, there was no way she could turn him down. So he waited patiently and confidently. His over-confidence was another similar character flaw that he shared with the Minister.

In her numerous discussions with Angie over brunches and spa treatments, and the like, Lydia discovered that the Minister shared the same affliction for golf that her husband did and she eagerly shared that information with him. She told him that she knew they wanted to get together and that Angie told her that he would be in Chicago at the same time as their visit, so she encouraged Donovan to invite him to play in the tournament. It would be good for them, she impressed upon him, and it would give her just cause to be close to him. She needed to be with him, so she thought.

So while the Minister had been spreading tulip petals and giving wine advice and howling into the night, making love to his passionate conquest, a private jet had raced to Chicago carrying two people whose presence would turn his trip inside out. He had actually passed them in the lobby as he walked by nearly comatose, his mind focused on sleep, and though they knew he was staying there in the hotel, with their backs turned they had missed the "romantic zombie." That was one of the secrets the blinking message light had guarded for him.

Donovan had actually called and left the Minister a message from the airplane, informing him that he would be in town shortly and extending an invitation to play a private tournament with him and a few other celebrity golfers. He said nothing about Lydia's presence and she had not made a call of her own. She reserved herself as a surprise.

By late afternoon, just when the Minister was changing gears and falling into an even deeper sleep, the phone startled him into consciousness. His first inclination was not to answer, but he thought that it might be Angie so he rolled over and answered in a voice that still slept. He was pleasantly surprised to hear Gemma on the other end.

"Well good afternoon sleeping handsome," she said in a voice that made him know she was smiling and showing her unforgettable dimples. "I'm so sorry to wake you. I just wanted to check on you, and thank you again for last night."

"Oh no; it's okay. I probably needed to be awake anyway. Thank you." He struggled to regain his vocal composure but never opened his eyes. The sleep still had him. "How are you today? And as far as last night goes, the pleasure was all mine."

"I'm absolutely fabulous. What are you doing tonight?"

"Well, what should I be doing?"

"You should be coming back to see me," she said coyly. He could see her girlish smile as his closed eyes beheld in beautiful pictures of her.

"Well if that's what I should be doing; that's what I'm doing," he responded with a quiet laugh. "And I can't think of anything that I'd rather do more."

"Okay, great! Showtime's nine o'clock and I'll send the car for you." She sounded like a happy kid who had just been promised ice cream, and the Minister loved the sound of that youthful energy even though it seemed that his escaped him.

"I'll be ready and waiting." There was a brief pause.

"And can we go straight to dessert right after the show?" The little girl had gone away and the grown up woman had taken over.

"I can't wait," he said seductively in a quiet voice that conveyed passion, knowing exactly what she meant.

He could feel his organ stiffening as he thought about her and saw memorable images of her body in his mind. There was so much that he tried to hold on to; her smell, her taste, her touch, her manicured hands, the way her hair bounced as he pounded her from behind, the sparkle of her smile as she rode him with her eyes closed, appearing to savor every powerful stroke of his manhood. He would remember and try never to forget.

The Minister hung up the phone, never opening his eyes. He knew that he had messages but he was still in the grasp of faded strength, so he obliged his body's call, and this time he would dream. Gemma's call injected his sleep with conceptual visions that would fondle his dreams and energize his instinct.

The Minister had not forgotten about his commitment to Crawford which was why he was supposed to be there in the first place. He had been faxed all the necessary information. He figured, although one of the messages that the blinking light held was probably from Crawford, he would most definitely understand that the Minister was very busy and that his call might not be returned as promptly as expected. But it was not Crawford's message that needed utmost concern. It was the missing message that was most important. Angie had not called; at least she had not called his room at the Drake.

At about seven-thirty in the evening, fate and coincidence knocked on the door of the Minister's world. He had finally dragged himself from bed, showered, groomed himself impeccably and headed downstairs for a quick meal. Tonight he felt that he and Gemma would go straight to dessert so it might be a good idea to eat real food before leaving. As he sat solo at his table in the hotel restaurant, he looked out into the lobby area, near the gift shop and saw Lydia. His mouth dropped. He had displaced the expectation of her presence and was not pleased to see that she had tracked him down. He had been through something similar with Alex, but with Lydia, the dynamic was very different. Donovan was not far behind but the Minister did not see him. The Minister dropped his fork, wiped his mouth and then rushed out to confront her.

"Lydia," he said startling her with his serious voice, "what are you doing here? I thought I told you not to come." The look on his face was not the most welcoming and she recognized that immediately. She was an intuitive woman and could feel that there was more behind his demeanor than just his surprise at her presence. All women seem to know when a man's behavior is suspect and has meaning beyond what is immediately visible. Lydia was also aware of her own irresistibility when she was in his presence and her thought was that his feelings would change once he saw her. She was quite unprepared for his contrary behavior.

"First of all, please let go of my arm," she said as he looked down almost surprised that he was holding onto her. "I told you I was coming, didn't I?" She pulled away and looked directly in his eyes with a look that was longing and somewhat unstable. It softened him somewhat, and he was surprised, himself, to see that he had her by the arm. That was not his style.

"I'm sorry, Lydia. I didn't mean to grab you like that. I, I was just really shocked that you came and I did not expect you." He put both of his hands on her shoulders as he spoke to her.

"Well, I probably wasn't coming, but then some things changed and you know how I told you I needed you, so here I am."

Her eyes began to well with tears and her light complexion made the reddening of her nose very apparent. Again, the fragility of her psyche was clearly visible and the Minister could only think of the contradiction of her person. She was so beautiful on the outside, confident, sure and secure, but obviously something had worn her insides away and it was that portion of her crumbling soul that reached out to him in a considerably inappropriate way. He searched himself for a balm of healing compassion.

"Lydia, it's okay," the Minister said as he took her into his arms. "Whatever is going on can be worked out, but I just think it's best if we handle it at home, don't you? Do you really think it was a good idea to follow me here?" He spoke softly and pushed her back gently to look directly into her eyes as he spoke. The trained psychologist was coming out and he was beginning therapy at that very moment that he hoped would turn her around and send her home.

Before she could answer, Donovan rounded the corner speaking loudly into his cell phone and laughing. He was not paying much attention to what he saw until he saw Lydia in the Minister's arms.

"Well, hey folks, quite a tearful reunion I'd say," he said as he approached them with a smile. He had not yet seen Lydia's face so his statement was somewhat assumed but correct. He could on the other hand, see that the Minister's face did not offer a cheery grin that should have been expected. He turned back to his wife. "Everything okay, 'Lyd'?"

"Oh yeah, honey. I was just so happy to see the Reverend here, and I thought his last sermon deserved a hug," she said as she pulled away. "You know I've been telling you that you need to come and hear him."

Donovan noticed her red eyes but made no immediate comment. He was almost sure that she had not mentioned anything about their personal issues in such a short time, and so he simply looked past her, much to the Minister's relief, and launched into a hearty greeting of his own. He knew that his wife had issues and that he was the cause of most, if not all of her stress, so he guarded his own embarrassment by not addressing what he saw and moving forward.

"Donovan, it's great to see you both," the Minister said as he also bypassed Lydia and extended his hand. Donovan caught his hand and pulled him into a friendly hug. It was as if they both skirted Lydia, knowing not to address her, for their own good.

"Hey man, it's great to see you too!" Donovan's greeting was excitedly sincere. "I thought it was a wild coincidence that you were in Chicago. 'Lyd' told me that she talked to Angie the other day, and she told her you were here for some kind of conference or something, and then when I told her about the tournament, she decided she was coming. She never wanted to tag along before but I said, 'hey what the hell; come on.'" He was full of smiles and laughter while Lydia stood to the side trying to force a smile and avoid covertly darted looks from the Minister.

"Oh, I see. Well, you know those two have become spa, shopping and brunch buddies and I guess we've graduated to their conversation list," the Minister said smiling at Donovan but using his peripheral vision to shoot the look to Lydia that she did not want to receive.

"Yeah, I know. I probably need to check my account balance. I don't know about Angie but knowing Lydia, I might be bankrupt." They both laughed.

Lydia turned her head to window shop a bit, and moved a couple of steps away but purposely not far enough to miss any of the conversation between the men.

"Did you say you were here for a tournament?"

"Yeah, a golf tournament. You didn't get my message about it?"

"No, where'd you call me?" The Minister figured that Donovan had called his cell phone and he remembered he had turned it off the day before after his frustrations with Alex, and had not turned it on since. Angie had probably given the number to Lydia.

"No, I left the message here at the hotel," Donovan said.

"Oh, you know I saw the light blinking on the phone but I just never got around to checking the messages. I was probably preparing for this workshop that I'm speaking at tomorrow night, and sometimes when I'm focused like that, I have tunnel vision and everything else gets shut out."

"Yeah buddy, I want you to play the tourney with me. Your wife let the cat out of the bag and said you have the same golf illness that I do, so why don't you come on out with me?" Donovan's smile was so outgoing and friendly that it was difficult for anyone to say no to him.

"Oh, I wouldn't want to impose on you like that. Besides I don't have my sticks, and I didn't bring any golf attire, and—"

"Ed, please man. It's no imposition at all. Be my guest. We'll get you all set up in the morning and you'll love the guys. It would be my pleasure after all you've done for Lydia. She can't stop talking about you and the church, and Angie's friendship has been great as well."

Donovan was not taking no for an answer and although the Minister loved golf and thought about the fact that he would probably be playing with a pro athlete dream team foursome. He was somewhat concerned about Lydia, and what she might do while he was away with her husband. He still reserved questionable feelings about her and Donovan's relationship, and what was going on behind closed doors that had Lydia on edge, and then she chimed in.

"Aw, go ahead, Reverend. You'll enjoy it, and you look like you could use a little stress relief on the golf course," she said looking beyond his eyes.

"My lady has spoken," Donovan said with a smile, swallowing her into his arms. "So what's your suite number? I'll make sure I give you a wake up call."

"1825," he said slowly, forcing congeniality.

"Really? We're right down the hall in 1801 so I'm sure we'll be seeing each other," Donovan said.

"Great." The Minister's response was noticeably flat. "Well it was great seeing you two, and Donovan I can't thank you enough for the invitation. I'm really looking forward to tomorrow." Looking at his watch, he slowly began to move away from them.

"So what's on your agenda this evening?" Lydia caught his eye before he could completely turn around.

"Well actually, I'm going to a stage play."

"Really the one at the Court Theater?" She said with recognizable excitement.

"Yes, that's the very one. The granddaughter of one of my faithful members has a tiny little role in it and I promised Miss Hattie that if I was ever in Chicago, I would go by for a moment, show my face and root for her baby. I try to support the endeavors of my people, you know."

"Wow, that's great, man. Lydia told me that you were some kind of pastor and how much the people loved you. I guess that's because you really go out of your way to show your support. I like that."

The Minister did his best to play the whole thing down and obviously not mention the performer's name. He was always self-protective.

"Well, I had to be here anyway so I said, why not bring a smile to the face of one of my members? Anyway guys, I'm going to be late, so again, it was great seeing you and Donovan, I'll try to get some rest tonight so I'll have some kind of swing in the morning. I wouldn't want to embarrass my sponsor." The Minister, again, glanced down at his watch, laughed pleasantly and left them there.

As she watched him walk away, Lydia moved close to Donovan and rubbed his chest.

"Honey, I want to go see that play tonight," she said with a longing grin. She knew that her husband had nothing against theater, but it was not what he probably would have chosen for the evening's entertainment. This was his trip and she was just tagging along, but in light of recent events in their relationship, she knew that he was willing to acquiesce to her wishes without much resistance.

"Baby, you really want to see that?" He was hoping she would change her mind but knew she would not. "It's such late notice, and everything."

"Oh, come on. It'll be fun. We can surprise the Reverend with some company and maybe meet his church member with the little part and make the person feel like a star. We can make it our good deed for the day." She smiled with the smile that always tugged at his innards.

"Okay," Donovan said giving in, "I know who I can call to get us some tickets. You head on up and start getting ready, and I'll be right there."

Lydia scampered away with a smile, satisfied that she had diverted her husband's attention enough to move him away from questioning her about what he saw when he walked up. She also found a way to be close to the Minister. That was all she really wanted. Maybe not be as close as she desired, but she would be close enough to make her wishes known.

Donovan, true to his word and desire to appease his wife, immediately got back on his cell phone and called one of his old contacts in Chicago that he knew had connections with the theater arts community. It was not a player, former teammate, agent or anyone of the sort. Donovan had other contacts, other people who led other lives in a world in which he only occasionally existed. As he dialed, he casually walked into the main lobby area of the hotel and noticed the Minister as he exited the hotel and got into the limousine that Gemma had sent for him. He found it quite interesting and somewhat strange, but he was glad that he saw it, and had no intentions of sharing what he saw with Lydia. He somehow got the feeling that the events surrounding that limo ride were very personal and very private. There was more to it than what he saw, that he knew, but he would save his comments and discussions for another time, maybe for the golf course.

CHAPTER 40

The Minister entered the comfortable confines of the limo shaking off the scene from which he had narrowly escaped. He had left without his overcoat because his plans were to go back to his suite after his meal, but running into Lydia and Donovan made him late, and he could not be late to watch his flower bloom. He also did not want to risk anything further with Lydia. She was looking very scrumptious to him even though he could see the danger behind her eyes.

Fate, not haste as one might expect, had caused several pieces of his puzzled existence to fall in the most unlikely places, and soon those pieces would begin to illuminate themselves to the most unlikely people, as they always do. Tonight however, the Minister would inhale the brisk air that should have chilled him without his overcoat, and feel inner warmth kindled by his own lust.

He thought about calling Angie but decided against the idea, as some of his concern about possible conversations with Lydia might bleed through. She was too perceptive and intuitive, and her ability to read him was only getting better with time. Though he did not have romantic feelings for Lydia, Angie could see that she was his kind of woman physically, and her second look at him was a bit more than perceptible. He wanted nothing to slip that would indicate any insightful suspicion of their encounters. He also remembered that he did not have his cell phone anyway. It was still in the inside pocket of his overcoat, at least that was the last he had seen it. It was not there but it would find him later.

He decided to clear his head, relax and enjoy his ride. He had successfully managed to stay one step ahead of the game tonight, and that was all that mattered; tomorrow would take care of itself. Gemma was his focus, now, and he had fortuitously sunken his teeth into her heart, and he was ready for more.

Everything went as expected, for the most part, when the Minister arrived at the theater. Jason, the man with the clipboard and headset, met him at the rear entrance just like he had the night before.

"Ah, it's *Reverend: the Sequel*," he said as he approached the Minister with a twisted smile.

"How are you Jason?" The Minister was unable to hold his smile and giggle. "Am I on your little clipboard tonight?"

"Why indeed you are," he said looking down. "And if you weren't, you know if I'm here, you're in."

"Yeah, but will I have to come to the back door?"

"I see nothing wrong with the rear entrance, 'Rev;' now come on in and let's get you seated."

The Minister laughed as he followed Jason to his seat. He appreciated his quick wit and unassumingly dry humor, and he respected the fact that he was willing to be himself in front of all he encountered. He reminded the Minister of Crawford.

"Crawford!" The Minister slipped, thinking out loud.

"I'm sorry?" Jason said, thinking he was talking to him.

"Oh nothing; I was just thinking out loud."

"Oh, well don't let me interrupt you; something juicy is bound to slip out," Jason said with a grin, as they arrived at the Minister's seat.

"Thanks Jason," the Minister said as he sat down, returning the smile. Jason stood there for a moment as if he were waiting to hear what was on the Minister's mind, and when he saw that there was nothing for him, he walked away. There were other guests to tend to, very special guests.

The Minister thought about calling Crawford right then and there. That is why his name escaped from the confines of his mind. He at least, deserved to know that the Minister had received the fax and would be there tomorrow night. But he again remembered that he did not have his cell phone, and decided that it was time to cease from worry and focus on the rising curtain. Because he was later than the night before, there was no time for Jason to come back to offer him refreshments, which was fine with him. He wanted no more interruptions, no more delays. He was ready for the lights to dim and his fantasy to begin.

Gemma was magnificent, just as she was the night before, and every other night that she had performed. Again, her skill and talent captivated the Minister and the unending ovations signified the audience's agreement with the Minister's assessment. When she sang, there was something in him that melted, and when she danced, it stirred his inner man into a frenzy of emotional anticipation.

Lydia and Donovan were also impressed. Donovan's contact had not only managed to get them tickets, but to also get their names placed on Jason's clipboard. The darkness cloaked their escorted late arrival and obscured them from the Minister's view. They were seated a few rows behind him and on the other side of the theater. It is always interesting to see what light reveals. At the intermission, the couple still had not seen the Minister, but many people nearby recognized them, and as Donovan entertained light conversation with husbands who welcomed the chance to chat with the NFL star about things other than the play. Lydia sat as the premiere picture wife, smiling beautifully, speaking intelligently and agreeing with the compliments on the show that came from the other wives.

The Minister could see the gathered group, but they shielded the duo inside. He was not really interested in what was going on there, anyway. He waited patiently for the curtain to rise and fall, the show to end and the chance to hold Gemma again.

Life never completely goes as expected. The gears of time have been placed in a shifting pattern by the author of the universe, and mankind is almost never prepared for twists, turns and changes.

At the close of the show, the ovation was powerful just before the crowd began to disburse. The Minister waited for Jason to come over and escort him backstage and share some dry humor on the way. As he stood and stretched, the lights finally revealed the unexpected couple. Donovan and Lydia had not spotted him yet but it was clear that she was scanning the room to see if he was there. She knew he was there, and it was not because he said he was coming; she could feel his presence. The Minister turned and faced the stage hoping she would not see his face. Maybe Jason would come quickly; he would go back and whisk Gemma away before the couple could get backstage to make the awkward meeting even more awkward. They could just wonder why they had missed him. But it would not happen that way. On a quick glance back, the Minister noticed that Lydia had seen him and was pointing him out to Donovan who eagerly shot a smile his way. The Minister sighed and prepared himself. He had always been cool and handled the pressure well, and this time was not going to be any different, if he could help it. In his mind, this was not the time to be concerned about their reactions. They had seen nothing and knew nothing.

He tried not to think about Lydia, who looked absolutely stunning despite her well hidden emotional instability. She wore another version of the simple black dress that all women either dress up or down, and she had definitely dressed it up to its highest possible degree. Cut high above the knee, he watched them approach and imagined how it looked when she sat down and it rode up exposing her supple thighs. Her appearance was the epitome of historic style and grace, and it was clear that she had been trained well before she came into her husband's wealth. Her jewelry was tastefully appropriate and complimentary, clearly expensive but not gaudy or overkill. She came from an ancestry with means beyond most and it was Donovan who really had to buy his way into the family caste system, seeing that he did not come from the Black version of blue blood. But his money and fame had cleaned him up well and keyed his entry into the clan.

"Well, hey you two," the Minister said with a smile as they approached, "I didn't know you were interested in coming; great to see you. When did you become a theater buff, big guy?" He joked with Donovan. Lydia hugged him tightly, but did not hold it too long.

"Hey buddy," Donovan said looking around. "She decided at the last minute that she wanted to come so I called an old friend who got us some tickets. So here we are."

It was clear that Donovan probably would have preferred to be somewhere else and had indulged his wife on this one, and the Minister was not sure if he liked that. He felt that her desire to be with him might be bleeding through and that would not be good for Donovan to see.

"So Ed, did you enjoy the show? My God, orchestra level seats; I guess you did," she said before he could answer.

"Oh yeah it was great," he answered smiling.

"And how did your little church member do? What part did she play?" She was leaning into the Minister's face.

"Oh hold on folks, here comes the guy to take us backstage," Donovan interrupted.

"You guys going backstage too?" The Minister thought maybe they would just say hello to him and leave, but Lydia was clinging tightly.

"Okay 'Rev', I think she's ready for you," Jason said. They all smiled back at him. "Oh you all know each other?"

"Oh yes," the Minister said clearing his throat. "Jason this is Donovan Davis and his wife Lydia. We're all new friends from home," he said smiling somewhat nervously.

"I know who they are 'Rev'; they're on my little clipboard that you teased me about. Okay, if you all are ready, we can go on back. I'm sure Miss Kimbro would love to meet the Davis' as well."

Jason switched away on the lead, the Minister followed right behind him, with Donovan and Lydia trailing. He did not want to see Lydia's face as she put together the fact that the Minister's little church member that he had come to support was actually the star of the show. It is always best for the accused to look away from the jury once the evidence confirms guilt. Jason announced their arrival as he knocked on Gemma's door.

"Miss Kimbro, I've got the Reverend here," he said.

"And the Davis'," the Minister jumped in. He did not want her to do something unexpected like fall into his arms in the presence of Lydia, especially.

When she opened the door, his eyes flickered as she again stood like a precious flower, beautiful and delicate.

"Gemma, I'd like you to meet some friends of mine, Donovan and Lydia Davis. They were in town and decided to check out the hottest play in Chicago." The Minister purposely spoke before Gemma.

"You were absolutely wonderful," Lydia said with Donovan signifying agreement. She looked around the room at all of the flowers and hors d'oeuvre platters and then glanced back at the Minister. He was not sure what her look meant but he began to get the idea as she moved closer to Gemma.

"Why, I thank you so much for that compliment, and I'm just honored that you came."

She was the perfectly humble diva, as she gently bowed her head gracefully. Even Donovan was impressed and felt that there was something special beyond special about Gemma. He stood quietly, smiling as his wife handled the covert interrogation.

"Ed didn't tell us that he had a member of his church that was the *star* of the show. It was almost like he was trying to keep you all to himself," Lydia said smiling falsely. "I wish I had known; I would have made it here to see you sooner."

"Oh well, I'm sure he's so busy with other things that he doesn't have time to talk about little 'ole me. I'm just glad that he took time out to see the show and enjoyed it. Are you two members of the church?"

"Well not yet but we certainly are thinking about it. Mrs. Hebert and I have become such good friends that I'm sure it's just a matter of time, and the Reverend here is such a great pastor that I don't think we can hold out and stay away much longer."

The dynamic that was going on between the women had become so thick that it could have been cut with a knife, and had silenced the men. They stood by as spectators in a battle of formidable wills. Finally Donovan jumped.

"Hey, let's all go out for a late dinner. What do you think Ed? Are you up for it? How 'bout it Gemma? It would be my honor to take out the star of the show."

Gemma looked at the Minister and in her glance was the desire to be with him only; along with a question about what was going on and why Lydia was so inquisitive. She could tell that the Minister did not expect the Davis' backstage visit, and she could also see that Lydia was more than a fan of the play; she was a fan of the Minister's. She could not tell however, if she was being protective in the absence of his wife or if she was being protective because she wanted him for herself. Gemma held herself from activating *Geronimo*, side of character. Instead, she was patient and just played along; allowing him to resolve whatever was in process.

"Well it's fine with me, but if Gemma is too tired I'll understand. She should probably get some rest. I don't want to keep her up all night and have the audience blame me when she can't hit those high notes," the Minister said laughing. "How do you feel Gemma? Do you want to go out?"

His communication was coded but he was not sure if Gemma was reading between the lines. Lydia made her presence known in a very obvious way, and as a woman she felt something, grabbed hold to it, and would not let it go. It was a woman thing, and Gemma could see it in Lydia. Her good instincts would have told her to cut her losses and go no deeper into something that was clearly not in her best interest, but what the Minister had created in her, the night before made her think with her heart and not with her head.

There was a dangerous aura about him, but that made him only more attractive, and she was drawn to that identity. Every woman finds it difficult to resist bad boys, especially when they operate under cloaks of goodness.

"Well," she contemplated, "I have a lot of Press to entertain and the director and producers will be sending their people back momentarily, so I think I should pass for now because I would not want to hold you up."

Lydia jumped right in, "Oh it's no problem if you want us to wait. I'd love to sit down and talk over dinner."

"No that's okay. I'd prefer that you went without me, but I tell you what," she said as she turned to her dressing table and retrieved pen and paper, "I'll give you guys Jason's number and you can give him a call once you settle at a restaurant, and if I'm available to come by, I will."

She wrote as she spoke and it was clear to Lydia that she had written down more than a phone number before handing the note to the Minister.

"Okay, that sounds fair," Donovan, said as he placed his large hands on the shoulders of his wife. "Gemma, again it was our pleasure meeting you and your performance this evening was magnificent." He tugged at Lydia to get her moving toward the door but she was not budging until she said her final salutation as well.

"Yes it was great. You were great and the show was great. I just wish you were able to go out with us, but hopefully we'll see you later." She continued to subtly evaluate her as she spoke.

Gemma nodded in thanks to them both and expressed her desire to do her best to finish up and make it, at least, for dessert. The Minister spoke to her with his eyes and hoped that she heard him tell her that she was beautiful, her performance was spectacular, and that he would see her later.

The trio exited and as he walked out, the Minister tried to keep his thoughts of having the two women in a hot oil wrestling match to a minimum, but he had to think of something amusing to try to shake off the intensity of the scene.

"So how 'bout it Ed; you up for bite to eat?" Donovan walked beside him, both of them trailing Lydia as they moved down the corridor.

"Well, not really. You know when you guys ran into me at the hotel? I was just finishing up dinner."

"Oh come on, at least have some dessert or something with us," Lydia said as she turned around.

"Yeah Ed, you might need something sweet to jump start your swing in the morning."

The Minister laughed, commenting internally on the depth of Donovan's Freudian slip, and after minimal resistance gave into joining them for dessert. Something in Lydia's heart made her know that he was not ready to leave Gemma but she had not tagged along to Chicago with the husband she did not want to share the Minister with another woman. She would be with him one way or another. As they came to an intersecting corridor just before exiting the theater, the group passed Jason in the hallway, hustling quickly with his clipboard in hand and headset securely mounted.

"See you *Rev*, and thanks for bringing your friends. Will we see you again tomorrow night?"

"Oh I don't know about that, Jason," the Minister said laughing and looking to the floor. "Thanks for everything."

"Oh, no problem. It's been my pleasure and I hope you all enjoyed the show," he said to the group. Before he continued down the hall to his myriad of destinations, he took a second look at Donovan. "Gee, Mr. Davis, have we met before? You look so familiar to me. I know I've seen you on television countless times but it seems I've seen you somewhere, maybe at a club here in Chicago?" Jason squinted as he quickly searched his memory, but the evening's tight schedule forced him to soon leave the process.

"Well, I don't know. Maybe you have; we've played the Bear's a few times, over the years, you know." Donovan glanced at Lydia who had a plastic smile on her face. He had seen that look before and tried to play down Jason's query. "Thanks again Jason for all your help this evening. My wife and I had a great time," Donovan said as he moved aside to allow Jason to continue to his destination.

The ice on which the Minister skated was thinning, and he knew it, but he was far from sinking. He was glad that Jason had not asked about him waiting for Gemma and the limo in front of Donovan and Lydia. As they stood in the brisk air, Donovan's powerful arms wrapped around Lydia and the Minister absent his overcoat, he took the opportunity to use the excuse to decline the dessert offer. He really wanted to read Gemma's note and find a way to be with her.

"You know what folks? I think I'm going to pass on going out tonight. I forgot my overcoat in the room and this Chicago wind is starting to cut through me."

"Oh well. Why don't we all just go back to the hotel? We can eat there," Lydia chimed.

"No, no, no. You guys go ahead and enjoy. Besides, I don't want to look stupid on the course in the morning so I better get some rest."

Donovan laughed in agreement and as their limo pulled forward, he offered the Minister a ride back to the hotel, which he declined, thanking them and stating that he had already made transportation arrangements. As they left, he noticed Lydia's longing eyes. She had tried to stay close to him as long as she could, but finally she had to go.

"Maybe we'll see you later?" She said just before the driver closed the door.

"I'll call Jason in about an hour and see if Gemma's available, and maybe we can all still grab some dessert."

"That would be great," she said and then silently mouthed, "*please try*," as the car drove away. The Minister watched them disappear into the traffic and then pulled the note from his pocket.

> *Please call me as soon as you can and I'll have Jason send a car for you. Don't make me wait too long. 555-8923*
>
> *XOXO*

The Minister grinned as he read the note and hailed a cab to return him to his hotel. He would go back, freshen up, tie up a few loose ends and then call Gemma. He filled his lungs with excitement, invigorated by a breath of the brisk night air. Fantasy was now taking tangible form, tugging on the thread that tested his desire. The tension of earlier moments only charged him more and he could feel the evidence in his pants. Relief would be found only when he pressed himself inside Gemma.

CHAPTER 41

Donovan and Lydia did not look at or speak to each other as they drove away. Each had mental creations and desires that were not to be shared with the other. Jason had definitely seen Donovan before, and it was at a club for a very specific clientele. Donovan had made it a point to frequent certain all male bars that hosted high-end clientele for whom discretion was paramount. On more than a few occasions, he had danced the night away and continued his private parties into the early morning hours. There was a fraternity of athletes and celebrities that had underground memberships in several gender specific nightclubs all over the country, and Donovan was a charter member. He was not bothered by the thought of being recognized, as it was the catalyst to memories that he long wanted to revisit. Lydia sat quietly, superficially appearing content and satisfied, but inside she rode an emotional roller coaster, fighting back tears of despair and fits of anger.

Finally they looked at each other, smiled slightly, and again without a word turned their heads away, falling back into their thoughts. They were both very intelligent people, and although one did not know exactly what the other was thinking, both knew that they were an ocean away from one another.

The Minister dashed back to his room but took his time showering and changing clothes before calling Gemma. Again, he saw that his message indication light was blinking but he did not address it. It was probably Donovan's message that he never listened to, he thought, and if it was not, he was not interested in whatever the interruption might be. After getting into a pair of Hugo Boss jeans and a Sak's Fifth Avenue cashmere turtle neck sweater, the Minister made the call.

"Hi, beautiful. Are you ready for dessert?" His voice was seductive and music to her ears.

"You know I've been waiting on your call. Will we be dining with guests tonight?"

"Of course not, and I apologize for any discomfort you might have felt by their presence," he said.

"Don't worry about it. More than a few women before Lydia have sized me up. She was not the first and definitely won't be the last. Is she one of yours?"

Gemma's question caught the Minister totally off guard. He did not expect her crass lack of diplomacy but he did not really know the depth of her style. What came up always came out. She did not mean to startle him into a fit of stuttering and back pedaling. But his reaction was quite telling. There was a need for him to understand where she was, and the essence of her comment was meant more to make him comfortable than cause him to search for some revealing explanation to share. Though she was a lover of romance and fantasy and was easily swept away by both, there was a realistic part of Gemma's character, a grown up and mature side that reserved itself for fleeting moments like these to force illuminating observations on life. For a split second, the Minister was speechless, but it was not long enough to cause a terribly noticeable abyss in the conversation. Gemma could feel him struggle though.

"Is she one of my what?" He smiled nervously and swallowed hard.

"Is she one of your women?"

"Oh Gemma, come on," was his only response as he tried to maintain the seductive demeanor with a sly giggle.

"It's okay, Alan. This is our few days of fantasy, not judgment day. There is no need to be concerned. I'm the last person to whom you have to answer, and it won't change how I feel about you."

"How do you feel about me?" He sat on the bed and toyed with the crystal ashtray on his nightstand while he awaited her response.

"I'll have Jason send the car for you and I'll show you when I see you," she said with a smile that he could see with his eyes closed. "How does about thirty minutes sound?"

"It sounds perfect. I'll be downstairs." He smiled inside.

There was something about Gemma that puzzled him, and he had met no one like her. She was willing and uninhibited and he could not help himself in terms of his desire to be near her. The Minister slipped into his Bruno Magli's and grabbed his leather coat. He still had some time and he knew that he needed to call Angie. He had not spoken to her and the kids, and he figured that she also had tried to reach him. Reaching into the pocket of his overcoat that hung in the closet, he was surprised when he was unable to find his cell phone. He was sure that he had had it the night before and that he had turned it off and placed it in the pocket. It must have fallen out somewhere and that could mean trouble. Picking up the receiver of the hotel suite phone, he dialed his home number, hoping to get the answering machine to leave a quick un-detailed message, but Angie answered the phone. He explained to her that he had misplaced his cell phone and that it was probably somewhere in the room. She did not ask many questions and her distance was barely conspicuous. As far as the Minister was concerned, everything was fine. But nothing is ever fine.

Guilt brings forth evaluative radar that tests the territory at all times with loved ones. But Angie gave no indication that she suspected anything. He told her that he had run into Lydia and Donovan and sarcastically thanked her for informing them of his whereabouts. They both laughed and closed the conversation normally, with Angie reminding her husband to be safe and how much she loved him. There was one small issue however. She asked him more than once about his accommodations, making sure that he was at the Drake hotel. The Minister just blew it off as his mind was already in the lobby waiting for Gemma.

Once again, *fate* and *coincidence* had teamed up with *time* as the Minister was spotted getting into a limo and leaving the hotel as Donovan and Lydia pulled up, and once again, only Donovan saw him, or so he thought. Lydia had other expectations for the evening that would remain unmet.

The Minister turned to Gemma after entering the limo and his heart almost jumped out of his torso as she sat dressed in nothing more than an ankle length maxi coat and stiletto pumps. She smelled like honeysuckle on a southern summer night and it was not long before they were at each other while on the way to the Minister's other suite at the Ritz. They fed a hunger for one another, in the car, that served as an appetizer to what would come later. All inhibitions were cast away and the thrill of the moment charged them both. It was as if every sexual detail experienced was something reciprocally craved and they were both starved. She was like candy to him and the fact that she was forbidden fruit made her taste that much sweeter.

When they arrived at the Ritz, they headed to the elevator without stopping. He touched her gently as the elevator ascended, as something in both of them called for his delicate hands to examine her shoulders, neck and the base of her hairline. There had not been complete satisfaction in the limo, and their loins still called for attention.

In the suite, they again howled in the moonlight, making unrelenting love until they both fell asleep, spent and satisfied. They had engaged in foreplay within their own minds, and when it came time for sex, there was no waiting. He especially, slept like a lion satisfied and full after a meal of well-stalked prey. They were awakened by the Minister's cell phone. It had fallen out of the pocket of his overcoat the night before and had been placed on the table, most likely, by the maid. He wondered who could be calling him at that hour but he knew he needed to answer.

"Hello?"

"Ed?"

"Lydia?"

"Ed, can I come down and see you? Donovan went out with some of his football buddies and I thought we could get together for a moment."

"Well, no Lydia. I don't think that's a good idea," the Minister whispered.

"Why not? Didn't you enjoy seeing me tonight? I wore that dress especially for you. You didn't find me attractive? You do remember that dress, don't you?"

"Of course I did, Lydia. I thought you looked great but you were there with your husband and all, and—" He tried to hurry her off the line and his whisper was getting slightly louder.

"And you weren't attracted to me because Donovan was there? Well Donovan isn't here now and we really need to talk. You know I came here to see you, Ed. Remember, you opened that door and told me to call you 'Ed'. Remember that day in your office when we first met? Remember how you looked at me and I looked at you? You could tell then that I needed you, couldn't you? You saw what I needed even then."

"Lydia, please!"

"Where are you Ed? You're not in your suite, are you? I saw you leaving. Donovan doesn't think I saw you and I had to make it seem like I didn't but I saw you leave. Where are you Ed? Are you with the granddaughter of the church member; you know the one with the tiny little part in the play? Is that where you are? Are you counseling her like you counseled me?"

"Lydia, please don't do this to me, not now," he said sharply.

"Do what to you; take you up on your offer for personalized counseling?"

"No, stalk me!"

"You think I'm stalking you? I need you. I'm going through a crisis and I have only found comfort in talking to you. I'm on the brink of total self-destruction due to an enormous amount of stress and you think I'm stalking you? Okay Reverend. You enjoy your evening!"

"Lydia? Lydia!" He could hear that she slammed the phone down and he knew that he would have to deal with Lydia sooner or later. The volume of his whisper had noticeably increased and he closed his eyes in frustration with the whole situation.

There was a brief moment, a split second when he evaluated his position in the cosmos, and knew he was out of place. There was definitely something deeper to what was going on with Lydia and he knew it. He could hear the emotional roller coaster in her tone. She was angry, frustrated, hurt, happy, sad and confused all at the same time, and he could see that she was lashing out at him with her misdirected emotions. There was a vein of compassion that he could feel her reaching for, but he had decided before he left home to withdraw his availability, and in his heart, he knew he was wrong for that.

He kicked himself for ever opening that door, but there was something that she desperately needed to tell him, something that he really needed to know but was not prepared to accept.

CHAPTER 42

The Minister's internal war was intensifying and becoming more and more difficult to ignore. He did all he could to appear as though he controlled his own destiny, but self-destruction was imminent if his demons were left un-addressed. He sighed and turned around to head back into the bedroom with Gemma but was startled to see her standing right in front of him. She said nothing to him and simply looked into his eyes through the night, looking through his outer shell of superficiality and seeing his distress.

"You know my grandma always said I had the gift of reading people's eyes," she said as she stepped close to him and held his face with her right hand. Her touch was simple and soft.

"Really, and what do you read in my eyes?" He tried to make light of her statement, almost dismissing her with a conjured up smile.

The Minister was not expecting the depth of her analysis, nor the direction she was headed. He was the analyzer, the psychologist. People came to him to understand themselves, their motivations and their idiosyncrasies. It was not the other way around, and it especially was not to come from her, but he knew Miss Hattie Lee, and how she never bit her tongue when it came to sharing her feelings and beliefs, so he prepared himself.

"You have secrets, Alan, secrets that are eating you from the inside out," she said softly. "Was that the Lydia I met tonight at the play and asked you if she was one of yours?"

He stood contemplating his answer, trying to keep his mouth from falling open. As smooth a liar as he was, there was something in Gemma's countenance that did not demand the truth but welcomed it without consequence. With simplicity, she had cornered him and there was only one way out.

"Yes," he said dryly.

"And she and I aren't the only ones, are we?"

"No." He had no idea what had drawn him to speak candidly with Gemma, and she was unsure why she even brought the issues forward, herself.

She could have stayed in bed and simply ignored the single-sided conversation she overheard, waited for the Minister to return, kissed, made love again and slept the night away without regret. But something else seemed to have entered the dynamic of their brief courtship, an entity unfamiliar to both of them but one that could not be avoided, a conviction that had brought her from the bedroom.

"Why did you come here, Alan?"

"I came here for you," he said looking into her eyes and then glancing away.

"No you didn't; you came here for you." She turned her head to catch his gaze and bring his eyes back into focus with hers. "But it's okay. I'm here for me more than I am for you. I'm here because I'm probably even more attracted to you than you are to me, and there is something in me that you satisfy in a way that no one has satisfied before, and I like that. I love that. I love the romance, the flowers, the notes and the attention. I love the way you look at me and the way you hold me, and I feel like I've been waiting for this for a long time, and normally I would continue without fear of consequence or conscience, but there is something about you that makes me feel like you need to be saved from yourself. And I'm not angry or hurt about Lydia or anyone else for that matter because deep in my heart I know that I'm not the only one who has been waiting to be in your arms.

"There is something that you have that every woman wants, but you're running from something inside, and I think you ran to me to try to hide from yourself. I guess what I'm saying is that we all want a part of something that is not ours to give. Everything you are and everything you have belongs to someone and something else. I know you didn't come here to hear all this psycho-babble, and Lord knows I didn't plan on saying it, but I think it's true. I think I'm right. I know I'm not your savior, and I really don't want to be, but there's something inside me that won't allow me to participate any further in whatever you're going through. It's not that I don't want to; it's that I can't. I don't think I've ever been this honest with myself, in my life, and I'll probably kick myself tomorrow because this has not been my style, in the past, but 'what the hell.' There's something that's pulling me toward you this way."

The Minister did all he could to come up with something to say that would nullify Gemma's statements but he could not. She was right. He had several unresolved issues with which he had not dealt, and probably never would unless he felt cornered or threatened, and no one had ever cornered or threatened him. There was something about the way Gemma spoke to him. No one spoke to him like that, at least not any of his conquests, none of the women he had put his eye on and slowly, but deliberately reeled in. They were all willing victims and participated without conscience. They were all so appreciative of his attention that they only wanted to say *thank you* in their own special ways , and their expectations of his response were always clear. They only wanted him to be the man of fantasy that he presented.

In essence, Gemma had released him from the commitment that he felt he had to display with all of the women with whom he had made secret engagements. She had reached a place in his heart, on this particular night that had not been tapped; the part that called on him to be honest with himself. It was that corner of his soul that he had shut down for so long that he almost had no idea how to open it and examine its personal content of truth. Her comments served as a catalyst to an immediate need for introspective evaluation, and the Minister quickly realized that the demons that he often blamed for his indiscretions were historic issues that he simply chose not to face. Still he tried to fight, caught tightly in the web of his own deceit.

"Gemma, I don't think this is the time or the place for us to get into this kind of discussion," he said as he backed away.

"You are absolutely right," she said as her eyes welled with tears. "This is not what I want to talk about. This is not what I want to think about. I would rather be in the next room screwing my brains out, but there's something that is just not letting that happen. I agree; this is not the time or the place, but there is no time or place when it comes to overhauling your life or your lifestyle. I'm just welcoming the process for some reason, and if you need me, I'm here."

She turned and led him by the hand into the bedroom. Her naked body took on somewhat of an angelic luminosity as the Minister followed. It was perfect in a nonsexual way, a way in which he had not thought in a very long time. Gemma pulled him next to her as she sat on the edge of the bed. She never put on any clothing and she glowed in the moonlight that shone through the window. They sat for nearly half an hour before either of them said a word, her hand resting gently atop his.

"You're right, Gemma. I guess I am a runner, and I'm running from myself. All my life I have been what was expected of me; a good student, a good preacher, a good husband, a good counselor, but I always felt trapped in the confines of other people's desires for my life, and their ideals for my success. I was never fully satisfied and I guess I began to search for it in places that I should not have.

"There have been so many people living inside my head that I've almost gone insane. I've had to be someone different to so many people that I don't think I ever discovered who I was or learned to be myself, and somewhere in the process, I got lost. I lost myself and maybe I've attempted rediscovery between the legs of numerous women, and I don't know if I want to stop looking. I hear what you're saying, but I just don't know where I am anymore.

"For years I was pissed at my father for never getting to know me, always being '*down at the church*,' for never spending time with me to learn the things that I liked and what issues were important to me. He was always '*down at the church*' doing God knows what. But he was who he was and nothing I did seemed to ever change that. He had predetermined in his mind who and what I was going to be, and that was who he was. I guess he never felt he needed to get to know me because he figured he already knew me. I was going to be his creation. Sometimes I feel like we were never properly introduced. I didn't know him and he didn't know me. When I really think about it, I guess I blame him for knowing so much about me and not introducing me to myself. Gemma, with all the crap I've been through, sometimes I feel like I'm so far passed redemption now that I don't know where to go." He never turned his head to look at her while he spoke. And he could not believe what had just come out of his mouth.

"I think you do," she said holding his face and turning his face toward her. "I think you know enough about who you are and have discovered enough about who you aren't to know that you don't belong here. I can see it bothering you. I saw it the day backstage in Manhattan. Your eyes wanted me but they were clearly filled with torment. I ignored it because I wanted you too. I saw the fight in you, the struggle. I saw it last night when you chose not to go into the director's party with me. You wanted to be there but you knew you did not belong there, and to some degree, I guess I should feel very guilty about bringing you into this situation and satisfying my own lust, but maybe it was the catalyst to something greater than my selfish desires."

There was something that softened inside the Minister. He did not want Gemma to feel guilty about participating in the tryst. He was aware of his skills and how he used his manipulative abilities to bring people into his fold. He carefully sought those he desired and then placed them in positions that were almost impossible to escape. Gemma was no different. He had paid very close attention to her personality type in the brief encounters they had and tested her early to see how far she would go. In his estimation, she was a sure thing and the previous day and evening had proven him correct. He had specified his romance with her from the beginning, as he had done with every other woman he had ensnared, and just as he had planned to do with Lydia. But tonight, something had happened. Gemma had come full circle unexpectedly, and brought him to a place that he had no intention of going, at least not on this night. He had often preached about the inevitability of righteousness but had never truly seen himself as a participant in its virtuous essence.

"I knew there was something about you when I hugged you in Manhattan. I took it as a spark that ignited a sexual attraction, but I guess I was wrong. I guess what I felt had deeper meaning than I gave credit, and it was just another turn en route to a conversation that I never thought I'd be having with you." The Minister gripped her hand as they sat and finally turned and faced her. "God Gemma, I've done a lot of crap, and I mean *crap* in the most literal sense of the word, and I'm tired. I'm tired of doing it and running away from it. I don't know why I've come to this point now, at this very moment, but I'm here and I know I need to be in a very different place. I guess sometimes I get so caught up in 'stuff' that I feel that I can't get out and change the scenery. I feel trapped in my own foolishness sometimes. I just don't know."

"Go home, Reverend," Gemma said looking directly at him with a sincere grin of patience and breakthrough for the both of them. "Just finish your work here and go home. There's nothing to explain; nothing to do; nothing more to say. Go home."

She stood and headed for the shower, leaving the Minister alone on the bed for a moment. She knew better than to turn around and look at him, as she had fought and overcome a very lustful and whimsically guided part her being, deciding for once in her life to choose wisely based on what she knew was right.

"So where does this leave us?" He asked as he followed her.

"It leaves us right where we need to be."

He stood there with a puzzled look on his face but in his heart he knew exactly where it left them, and somewhere in his silence, he thanked her for his freedom. He thanked her for the strength and resolve that he should have had.

CHAPTER 43

Friday morning drew the cast of principals a little closer in their loosely knit circle. Very soon they would all meet face-to-face, and they would all play their respective roles in paving their individual journeys to a collective confrontation. Angela, the Minister, their children, Alex, Lydia, Donovan, the Watcher, the Caller and even Crawford were all well established on paths of coincidence and circumstance. All raced toward an unforeseen destiny. Advancing steps were already being taken by each person, in his or her, own stride. Some would run into each other at an alarming rate, while others would quietly bump, excuse themselves, and keep moving.

Staring into the cosmos by way of her kitchen table, Ivy sat over a cup of warm coffee that had once been hot. She had not given up completely on her new outlook on life, which advised her to go with the flow and to not ask questions that would stunt her enjoyment of the moment, but Donovan had thrown himself into her life, and then tossed a curve ball, in a way that caused the *old Ivy* to resurface. She sat there wondering what he expected from her and how he could possibly think that she would be willing to give up everything that she had worked so hard to achieve and concentrate solely on him. He obviously had no idea what she had been through to have arrived at her current destination. She thought about the money and how it made her skills look like a purchase, or at least an "auction-able" item. *Had he gone shopping for a lawyer and spoken to a dealer who told him that he needed to make a $50,000 down payment on an "Ivy" model? Was that what she was worth to him?* She was sure that there was more money down the way, and she could probably wink laughingly at the money she had saved in her 401k, in comparison to the fortune he, most likely, would offer. She could probably retire, she thought. But then she began to weigh the attributes and activities of their relationship against the innumerable factors about him that she was unaware.

It was clear that he was in some sort of legal trouble, and she knew that he knew enough about the law to know that she would soon find out one way or the other, and whatever was going on with him would be a decisive factor that would probably determine her answer.

There was also a side of her that was tired of the corporate struggle and consistently having to prove herself. Even though she was handling bigger cases and being looked at as one of the rising stars of corporate law, she knew that by the time she made partner at her present firm she would be wrinkled and gray, and would have given more of her life than she was willing, to unappreciative bosses who would pleasurably count the money she made for them.

Starting her own firm, or at least going into private practice would be the only way to ensure success the way she wanted it, and securing a flagship client like Donovan would be an excellent way to begin. She knew that she had a great rapport with male athletes and as long as she kept a keen mind for the law and was as shrewd as the other lawyers in the game, she would never be short of clients. She also knew that as long as she kept those runner's legs, tight buns, and pert boobs, she would have a definite leg up on the competition. Her light gray eyes would not hurt either.

Donovan's offer was even more tempting because she was falling in love with him and she believed that he was falling for her. She knew that Lydia existed but he made it seem like there was no relationship and that they were most likely headed for divorce. That did not bother her, as it was the climate of the day. She knew that most contemporary relationships did not work and the statistics that made divorce seem like an epidemic were simply an illumination of the fact that people were not afraid to admit that they had made mistakes in selecting their spouses.

She took a sip of her lukewarm coffee, which jarred her out of her trance and into movement. Placing the cup in the microwave, she decided that she would call Donovan to give him her answer. *What did she have to lose?* It was a whole new world where corporate kings took risks to make millions and stories of success out of adversity were all around her. She stood wearing nothing more than an extra large Columbia University Law School sweatshirt, leaning against the counter busying her hands with a few dishes and with the phone lodged between her shoulder and right ear. It rang to no answer.

Lydia watched it ring while Donovan showered, preparing for his round of golf. She sat at the table in the living room of her suite, just like Ivy in front of a cup of warm coffee that had once been hot. She too, searched the cosmos in thought. Ivy did not leave a message when the greeting came on; she simply hung up and retrieved her drink from the microwave. After a sip that showed she had left it in much too long, she called again. And again Lydia watched the phone ring while her husband showered, still searching for antiphons in the crowded regions of her mind. After that final attempt, Ivy felt that she could hear Aunt Cindy saying, *"Let it go, baby; just let it go. Somethin' just ain't right. Let it go."*

"Good morning. What's on the calendar?" Aunt Cindy's whisper stifled further attempts and shifted gears swiftly. Ivy called her assistant to begin the day. She knew there was more that she would have to deal with and maybe she would miss out on something that she might have enjoyed, but Aunt Cindy was the one person whom she knew she could trust. Even now, when she heard her voice from the heavens, she listened, knowing that she only had her best interest at heart.

"Well, the last time we talked you told me to schedule the magazine reporter for the new case for today, so I have her coming in at noon. I wanted to give you a little time to prepare, if you needed it. And I sent over a few documents on the case so you can familiarize yourself with the principals, and I've pulled all the related files for similar cases, including a few briefs and opinions and placed them on you desk."

Ivy's assistant was more than ready. She had tasted the spoils of victory with her boss and liked it, and she had learned to admire Ivy's tenacious efforts. They were becoming a forcefully powerful unit. She had also rented *Erin Brokovich* on DVD over the weekend, and was charged.

"Wow," Ivy replied. "You're really on it; thanks! By the way, did I have any calls from Donovan Davis this morning?"

"No, I haven't heard from him. Are you expecting his call?"

"No, no. Don't worry about it," Ivy's voice trailed off. "He's probably expecting mine though," she said almost inaudibly.

"I'm sorry, what did you say? I couldn't hear you."

"Oh, nothing. I'll see you soon. Thanks for getting things organized."

As Ivy drove toward her office, she fought against herself, as well as against the whispered admonishments of Aunt Cindy that still floated in her head. She picked up her cell phone several times, and even checked her home messages to see if he had called. He had not, and something would not allow her to call him. She decided to go back to her old method and hide from the torment of personal decision making by submersing herself deep within her work, but she was not prepared for what she met when she arrived at her office.

There was a part of her that expected, almost knew that Donovan would have some coercing gift waiting there at her desk, or maybe even be there in person, but there was a greater part of her that knew that they had come to a point of climax, and that the decision to move further with him would be hers. She almost blew by her assistant without speaking; she was so deep in thought, but she was caught quickly by her hearty "hello" momentarily bringing her back to earth.

"Good morning, Miss Page," she said with a smile. "I wanted to stop you before you went in. Miss Gaines is inside waiting for you. Did you have a chance to go over any of the files?"

"Miss, who?" Ivy knew the name sounded familiar but she could not place it.

"Miss Gaines; the lady from the magazine," her assistant said as she slowly pushed the door open, allowing Ivy to peek inside before walking inside to see a face that she had not seen in years, and really did not want to.

"Yavonne?" Ivy's assistant shut the door on her way out after noticing her boss's tone.

"Hey Ivy; it's been a long time hasn't it. You're looking great," the woman said somewhat sarcastically. Ivy had not yet come to grips with what she was seeing.

"Yavonne Gaines," she said slowly, just before biting her bottom lip and closing her eyes momentarily. "You're the reporter from the magazine with the big story about the sports celebrity? Why didn't I know that?"

"I don't know. It should have been in your files, but I guess it slipped out or something."

"So, how have you been?" Her tone showed a noticeable effort to convey nonexistent warmth.

Ivy was determined not to maintain her professionalism. She fought back the yearning to jump across her desk and tightly wrap her hands around the throat of the woman, who had almost gotten her raped in college. She thought about Donovan's offer again, and wished that she had just said "Yes!" immediately, and not come in to work at all. This was not the picture she was prepared to see. But there was still Uncle Henry's fighting spirit inside her and she was not going to let the past or especially this woman, knock her out of her zone. She could handle it; she knew it. The bad thing was that they were supposed to be on the same side.

Ivy was going to have to listen to her and fight for whatever it was that her magazine wanted, so she simply took a visual inventory of Yavonne, as she sat across from her desk, and picked out the things that she knew separated them and always would. She looked at the shoes she had obviously worn about three months too long, and the run that was soon to begin in her stockings because they were at least two sizes too small, the overkill business suit that exposed the absence of cleavage, and the hair-weave that was three shades different than her natural hair color and way too straight. Uncle Henry called it sizing up your opponent, and Ivy knew she had won this battle.

"I've been great, actually, and I see you have too," Yavonne said as she looked around the office, noticing several of Ivy's awards, commendations and pieces of art on the wall.

She seemed like she was waiting to get into the college incident and other sorted aspects of history but Ivy defused that bomb before it had a chance to explode. Ivy could also see through Yavonne well enough to see that she had not been as *great* as she claimed.

"Yavonne, listen," Ivy said matter-of-factly, placing both palms on her desk. "I did not expect you to be here today. To be honest," she said nearing laughter, "you're probably the last person in the world I expected to be in my office when I got here, but girl, you're here, and what happened, happened. I was pissed off at you for a long time. Come to think of it, I'm still pissed at you for leaving me with that fool, but we're grown-ups now and we're professionals. My company is working with your company and both of them expect the utmost professionalism from both of us, so I'm willing to let bye-gone's be bye-gone's, stow the drama, and handle our business like two 'sistah's' should."

Ivy extended her hand across her desk in a genuine gesture of kindness. Yavonne sat for a moment, silenced by Ivy's expression, and then she nearly burst. It was unexpected and caught Ivy totally off guard.

"Oh Ivy, I'm so sorry about what happened that night; you just don't know how sorry I am," she said loudly, as she placed her face in her hands, nearing tears. "You were my friend and you had everything I wanted. You were pretty, and smart, and tall and everybody liked you, and you were the only one in the 'in crowd' who was my friend." She started to sob and Ivy came over and placed her hand on her shoulder.

"It's okay Yavonne. It's over; that was a long time ago."

"I need to say this, Ivy. I really do." She pulled her tearful face away from her hands, sniffing, and looked up at her old friend. "Ivy, I was devastated that night. I was devastated because of what I did to you, selling you out like a piece of meat to a bunch of senseless dogs. I should have never brought you there; I should have never been there myself because when you left," she paused.

"What, Yavonne? What happened when I left?"

"They raped me; every one of them, those bastards." Yavonne dropped her head in shame.

"Oh my God." Ivy pulled Yavonne close to her, grabbing a handful of tissues from her desk, and hugged her tightly as she sobbed. All of a sudden, Ivy felt terrible about her mental comments about Yavonne's clothing and messed up hair weave. In a matter of moments, she needed tissues for her own tear filled eyes. The football players had taken their anger out on Yavonne after what Ivy had done to their star player.

"What about the other girls who were there? Didn't they help you?"

"No, after you left, they left and I was there all alone. I tried to get away but I couldn't; I just couldn't; I just—"

Ivy pulled her even closer and rocked her like Aunt Cindy used to do when she could not stop crying after some sort of disappointment. There was new understanding that came to Ivy about Yavonne, and other people like her. She had struggled so hard for so long to fit in that she had placed herself in costly positions, often losing people who genuinely cared about her, and generally driving her self-esteem and respect further and further into the gutter.

The moment stirred the fierceness in Ivy and she wished that she could turn back the hands of time and go back to the night of the incident. She wished that she had pulled Yavonne out with her and taken her home and saved her from the terror that happened to her. They were friends then; very good friends. They had shared many triumphs together; passed exams, classes secured, semesters survived, pranks pulled, and a host of other activities and emotions that came with college life and bonding friendships. She remembered that after that night she no longer saw Yavonne around campus, but captivated by her own anger, she never asked about her and simply wrote her off. Yavonne had spent nearly three weeks in the hospital because of injuries she sustained during the rape, and then several months of physical and psychological therapy. The young men were never charged which only added to her problems. Three of them were now professional football players, with one of them having even earned a Super Bowl Championship ring.

"Ivy, I knew you must have hated me. That's why I never tried to contact you," she said, as she appeared to use all her fortitude to state her peace. "But I watched you, and I knew where you were. That's why I brought this case to this firm; I knew you were here and would handle this case properly. I made sure that you were the requested attorney. I knew when you graduated law school that the world had to watch out because you were armed and dangerous. As a matter of fact, I was there."

"Where?" Ivy looked down at her.

"At your law school graduation. You were my friend and I loved you but I hated myself for what I had done, so I blended in with the sea of people and supported you from the rafters. I'm so sorry, Ivy; you just don't know. I was even at the funeral when your Aunt passed."

Ivy knelt down in front of Yavonne and grabbed by both shoulders. She needed her to sincerely know that she was forgiven. Ivy had no idea that Yavonne had been through such an ordeal, and she needed her to know that they could still be friends, even after all this time. Yavonne had come there for more than just legal issues; she had come to finally face her old friend, settle her conscience in some way, and say she was sorry.

"Yavonne, look girl," she said as she looked directly in her eyes, "it's over and I owe you an apology."

"For what?"

"For holding on to all this damn anger for so long. It wasn't fair to you or me, and as Aunt Cindy used to say, 'being mad ain't gonna help nobody,' and I'm not mad anymore. We can still be friends; I want that. How 'bout you?"

"Oh, Ivy," Yavonne said, and fell into her arms like old friends should. It was as if a load had been lifted off both of them.

"You know, whenever Aunt Cindy would say, 'being mad ain't gonna help nobody', my Uncle Henry would always chime in behind her and say, 'maybe not, but kickin' somebody's ass will', so let's kick some ass, girl. What do you have for me?" The two fell out laughing regained their composure hastily.

Whoever was at the other end of the legal stick was in trouble now because these two re-energized forces were about to converge on them. Charged by the renewal of their friendship, they set out on a path toward success and hopefully a courtroom victory, if it even got that far. But Ivy was unprepared for the shock she would feel later, when Yavonne explained the case to her. They would do that over lunch while Ivy's office, *The Confessional*, was allowed to cool down.

"Is it too early for a Margarita?" Yavonne asked.

"It's never too early for good tequila girl, and I know just the spot," Ivy replied as they exited her office. "We're going to go grab some lunch and continue our meeting, so you can reach my on my cell if there's anything important that happens here," she informed her assistant.

CHAPTER 44

By 9:00 a.m. on the same morning, the Minister was fully dressed, excited about his round of golf, but even more ecstatic about his newly imparted lease on life. He felt redeemed, in some way, and though he had not made a confessional announcement to anyone, he felt as though he had introspectively faced at least, some of his demons, which was a far greater feat of courage. He knew that there were still several issues with which he had to deal, but he was confident that he would handle them correctly, as a good minister should, spiritually and faithfully.

He had to also face the things that confronted him immediately, like Lydia. He knew that it was just a matter of time before she called or came by, and he would have to be strong and secure himself within to deal with whatever it was that she wanted to say or do. He thought about calling her but decided that there was no reason to rush the inevitable. Donovan made small talk on the way to the course. The other part of the time, he spent on his cell phone, presumably speaking to his agent. He was a joy to be around and the Minister had not laughed so much with another man in years. There was a comeback to every joke, and punch lines that kept the Minister in stitches and holding his stomach almost all of the time. He was abundantly complimentary and kind beyond compare. That helped relax his swing and keep him loose. He was having a great round and the other pro athlete golfers were great as well. They asked about his sporting days, as they could obviously see that the Minister was in excellent shape, and looked as if he could have suited up on any Sunday with them, and sprinted for the goal line after a reception.

There was a unique comfort that the clan offered, and he was made to feel as though he belonged. They were like a fraternity of zealously happy men, always congratulating each other on good shots converted, and offering encouraging comments on the ones that were not so good. It was quite different to see a group of men behave in that manner, and the psychology student within the Minister was coming out and taking notes for another dissertation. They had almost completely laid aside their innate competitiveness, even though there was plenty of side betting for fun, and genuinely pulled for one another.

The course was beautiful, with manicured fairways and greens that looked like brand new carpet. Each hole seemed isolated, and trees and other foliage surrounded the tee boxes, so that the group was hidden from onlookers and other golfers that might disturb concentration. The only sounds heard were the birds chirping and the whistle of swinging golf clubs as they cut through the air. A symphony of solitude and contentment was harmoniously being broadcast by the fowl of the air, and with a twist of the golfer's wrist, soul soothing music was being made, at least music to a golfer's soul.

It was one of those places that only a select group of people even knew existed, and outsiders were brought in by invitation only. The Minister enjoyed the celebrity treatment. He was one in his world, but this event signified a crossover that he enjoyed. He fit right in and the other gentlemen seemed to go out of their way to make him feel welcome. They were all that one would expect from celebrity athletes and more. It was not until the final hole that things got strange.

Donovan and the other two players teed off first and the Minister was last. Both of the first players sliced their shots severely and left to begin their ball search, leaving Donovan and the Minster alone on the tee. Taking his time, the Minister unleashed a massive drive of at least 300 yards, straight down the center of the fairway. Both men cheered like teens and were hand slapping happy. When they got into the golf cart, preparing to drive away, they continued their antics, with Donovan congratulating the Minister with a powerful wrap around the shoulder, and that is when it happened. Caught up in laughter and high jinks, Donovan quickly and clearly leaned over and kissed the Minister square on the lips.

CHAPTER 45

On the same morning, Angie sat in her bath next to a cup of something that had once been hot and contemplated a call she had gotten the night before, and the information she had in her hands. Normally, her moment of bath time solitude was a time to re-group after a culmination of the week's events, but the stirring thoughts that bounced against the partitions of her mind forced evaluative thought. Like most, she figured things out in the bathtub or shower, and if the dilemmas were not solved, a plan of action at least was developed. It was time to plan. She had learned patience from her husband and it had often been her greatest asset, especially when she felt, in her spirit, that something was just not right. The reward for her virtue came with a simple ring of her phone, and once again, truth teamed up with fate and found its way through the muck and mire of circumstance and deception. On some planets it is called Murphy's Law; on other's it is simply, intuitions reward.

A zealous new employee of the Ritz-Carton Hotel had found her husband's cell phone, and turned it in to the front desk. It was later nonchalantly placed on the desk, of the Front Desk manager, who at the time was busy with arriving guests. The cell phone was the exact type that the manager owned, and after completing her tasks, she quickly scurried to her office to retrieve some papers, and without thinking, picked up the phone. Deciding to make a quick call home to check on her husband and children, she simply depressed the number one on the keypad, which was the programmed speed-dial to her house, but the woman who answered was neither her husband nor her children. The number one on the keypad was also *home* for the Minister. Angie looked at his cell phone number on the caller I. D. display on her phone as it rang several times before she answered. She thought about allowing the call to go into voice mail, but something told her that she needed to field his call.

"Hey, honey," Angie, said softly.

"Steph?" The distracted hotel manager now focused on the voice that did not belong to her twelve-year-old daughter.

"No, this isn't Steph. Who might this be?"

"Huh? Oh, umm, this is Kathy Berkow at the Ritz in Chicago. I'm sorry, the lines must have gotten crossed or something."

"Yeah, something," Angie said as she sat up, in the tub, "because you're calling from my husband's cell phone."

"What?" Miss Berkow looked closely at the phone in her hand and noticed that although it was nearly a dead ringer to hers, it was missing a noticeable but easily overlooked scratch that along the side. "Oh, I'm sorry. This isn't my phone."

"I know that; it's my husband's, and I'd like to know why you have it," Angie said seriously.

"Ma'am, I'm sorry. It looks just like mine and must have been turned in by an employee. I'm the manager here at the Ritz, and I guess someone just put it on my desk, while I was tied up. Well, you'll be happy to know that we found your husband's cell phone," she said cheerily.

"Well, I'm sure he'll be glad to know that," Angie said.

"I'd be happy to FedEx it to you. Is he a guest staying with us or was he just here having lunch or dinner at one of the restaurants?"

Angie contemplated her answer quickly. "He's a guest," she said, casting her line to see what she might reel in. After giving Miss Berkow, the Minister's full name, she instructed her to just leave it there and secure it, knowing that he would be back to pick it up, but the cheery manager told Angie that he had already checked out. Angie reiterated her instructions, as she needed to plan her movements without suspicion.

"Okay, Mrs. Hebert. We'll hold on to it, and once again I apologize for the mix up. Is there anything else I can do for you today?"

"Actually, there is, Miss Berkow."

"Call me Kathy."

"Okay Kathy."

It was time to get out of the sudsy think tank of discovery, but just before she did, Angie asked that a copy of her husband's billing statement be faxed to her. Unfortunately for the Minister, Angie was speaking to a woman who understood what she needed and was more than happy to oblige her requests.

She could not believe what she saw on the faxed statements. Each night that the Minister had been there, he checked in during the day and checked out the next, placing large cash deposits as security in lieu of a credit card. He had billed dinner, gifts and flowers all to the suite and charged them against the cash on record. Angie also called the Drake Hotel and had them do the same, and once again, the female employees with whom she spoke were more than happy to assist. There, he had checked in with a credit card, as expected and made normal charges to the room; single meals, movies, room service, and the like. Angie was not sure if she wanted to go farther. *Should she press?*

The information she acquired was not difficult to obtain, and she feared the simplicity with which she found out that her husband had been screwing around in Chicago, might reveal someone she knew. She had been down this road before and she knew the end thereof. It was not pretty; it never had been. She was aware of his complexities and his need for some sort of gratification outside their marriage. She knew much more than he ever thought she did, and she had dealt with it in her own way. But in her heart, she felt that she had reached her limit, and the value in their relationship was fading.

They had vowed to stand by each other through good and bad times, but her survivability was becoming questionable. *Was this all she had to look forward to?* She sipped her, now cold tea, placed the papers on the ledge of the tub, and leaned back into the dissipating bubbles. She turned the hot water on with her toes and whispered out loud, more than once, "Ed, why do you keep doing this to us?" It was not a question love. She knew very well that he loved her, but she also knew that he had many issues that he never discussed that were yet unresolved. It was those things and many others that he always allowed to creep in and motivate him negatively. He had hurt her so many times, but she too, just like Lydia, was a part of a picture that was viewed by so many, as pristine, perfect and faultless. Even though she knew that was not the case, and knew that many with that view were also aware of his imperfection. She respected the fact that that was how they wanted to see their pastor and his family. Even though he was not perfect, they needed to see him as near to that as possible. That was just the way it was supposed to be.

Finally, she got out and stood before the mirror. As she moved in closer, she frowned, scrutinizing every part of her body. She was still beautiful, and she knew that, but she began to internally question herself, wondering if her husband was on a search for what she used to be. Her breasts were still full and supple after two children, and she had managed to keep her weight well under control. Her thighs and bottom showed that her efforts at the gym were not all for naught. Her smile was still radiant, her hair long still and flowing. But time was still a force that worked against her, as it does everything. She wondered if he was just tired of the old model and ready to trade her in for a new one. And then she stopped. She stopped evaluating and kicking herself for not being what she was not. He was out of line and he would pay for his insurrection. *"It may not be now,"* she thought to herself. *"But one day, very soon, he will pay."* Angie was unaware, but those gears had already begun to turn, and she and the children would be the sprocket that turned a painful chain of events that led to her husband's retribution.

CHAPTER 46

Yavonne had already guzzled her second Margarita by the time Ivy had consumed only two swallows of her own, and before she could order a third, Ivy gently proceeded to question her about the details of the case. She could see that Yavonne had been through quite a bit during the time that Ivy had missed, and it was probably a significant feat for her to secure a position at the magazine. The empty margarita glasses before her were the results of her efforts to contend with issues that still haunted her.

"You majored in Journalism, didn't you, Yavonne?" Ivy commented.

"Yes, I did and I'm still trying to break into the business like I want to. I guess I don't need to tell you how hard it is for a Black woman to get some respect in the business world. Maybe this story will be the one that really opens the door for me."

Ivy thought about it for a moment, and knew exactly what she meant. She had been struggling for years, to gain proper recognition for her work, which had always been superb and greatly depended upon. But it was not until her most recent courtroom victory in a very high profile case that she started to receive the, long over due, respect that she deserved. She knew that it only took one big win on a highly visible case to open doors historically locked from the inside.

"So tell me what's up with this sports personality who won't let you print his story. That's pretty unusual; most of them want to be in the news."

"Well this one doesn't," Yavonne said. "Let me first lay everything out and then I'll tell you all about it. This one is more visual than anything else."

Yavonne reached down to her briefcase and pulled out three large envelopes full of pictures and drafted articles. Slowly, she began laying the photos on the table. As Ivy looked closely, she could see that the pictures were of two men, and in most cases they were holding each other in some way. The shots had been taken in some of the most beautiful and romantic locations in the world. The men were beautiful and looked like models as they sat or stood in front of museums and ruins, on beaches and park benches, underneath palm trees and on exclusive golf courses. In all cases, they seemed genuinely happy and content with each other, almost like a dating couple. One of the men in the pictures was Donovan.

Ivy held her composure as best she could. She tried to shore up any areas that might have revealed an emotion leak. She was almost sure she knew where this was going and it was the last thing she wanted to face. She also did not want to let on that she was, in any way, involved with him personally.

The photos kept coming. He had obviously been under surveillance for several months, if not years. Some of the pictures showed him in questionable positions and scenarios, but it was not until she saw the one where he was kissing his male lover, that she had to excuse herself to the ladies room.

She blasted the stall door open and almost fell to her knees. The griping pain in her stomach was familiar, bringing back unwelcome similarities to the night after the party on the yacht. *How could anything bring that feeling back again?* Hovering over the toilet, she threw up profusely, gagging several times and holding on to the stall partitions for stability. Ivy did not see it coming, and her insides churned. She could feel herself reaching but there was nothing she could grab onto to mend the painful destruction of her insides.

Ivy was in a terrible dilemma because it was taking everything in her to keep her from leaving the restaurant, going home, and burying herself beneath her blankets. But she had been called on to be a professional, and that was what she was going to do. She tried to gather herself, and not figure things out too far ahead of the game. She knew how her mind worked, and her methodical review of past events would only bring questionable issues to light and make things worse.

Yavonne was waiting outside and she had a host of details to share, and they would probably be things that might send her back to the toilet, but the situation called for her to call on something deeper than herself. As she washed her hands and rinsed her mouth, she looked into the mirror and could somehow see and feel her Aunt and Uncle joining her reflection.

She closed her eyes and whispered to the silhouettes of the souls she loved, "*thank you*," and then she walked out and rejoined Yavonne.

"You okay?" Yavonne asked as she crunched away on a tortilla chip.

"Yeah, I'm fine. Maybe it *is* too early for a Margarita. Anyway, what's up? What do we have here with Mr. Davis?"

"Oh, you know him?"

"Well, who doesn't; he's a super star football player, isn't he?"

"Oh, no; I thought you knew him personally or something," Yavonne said, dipping into the salsa.

"Well we've met at a charity event, a time or two, but—." Ivy's voice trailed off as she looked through the photos. "So who's the boyfriend in the pictures here?"

"That would be, Mr. Ermacio Dolceviso. He's an artist, a sculptor actually, and he's an ostracized member of the royal family of Monte Carlo in some way. But the main thing that he is, as far as this case is concerned, is the lover of one of the most celebrated linebacker's in the National Football League. That still is not even what this whole thing is all about. This is one of the hottest, non-death, destruction, or terror stories, in a very long time and we've been slapped silly with injunctions, threats and everything else you could think of, to keep these pictures and the story from going to press. It's like Davis is some kind of preciously protected American commodity, and I guess you could understand where the other guy's people are."

Ivy simply nodded her head as she listened to Yavonne talk. She was doing her best to concentrate but she was putting historical events together and beginning to understand things more and more. She gulped the balance of her Margarita, hoping that it might help settle her stomach, and if not, at least give her a reason to escape to the ladies room again.

"So, how long have you been following this story?"

"Well, we've known about Donovan for a long time. Well actually, we've suspected him for a long time. He and his plastic wife are all over the television doing PSA's and Nike commercials, when in reality this guy is living two or three separate lives."

"What do you mean?" Ivy played in the refried beans that had come with her taco and enchilada combination. Her appetite was gone, and looking at the plate only put her one step closer to another dash to the ladies room.

"Well, he has a house where he stashes his wife in Myrtle Beach or somewhere but he actually lives up in a place up in the hills of upstate New York with the Ermacio guy. They've even got a Spanish name for it, *La Ventana de Bonita*. Anyway, he's gay and his life's a lie and we've got pictures and documentation to prove it. This story is my big break. The magazine is loving it so much, they're in negotiations with a couple networks to develop an investigative tell all television show, and they've done that based on the solid strength of this story. *20/20, Hard Copy, 60 Minutes* and a bunch of others all want it. Hell, even *BET* has called my office. That's why we contacted your firm. For them it's all about dollars and making more of them in, and they don't want anyone or anything to stand in their way. For me, it's about an opportunity to show that I can actually do something on my own, something solid.

"Davis has lawyers up the 'ying-yang' trying to keep this whole thing closed down but apparently, his legal counsel is weakening and threatening even to quit on him. So much new information is coming out that the guy had not been honest about, and I guess his lawyers, don't want to deal with his crap anymore. The real issue is that he stands to lose, damn near, all his endorsements if this comes out, and if he can't make any money for them, they're through with him. Serve's him right, if you ask me."

"Well God, Yavonne," Ivy said. "I know it's your big break and all, but would you really want to do that to this guy? I mean, you're going to destroy him."

"Destroy him? I don't think so; he's already done that to himself," Yavonne said as she gestured to the server bring her another Margarita.

"Why do you say that? I mean, being gay in the NFL is bad but I'm sure he could get through it some way." Ivy really didn't know why she even said that. Her mind was beginning to twist and writhe in a very weird way.

"Ivy, the man is also broke," Yavonne said looking directly into Ivy's eyes. "I mean broke, as in *no money*. Apparently, Mr. Davis gambled one time too many with his little European boyfriend and lost everything."

"He's a gambler?"

"Yeah, but not in the casinos. He gambled with an investment that blew up in his face. The boyfriend is actually the nephew of some research scientist in France who started a pharmaceutical research company that was delving in to some uncharted territory by way of unauthorized genetic experimentation. It was supposed to be a goldmine and Donovan Davis was the cash cow that put every penny he could find into it. I guess the plan was to make an ungodly bundle and then tell the world to kiss his butt. It didn't quite work that way. The uncle got busted for some serious legal and political improprieties and any assets that were left have been indefinitely frozen."

Ivy sat speechless, trying to manage the onslaught of emotions that tried to overtake her.

"Ivy, think about his wife, for God's sakes," Yavonne said, breaking the glass of Ivy's trance. "What do you think she's going through behind all this?"

"Does she know?" Ivy looked up from the pictures by her plate through which she was still thumbing.

"Of course she knows. She spent a few months in a mental rehab retreat because of a nervous breakdown behind it. And apparently, she's still sick. I hear that she is still in constant therapy and has had several bouts with manic depression."

"So why is she still with him?"

"She's part of the package. And she's a professional at what she does. You know; she's one of those women who have been trained for a life in sports royalty, like the princess who had been trained all her life to marry the king. It's all she knows and all she does."

Ivy took a deep breath, trying to internalize all the information that her old friend was sharing. There were so many things going on in Ivy's head that she felt like she was going to explode. She was terribly torn between anger and frustration. She was angry because the man she had fallen in love with was a homosexual, and their relationship was built on lies that could probably have her headed to an early grave. She was frustrated for almost the same reason that she was angry, but because she thought she might be in love with him, there was a part of her that genuinely wanted to protect him.

"Well, isn't he between football contracts right now? I heard he was negotiating something with the Giants." Ivy knew very well of Donovan's contract status, but since Yavonne seemed to have so much information on his personal affairs, she thought she would throw it on the table and see what came back.

"Exactly. Right now he doesn't have a contract, and if this goes to print he probably won't get one," Yavonne said in a way that seemed like she got some strange pleasure out of tormenting the man.

"Yavonne, this story then, could ruin his career. Couldn't it?"

"Exactly."

"You would want this on your conscience? You reveal some truth about a very personal and private lifestyle of a celebrity and then they can't work anymore; that doesn't bother you in any way? Did you ever just consider walking away from this one?" Ivy was doing her best not to sound like the issue was personal but her feelings were beginning to surface.

"Ivy, please. I'm not taking bread out of this guy's pantry. He'll probably still get his *f-ing* contract and he'll get to play. These sports guy's always get away with murder. They do what they want, live the way they want to live, step all over people and do them wrong, and then come out smelling like roses, and the public still loves them. I know that first hand; remember? I'm not talking about what I think; I'm talking about what I know. Well it's my turn, now. Those assholes took, damn near, my whole life away, and if I can't get them, I'll get one of their bastard buddies. They're all the same."

"No, they're not all the same, Yavonne, and you can't just randomly select someone to persecute for crimes perpetrated against you, by someone else."

Ivy could see what this was about. Yavonne was vindictive and bitter, and she had been for a long time. This was not just about the guy's who raped her or even Donovan, for that matter; it was about every person in the *in crowd* who ever kept her out.

"Well, I'm not letting this one slip away," Yavonne said as she took another sip of her third Margarita and looked away.

Her eyes found their way back to Ivy in a brief second when it seemed like something clicked in her head.

"Why does it seem like you're taking this guy's side? It almost seems like you don't want to go after him, and as our lawyer, it shouldn't really matter. Is there something that I should know? Did I make a mistake in bringing this case to your firm?"

"No, Yavonne. I have to play 'devil's advocate' and look at this thing from all sides, and besides, don't you sometimes want to see if there are ways you can help our *brotha's* out? Jesus, they're becoming a dying breed."

"Well, let 'em die!" Yavonne was unrelenting. She took the last swallow of her Margarita, slammed her glass down on the table, and looked directly into Ivy's eyes, as if she were staring her down in the street scene of an old television Western. It was a look that seemed to say, "*I'm expecting you to pull your guns and fire every bullet you have, partner.*"

CHAPTER 47

The Minister truly felt that his day with Donovan should have ended after the golf cart incident, but it did not. He felt that something should have been said right then and there, but it was not. He felt that he should have been angry, and behaved in a misunderstanding way, and should have considered himself violated as a man, and made some sort of physical gesture that might re-affirm his masculinity; he did not. There was even an introspective part of him that sought answers, in terms of the presumption of this other man. Maybe there was some sound, scent or action, that led to the unexpected behavior; maybe he needed to psycho-analyze himself; he did not. A voice inside him screamed, *"Foul!"* But it was quieted by another that said, *"No harm; no foul."* And so he carried on, even within the moment, without immediate self-searching and without confrontation, and he did not completely, know why.

There was some weird essence of Donovan's character that made it such a natural part of his being that it did not call for any of the responses the Minister held within, neither did it call for his professional services. It was not a desperate cry for help or understanding; he had never seen a man, or men for that matter, more relaxed and genuinely enjoying each other's company, without regard for sexual preference, and the physical gesture was no more than a harmless question. It was almost like asking a girl to dance, at the freshman social. There are no hard feelings when she says *"no."* It was a simple offer from Donovan to the Minister, a very forward offer, but yet a simple one that said, *"Here I am. Where are you?"* The Minister knew that all he had to do was answer and then move on. The question would never be asked again.

The gentlemen completed their golf round and headed for the clubhouse. Donovan continued in his consistently jovial mood and made no mention about what had happened. The Minister did not expect him to, at that point. His response did not warrant a verbal address. The Minister was a suave character and it took more than what happened on the course to knock him sideways, even if he was somewhat disturbed and unclear. Donovan moved right through it, and acted almost, as if nothing happened.

They sat down, like every foursome does after a round, and laughingly discussed the triumphs and defeats of the day, how the course robbed them of pars and birdies, and how they could conquer it with one more chance. It was a ritual, and the clubhouse like the three men seated with the Minister, seemed rich with tradition and ritual. But there was a recognizable newness in the ambience of the place. The wood was lighter and the furniture uniquely modern. It serviced a different golfer. The membership was younger and more athletic looking, signifying the new breed of participant in the old sport. It would seem that this group of men might not belong, based on the color of their skin, as golf is a sport that still struggles to maintain its prejudice, even *with* Tiger Woods. But their status granted them both access and respect, and their comradery easily held outside opinion at bay. They were sports royalty.

The female server was at their beck and call, and was so accommodating that it seemed only a matter of request before she stood on her head atop the table or did back flips across the room. She eyed the Minister with a welcoming grin; as if she knew something he did not. He accepted her glances and returned them with his own, making sure that she understood that he was aware of what she might be alluding to, but was not phased by it. In reality, he knew little to nothing, but it was always his policy to appear that he was in the know.

The Minister drank no alcohol in front of the group, as was also his normal policy. He did not know if they even knew he was a minister, or if they even cared, but he was striving to maintain his re-emerging morality, at least in front of these guys. After a few rounds, the conversation seemed to die down and a door was opened to other issues of discussion. The Minister wondered if this was the time that the events of the 18th tee would be discussed.

The door was opened, but for more than dialogue about the 18th tee. He was definitely not going to bring it up in front of the other men. He had no intention of embarrassing Donovan or himself, for that matter; and besides, these guys were jocks and although they slapped one another on the butt after a good play, adjusted their jock straps and protective cups on national television, showered together and probably washed each other's backs on occasion, homosexuality was still taboo in their world. Donovan was first to head off the oncoming silence.

"Ed, Lydia told me that you're here to speak at a Music Workshop. Is that what's on your plate tonight?" The other men were becoming engrossed in sports highlights being shown on a nearby big screen and Donovan took advantage of their distraction.

"Yeah, that's why I'm here, actually. The Music Director at my church is conducting it, and he asked if I would come and say a few words," the Minister responded, coolly.

Donovan made a bit more small talk about the event and then asked where it was being held. The Minister hoped that this was not another preliminary investigation that would lead to a surprise visit, but then he really did not care. There was nothing to hide and nothing to be exposed. If they decided to come, it would be fine with him. He was holding fast to his regained righteousness, and they would have the pleasure of seeing him in his element.

"Well you know, I was thinking about coming and checking you out. I haven't mentioned anything to Lydia, but she's been telling me what a great speaker you are, and I haven't made it to the church, so what do you say?"

"I say you are both welcome to come. I'd be glad to have you." The Minister tried to place special emphasis on *both* without sounding strange.

He wanted to subtly, but continually impress to Donovan that he was not interested in any 18th tee encounters. There had not been anything mentioned but the Minister was paying close attention to any gesture that might indicate that he had not been clear. He was probably beginning to think too much but he soon found out that he was correct to be on guard. There was more to Donovan's query than what appeared superficially. He paused for a moment as if he were gathering himself to say something or ask a very personal question, and the Minister prepared himself.

"So what did you and your *showgirl* get into last night?" Donovan's question was almost whispered, and his suspicious grin looked like that of some of the gossiping old women at the church who fed on juicy morsels of rumored truths. It was, again, not what the Minister expected.

"What do you mean?"

"C'mon man, you know what I mean. I could see through the smoke you and Gemma tried to bring up; 'Lyd' could too. But it's cool; don't worry about it," Donovan leaned in even closer to the Minister.

"She is fine as hell. I can understand you fully and completely. If I were in your shoes, I'd be all over that too."

"I told you guys she was a member of the church and I just came to support her as a very special favor to her grandmother." A slight *men's club* smile crept onto his face.

"Okay, 'Rev', I got it." Donovan laughed and then lowered his voice. "But it's no big deal to have a secret or two, and don't worry; your little secret is safe with me. I can't say that I don't have a few of my own."

Their eyes caught one another's in a very different way, and the Minister could see that he had just had the conversation about the incident on the 18th tee. It was brief and indirect, even somewhat camouflaged, but another obvious invitation had been extended. Donovan had used an attempt at exposing knowledge of some common ground to offer support to his query, and the Minister wanted to deny the allegations of a relationship with Gemma and very clearly state his lack of interest in Donovan, but he thought it best to cut his losses and remain quiet.

The other men returned their attention to the table and conversation; they seemed to signal each other, in some way, and informed Donovan and the Minister that they were going down to the men's locker room to shower and change. Donovan spoke for the Minister and informed them that they would be right down to join them.

The Minister had been comfortable all afternoon, had a great round of golf with a great guy, and enjoyed the company of the other fellows, and really had not been shaken, or made to feel uncomfortable by the kiss. There was a part of him that thought he should have been, but he was not. But now, he felt uncomfortable and the awkwardness of the moment was heavy. Something inside him told him that there were other aspects of tradition in which these men were about to engage, and he felt as though he was being drafted into a club that he had no interest in joining.

There was no time for introspective reasoning at this point. He trusted in the fact that he had not released a vibe that in some way signaled a sexual interest in Donovan, and he could see that Donavan's motivation had nothing to do with that. His actions were not reactions to something he had seen in the Minister, they were simply proactive gestures that subtly stated who he really was.

"Hey Donovan, man I think I'm going to head back into town and prepare for tonight. I'll just shower back at the hotel." The Minister was cool, but a sharp eye could see that he was back-pedaling like Fred Flintstone attempting to stop his car with his feet. "I really appreciate the offer, but I have had too much fun today. I better get some work done so the folks that I speak to tonight won't be able to tell that I've been playing golf all day."

"You sure, Ed? They've got a dynamite facility here; whirlpool, sauna, massage, aroma-therapy, the works. You sure you're not interested?"

The same look was in his eyes that he had on the 18th tee. It was another clear offer. The other men had not gotten up yet. It was almost as if they were waiting on the Minister's response as well, employing a healthy amount of peer pressure.

"I'm sure; I really think I should get back."

The other men stood and excused themselves, thanking the Minister for the round and again showering him with accolades about his play and what a pleasure it was to meet him. They also extended invitations to him to join them on other occasions and to get in touch with them and they would gladly share complimentary tickets to their respective sporting events. The Minister stood and shook hands with them like men do, and reciprocated the sentiments they had graciously shared. He remained standing on purpose, to show Donovan that he was truly leaving. The move was subtle but clear. Before Donovan could get up, he thanked him for the invitation and told him what a wonderful time he had. For a split second, he thought about saying something about the kiss, but he just wanted to leave. Enough had been said.

Finally, Donovan stood and looked into the Minister's eyes, smiling and thanking him for coming and said only one thing, "It's all good."

The Minster could feel that there was quite a bit of weight in the phrase, and in someway, he was okay with it. It seemed to indicate that it was okay if his advance was not reciprocated; life would go on. But he did not feel the same respect for Donovan that he felt for Crawford, or even Jason. Donovan was living a painful lie that was involving and hurting his wife, and it seemed that he behaved in such a manner because his name and his finances gave him license.

"Thanks again, Donovan; and maybe we'll see you and Lydia tonight," the Minster said as he walked away.

"Oh yeah, Ed; it was my pleasure. When you get back to the hotel, why don't you stop by my suite and give Lydia all the details about tonight. I'm sure she's there. Hell, she's probably waiting for you." Donovan released a devilish chuckle as he turned and headed for the stairs, and his volume increased as he moved away.

The Minister stood there a while and tried not to think about the many things that were coming to haunt him, but he could not help it. He thought about the time he spent with Lydia in his office and how he thought he heard someone at the window. He wondered if that was Donovan and if it was, why he did nothing. That thought was dismissed and chalked up to paranoia, but there was something more than dangerous about the Davis', both of them, and the Minister was more than ready to steer clear.

CHAPTER 48

Gemma felt that a walk in the brisk evening air would do her some good. She needed to clear her head, and even though she knew that the night would fall quickly and that she was nearing her pickup time for her evening performance. She needed to feel the pulse and energy of the city. She needed to hear the bristling of leaves of the trees that stood in the concrete jungle. She needed to hear the car horns of impatient cab drivers who knew they would get no farther by blowing, but merely served some inner part of their being that found phallic masculinity in the gesture.

The sights and sounds of the city were a very particular medicine for her; it always had been. While some people sought peace and quiet to ease their troubled minds, Gemma found solace in the silence of noise. That was who she was, and if she did anything different, she would be denying herself a part of the spirit that had existed within her since childhood. She was *lights, camera, action,* and often lived impulsively and impatiently. Her grandmother always said that when she was born, *"she hit the ground runnin'; singin', dancin' and performin',"* and she would, most likely leave that way. Miss Hattie Lee had no idea how right she was.

She walked with a smile on her face, which properly portrayed the consistency of her character. It was not that she did not realize that there were serious aspects of life that warranted frowns and winces, but Gemma had never chosen to deal with those issues, often overlooking things that would later prove devastating. Even her best friend, Ivy would often get on her about not planning certain aspects of her life and wondering how she got herself into so many sticky situations.

Gemma was a shining star of talent that was placed on earth to simply shine and bring light to overcast faces and clouded hearts. With her hands in the pockets of her overcoat, she sauntered down Michigan

Avenue and thought about the Minister. She did not think so much about the sexual episodes that they shared, although they were the best that she had ever had; she thought about herself and what she believed she had done for him, and there was some part of her that made her proud of her actions.

It was a significant first in her life, one where she looked beyond herself, and personal desires and saw something past momentary bliss and carnal satisfaction. She had stopped, and helped to retrieve a falling star, placing it back into proper celestial alignment, and she commended herself for the will power to do so. She felt that she too, had reached a turning point in her life, and was ready to focus fully and completely on her career. Her lust would no longer be allowed to interrupt her again, and she had proven to herself that she had what it took to hold fast to the true desires of her heart, and not be swept away into the oblivion of fantasy. And it was at this time of triumphant personal discovery and strength, this time of realization and internal victory, this time of breakthrough and spiritual discernment, this pinnacle moment of insight that her life would change forever.

Stopping for a moment, Gemma gazed into the sky, noticing a uniquely beautiful crescent moon. The view was breathtaking and the darkening sky made a surreal canvas backdrop for the skyline in front of it. She had seen crescent moons in some of the most remote and romantic corners of the world and could not escape feeling like she had always been missing something. There was an especially different feeling this time. Maybe it was another breakthrough, as this was the first time she had enjoyed this unclouded view alone, without feeling lonely. Warmth like none before overcame her, a rejuvenating freedom of heart, soul, body and mind.

She never saw him coming, even with her senses fully alert and her mind sharp and her intuition cresting. He must have come out of a nearby alley, and before Gemma could react, she felt the sharpness of the blade penetrate her lower back. His large gloved hand smothered her as he pulled her back into the darkness of the alley from which he came. Of all the targets on the street that evening, he chose her for no particular reason. He was a member of the statistic that defines random violence, and Gemma had been inaugurated into a fraternity of victims. But no violence is random; it is always calculated and specific. She struggled to breathe as she tried to wrestle against him, but he was too strong. With her own strong legs, she tried to kick him but he had his legs wrapped around hers, rendering her nearly motionless. Now her wishes were different and her thoughts of personal congratulations on re-establishing a spiritual life were gone.

Gemma screamed the Minister's name within herself and against her assailant's hand, hoping someway that he would amazingly appear, as he had a few days prior, and save her. He did not, and her crazed attacker did not let up. She wanted desperately to speak, so that she could offer him whatever he wanted, and maybe he would release her. She would willingly give him all of her money, if that were what he wanted, or if he just wanted her to submit to a sex act, she was reluctantly willing. But it seemed that he had interest in neither. He wanted to hurt her and then kill her. His crime was one of violence and power, not sex. With the tip of the knife buried in the small of her back, Gemma could feel him writhing his nakedness against her. He wore no pants, stylish athletic shoes, a shirt and tie, leather gloves and a black cashmere overcoat. Again she wished that he would allow her to speak, so that she could negotiate with him, but the more she struggled against him, the tighter he held her.

Finally, with a loud moan she could feel that he was ejaculating, and she thought that it was over, but it was not. He then drove the length of the blade into her flesh. Gemma collapsed behind a dumpster, paralyzed by pain, fear and a lack of consciousness, bleeding and struggling to breathe, as her assailant watched. He walked to another dumpster in the alley and retrieved a briefcase. From it, he removed a pair of black dress shoes and gray slacks, and put them on. He put his athletic shoes, and the blade into the briefcase, tucked his shirt in nicely, adjusted his tie and smoothed his clothes. And then without another glance at his victim, he walked back onto the sidewalk, disappearing inconspicuously into the sea of people.

CHAPTER 49

The Minister had no intention of calling Lydia when he returned to the hotel. Another situation of ill substance was not what he was looking for. He was ready to prepare for his homily to Crawford's workshop participants, and he honestly, just wanted to go home. He had had enough of his own demons, and was ready to focus on his ministry. He thanked Gemma, in his heart, for what she had done; which was nothing more than open his eyes to some facts about his life that he had chosen not to face. Whatever had happened, he was glad about it. Even though he did not want to talk to Lydia, initially fearing his own relapse into lust, he felt that he could, and he knew that he would get his chance. He knew that she was out there somewhere waiting for him, and whatever the situation was between her and her husband, the Minister knew that he was in for unsolicited details.

Donovan had knocked him for a loop even though the Minister was a man who truly tried to understand the world, and the people in it. He was not surprised by much and did not hold prejudicial views against people even if he did not agree with their behavior, but Donovan and his friends were somewhat shocking. There was no admission, on anyone's part, that they were gay, or going to engage in homosexual activities in the locker room, but the Minister had intuition of his own; a spiritual intuition, and it was at that moment in the clubhouse restaurant that he remembered the words of his Uncle, the former pastor of the church where he was now pastor, when he admonished him to stay away from anything that even looked sinful. He remembered a sermon he preached in which he used a Biblical quote that said to, "*Shun the very appearance of evil,*" and he felt that something evil was about to transpire.

When the Minister finally reached the security of his hotel suite, he felt an enigmatic sense of relief. It was almost as if he was on the run from the devil, and he needed to hide out and regroup. He thought of the calls he needed to make and saw that his message indicator light was blinking, but he followed through with his most pressing desire. He fell on his knees and prayed. He felt as though he had not sincerely done that in quite a long time and he needed to reintroduce himself to the benefits of prayer that he so often preached about. He prayed for his family, his church, his relationships, his strengths, his weaknesses, and he prayed for forgiveness. He knew that he had come to Chicago without the most Godly of intentions, and for that he was sorry. He felt refreshed and re-energized when he stood, like a burden had been lifted from him. He felt that he could see with renewed vision and that there was a new sense of hope in his heart, and then he heard the knock on his door.

Quietly looking out the peephole, he saw Lydia, and he salivated. The Minister fought with himself as he allowed her in. She was exceptionally beautiful, this time; there was something about her that captivated him more than the times he had seen her before. He looked down at her feet and noticed her recent pedicure, as she walked in. Her legs glistened with herbal oils that had been massaged into her fair skin. His eyes made their way up to her hands, and he could see that she had a manicure to match. He tried to control his mind, knowing that a pampered and prepared woman of beauty was one of the very things that tickled the most erogenous parts of his being. He thought of the skilled hands that had massaged her supple skin and anointed her most private regions with sensual oils, and mentally replaced them with his own.

"How was the round?"

The Minister caught her recognizable fragrance as she brushed by him. That was another one of his issues; he often remembered his most passionate sexual escapades based on the fragrance the woman was wearing. He did not know if Lydia knew that or if it was coincidental. If she he did, that was just another erotic ingredient to the bubbling mixture in his mind, that was driving him crazy.

"The course was spectacular. I can't thank Donovan enough for inviting me. It was an absolutely marvelous day; I wouldn't change a thing."

"Really?" Lydia walked toward him as she spoke, seeming like she was suspect, in some way, of his statement.

"Really; everything was great," he said. There was a brief moment of silence.

"Ed, why have you been avoiding me?" She touched his shoulder as she moved closer to him. He could feel something rising inside him, and he was a bit perplexed because he thought that he had made a breakthrough the night before. He struggled against himself.

"Lydia, Donovan is finished with his round also, and I'm sure he'll be coming up right behind me, so maybe you shouldn't be here," he said as coolly as he could.

He said that more for his own sake than for Lydia's. Her presence was successfully gnawing at him, chipping away at his righteous foundation.

"Donovan won't be here for hours, and you know it," she said.

"And how, and why would I know that?"

"He's with the guys, and the guys have things to do, with each other, before they go home to their wives."

The Minister did his best to look as far ahead of the developing situation as he could, and he could see that he and Lydia were moving toward a familiar place. She paced around him like a purring cat rubbing its tail against his leg. He knew that this was the way that she behaved when there was something that troubled her, and she translated her lack of ability to express the depths of her heart into episodes of lust and meaningless passion. He had given in to her advances and his own desire before, without hesitation, but this time he tried to be careful about the way he would respond to her, especially considering what he suspected about Donovan.

"Well, I still don't think it's that great an idea for you to be here," the Minister said.

"What are you afraid of, Ed? I thought you liked me; I thought we were developing a very special relationship, where only you and I could share intimate moments, and no one else would know. Are you afraid of what's under my skirt? I saw you looking when I came in the door, and that's exactly what I wanted you to do. This is all for you; I've been preparing for you all day, since you guys left this morning. Are you afraid that you will do something you don't think you should? Well, I'm here and it's okay. It really is. This has nothing to do with Angie or Donovan, and you'll never have to worry about me telling either of them, if that's what you're worried about. It's just you and me and that's all that matters. What happens here stays here, just like what happened in your office."

He could feel himself weakening as he looked at her legs, and he was most definitely afraid of what was under her skirt, not because of Angie or Donovan or any repercussions, but simply because he knew enough about what was under there to want her like a madman. The fact that she brought up the escapades in his office made beads of sweat form on his brow, and he loved the fact that she still had vivid memories. She was doing and saying the exact things that tore at his soul, and he could feel the thoughtless man in his pants stiffening, trying to say the things his mouth would not. His renewed inner man was losing a battle of will in the fight against carnal lust. He searched himself as quickly as he could to try to find something to hold onto; something that might momentarily halt his desires. He looked within because there were no offers of restraint coming from the woman who stared into his face. He looked away from her, hoping that the chair at which he stared might offer help with his dilemma.

"There's nothing to worry about with him. He doesn't want me, and he hasn't wanted me in years. Didn't you find that out, today?"

She looked down momentarily to find some resolve in her demeanor; there was obvious pain in her countenance, but Lydia looked through it, and directly into his eyes.

"You mean to tell me that a man with your intelligence could not figure out what the little boys club is all about. I'm sure you were invited to participate, and the fact that he's there and you're here let's me know that that's not what you're about. So, why can't we just go from here? There is not a more perfect situation, is there?"

The Minister moved away from her and sat in the lounging chair at the foot of the bed, the very one he had just knelt before, praying for strength and redemption. It was not the smartest move, in terms of true escape, because it was not long before she went to him, raised her skirt and straddled him. He felt intoxicated as he placed his hands on her thighs, fighting himself and losing the battle against rubbing and touching her. She was milky soft and he could feel a light perspiration on her body. It was anticipation, and it only stirred her scent, sending him to another place in his mind. Thoughts of Gemma were gone; they had left along with the breakthrough. It was Lydia's turn again. She planted her mouth on his as she continued to grind her panty-less crotch against his. He wanted to do nothing more than to unzip his pants and release his stiffness inside her. Her bottom felt like two heated silk pillows in his hands, and he could feel her erotic wetness seeping through his pants. Again a fleeting moment of righteousness crept in the Minister's heart just before he went for his belt buckle, and this time he was determined to take hold to it.

"Stop, Lydia!" He shouted at the top of his lungs and threw her onto the floor. The burst of energy even startled a pigeon that had alighted just outside the window and watched the hungry lovers play. She looked at him with crazed eyes, her chest quickly rising and falling as she panted, and then she broke into tears. She jumped up and ran for the door. The Minister jumped up and ran right behind her; overtaking her just enough to slam his hand against the door before she could open it and escape. He had let her go before, but this time he would not.

"Lydia, I'm sorry," he said as he picked her up after she fell against the door, then crumbled to the floor.

He placed his hands on her shoulders after he straightened out her clothing, and looked at her with very different eyes; the true eyes of a changed man.

"I can't. I can't do this to you or me, and in your heart, I know this is not what you want. Now tell me what's wrong because I'm ready to listen; I'm ready to try to help you."

She fell into his arms and cried for quite a while. It was as if she had been holding her tears behind an emotional dam that had built, over years of grief. The Minister could hear the pain of relief and release in her wailing, and he did not stop her. He knew that whatever was inside her needed to come out, and as gratifying as the sex was, it only would have only made things worse.

After she was somewhat composed, the Minister took her by the hand and led her to the table in the living room area of the suite. Lydia told him everything, even more than Yavonne told Ivy, over margaritas. She told him about how she found it strange when they first met that he was so close to several of his male friends but she dismissed thoughts of it anything outside normalcy until she noticed him hugging one of them and something was strange about their contact. She could not put her finger on it at the time and did not know whether it was that they held their embrace too long or that their hands in some way, seemed out of place. But whatever it was, she could sense that there was more to it than a simple hug. She had written it off, as there were so many other fairytale aspects of their relationship on which to focus.

Lydia was married to a celebrity athlete, and the fringe benefits that came with that were without comprehension or description. Even her most outlandish wishes and dreams were made realities, sometimes before she could even complete the thought. So thoughts of her husband's inordinate friendships were quickly abolished. Besides, he was not like any other jock she had known.

He was handsome and highly intelligent, and could have chosen any career and any woman, and she was still flattered that he had chosen her.

It had begun rather innocently, as far as she knew. The various homes that they had lived in over the years had always been filled with

Donovan's friends, many of whom were professional athletes, celebrities, and other entertainment people. It was part of the package, and with it privacy became foreign, but she learned to tolerate the traffic. They had become part of an elite crowd of modern fame, and that was something that she and her family had planned for her, and she had learned how to functionally accept her role. She was a well trained Celebrity Princess much like Angie, and when she got tired of entertaining, she simply went to bed or retired to another part of their large home, which always seemed full. The guests were allowed to stay as long as they liked, and with plenty amenities, they usually continued to entertain themselves for quite a while before going home, if they went home at all. She never suspected anything strange until the night she walked in on the sight she would never forget.

The weekends at the Davis' house were all the same; every evening, they entertained friends, and friends of friends until the sun came up, but on this particular night, everybody did not go home. One of Donovan's friends stayed a bit longer than usual. After numerous drinks in their entertainment room, which was furnished for ultimate comfort, equipped with an unbelievable sound system, two pool tables, several arcade style video games and three large screen televisions, the crowd finally thinned and Lydia said "goodnight" to her husband and his lone friend. She was not sure if she had seen him before, but that was nothing new. It seemed that every weekend since they had gotten married, new people were brought into their lives. For all she knew, he could have been another ball player, even though he did not seem as large as the other players. *"Maybe he's the kicker,"* she remembered thinking to herself as she made her way up the stairs.

From her bedroom window, she noticed that the men had decided to take a swim, and instead of her continuing with her preparations for bed, something made Lydia go to the huge sliding glass window of her bedroom, that overlooked the rear portions of their estate, and watch. She watched them swim, and very playfully touch each other, with obvious apprehension about the noise. They whispered to one another, about what, she would never know. But without hearing, her other senses had become sensitively keen, and watching the frolicsome conversation between her husband and the *kicker* she was able to interpret a meaning beyond two guys going for an evening swim. She moved away from the window at the initial shock of what she suspected, but something would not allow her to take her eyes away from the activity that stirred the water.

Lydia took a seat on the edge of her bed, tried to slow her racing heart, and watched the performance unfold. It began with the frolicsome play turning into exploratory hands with which the men began to caress and stroke each other. Her mouth dropped when she saw them kiss with a passion that she had not seen in her husband, at least not with her. He was a great lover and she had never been dissatisfied, but she could see that there had been something in Donovan that had been held from her; a craving that seemed to more than satisfyingly charge him. She watched their tongues play like two children sharing a melting soft serve ice cream cone on a sweltering summer day. After the kiss, the men swam away from one another, and it was then that she wanted to turn away, hoping in her heart that the show was over, but she was held in position by a force greater than herself.

Within seconds the men swam to a position near the steps of the pool, and back into each other's arms, but this time they were absent any swim attire. She watched them play, and it was like nothing she had ever seen before. They touched, caressed, kissed, stroked, fondled, and toyed with each other before the *kicker* finally crouched near the steps of the pool, holding onto the rail for stability. Donovan positioned himself behind him, and although he might have looked like he was performing a version of the *Heimlich maneuver*, Lydia could clearly see that the man was not choking. She watched them have sex twice that night.

When Donovan finally came to bed, he quietly entered the room, as usual and headed to the shower. For some reason, Lydia was frozen with fear and shock, and she could not say or do anything. Her mind raced as she felt his large body enter the bed, making it bounce dramatically. He leaned over and kissed her on the temple, thinking that she was fast asleep, turned over and began snoring almost immediately. Lydia lay there in a state of near catalepsy until morning, wondering where she had gone wrong and why she had never known that this part of her husband existed.

The Minister listened intently, as she spoke. Often she looked out the window or at the floor, but almost never into his eyes. He wanted to stop her and ask if she needed something to eat or drink, but he could see that she was engaged in a free flow of all that was inside her, and he was not about to stop her. He could only think of her obvious pain, which made him consider the pain that he knew he had often caused.

Her grievous discourse was another stepping stone in his redemptive deliverance. His thoughts of her sexuality were decreasing as she spoke, and he was beginning to better understand her needs beyond meaningless fornication.

Lydia continued to tell the Minister story after story about times that she found her husband engaging in sexual exploits with men, until he finally interrupted her and asked why they were still together.

315

"First he promised me that he would stop, but he wouldn't," she said as she stared out into the evening light. "I kick myself everyday for not doing something the first night I saw him. There were so many things I wanted to do but I was frozen and couldn't move, and couldn't bring myself to even talk about it. But I think what bothered me most was that when I finally confronted him about it, he acted like it was nothing. He didn't seem to even care that I knew, by that point. He said it was just *sex* and that it didn't mean anything, and that I shouldn't worry about it, and that he always wore a condom, and a whole bunch of other *BS* that I should have taken to the judge and sued the hell out of him for."

"Why didn't you?" There was a long pause before Lydia answered.

"Because I loved him, at least I thought I did" she said. "I still think I love him, sometimes. But I hate what he does and I hate what he did. I was a fool for not leaving back then, and now I'm a fool because I have nothing of my own, and he doesn't have jack to give me." She shamefully looked to the floor.

"What do you mean by that?"

"I mean exactly what I said. He's screwed away over 250 million dollars in some kind of *sure thing* investment deal. I want to kill myself every time I think about what he doesn't think I know. But I almost don't give a damn anymore. I'm just beat."

"So is that why you're so torn up inside, and why you came at me like you did when we first met in my office?" The Minister brought her eyes to his.

"I'm torn up for a lot of reasons, Ed, and I came at you that way in your office because I saw something in your eyes that told me that I could. I knew that you would hold me and caress me and make me feel like a woman, and beyond that, you'd let me make you feel like a man."

"There are probably plenty of men that would be more than willing to do that. You're a beautiful woman and I'm sure I'm not the only man you drive crazy when you walk into a room." He had hoped his comment might bring a smile; it did not.

"Well if I'm so beautiful, why is my husband a fucking fag?"

The Minister searched for an appropriate answer that would place things in a helpful perspective for her; he could not. They both stared out the window for several minutes without saying a word. Luckily, she started speaking again, as the Minister still had not yet formulated his response to her last statement.

"I'm sorry; I shouldn't have said that," she said, as she looked away, her eyes still swollen with tears, but still extraordinarily gorgeous.

"It's okay; say what you feel, Lydia." He brushed a stray hair lightly out of her face.

"I guess the thing that bothers me most is that I saw something that first night that I had not seen before. I saw passion for someone and something else that I thought should have been for me, and there was nothing that I could do about it. I had spent years being what I thought he wanted me to be, and then looking out my bedroom window, of all places, I discover that I cannot be, or give him what he truly wants. I was jealous and simply outdone, and I was pissed that someone else had the strength to come in and take from me, the man I had worked so hard to get. And instead of leaving him, I tried harder and harder to please him, allowing him to keep his side satisfaction in exchange for the storybook life that we've led in the media, and now it's about to all crumble in front of my eyes."

"What do you mean?"

"Well, what I thought would never happen has happened, and apparently, has been happening without my knowledge. He's in love with a man, and some magazine has files full of career ending photos and records of his overseas financial dealings that document their involvement."

"What?" The Minister's shock was obvious, even though he did his best to maintain his calm. Despite the incident with Donovan on the 18th tee, he never in his wildest imagination thought that he would be having this conversation with Lydia.

"Yes, they have even bought a ranch somewhere in upstate New York."

"And how do you know all of this now?"

"He finally told me himself and tried to brainwash me into believing that I should accept and deal with it. He told me how much he loved me, and how he needed me, and how this was something he just needed to get a grasp on and that our marriage would not suffer behind it. He made me start seeing a psychiatrist who prescribed a bunch of medications I can't pronounce and several spa treatments, to supposedly help me deal with the stress of celebrity life. I don't know what Donovan told him about our lives, and at that point, it really didn't matter. I guess it wouldn't really matter now either, but I know I just can't take it anymore. I don't know what to do or where to go, and I have never spoken to anyone about anything, not even Angie.

"Some women would probably hear my story and think it's easy to mend, and they'd probably have a ready-made solution for all of my problems, but no one can understand the emotional torment that I've been in for the last few years. I've had to smile for the camera everyday and cry myself to sleep every night. Donovan has moved farther and farther away from me and closer and closer to his lover, and with this big lawsuit in our face, he stands to lose out on probably, all of his endorsement contracts."

"Well wouldn't you be okay financially if you divorced him?" The Minister searched for positive options.

"His agent forced a *pre-nup* on me that leaves me virtually penniless, and like I said, there's nothing really to give." After a few moments, Lydia stood up and sighed deeply.

"I'm going to leave now, Ed. I'm sure Donovan will be coming back soon. Can we come hear you speak tonight?"

Her voice carried a sympathetic longing that tugged on the Minister's compassion. It was as if speaking to him that evening had released her from the internal bondage of secrecy, and she had not been cured, but certainly helped. There was definitely more, but she abruptly halted her discourse, having said all she was going to say.

"Of course," he replied.

The Minister followed Lydia to the door and watched her solemnly. When they got there, she turned around and thanked him for whatever he had done for her. She was not entirely sure why she had exposed the depths of her heart to him but she thanked him for whatever the catalyst was to her release, and then she put her arms around his neck and kissed him deeply. He responded accordingly, but had not expected her to go to such a degree. As he opened his mouth slightly, her tongue moved in slowly as if his heat was feeding her. Finally she released him and looked in his eyes without a word, opened the door, and left. He stood there for a moment trying to digest all that had happened that day, and all that Lydia had just said and done.

There were many things that the Minister did not understand, and he was not sure if he even wanted to try. He wished that he had never engaged her when they first met, but that had been the story of his adult life with women. He had been so sexually charged that very often, he was not discriminating enough to save himself from the inevitable trauma that the relationships he pursued would later bring.

He thanked God for Angie and often wondered how he was able to secure such an undeserved jewel of a wife. He closed his eyes and briefly whispered a prayer of thanks for her, and one of mercy for Lydia. The information she shared was so unbelievable that the Minister grappled with its authenticity.

Donovan's escapades defied reality, and although he believed Lydia, he struggled, with reconciling her stories against his own perceptions of the man. But soon, he would receive confirmation from one of the most unlikely sources.

With his back against the door, he sighed heavily with his eyes closed; feeling some sense of relief and closure, but the worst of his troubles had not yet come full circle. They would wait for him, patiently and meet him at home, like troubles always do.

CHAPTER 50

He truly did not expect them and was somewhat surprised to see that the couple actually did make their way to the large church where Crawford was conducting his workshop and the Minister was speaking. They actually arrived before the Minister, took their seats and were privy to listen to some of the most beautiful and soul stirring gospel music they had ever heard. Lydia was on her feet, waving and clapping her hands to the soulful beats, with tears running down her cheeks. She had been touched all right, but by more than the music she heard. Her emotional display was more a continued outpouring from her earlier conversation with the Minister. It was another stretch toward the thread that she sought to cleanse her soul.

The music was phenomenal. Crawford however, was not playing; he was too grand for that as the workshop clinician. Instead, he gave direction to the choir and band, in his most colorful and eclectic manner. Before long, the entire crowd was on its feet shouting and dancing like their shoes were on fire. Even Donovan stood and waved his hands a time or two, his large muscular body shadowing the smaller people around him. There were a few people who recognized him but their focus was not on celebrity, this night; Crawford and his cast held the spotlight, until he introduced his very special guest speaker.

When the Minister came onto the dais, the crowd again went wild, as his entrance was on the heels of a soulful gospel tune that again had the people on their feet. He picked up the tune, carried it to another level and then preached like never before. It seemed that an unfilled vial in his soul that had long been capped, was now opened, and he allowed him self to be filled with a portion of Spirit that had long been absent from his life. It was as though he were preaching to himself, words that healed him. When he finished, the crowd congratulated him for being dynamic and uniquely charismatic, as always, but even without the accolades, he knew that there was something different about this sermon.

It had the same feeling as his first, the trial sermon as it was traditionally called. He had preached with a renewed zeal and spiritual power. It had been a long time since he felt that charge within himself, and for that he was thankful.

Everything was normal until Lydia and Donovan came up, and wanted to meet Crawford. They had nothing but great things to say about him, as they listened to him from a distance, but when they finally made their way through the crowd and Crawford turned around to face the couple, both men were speechless. The recognizably awkward few seconds of silence left the Minister and Lydia clueless, but it grabbed Donovan and Crawford by the throats, until Crawford broke the silence.

"Oh wow, Pastor, you didn't tell me that you were bringing celebrities with you tonight. Had I known that, I would have put on my good suit," he said laughingly to the group.

Crawford of course was outrageously dressed to the T in a black patent leather suit with a crocodile print pattern and a bright lime green silk shirt that had an over sized collar and cuffs. His effervescent reptile skin shoes seemed to change colors depending on the angle viewed, and were so bright and reflective that they could have been easily used as roadway signals.

"Your music was magnificent, and it always is every time I've come to the church." Lydia leaned in, extending her hand.

"Thank you; I'm glad you enjoyed it. I thought I'd seen you at the church, but I don't think I've seen your husband here. Have you been to Calvary?" Crawford's question was heavy with sarcastic undertow, and his eyes taunted the linebacker.

"Well not yet, buddy, but I'm sure I'll get there one of these days," Donovan answered.

"Well, I'll look forward to it."

It was not long before the Minister was distracted from the immediate conversation as people from all over the building made their way to him to thank him for coming, express their enjoyment of his sermon and to just be next to him. Donovan took notice of his celebrity in this forum and found it very interesting. It was an arena with which he was unfamiliar, as it had not been a part of his life for a long time. This was where the Minister was a star, and everyone, especially women, magnetically flocked to him. Lydia recognized it as well, and casually attached herself to him as he moved through the crowd. It was at this time that she and the Minister had moved far enough away from Crawford and Donovan for them to have a brief conversation, and true reunion that no one else was to hear.

"*Triple D*," Crawford said as he smiled and looked Donovan up and down.

"What's up, *Centipede*. It's been a long time."

"I see you've been hiding out in matrimony, huh?" Crawford was known for the brutality of his honesty. Donovan responded only with a laugh.

"Haven't heard from you in quite a while," Donovan said as he stood back displaying himself with a smile.

"And you're not going to hear from me anytime soon. I told you that I was finished and out of the game."

"Centipede, out of the game? No way; I know I haven't seen you in forever, but you look like you're still in the game to me," Donovan said. He took notice of Crawford's outfit, especially his eye-grabbing shoes.

"Well, don't let the look trick you." Crawford spoke out of the side of his smile as he continued to wave and blow kisses to people as they exited. "I have no more interest in the life, and seeing you does nothing more for me than seeing anyone else. I mean it's great to see you, D, but if you were thinking anything else, I'm going to have to disappoint you tonight, baby."

"Okay, Centipede; no need to get your panties in a bunch. Congratulations on your new life, but you still know how to get in touch with me, don't you?" Donovan smiled as he noticed Crawford's grin of consent.

Crawford used all the will power he could muster to say what he did to Donovan, as the sheer sight of him made him salivate with memories of several episodes long ago. He was not really shocked that he was married because he had always known him as a closet freak, and he understood that he had an image to maintain. But he was shocked that the world was so small that he and his wife, or whatever she was, showed up in Chicago at his music workshop, with the Minister.

Triple D and Centipede had met at an underground party where a lot of "double-lived" male celebrities expressed themselves freely. Once Donovan had had a piece of him, Crawford became a celebrity in his own right, dealing with quite a few of Donovan's secret friends who were soon hooked on the ways of the *Centipede*. Crawford had been equally hooked on Donovan's attributes. He was called *Triple D* for his rare ability to climax three times in a row, giving his lovers pleasure beyond compare.

This sensual benefit was another that Lydia had never known and probably never would.

Out of the corner of his eye, the Minister noticed Crawford and Donovan's conversation. It did not take much to figure out that there was something between them, even without hearing a word. He saw hidden giggles and sneers, and there was a very familiar smile on Donovan's face every time he looked at Crawford who in turn, seemed to almost never look directly at him.

Suddenly things began to come together, and the unbelievable story that Lydia told began to take new meaning. He thought about the kiss and the stressed invitation, and now he saw a conversation between the two men, and there was just something that intuitively clicked, far beyond the simple complexities of a man being gay. He glanced at Lydia and could see pain beneath her layers of polished beauty, and it tugged at his compassion.

He made his way back to Donovan and Crawford, with Lydia in nearby tow, to say his good byes. Donovan expressed his somewhat transparent gratefulness for having met Crawford, and also gave him an obvious eye, and Lydia shared her accolades as well. She did her best to ignore her husband, hiding her discomfort within her congeniality.

"Thank you so much coming, and I hope you enjoyed it," Crawford said to Lydia and Donovan as he bowed slightly before them. "I'll call you, Pastor," were his final words before strutting away.

The Minister knew what Crawford meant, and that there was probably some aspect of the conversation between him and Donovan that he wanted to share. The only thing the Minister wanted to do was to tell Crawford that a call was not necessary. As they walked out of the auditorium, each with an awkward need to say something, the Minister only thought more of going home.

"So Ed, can we take you out to dinner?" Lydia offered. She was trying to hold on to him for as long as she could.

"Yeah, how 'bout it Reverend? After that powerful preaching, I'm sure you've worked up an appetite," Donovan chimed in.

"No, I think I'm just going to go back to the hotel and rest. Thank you both, though."

"Your plane doesn't leave until Sunday morning, right?" Donovan asked.

"Right."

"Well how 'bout another round of golf? The guys and I are playing at the same place tomorrow."

"Actually Donovan, I think I'm going to see if I can get a flight out tomorrow some time. Something tells me I need to get home."

"Well I understand the feeling, and if you feel it inside, you'd better go with what you feel. Who knows what's waiting for you at home?"

The Minister could see the disappointment on Lydia's face, even though she tried to hide it from her husband. There was more that she needed and wanted to say, but the Minister had seen and heard enough.

As they stood outside with the Minister waiting for the car that had been arranged for him, he expressed his thanks to them both for coming and to Donovan for the golf invitation. When the car rolled up, he hugged them each, but when he hugged Lydia she whispered into his ear, "Please don't leave me tonight." But it was too late; the Minister had already gone to a different place in his mind and heart. He had already gone home.

Lydia watched the car turn out of the driveway and disappear down the street. All smiles faded away and she turned her attention to her husband.

"So I take it you know Crawford?" She continued to look into the distance where the Minister's car once was. She was determined not to let things slip away without being addressed anymore. Maybe that had been her biggest mistake, but now it really did not matter.

"Why would you say that?"

"Donovan, please; we're past that aren't we? There's no need to lie; I could see you guys talking, and it was obvious that this was not the first time you two had met. So c'mon, we can keep it real."

"That was a long time ago, baby; a long time ago." He never looked at Lydia, continuing to stare into the distance. After a few silent moments, she slipped her arm around his, and they walked to their vehicle.

"I want to go home," were the first words she said as they drove.

"I honestly don't even know why you came, Lyd."

"I did what I came to do, and now I want to go home." She stared out the window and watched the road go by.

"No problem, I can have you on the first plane out of here, in the morning, if that's what you want," Donovan said.

"That's what I want."

CHAPTER 51

Gemma's nearly dead body was not found until Saturday morning by a trash collection crew. Normally they did not work on Saturday's but due to the remodeling of a nearby office building, they had been called out to haul away an unsightly tonnage of trash that was beginning to block the alley where Gemma had been snatched away, attacked and left to die. It was miraculous that she had made it through the night with such serious injuries, and her struggle to live would have been all for naught had one of the trash workers not heard her ringing cell phone. It was Jason; he had been trying to call her all night.

The show had gone on with her understudy, but he had been searching for her all evening long. That was his job; he was expected to know where everyone was and make sure that they were where they were supposed to be when they were supposed to be there. But she was more than his job; she was his friend. He had even come to her hotel where she had last been seen, but no one had paid any closer attention to her activity than any other time, and no specific information about her whereabouts could be obtained.

The paramedics worked frantically to save Gemma; her pulse was sporadic and her respiration faint. The police had been notified soon after the ambulance had arrived at the crime scene, and the officers worked diligently to collect scarce evidence. It was their job to notify her next of kin, but they had not made a positive identification yet, and that was not their immediate priority. She flat lined twice, in the ambulance. When she arrived at the hospital, the doctors immediately began working on the victim without any thought of her identity. But one of the nurses recognized Gemma's unblemished face from the play she had seen the week before, and soon made her way to the nearest phone, calling the theater to inform them that they had their star, and that she was barely hanging on to life. The doctor's worked furiously to save her, but despite their efforts, she slipped into a coma. Only time would tell; and time was not on her side.

The nurse had not been motivated by the need to notify Gemma's next of kin, instead she wanted to be the one who might receive some accolade for breaking a very important news story to the press. It was not the press that immediately showed up; Jason led the way, with several cast members and the director, to the hospital to find the star for whom he held the utmost admiration in the Intensive Care Unit, and near death.

He could not believe his eyes when he saw her. It was not that she looked so bad; her face was barely even bruised. It was that he was seeing her in a position so foreign to her character. She was a live wire, full of passion and electricity, and now she was still and silent. Her fire had been cooled to such a degree that there was barely a flicker of hope to light the darkening skies. He, and all those who came with him to see her, left broken hearted, feeling cheated of their happiness by the brutal circumstances of life.

CHAPTER 52

The drive up to *One Larke Ellen Circle*, took novel meaning for the Minister, this time. He had been away many times before, and had been involved several secret affairs without a true sense of conscience or consequence, and had come home to resume a life of normalcy, absent of any semblance of remorse, but something had changed him. This time something was different and he could feel it. He was looking at very familiar sites with very different eyes now, and the things that he saw spoke to his heart in a way that his loins did not comprehend.

The vibrant color of the flowers in the courtyard had new significance. They were flowers that he and Angie planted years ago, and color that was once faded, was now bright again. The light breeze made them sensitively sway, and gently carry their essence to a freshly reawakened place in his heart. He was a new man, he thought, or at least there was an igniting spark of righteousness within him. That spark was guiding his inner man to a place that he could sincerely call home.

He glanced over at Brown, who was at his post, on time and at his beck and call. He had to smile to himself, seeing the subtle, but forced disappointment on Brown's face. It was obvious that he wanted his feelings noticed, and the Minister knew exactly what the look was all about; he had let the air right out of Brown's plans for Sunday service. Since the Minister was going to be out of town, Brown had been scheduled to preach, and he had rehearsed his show since the day he found out that he was leaving. The Minister also knew how much he was looking forward to a nice check from the church and an offering from the congregation, guaranteed to fatten his wallet.

He had already gone as far as to choose the solos that would precede and close out his sermon, and had made his wardrobe selections with meticulous care. He had planned to wear a light blue, pin-striped suit and two toned silk shirt and tie set; his cuff links would match the gaudy, gold nugget bracelet that he wore on his right wrist, and his shiny blue, square toe "gators" were the shoes that were to set the whole outfit off. When he sat in the pulpit, his pant leg would rise to expose his nylon socks that had his initials embroidered on the outer ankle. The Minister's early return had spoiled his plans.

"Well Pastor, here we are, back at the *Ponderosa*," Brown said as he pulled the bags out of the trunk. "I know you're glad to be home, especially early, on a beautiful Saturday like this. Maybe you can get a few holes in at the golf course."

"No; not today, Henry. I heard this house calling me all the way from Chicago, telling me to get my tail in it and sit down, so that's exactly what I'm going to do."

"I heard that, Pastor. I know you'll be glad to get some rest, and I'm sure it's much needed," Brown said smiling.

The Minister did not know whether or not he was insinuating that he knew or suspected something about his Chicago trip, but instead of pursuing it he simply let it go. Brown was free to think whatever he desired, as the Minister sought the comfort of the truth within his heart.

"Oh thank you, man. I don't know what I'd do without you, 'Br' Brown'." The Minister grabbed the small over night bag that he was about to leave in the car until Brown brought it to his attention.

"Oh well, you know I'm here to support my pastor, and whatever you need, I'm there. Whatever you need," Brown repeated, "I'll handle it for you. If you need me to teach or preach, or anything, you know you can count on me."

The Minister could see that Brown was making a concerted effort to both, show his disappointment and make a charitable request, with his twisted smile, so he decided to give him what he knew he wanted. It was almost like allowing a child to have the toy they had saved all their Christmas gift money to purchase. It was also a matter of church politics and political correctness. Though Brown might not ever say, the Minister knew that if he were not allowed to see his desires to fruition, he would hold an unhealthy grudge that would be more of a problem than it was worth. The Minister also knew that he had much more important issues with which to deal, and having to see Brown's sulking face week after week was not going to help his efforts in any way.

"Well Henry, there is something I probably need you to do for me, and I hope it's not too much."

"Oh, what? Whatever it is Pastor, you know I'll take care of it," Brown interrupted. His fingers were crossed behind his back.

"If it's not too much, I still want you to preach on Sunday. I kind of had a lot going on this week and I didn't really focus on home, so if you wouldn't mind, I'd like you to go ahead and handle it. I know the folks haven't heard you in a while, and I'm sure they want to hear from my right hand man." The Minister used his confident and embracing smile, and placed his hand on Brown's shoulder.

"Well," Brown said slowly, "I guess I could throw something together. You know I've been kind of busy here too, and I was kind of glad you were back to preach. You know, I have been so involved in this local Minister's Seminar that I really haven't had a chance to get myself together, but if my Pastor needs me, I'm there."

"Well if it's too much, don't worry about it; I can get someone—"

"Oh no, no, no, I got it," Brown jumped in before the Minister could even finish.

"Good, I knew I could depend on you," the Minister said, knowing that he had just made Brown's day.

"Okay Pastor, that's fine. Let me get on out of here so I can start working on something. You know I need to give myself to study for a while." Brown could not hold back his ear-to-ear smile, as he moved quickly to the front door with the Ministers bags.

"Thanks, Henry," the Minister said, knowing that Brown was probably not on his way to study at all, but probably on his way home to get on the phone and continue to invite his supporters, and anyone else who might help fill up the church sanctuary, and shout an Amen or two, in his direction. He also knew that there was no Minster's Seminar in town.

It did not matter to the Minister. He knew that Brown really had very few supporters, and most of the parishioner's knew of his opportunistic personality. He was one who sought to create moments of attention as often as he could, and his escapades never took away from the Minister's powerful draw. He could turn flips while juggling three baby pigs in one hand, and flying a kite with the other, and his audience would leave him, if the Minister walked into the room. Brown had never been, and never would be a threat to his confidence.

He entered the empty house, knowing that Angie and the children would not be at home. It was Saturday, and Angie still had chauffeur duty for their various activities, and unlike most weekends when they shared the load, she had to handle it alone. She would not be home for a while and that was fine with him. He knew that he needed time to himself before he greeted the family, so after he put his bags down, he made his way to his study.

There was something comforting and secure about that room. It was a place that he always had to visit alone to know that he was home. He sat behind his large desk, noticing that nothing had been moved or displaced, at least not to his knowledge. Even Tila, the housekeeper, had been instructed to only vacuum and dust, and never touch anything on the Minister's desk. And no one dared open his drawers, where many disjointed clues to his secrets were secured.

He sat looking at a picture of his family, and he knew that there were things that he needed to express to them, to his children, to Angie, to Lydia, and even to Alex, for that matter, but he knew there was a stone in his heart that had often blocked his ability to verbalize his feelings. He spoke most candidly with his pen.

He removed his journal from his top, right drawer, and placed it on the desk. With his hands clasped before him, he glanced again at the family portrait immediately before him, and then at some other photos he had lying in the open drawer, and then he shut his eyes. The Minister allowed his mind to flow freely with thoughts that ranged from past to present, but rarely did his cognition wander into the future. He thought about the plethora of nameless faces and shapes that occupied the most hidden and guarded places in his psyche, and he released them, something he had never done before. They were free to escape his memory, as he decided to no longer hold them captive for an occasional fantasy. Finally he opened his journal and began to write. This time, it was a familiar passage from the book of Ecclesiastes.

To every thing there is a season, and a time to every purpose under the heaven:

A time to be born, and a time to die; a time to plant, and a time to pluck up that which is planted;

A time to kill, and a time to heal; a time to break down, and a time to build ;

A time to weep, and a time to laugh; a time to mourn, and a time to dance;

A time to cast away stones, and a time to gather stones together; a time to embrace, and a time to refrain from embracing;

A time to get, and a time to lose; a time to keep, and a time to cast away;

A time to rend, and a time to sew; a time to keep silence, and a time to speak;

A time to love, and a time to hate; a time of war, and a time of peace.

The Minister closed the journal after writing the passage, feeling in is heart that he had completed a season of his life, but knowing that there was still much more to come from his pen. He inhaled and exhaled slowly feeling in some way, transformed and renewed, but he neglected to attend to the fact that transformation is rarely complete without tragedy, and in most cases, tragedy is its catalyst. His tragedy was all around him without his knowledge, as it waits for all humanity, and at that very moment, the shrill of his ringing cell phone cut deep into his solitude, bringing him into submission to the rules of the universe.

"Ed!" Angie's voice screeched with shock.

"Yeah, baby; what's wrong? Are you and the kids all right?"

"No," she yelled over the background noise. "We've been in a terrible accident. You need to come home right away!" She was nearing hysteria. "Oh God!" She screamed again.

"Baby, calm down; I *am* home. Where are you? What happened?"

"Just come down to the hospital right away. The ambulance is here and they're ready to transport."

The Minister's heart began to race as he heard the sirens in the background and the officials talking to Angie, trying to assess her condition. He also heard broken conversations between emergency personnel as they discussed the extraction of a trapped victim.

"Angela, what hospital are you going to?" He was almost yelling over the noise, as he ran to get his keys.

"We're going to *Mercy*, downtown."

"Are the kids okay? There was no response. "Angela, are the kids okay?" The Minister yelled again.

"No," she said quietly, with obvious pain. "Junior is all banged up and bruised, but it's Shelby; she's been hurt badly, Ed. They don't know if she's going to make it."

The Minister's heart skipped a beat as he heard his wife beginning to cry, just before hanging up the phone. He was a freak when it came to his sexual exploits, but still a man who loved his family, especially his budding little flower Shelby, who had secured her place in his heart long before exiting her mother's womb. His eyes welled up with tears, as he ran to the car, praying all the way. He would, without hesitation, trade places with her if he could. He felt that none of them deserved this, but especially not Shelby. She was the most innocent of victims.

He drove like a mad man, pushing Angie's convertible and his psyche to the limit, and when he got to the hospital, he could not believe the tragedy that beheld him. Just as he broke through the emergency room doors, Angie rushed to him with bandages on her arms and forehead, and fell into his arms. She sobbed uncontrollably for a while that seemed like an eternity. There were two things that always broke the Minister's heart: seeing his mother cry and witnessing the tears of his loving wife. He had seen both before and both grabbed his heart by its throat and brought him to his knees. He did his best to display a strength from which they both could draw, but it was almost impossible.

"Where are the kids, Angie?" The Minister whispered to her before she was able to gain full composure. His heart was already aching but he needed to see his children.

"Junior is right in there, and they have Shelby in the next room," she said as she pointed and sobbed.

"Have you spoken to the doctors?"

"Yes, Junior is going to be fine. His ankles are fractured and he broke one of his wrists, but they think he'll be okay. It's Shelby they're still working on. Ed, I don't know how it happened; one minute we were just driving down State Avenue minding our own business, and the next thing I knew, this car came out of nowhere, and before I could react, we were all tangled and mangled. I just didn't see it coming. I tried all I could but I just couldn't..." She began to cry again, and fell against his chest.

"Shh, everything is going to be fine."

The Minister tried to calm her as he surveyed the outer triage area, trying to find a nurse or doctor to speak to about the condition of the children. He sat Angie down in the nearest comfortable chair and headed for the information desk. As he approached, he noticed that one of the paramedics who rescued his family had a familiar face that he could not place.

"Pastor Hebert," the young man shouted.

"Yes?"

"How are you? I'm Earl Graves; I've been to your church and I've heard you on the radio. I think I've even seen you on television. Wow it's an honor; can I help you with something?"

"Oh, hello Earl," the Minister said without giving him much attention. "I'm trying to find out some information about my family. They were in a serious accident today and my little girl is hurt, and I can't seem to find anyone around here to help me."

The Minister's voice was shaky and getting uncharacteristically loud, with noticeable desperation, and right then the young paramedic seemed to mentally put two and two together and realized that the mother and children he had just rescued were the wife and children of the big time minister whose church he had often visited. He did not recognize them because he had never been close enough, during the service, to see them or privy to the inner circle of the Calvary Baptist Church. But he was determined to make an unforgettable impression on this particular day.

"Oh Reverend, I'm sorry. I didn't know. Come with me."

Earl took the Minister by the arm and took him behind the closed doors, leading him down the corridor to the rooms where the children were being treated. The Minister knew, and was thankful, that the children were in the best hospital in the city. It had a high profile reputation and was known for catering to the rich and famous, but as much confidence as those thoughts gave him, he would not be satisfied until he saw his children for himself.

"Earl, what the hell happened out there; do you know?" The Minister walked swiftly as he glanced at the paramedic.

"Well sir, it was just one of those things that seem to happen everyday, but never to someone you know. Your wife was driving up State Avenue, approaching the Fifth Street intersection, and a vehicle traveling at a very high rate of speed ran the light and broad sided her. She was lucky she was in that heavy Range Rover because the impact probably would have taken the lives of your family members in any other vehicle."

"What about my daughter, Earl?" The Minister stopped and held him by the arm, halting his pace. "When my wife called me from the scene, I could hear you guys talking about someone being trapped. Was that Shelby?"

"Well, yes sir," Earl said as he dropped his head. "She was actually trapped because of some golf clubs that were in the back of the S.U.V. Some kind of way, one of those clubs flew out of the bag and impaled her, and I think it tore through some vital abdominal organs. She's in surgery now, and that's probably why the doctor isn't back yet. I know they're doing all they can Reverend, and I'm sure you know that this is the best hospital in the city."

The Minister fell against the hallway wall, and Earl Graves grabbed him by the arm to steady him. He could see that this was a father

335

going into shock but struggling to maintain his strength for his family. The Minister pushed away from the wall and righted himself, wiping his tear-filled eyes. He struggled to breathe, as his throat stressfully constricted.

"Where's my son? Take me to see my son."

"He's right in there," Earl said, pointing through the window of an ER alcove.

The Minister looked through and saw his bandaged son lying on a gurney. He was able to get the attention of the attending nurse who let him in for a brief moment. Junior was sleeping, having been sedated so that his injuries could be properly attended without him moving around unnecessarily. When the Minister rubbed his hand through his son's curly hair, he briefly opened his eyes and smiled.

"Daddy, my ankles hurt," he whispered as his eyes shut again.

"I know they do son, but you're going to be fine. You're going to be shooting jumpers in no time at all," he whispered into his ear. "Now go back to sleep, while I go check on your sister and your mother. You were very brave today buddy, and I know it was scary, but you made it and you're going to be fine. I'm so proud of you."

Before he could finish, Junior was fast asleep. A slight smile came over his face, bringing some ease to the pain in the Minister's heart. He was happy that his son felt some sense of security, knowing that his father was there.

After being assured by the nurse that he was going to be okay and that she would stay right by his side, the Minister left the room. He headed back down the corridor to sit with Angie and wait for the doctor to complete Shelby's surgery, and give them some kind of report. As they walked, the Minister thanked Earl from the bottom of his heart and told him to make sure that the next time he was at the church to come down front and also visit his office before leaving. The Minister was big on gratitude and loyalty, and he had intentions on doing something for Earl Graves that would show both. When they got to Angie, they saw that the doctor had beaten them there, and the Minister rushed to join the conversation; he knew that information was being shared about Shelby's condition.

The doctor introduced himself to the Minister and again sang the accolades to the protective qualities of the heavy S.U.V. that Angie was driving. But he also explained that Shelby's condition was grave. The impact of the other vehicle that crashed into them had shaken the contents of the car so violently that the Minister's golf clubs flew wildly about the back of the vehicle, where Shelby was sitting. She was fortunate in that none of them crashed into her head, but a sand wedge had gorily pierced through her abdomen, damaging several organs and practically destroying her kidneys. Angie and the Minister held each other as the doctor spoke.

"Reverend and Mrs. Hebert, I do not want to lie to you and tell you that Shelby is going to be okay. We're doing the very best we can to stabilize her. We were successful removing the object and we were able to close without severe hemorrhaging during the surgery, but as I am sure you could tell, Shelby had lost quite a bit of blood before she arrived. To some degree, I feel some glimmer of confidence simply because of her miraculous survival. Your daughter is an amazing child, and probably stronger than most adults that we have seen come through here with traumatic injuries. I'm hoping for the best with her and I guess since you're religious folks, a little prayer won't hurt either. I'd better get back to her now, and also check on your son. You've probably already seen him; he's a trooper also, and I can almost guarantee a full recovery for him."

"Thank you doctor," the Minister said. "I appreciate everything that you're doing for my children, and have done for my wife. We'll be doing a lot of praying, and I'm sure that my baby will be okay. Can we see her yet?"

"Well, not yet but I'll send the nurse out shortly to let you know when you can."

The doctor walked away, looking over the medical chart in his hand, and the Minister whispered a prayer on his behalf.

"Bless the hands that touch my babies," he whispered.

Angie fell deeper into his chest, and without saying a word, she spoke to her husband, and he heard her and understood every unspoken sentiment. They sought and found refuge in one another. The two were a dynamic and unstoppable duo when the Minister allowed his wife to truly be his teammate. Up until now, he picked and chose the issues that they would face together, but now he was ready to re-establish the heavenly match that had been formed before time and face life as they should have all along, as one. Like the flowers in the courtyard that spoke to him earlier in the day, the passion of Angie's heart was bringing light to his soul.

"Oh God, Ed! Why did this have to happen?" She whispered, as she grabbed his shirt right where she was laying her head against his powerful chest.

The Minister did not respond and could not escape an overwhelming feeling of guilt. He was devastated by what he heard and felt especially guilty because Angie had so often told him not to leave his clubs laying around in the car. His dismissal of her request had nearly ended his daughter's life. It was just another issue that pinched hard at his conscience. He did his best to display the strength that was his character but the man inside him was screaming, reaching and pulling for something to which he could hold. As they sat huddled closely, the Minister mentally fought to keep his mind from drifting backward, chastising himself for his escapades in Chicago, for his motivations, for his encounters with Lydia, and his lustful desire for Gemma. Even the situation with Donovan crept into his mind, probably because of the association with golf. It was at that very moment that Angie raised her head from his chest to catch his eyes.

"How was Chicago?" She whispered, catching him completely off guard but reminding him of her intuitive nature.

"It was fine, but I should have been here. I should have been here, Angie, and I'm sorry."

Angie kissed him gently on the cheek and nestled her head back in his chest. She loved him but she could not feel for him right now. She knew that there was much more to his trip than he would probably ever tell, but she could not be concerned about that right now. She was a mother concerned about her children, and she needed his strength to help pull them through this season of pain. A new teardrop rolled down her cheek and cascaded untouched, off her chin, disappearing into the fabric of the Minister's shirt.

CHAPTER 53

Ivy had a lot on her mind when Saturday rolled around. She was to have already given her answer to Donovan but she had not even bothered to call after the events and revelations of late. He had not called her either. She did not know why, nor did she care.

Now was the time to again secure her emotions and deal with the responsibilities of the case before her, she thought. But the task was utterly torturous. If she had not pursued her personal interest and kept him emotionally at bay, she would not be facing this dilemma. It would just be another *told you so case* and she would attack him just like any other victim of her legalese. But this was difficult because she continued to search and brow beat herself for not having embraced the portion of her intuition that should have alerted her to the type of man with which she was dealing. She had been a master throughout her career, and life for that matter, of disallowing her romantic or personal interests to interfere with her professional life.

Initially, her intentions were well controlled with Donovan, and she heeded every red flag that came with his suave presentation. She had seen it all before, but this time something happened, something that she could not explain, and that was a problem for a master of rational and logical thinking. Something inside her had spoken with unyielding clarity, telling her that it was okay to fall for him as long as she exercised will power, strength and well defined parameters. But something had gone terribly wrong when she decided that it was time to discard that box which held her infatuation; she discovered that it held more passion and desire than she would admit, and as hard as she tried, it just would not go away.

She was bothered most by the fact that in past instances, she had been able to turn off her feelings like a light switch and choose her emotional state with ease. But with Donovan, her controls were not working, and as hard as she tried to flick the switches, things just were not that simple.

She sat in her apartment with a cup of tea, in front of a television that watched her. Her mind had taken her to places unknown. She had been assigned a case and she was going to do her very best to represent her client to the best of her ability, but she honestly wondered if she had the strength to face Donovan, and still function professionally.

Ivy felt betrayed beyond measure, stupid and just plain duped. Her mental basket was being filled with a potpourri of emotions that ranged from anger to embarrassment. She felt terribly hurt for having trusted him. She had had her guard up, as was her style, for quite a while but then finally decided to allow herself to feel for him, and her feelings had been stepped on, and kicked to the curbside.

Ivy got up and stood in front of her full length mirror, analyzed her reflection, and wondered if there was something physical that he could see that could have made him think that she deserved to be treated this way. She thought back to the night they met and wondered if she had simply acted like an upscale groupie. *"Did he see that in me?"* She thought pitifully to herself. *"I was brilliantly professional and I have never acted in a manner that made me look like the groupie girls. He should have been impressed with me,"* she continued in her mind, inhaling what she hoped was a breath of confidence.

She finally decided that she had had enough of feeling the way she felt, and instead of reaching for the case file that she had brought home with her, with copies of the pictures that Yavonne had shown, she felt the need for a run. It had always worked in law school, so she was sure it would work now. She was a fighter and always had been. It was time to put him on his heels and against the ropes, and make him pay. She went into her bedroom and removed the extra large sweatshirt that she was wearing, and donned leggings and a T-shirt. She tied her shoes and headed for the door, and just as she reached for the handle, the phone began to ring. She felt in her heart that it was Donovan, and her initial intention was to let it go into voice mail, but she was angry and she felt that he deserved a piece of her mind. She knew that she should not speak to him because he was now a respondent in the case, but she threw all matters and issues of protocol out the window. The fighter inside her was coming back and Ivy was going to make sure that he would wish he had never called. She marched over to the phone and snatched it into her hand, but was surprised to hear the disturbingly weak voce of voice of Miss Hattie Lee, on the other end.

"Miss Hattie, what's wrong? Are you okay?" Ivy could hear in her breathing that she had been crying.

"Baby," Miss Hattie Lee sang, " I got some real bad news about Gemma, this mornin'." She was struggling to speak.

"What happened?" There was a long pause.

"They called and told me that Gemma was attacked the other night and she's in the hospital. They say she's hurt real bad and they don't think she's going to make it." Miss Hattie's voice trailed off.

"What?" Ivy was caught completely off guard, moving toward the shock of disbelief. "Are you sure Miss Hattie; are you sure they had the right person?"

It was not so much that Ivy did not trust Miss Hattie Lee's judgment, thinking that her senior years were playing tricks on her mind. She had always been as sharp as a tack; it was simply that her statement was so far out of place that Ivy did not know how to respond. It was like a note in a symphony performance that was so horribly wrong that it soured every musical effort around it, the kind that made all the other musicians drop their instruments hopelessly to the floor and reluctantly turn their heads toward the author of the sound.

"Miss Hattie, I want you to sit down and tell me exactly what happened, and who you talked to, and take your time. Are you sure they were talking about our Gemma?"

"The boy who called said his name was Jason and he was some kind of a coordinator or something on that play she's doing out there, in Chicago. He said that somebody snatched her off the street and hurt her." Miss Hattie Lee started to cry but continued. "He put me through to the hospital and I talked to the doctors and the police, myself."

"Okay Big Mama, don't worry; everything is going to be all right," Ivy said, trying to calm her while falling apart inside, herself.

"Ivy, I have to go to Chicago and I need you to go with me. I need to look on her with my own two eyes and I need my strongest girl with me. I don't mean to be no burden, but you know Gemma would want you with me in a time like this."

"Oh, Miss Hattie, I wouldn't have it any other way. I'll book two seats on the first flight out," Ivy retorted quickly.

"Thank you, baby. Call me back as soon as you get it together."

Ivy put the phone down and immediately ran to her purse to retrieve her credit card. She was frightened, confused, angry, disoriented, and mentally exhausted. She tried not to begin kicking and blaming herself for something over which she had no control, but that too was her style. She had been born with an overwhelming sense of responsibility, and that was one of the things that made her and Gemma's relationship work so well. Ivy's responsibility was balanced by Gemma's spontaneity, and Ivy always believed in the back of her head, that that quality of Gemma's would someday contribute to her demise.

Her anger intensified and found its way toward Gemma, for some reason. She just knew that she was doing something that she should not have, on the mean streets of Chicago. She must have gotten herself into an inescapable situation, or reacted too slowly to a situation that developed around her. All of a sudden, it was all Gemma's fault, and then Ivy brought the blame back to herself, feeling that she should have been there; she should have done something; she should have said something, and she was wrong for not being Gemma's on call savior.

She struggled to control her wayward thoughts and the myriad of emotions that raced through her mind. She retrieved her credit card even with her hands shaking out of control, and just as she was about to dial the airline, her phone rang again. Without thinking about who it might be, she picked it up before it had even completed the first ring.

"I thought I would have heard from you by now," the voice said just after her hurried greeting.

"Jesus H. Christ! I can't deal with you right now, Donovan," Ivy yelled after she recognized the voice.

"Hey, take it easy. What did I do to deserve all this?"

"You know exactly what you did, and if you don't, I have a file full of photos and articles that will explain it all to you; every sorted fucking detail!"

"Ivy, we need to talk—"

"You are damn right we need to talk, but not now. You will be hearing from me, and I can pretty much guarantee that," she yelled.

"Ivy wait. At least give me a chance to explain."

"Donovan," she said slowly, "you will have all the time you need, but you will not have it now. I have had a trying past couple of days, and I don't need my emotions frosted with bullshit, right now. My insides just can't handle any more information, so I'm going to hang up now and ask you very nicely not to ever call me back." Ivy could hear him asking her to wait and hold on before she cut him off. Within two hours she was packed, and was walking through the airport with Miss Hattie in tow.

There was something inside her that made her always think that the day would come when she would have to say goodbye to her dearest friend but she had never been ready, and she was not prepared for what she would find in Chicago. When they finally boarded the plane and were seated, Miss Hattie Lee Ross went for what she believed in most, grabbing Ivy's hand and squeezing it like a vice, she prayed all the way to Chicago.

CHAPTER 54

Sunday morning was a most frustrating day for Brown. It was his big chance to shine and perhaps arouse the coup that he had always played with in the back of his feeble little mind, but the news of the *First Family's* tragedy had spread like wildfire, engaging a somber mood throughout the congregation. The result was a complete lack of focus or attention on anything the *great* Reverend Brown had to say. What made things worse was the fact that most of the important people in the congregation, the ones that Brown truly wanted to hear his singing, crooning and attempt at a sermon, were either already at the hospital, or on their way. They all wanted to be with Angie and the Minister. It just was not fair, in Brown's mind; everything he tried to do never worked out the way he wanted. But he was determined to have the spotlight and upstage the Minister one good time; maybe one day, but not today.

Brown struggled as best he could to sing, and preach, and scream, and yell, but his responses from the crowd were very weak. Even Brown's flashy new suit and shoes were not enough to bring the group under submission of his antics. Finally frustrated and tired, he gave in and decided that he should lead the church into prayer for the Minister and his family. It was his most intelligent decision in ages, but it was still frustrating. It was not at all, what he wanted, and he clinched his teeth, festering resentment in his heart with every word. After the service, it could have been assumed that Brown would hustle over to the hospital and begin attempting to regulate the traffic that came to comfort the family, but he did not. He retired to his small office at the church and kindled his anger.

He was jealous and angry about the family dynasty that had been established over the years at the Calvary Baptist Church. First it was the

Minister's uncle, and now he was there. The fact that Brown's father had assisted the Minister's uncle, while he was alive and had faithfully accepted the role of being the *number two* man only added fuel to the fire. He did whatever he was asked, and made it his life's work to take care of his pastor. In Brown's mind, that belittled him and made him feel that his father never received the respect he deserved, and although he tried to hide it from the Minister, he voiced his deep seeded resentment to the few who would listen. Over time, his feelings had grown from resentment to anger, and it was just a matter of time before Brown exploded. The tragedy involving the Minister's family re-ignited the very short fuse of a bomb that had been lit long ago.

Brown stayed in his office and grieved within the context of his acrimony, until all of the parishioners left. He greeted no one, not even those who would tell him that he had done a nice job during the service. He sat behind his desk with a look of disgust plastered on his face, made one very significant telephone call, and then casually left the church. He headed for the hospital, feeling that was where he should be. While he drove, he did his best to reconstruct his composure in order to offer the Minister a posture of perfidious loyalty.

About the same time that Brown was making his call, Detective Alexandra Heart received an important one from a colleague at the Chicago Police Department. Actually the caller was more than a colleague, at one time in their history. Her presence was privately requested for assistance in investigation of an assault on a theater diva that was, most likely going to turn into a homicide. Her academy classmate that was now a high-ranking official in the department, knew very well of Alex's reputation and experience in such cases and her skills would be a definite asset. There were also undisclosed issues surrounding this case that called for Alex to make her way to Chicago.

Permission was granted by Alex's department brass to take what would be labeled a *vacation*. They were not always willing to allow her to assist on cases all over the country, even though she was a perfect showpiece and public relations tool. The press had fallen in love with her face after her success with a high profile drug smuggling case, and with her headlines came fame for her department and superiors. Historically, detectives are territorial beasts and the welcoming of an outsider was unheard of. This was no different and there were several concerns that floated around in Alex's head. There were always strange things floating around in her head, though.

Alex thought about calling the Minister, for no reason but to simply get under his skin. Only for him would she consider pleasure before business, but not this time. Even though her thoughts of him were unrelenting, she managed to control herself. She halted her workout and headed to her fax machine to receive preliminary confidential details that she was told would arrive shortly. By Monday afternoon, she too, would be in Chicago aside the bed of a woman with whom she had more in common than she would ever believe.

CHAPTER 55

Angela was not leaving the hospital; she had been there for three days, and was determined not to leave without her daughter. That was the kind of mother she was. Junior had been treated and released after a twenty-four hour observation period, and the Minister took him home, to allow him to recover within secure and familiar surroundings. He had Angie's mother to come and stay with him while he traveled back and forth between home and the hospital.

There was nothing like the comfort of a loving grandmother, and both Angie and the Minister knew that. Junior would be fine, but little Shelby's condition had not improved, and after speaking to the doctor's, they were sure that she would need nothing short of a multiple organ transplant and a miracle to survive.

The news was devastating, and the Minister's heart was breaking into pieces, even though he did his best to maintain a positive outlook. His stomach was in knots and he could not escape the onslaught of a migraine headache. He searched himself for the faith that he knew was lodged somewhere in his soul; for the well of scriptural edicts from which he could draw a word of encouragement, but it was difficult. He was staring at the destruction of his family right before his eyes. There was no recovery from the loss of a child, and he knew it. His wife was in agony and her puffy eyes aged her overnight. His son was both in physical and emotional pain, and there was nothing that he could do about it.

He struggled to answer his questions honestly and positively, knowing that the situation was nearing a stage of hopelessness. He thought about all of the counseling and consoling he had done for others and how he had told them not to worry and that things would work out, but it was difficult, if not impossible to personally administer the same therapeutic measures. He was a spiritual healer of the heart, soul and mind, yet he was struggling to find the medicine he had so confidently offered to others. *"Is there no balm in Gilead?"* The Old Testament scripture played over and over in his head. *"Where was the solace for his pain?"* he pleaded.

Finally, he left and headed for his church office; he could not take it any more, and he needed to hide from himself. He knew that no one was there; India, his secretary, was at the hospital with Angie, and she had been a Godsend, putting her envious feelings aside, and genuinely caring for the Minister's wife. She really did love them, maybe too much; that was really her only fault.

Angie understood his need to go, and even though she wanted no other person by her side, she knew that she had to allow him to manage his pain in the best way he could. She understood the reality and loneliness of worry, and the fact that it had to be dealt with in a very personal way to ever be brought under control.

"Go," she told him quietly. "Just make sure you come back."

He kissed her gently on the forehead, holding his lips to her skin for an extended period of time, as if he were drawing strength from her spirit. India longingly watched the interaction, and for a brief second, she closed her eyes and imagined her lips on his. She knew that this situation was not the time or place for such thoughts, but she also knew that her fantasies had to consist of stolen moments of cognitive imagery.

As the Minister drove to the church, his mind was in a virtual fog. He was doing his best to re-establish his expectations and hold to his faith, but he was fighting a losing battle. His stomach ached more as he thought of his children, especially Shelby, and his guilt about the whole situation was rapidly consuming him. Several scenes kept replaying in his mind like a highlight reel: pictures of the crash, Angie with a bandaged forehead, and the children lying in the hospital with a team of doctor's and nurses around them. He saw himself in the corner of the frame, standing with out-stretched arms, but much too far away to help, and his muted voice screamed in anguish. What was even worse was the disturbing integration of numerous flashbacks to the women whose arms entangled him and whose lustful expressions gripped him so tightly that he appeared to be suffocating and struggling to live. There were so many pictures speeding through his mind, and every now and then he squeezed his eyes shut, hoping that he would open them to something different. They would eventually, but not now.

The Minister entered the administrative office building of the church but did not stop at his office. He would get there eventually, but this was not a moment for sitting behind his desk, shuffling papers, or making calls. There was a need to communicate, but not with another human being. He walked down the long corridor that led to the sanctuary of the church, and made his way to the altar. He first fell to his knees affront the large gold cross that sat majestically on the communion table, and then went completely prostrate on the floor. This was not the first time he had assumed this position for prayer, but it was probably one of the most sincere.

The scene was amazingly surreal and looked like an orchestrated film scene depicting a lone vicar praying in a medieval cathedral. The light that poured through the multicolored stained glass windows cast effervescent shades and lines that struck the Minister and the altar, making both appear that they were in the very presence of the Almighty. He prayed out loud, asking God for a miracle for his daughter and for mercy on his family. He said that he would be willing to give anything to see things back the way they were, and he asked forgiveness for his sinful acts that he believed caused the tragedy, promising that he would never do them again. But what he failed to realize, as most men do, was that his promises meant nothing without challenge, and he would soon have the opportunity to prove himself. He stayed in that position for nearly an hour, his body lifeless and frozen by the sincerity of his posture, his mind tuned completely to a singular directive.

"I thought I might find you here, but I thought you would be in your office," an approaching voice said, startling the Minister. He did not move.

Lydia made her way down the center aisle and took a seat on a pew near the front, about fifteen feet away from the Minister. He knew who it was without another word because of her scent, and he waited for her questions about what he was doing. She said nothing, and allowed him to finish praying, which he did silently. Finally he stood and spoke, but did not turn around to allow her to see his face.

"Lydia, what are you doing here?" His voice was clearly shaky even though he tried his best to camouflage it, and his outstretched hands held tightly to the table before him, steadying his weak legs.

"Ed, what's wrong? Are you all right?" She moved quickly from her seat and grabbed him by the shoulder, turning him around.

"No, I'm not all right, and I don't know if I'm going to be all right," he said with a face full of dried tears.

"What happened?" She thought that Angie may have found out about them, and he was in a state of guilt-motivated repentance. She had never seen him look like this before and she was afraid.

"My family has been in an accident, and my baby is hurt real bad," he said as he fell into her bosom.

"Oh my God!"

Lydia stroked the back of his head as she held him, terribly sorry about the news, but relieved that it was not what she had suspected, especially knowing that he had returned home from Chicago early and seemed to be in an honest and redemptive mood when they were together last.

She had not come to the church expecting what she found, but the Minister's catastrophic announcement had pocketed her lust. Even though they had had an expressive conversation in Chicago and there had been understanding and resolution, she was still hooked on him and wanted nothing more than to be near him. The honest revelations and heart felt communication in Chicago had only made her want him more, and she was ready to tell him just that. She was ready to express her desire to be with him completely even if he could only give part of himself; that would be enough for now. She had waited as long as she could and had been driving in the area of the church almost daily since her return looking to seize the opportunity to see him. She was going to try to convince him to reconsider the suppression of his lust and reaffirm her desire for him, but the events of the last few days had been larger than the Minister's amorous appetite, and Lydia was now pulled into his pain.

"What can I do, Ed?" She whispered into his ear. "I'm so sorry."

"Just go to the hospital and be with Angie. I know she'd love to see you. Go, and do for her, what you're doing for me."

They finally released their embrace and as Lydia headed out the main doors of the church, the Minister glanced at her gait as she moved swiftly. She had come prepared to tease him, and if the circumstances had been different, the one-piece denim dress that she wore, with splits in front and back, would have most likely been on his office floor. But today crisis overrode carnality, and a little one stood in the way of her father's lasciviousness, forcing him into righteousness. He watched Lydia leave, and then again fell to his knees, and then completely prostrate before the altar, and prayed for his child. Lydia brushed tears from her face that had fallen for the wrong reasons and tried desperately not to be over-evaluative. It was time now, to go and do her best to comfort her friend, the friend whose husband she now loved.

CHAPTER 56

Miss Hattie Lee Ross fervently prayed for her child also, with her surrogate granddaughter's hand in hers. They stood at Gemma's bedside, stroked her beautiful face that still seemed to be radiant and smiling, and whispered prayers. Gemma was slowly leaving them, and they both knew that. She had bled excessively, and had the garbage men not found her, she would have bled to death, but although she was alive, she had suffered such severe blood loss that her brain was damaged due to lack of oxygen.

As they looked on, both Ivy and Miss Hattie Lee were stricken with feelings of guilt and pain. They did not communicate them out loud, but their thoughts were clear, and each could feel the other. They felt that they should have been there to save her, and because they were involved in other things, they let Gemma down.

Ivy especially, felt that way. She tortured herself about her relationship with Donovan, and knew that she should have confided in her friend long time ago, but when she really thought about it, there was nothing that she could have told Gemma, because she had no idea that the man she had fallen in love with was gay. What bothered her most was that she had become consumed by her feelings for him, and when she was not with him physically, she was with him mentally, leaving little to no room for anything else.

Ivy screamed inside because she had always been there for Gemma. Whenever she got herself into any kind of trouble, even trouble that they thought Miss Hattie Lee knew nothing about, she had been there. Ivy had bailed Gemma out of bad relationships, bad business deals, and some plain bad choices, as long as they had known each other, but when she was attacked that fateful evening, she was not there to bail her out, and something inside her made her feel that she should have been. She was being eaten up by the psychological guilt of a rescuer who was too far away to save a flailing victim.

Ivy and Miss Hattie Lee sat in Gemma's room all afternoon, and that evening they had the pleasure of meeting Detective Alexandra Heart. They were stunned when they saw her, as she looked like no female police officer either of them had ever seen. She looked as though she belonged on stage or in a film with Gemma, instead of being there to investigate a crime. She had a look that placed her easily in places that cops just did not belong, and being a beautiful woman gave her privilege to information that lesser women never received. Her beauty was the most useful part of her uniform. It was amazing how much information and often incriminating evidence had just been volunteered to her, over the years by both men and women, who were mesmerized by her beauty and edgy charm.

Ivy looked her over carefully, and allowed the attorney inside her to leap forward to guard her dying friend, at all costs, even from the police. But soon she could see that Alex was an ally, at least she presented herself in that manner, and thereby evoked Ivy's trust. The only problem not exposed was the fact that neither of them knew how close they were to this case.

"I know this is an extremely difficult time for you both, especially for you ma'am," Alex said as she glanced at Miss Hattie Lee, "but I want to assure you that I will do all within my power to find who did this and bring them to justice."

"You know, I 'preciate that, baby, and I know that you'll do all you can," Miss Hattie Lee said, looking at Alex with wise eyes, "but ain't nothin' you can do about bringing my baby back, and right now, if I could have anything I wanted, that would be it. *'Vengeance is mine saith the Lord'*, and He's gonna deal with the one who did this, so you do what you need to do but right now, I'm gonna keep praying, and let God handle the rest. I'm gonna call my pastor and he's gonna pray; I'm gonna call everybody I know and get them praying too. Oh Lord, we need to pray."

Miss Hattie Lee went back to Gemma's bedside, fighting tears and exhibiting the strength and wisdom that she had been known for. Ivy stayed just outside the door with Alex, after walking her out of the room. There was no need to interrogate Miss Hattie Lee; she knew nothing and had nothing to give, except her prayers.

"So what are your thoughts on this? Where do you go from here?" Ivy was focused and direct, looking into Alex's eyes.

"Well, I really just got here a few hours ago and I probably would not have even come to the hospital tonight, had it been any other case, but after hearing the circumstances and the fact that it was a talented young sister, I came as soon as I could. I really haven't even had a chance to review the police report or interview any witnesses, but I am on it tonight and first thing in the morning. The only thing that I do know is that there has been a serial rapist at work, with a similar *MO*, according to the detective who brought me over. But he had never gone homicidal, so we have no idea if this is the same person and he has upped the intensity of his crimes, or if it is someone completely new. "

Alex's comment took Ivy back, a bit. The word, *homicide*, cut through her spirit like the blade that had pierced her dear friend's flesh. Even though the situation was grave and relatively hopeless, there was something inside Ivy that made her think that Gemma would bounce back, like she always had. She had been in some of the most trying situations and always found a way to re-emerge with an even more radiant smile. But that word was finite and it stepped on Gemma's recovery chances, and relatively closed the door, on Ivy's heart.

"Well, if there is anything that you need, I'm here and I can assure you that her grandmother will be as helpful as possible, as well," Ivy said after a thoughtful pause.

"I appreciate your cooperation and we'll get back to both of you as soon as possible. I'll probably start going through the evidence first thing in the morning, and I want you both to know that, if there is anything that you need, any question that you have, please don't hesitate to call."

Ivy thanked Alex and as she watched her walk away, she tried to think; she tried to concentrate on anything that might help her to, not so much solve the case, but to ease the pain and anguish of feeling so helpless. She felt that she had so many tools that were of no use in the current situation. Her best friend laid less than three feet away from her; Ivy could touch her, caress her, talk to her and tell her how much she loved and needed her, but she could do nothing to change the events that put her down.

The surrogate grandmother, who had taken her in and cared for her, who had loved her like she was her own child, who had advised and consoled her in some of her most difficult times, was seated at the bedside of her child, and in indescribable pain, and Ivy felt that she could do nothing. She could do nothing but wait for whatever was next, and there was a sure guarantee that things would unfold in a way that would be shockingly strange to everyone involved. A noose-like drawstring was being tightened around the necks of a cast of players that would soon find disturbing commonality. Their lives were now provocatively entangled, and none of them would breathe freely until the life was nearly choked out of them.

CHAPTER 57

When Alex left the hospital, she had every intention of going straight to her hotel to get some rest and prepare for a full day of investigation the next day, but something inside her would not allow that plan. She went to her hotel but instead of staying there for the night, she called her friend on the force who had requested her presence, and asked her to meet her at the precinct. Alex was one of the most instinctive detectives around, and something bothered her about this case. Gemma's beautiful face stayed on her mind. There was something beyond allurement and curiosity that had to be satisfied.

She was pleased to find Gemma's clothing in the evidence room and hoped that hair or clothing fibers from her assailant might still be detectable. Maybe she would get even lucky and see that Gemma had struggled and was able to wound him, leaving traces of his blood on her clothes. The DNA investigation could begin. Although the crime lab would soon be processing all this evidence, Alex took it upon herself to do her own preliminary search. What she found knocked her sideways, and as strong, instinctive and intense as she was, she was not prepared for what she found in the pocket of Gemma's jacket.

> *Dearest Gemma,*
> *I can't tell you how much I thank you for the time we spent together. I looked forward to it with legions of anticipation, and there was nothing about you that fell short of my anticipation. The picture of us howling in the moonlight, as our bodies worked in sensual tandem is something that will remain etched in the most secret part of my memory, and every time I gaze upon a full moon, I will bring you forward in my*

fantasy. But you did something for me beyond the satisfaction of my physical cravings for your fire, you gave me something that I did not expect, but needed greatly. I remember your last words for me were simply, 'go home,' but I just could not leave things the way they were. That statement opened my eyes to an aspect of my being that had been dormant for what seemed to be an eternity. You need to know how unequivocally special I believe you are. You are truly a talented jewel, and your gifts go far beyond the stage. You gave your gift to me on the last night we were together, and for that I thank you. I will cherish forever, the diamond between your thighs, but hold even more dear, the diamond within your heart. Thank you for opening my eyes and making me see. You are the first to ever send me to the place I most desperately needed to be. Eternally grateful for all that you are.

Ciao Bella,

EAH

Alex read the letter and then read it again. She put it down on the table where she had all of Gemma's items spread, and then she picked it up again. She was a detective and there were things that detectives knew and never forgot, but beyond that, she was a woman, one who loved a man whose prose was his signature. And she could hear his voice in her mind, as the closing salutation rolled off his lips, "*Ciao Bella.*"

She struggled to maintain her composure, as this discovery grabbed her by the throat. She could feel her pulse beginning to race and her mouth watering, and there was only one person who had that effect on her. Alex reached into Gemma's other pocket and found two other notes that made her certain that Miss Kimbro had spent the weekend with one, Reverend Doctor Edward Alan Hebert, and the flood gates that held back her emotions swung wide open. She glanced around the room, especially checking to see if the officer on duty was paying attention, and against all that she knew was right, she placed the letters into her pocket. After turning Gemma's clothing back into the security of the evidence vault, she rejoined her friend upstairs.

"Find anything helpful?" The other detective broke away from her nonchalant conversation with a uniformed officer to address Alex. To her, the case was highly important because of the terrible press her city was already receiving behind the horrifying crime. The attacker had been choosing nameless and nondescript victims, but now things were different. A celebrity had been touched, and even though she was an African-American, which almost never made the news, she was a budding beauty in the lime-light, and that meant that all eyes would turn in her department's direction. That was another reason Alex was called. If the press was going to look, they might as well have something to look at. But Alex's mind had been turned from crime solving after her breathtaking discovery. She had a new motivation.

"Not much, but I think I have some ideas, and somewhere to start. I think I'm going to head to the hotel and get some sleep if I'm going to jump into this with both feet in the morning."

Alex exited the building and entered a waiting patrol car that had been assigned to deliver her to her hotel. On the ride over, she said nothing, and simply looked out the window, watching the city roll by. She had been involved in a number of sensitive cases over the years but this situation was a first, and it struck her like a ton of bricks, evoking feelings inside her that she did not think she had anymore. The Minister stirred the emotions she had once stowed, when she removed herself from all interaction with him, but now he was back, she was back, and the antagonistic toying that she was doing with him was surreal in comparison to the true depth of her re-discovered feelings.

She had always been an instinctive cop, usually being able to plan her moves several steps before the criminals; that was how she caught them, but now an unexpected bomb of tumultuous emotion had blown up in her face, and as she watched the scenery race by, she had no idea what she was going to do next.

After checking in and stowing her luggage, Alex thought about eating. But she had left her appetite in the evidence room. "*The notes could be meaningless*," she tried to convince herself, but she knew in her heart, that they were not. Something instinctive was speaking to her, and she had not yet decided to listen.

Alex headed for the shower, where cognitive issues could be rationally sorted, but rational thinking was not what she was known for, when it came to the Minister. As the water cascaded through her long hair, she closed her eyes and called on everything that she knew, to give her guidance. She was not a religious person by any means, but she did respect the higher powers that be, whoever or whatever they were, and she needed help with this one. After about thirty minutes of mental silence and labored breathing through the humidity of steam-filled capsule, Alex decided on a plan of action.

She would move quickly and meticulously, first solving the crime of passion that she felt had, in some way, been committed against her, and then the crime of violence, hoping that the suspects were not one in the same. There was a rush that overcame her, one that only happened as a result of one particular individual. When he was involved, she could not think straight and her actions were dictated by unbalanced emotion. Alex was entering a fight of internal wills, engaging in terrifying battles between her disconnected heart, troubled mind and wayward spirit.

CHAPTER 58

The Minister was devastated when he received the call from Miss Hattie Lee. It hurt worse because he could not really show the depth of his devastation for several reasons, so he did his best to offer pastoral words of comfort and encouragement, while he screamed inside. He was numb with the pain of disbelief, and it hurt even more deeply because of the issue with which he was currently dealing. There was an amazing closeness that he had developed with Gemma, far beyond the sexual encounters, although he knew that there was a part of him that remained in constant craving for her passion. He had been affected in an unforgettable way, and he could not share the depth of that sentiment with anyone, especially not Miss Hattie Lee. He had to force himself to be strength filled spiritual sage she needed him to be. However that persona was light-years away from the broken man he truly was.

He had most of his calls forwarded to his cell phone, which could be dangerous, because he was spending so much time at the hospital, and with Angie right by his side, but it did not matter at this point. Miss Hattie Lee explained the gory details of the assault as best she could, and with every word and detail, the Minister could feel his heart being stabbed and drained of its life force. Standing and walking around, he thought might help, but it only made him want to fall to his knees. It was getting harder and harder for him to mask his emotions and he was nearing a significant breakdown. He gingerly shared the bad news with his wife, doing his best not to add stress to her already troubled heart and mind, but she needed to know. She needed to know that it happened but he could not allow her to see how the news had really affected him. Gemma's circumstance had to be treated like that of any other member in crisis, and Miss Hattie Lee had to be made to feel like any other mother who came to her pastor, mourning the injury or death of her child. It was difficult but that was the way it had to be.

"Oh my God, Ed. Where was she?"

"Chicago," the Minister answered sheepishly.

"Chicago?" Angie looked at him directly.

"Yes." The Minister swallowed hard, as he could see that there would be no way out of a possible guillotine of questions.

"When did it happen?"

"Last Friday," he said, staring blankly forward.

He tried to prepare himself for whatever she had to say, because he knew it was coming and it was going to be fierce. He watched her mind work, establishing a line of time and place, and then pasting figures and pictures in perspective. But her response was not what he expected. Angie did something much worse; she said absolutely nothing.

The Minister could feel his stomach churning as she expressed her sentiments with body language that moved her slightly away from him. The movement may have only been a matter of inches, but it may well have been miles. It was effective and very well understood. Angie's instinctive juices were also flowing, and he knew it. It was bad enough to be within the vision one woman's intuition, but two could be more than overwhelming.

He sank as he looked at her because he did not see the pain that he expected on her face. Instead, he saw that she was fortifying herself, and it was that stockpiling of inner-strength that he feared the most.

CHAPTER 59

Detective Heart made her way back to the hospital first thing in the morning to look in on Gemma and her family, and to look more closely at Gemma's medical records and reports. She wanted especially, to see the results of a battery of tests that are performed on all women who are brought in after a sexual assault. Because the tests were done at the hospital lab, she knew that she would not have to wait as long for a definitive word to possibly satisfy her suspicions.

According to the tests, Gemma had recently had very rough sexual intercourse, which probably indicated that her assailant had raped her. DNA samples had also been obtained. To any other detective, these items would have only found meaning in the police crime laboratory as pieces to a puzzle that might eventually lead to the District Attorney's office, but the evidence Alex had led some place else. She needed to leave Chicago for a moment and pay an uncharacteristically professional visit, to an old friend whom she knew would not be very happy to see her. Alex was being driven by a part of her that had been rudely awakened, but was by no means dead.

There was something inside her that found the whole situation almost unbelievable. She knew that the world was small and it seemed that paths crossed that she would have never comprehended, but she just could not place the man that she loved, or at least lusted, in the path of this crime scene. He was not a killer and would have never been involved in such an act of violence. He was a lover, an incredibly skilled and attentive one at that, one who would, however, go to great lengths to satisfy his cravings. That she knew very well, as it was their common denominator; they had played unbelievably memorable games in their day, and she always knew that just because he was not playing with her, did not mean that he was not playing with someone.

She tried, for a moment, to sort through it in her head but her head and heart were not working in tandem. Her thoughts and decisions were being directed by the most obsessive and compulsive parts of her psyche. He would have been the last person on her mind, in terms of any involvement with Gemma's circumstance, but after a conversation with Miss Hattie Lee in which she learned of their church affiliation, and with one look at Gemma's beautiful face and body, and now the letters, Alex knew that the Minister had been there. He had been more than *in Chicago*; he had been *in Gemma*.

Alex decided that she would keep the information to herself, for now. There were things that she had to place in order to settle a raging psyche before any distribution of information. It was not proper police procedure, but it was in adherence to emotional protocol. She took what she had learned very personally, and would have to resolve it in her own way. She did not want to view the Minister as a suspect in the case and she could see how religious and spiritual Miss Hattie Lee was. One of the first things she mentioned doing after prayer was calling her pastor, so Alex could also see the high regard with which the Minister was held. It would be counter productive and unnecessarily hurtful to reveal this discovery to Gemma's faith-filled grandmother, but all secrets would be revealed in time.

Alex knew how people thought of him, especially his church membership. They loved, respected and adored him; some nearly worshipped him. It was that enigmatic magnetic power that often spilled over into other aspects of his life and had drawn her in so tightly that she could not let go. She had stopped trying, thinking that her obsession was contained, but she had become overwhelmed in recent weeks with thoughts of their time together, and the heat that tormented her mind was relentless. She had been pleasantly sustained over the years, with her memories and assumptions, but the discovery of the letters was driving her over the edge, and she did not want to honestly face the reason why it was happening. That might be even more painful.

Detective Heart briefly shared her plans to leave and return in a day or so, with Ivy during a hallway conversation, just outside Gemma's room. Miss Hattie Lee had been doing the same thing she had been doing since she arrived, praying, and did not pay much attention to Alex. She was doing what she knew to do. But the detective that lived in Ivy came to life, wondering why Alex was leaving so abruptly, after having been especially brought to Chicago on a moments notice. She was unaware of the explicitness of Alex's instructions, not knowing that she was to quietly do what she did best, turn that information over to her colleague and then leave.

"So you have a lead, detective?" Ivy's subtle desperation and suspicion was obvious.

"Call me Alex, and no, I really don't. There's just something that I need to check into back at home before I proceed. I'll be back before you know it, and if there's anything that you or Miss Kimbro's grandmother need, you know how to get in touch with me or Detective Bradford, at the Chicago P.D." She was short and her tense was recognizably hurried.

Ivy watched the athletically sultry detective leave and could not fight feeling that there was something that she had not disclosed. Her senses were keen, especially now. Detective Heart was hiding something, and Ivy knew it. She did not know what it was, but she could feel in her bones that there was just something different about the way the detective spoke, and looked, and behaved. Ivy was a woman too, and could feel and see things that only women can feel and see. She sharpened her senses and prepared herself, feeling the inevitability of the unknown approaching swiftly with a package of brand new complexities.

CHAPTER 60

There was always an essence of circumstantial enormity that seemed to constantly surround Ivy, and somehow she managed not to be consumed. She was still in the midst of one of the biggest, and most emotionally dramatic cases in her life, but she had no intention of leaving her friend. Gemma was the sister she never had, and *"sisters don't leave sisters,"* she thought to herself. She called her assistant, arranging a series of conference calls, and had several important files faxed to the business center of her Chicago hotel. She called her boss and apprised him of the whole situation, to which he was sympathetic and conditionally understanding, reminding her however, of her case load and deadlines soon after his expressions of sympathy. He gave her a few days of family care leave, knowing that he could depend on Ivy's work ethic, and the fact that she would find a way to get the job done and keep things moving. Just as Ivy finished her last call, running down final instructions to her assistant, her cell phone rang.

"Can we talk now?" Donovan's voice was quiet, deliberate and still.

"Talk about what, Donovan," she retorted sharply. "I think I've seen enough and read enough, and there's nothing that you need to say right now."

Right then Donovan knew that Ivy had been informed about his issues. He was not sure what she knew or where she had obtained her information, but he had gambled and lost. He just knew that she would jump at the chance to, not only make incredible money but also, be with him. His plan was for her to feel about him exactly the way she did, but even more; he wanted to evoke from her, enough loyal emotion to disregard anything that she might see or hear in the press, and stand by him.

"But Ivy you said we could talk. Don't I deserve that?"

"Well, I've changed my mind and I don't think you really want to discuss what you deserve," she said as she attempted to keep her voice down while peeking in at Gemma and Miss Hattie Lee.

"Ivy listen; I'm not a bad person. You know that; we've spent quality time together and you've seen the kind of man I am."

"No Donovan, you're a very bad person. You're a liar and a cheat, and I think you deserve everything they take from you, and I'm going to help them do it!"

"So you know about the lawsuit?" His tone changed slightly.

"Yes I know very well about the lawsuit, and yes, I thought I had gotten to know you pretty well, but I was foolish; that's forgivable, but I'm not going to be stupid, from which there is no recovery," she preached.

"Ivy, please—"

"Donovan, save it!" She clinched her teeth, trying to keep her volume controlled. "You're right, I got to know who I thought you were, but now you're going to get to know me very well, and you're going to wish you had never even said 'hello'."

"Ivy, we can work this out. You're angry about things you don't even know about, and if you'd just give me a chance to explain, I—"

"Explain? No, let me explain something to you, Mr. Davis. You have messed with the wrong attorney, and I gave you a chance, a chance that I never should have, and I'm paying for that, but you're not going to make me pay for your sins as well. Don't think for a moment that I'm not going to have my day in court!"

She hung up with him calling her name. Ivy's intent was to never speak to him again, while planning to levy a horrifically vindictive, legal boom on him. There were tears in her eyes that she knew were from the pain of having fallen for him, but she did her best to fight them and apply them to something else, trying to legitimize their presence for reasons other than Donovan Davis. There might have been a remote chance of redemption for Donovan if the circumstances were different, but Ivy felt painfully backed into a corner and it was just a matter of time before she came out kicking and scratching.

After the conversation, Donovan pressed, *stop* on his tape recorder. He would call Ivy again later, but he had enough, for now. He stowed the tape in a safe place and left it unmarked; it would be retrieved only if necessary.

Hell hath no fury like a woman scorned, until that woman runs into an ingeniously conniving snake of a man with a stellar smile, disguised as an all American football player. Ivy was smart, and a worthy adversary to his intellect, but she was distracted by her pain, and was simply doing all she could to emotionally survive. As far as she was concerned, it was over, for now, but she would find out later that things were just beginning, and her entanglement with Donovan would scar her for life.

Ivy closed her eyes and rubbed her brow; she was mentally exhausted but she could not stop now. That was not her style and not what her friend, Gemma, needed from her. She decided to make a call to the Chicago Police Department, and take Alex's advice about speaking to Detective Bradford. She was convinced that Alex knew something she was not sharing with her and Miss Hattie Lee, and she was determined to find out what, before the rest of the world did.

The press was coming and she knew it, and soon Gemma's personal life would be dissected and served on a media platter for the public to devour. Ivy was going to protect her friend, at all costs, especially at a time when she could not defend herself. She knew that several of Gemma's issues of the past would be resurrected and scrutinized as part of the story, and many of those issues were truly tabloid material.

It was time to dawn Uncle Henry's boxing gloves and prepare to fight. The irony was that Ivy and Gemma were still on common territory, as the both engaged in fights for their respective lives.

CHAPTER 61

There had been so many transitional events, in the lives of the Minister and his wife that they had stopped counting the times their lives were turned sideways or upside down. They had been through so much together and survived so many secrets, while always finding the fortitude to camouflage reality and present a storybook façade. Sometimes reality was difficult to grasp and had often become elusive, but then at other times it had slapped them both in the face, almost always catching Angie when her guard was down. Wednesday night would begin a series of pivotal events that would change their lives forever, and would challenge them to the farthest borders of their existence.

One of the problems with *Time* is that it exists concurrently, and its one-way motion affects things as momentous as the breaking of glaciers into the open sea, and as miniscule as the blinking of the eyes of a humming bird. It also has a very predictable patience, by which many plan and attempt to operate ahead of its changeless patterns, but no matter how far ahead one might believe they get, *Time* has a way of catching up and consuming all in its path. On Wednesday night, that moment of realization visited the Minister's house.

The doctor had finally convinced the Hebert's to leave the hospital, and go home for a while. Shelby's condition was still grave but it was stable, and they were torturing themselves by being there. It was clear that her survival was probably going to depend on multiple organ transplants, and the news was devastating. They needed a break, especially Angie. There were things that they needed to deal with, in comfortable, family surroundings and they needed to spend some time with Junior, to let him know that they were still a family. As they drove home, the weight of the entire situation was clear, and though they wanted to speak, they could not. There was something that probably needed to be said, but words seemed strained at best.

The Minister reached over very gently and held Angie's hand. The gesture said more than any words ever could. It made her know that they were facing their challenges together and that he was still her willing support. They walked into the house that way, greeting Angie's mother at the door. She had been there the whole time, doing what she could to comfort Junior, pampering and consoling him in ways that only a grandmother could. They all came into the Minister's large embrace, and he comforted them, reminding them that everything was going to be all right, and then they all went their separate ways.

Angie and her mother went to look in on Junior, who was fast asleep with a noticeable frown on his brow, possibly being tormented in his dreams of the accident. His mother sat on his bed and began stroking his hair and kissing his cheek, and soon the scowl disappeared.

The Minister retired to the den where he sat on the large sofa with his head back and his eyes closed. He tried not to think about anything but he knew that there were difficult decisions ahead. Quickly glancing around the beautifully appointed room, he noticed its neatness. Everything was specifically and appropriately placed. The room was set up for comfort and nurture of the family. He wondered how things in his life had become so misplaced and chaotic. The room's order was a complete contradiction of who he truly was. And then there was the all too familiar wish for the ability to turn back the hands of time, replaying the events that had led to this circumstance. As he tried to clear his mind, praying briefly for a mental reprieve, the last thing in the world that he expected happened.

The doorbell rang, and though it was not very late and he did not expect anyone, he made no attempt to head for the door. He figured it was probably just a member of the extended family, coming to get first hand information and offer a bit of consolation for Angie. That would probably be happening all night. He was startled when he recognized the voice, however. It was one that he had never heard in his house before, and never thought he would. Before he could get up to make his way to the entryway, Detective Alexandra Heart was ushered into the den, by his mother-in-law. Angie was still in Junior's bedroom and would be along shortly. The Minister did his best to maintain his cool demeanor, but the events of late had sucked out almost all of his deceptive capabilities, and real life was dead in his face. His mouth dropped, and his mother-in-law read clearly that something was not right.

"Ed, this is Detective Alexandra Heart. She says that you two know each other and she has something very important to discuss with you." His mother-in-law had a strange look on her face and did not appear like she was going to budge, wanting to know exactly what the discussion was about.

"Thank you, Mom," the Minister said, his voice recognizably shaky. He and Alex looked at Angie's mom as if they were waiting for her to get the message to exit the room.

"Thank you ma'am. Would you excuse us please?" Alex smiled slightly.

"Yes, I'll go get my daughter," she said as she turned and left.

"Alex, what the hell are you doing in my house? You have never been here and you were never supposed to come here! What is this all about?" He did his best to keep his voice low, but even with his teeth clinched, the volume was noticeably increasing.

"Maybe I should wait for the 'Mrs.', especially if that's how you're going to come at me."

"Alex, this is no time for games, and you know better than to be here. Don't push me, not now! I'm dealing with some very serious issues."

"Well, I'm here to talk about some serious issues," she said rather sarcastically.

"Alex, please don't do this. This is not the time or place, and you don't want to upset me anymore than I am already."

"Or what, you'll strangle and stab me, and throw my body into an alley and wait for me to die?"

"What the hell are you talking about? I think you've lost your mind," he said.

"No, I think you've lost yours, but I see you haven't lost your appetite," she bit back.

"I think you need to tell me what the hell you want, and then get out of my house and never come back."

"Where were you last weekend, Eddie?"

"If you're asking me; you must already know," he said looking to the ceiling, frustrated, angry and confused about her motives. He had not placed her with Gemma's case and was quite a bit off balance. "I was in Chicago, why?" He threw his hands in the air.

"Are you aware that one of your church members, a Miss Gemma Kimbro, is laying in the hospital, hours away from death, after having been raped and left to die?"

"Of course, I spoke to her grandmother and she told me all about it. Why are you asking me about it; you think I did it? Is that why you're here, Alex? You think I went to Chicago to rape and try to kill my church member? If that's what you think and why you're here, you're even crazier than I thought."

"No, I don't think you did it, but there are certainly those who will think you did, if they so choose and are steered in that direction," she said stepping into him and speaking inches away from his face. "You were there, weren't you?" There was a possessed and neurotic look in her eyes.

"And what if I was?"

"I'm going back to get some DNA results that might place you in a very bad place, and they can either be placed at the center of the investigation, or in a very far away and insignificant place. That's what I'm here to talk to you about." She was more intense than he had ever seen her, and the look in her eyes was beginning to make him nervous.

"So what are you doing, threatening to blackmail me or ruin my life with some scandalous misinformation, or something? What do you want from me, Alex?" The Minister's stare became cold, as he spoke. He could see where she was going.

"You know exactly what I want, Eddie." Right then, Angie walked into the room.

"*Yes*, he might, but I'd like to know what you want, detective?" Angie interrupted with a concerned, *what now*? tone. They both turned and looked at her simultaneously, and then Alex focused her attention back to the Minister.

"I just came from Chicago. They called me out as a special investigator on the case, and I found these." Without any regard for Angie, Alex reached into her pocket and pulled out the three letters that she had taken from Gemma's coat pocket.

Angie would not be ignored, and before the Minister could extend his hand to accept them, she grabbed them out of Alex's hand, and began reading them. She almost fell to her knees but was determined not to have her pain show through that easily.

"I came here tonight, Ed, because the heat of this thing is going to come your way, and though I don't think you're a suspect, I think you'd better get ready for some serious questioning," Alex said while Angie read.

"No you didn't; you came here tonight because you're a sadistic individual and you want to ruin my life!" The Minister was beginning to lose control. "Get the hell out of my house, Alex, and don't come back! Don't you ever come back!"

Alex turned to Angie as if she had not even heard the Minister's powerful directive and introduced herself, extending her hand. She did not know it but Angie knew exactly who she was.

"Mrs. Hebert, I'm sure you're aware of what happened in Chicago with Miss Kimbro, but you may not be aware of your husband's involvement. That's why I came here tonight. I wanted to discuss his options with him, and of course, with you also."

"Get out, Alex!" The Minister interrupted, but Alex continued, looking directly at Angie.

"I don't think he's a suspect, personally, but there could be a few issues if the DNA results come back and show that—"

"Get out, Alex," the Minister interrupted again, this time with a near blood-curdling yell.

"Your husband knows that I can help him work this thing out and I'm sure you'll encourage him to discuss things with me, so that no disharmony comes to your home. He knows exactly how to reach me."

"Detective Heart, I think you better leave now," Angie said in a tone of surreal calm that caught Alex's attention and made her recognize Angie's uncanny strength and control.

Angie could see that they were dealing with a volatile individual whose behavior was moving toward the edge. She had seen women develop obsessions with her husband after flirtatious behavior got out of control, but this was an entirely new level. Angie shook her head within herself, frustrated, hurt and angry that her husband's actions or lack there of, had brought such a horrific scene into their home.

"They're going to come for him; you know that. I was just trying to help him, as a friend. I wasn't trying to hurt him," Alex said in a weird sort of way.

"Goodnight, detective," Angie said, looking directly into her eyes. "My mother will see you out." Angie knew that her mother was listening just outside the door, even though she was not supposed to be there. Alex received the message loud and clear and was actually afraid. Angie spoke from a powerful place within herself, a place with which Alex was unfamiliar. Angie was not simply a fighter, she was a gladiator. Silence was her sword and calm was her shield. Alex had never met a woman like Angie.

The Minister was right; Alex was sadistic and had been motivated by her own lust. She had crossed a line that the Minister had crossed years ago, and he knew then that she was not the kind of person with whom he should have been involved, but he satisfied the most carnal part of his being whenever he was with her, and she could always depend on his yielding to her temptation.

Alex was escorted out of the house by Angie's mother and went directly to her unmarked patrol car, where she sat for nearly an hour, staring at the upstairs windows of the house. Alex really did not know what to expect by paying him a visit, and did not consider him a suspect. She was driven more by her own anger about his conquests. There was a consuming part of her that was terribly jealous of the life he lived with Angie, and the Minister never knew the contempt she had for his wife. He thought that what they had was securely fastened in well-defined parameters but Alex had proven that that was not the case. That reckless way of thinking and living that he thought was confined to the sensual aspect of her being had spilled over its borders and manifested itself in a compulsive and painful obsession. There were things that he would never know or understand about her. She had been watching his every move for months now. She knew that he was in Chicago with Gemma just as she had known about his tryst in his office with Lydia. That one she had had the pleasure of capturing on video, and watching over and over. She had crossed a bridge and had lost grasp of the thread that held her mind and heart together. Her visit had been scheduled long ago, fueled by anger, frustration and envy. The Minister's problems with Alex were deeper than he ever could have analyzed.

Alex could deal with his lust but not his love, and that was why the letters to Gemma had sent her over the edge. She knew that Angie had what she could never, and she managed to accept that because she was his wife, and it had always been that way. But when she saw the letters to Gemma that expressed loving and romantic emotions, she was sent into a tailspin; he had never done that for her. He had sent her a letter all right, but she knew as well as he did that it was simply a means to an end, and all he was doing with it was making sure that he could reel her in tightly, making sure that she would never let go. Their relationship had never been romantic; it had been charged and exciting, but never romantic, never soft. He had never looked at her with the eyes that she assumed looked at Gemma, and she was angry.

She had been working for years to quietly captivate him, and make him think of her in the way that no other man had, and along came this other woman, who had in no way made the efforts she had, and was able to steal his heart. She had been good enough for whips and chains, and for fulfilling his most erotic fantasies. She had been good enough to engage in passionate encounters in obscure hotels off the interstate, and for that matter, to feel the rush of having sex with her in his lap while nearing one hundred miles per hour, on that very interstate. She had been good enough for bondage games, and for midnight skinny dipping after a stake out and a counseling session, and for intense sexual role playing escapades that would put the wildest porno movie to shame, but never good enough to love, even secretly. She wanted to hurt him if she could not have him, and she had done just that. Finally she left, headed straight to the airport to catch the next flight back to Chicago.

CHAPTER 62

Angie turned to the Minister, whose eyes were filled with tears that had been generated by rage, embarrassment, and pain, and said nothing. She simply looked at him, leaned over the entertainment center and tried to find a merciful spark somewhere in her heart to curb the inevitable onset of an all-consuming fury. She could not. There was no pity there either.

"Angie, I can explain," he said sorrowfully.

"No you can't, Ed," she said with a painful smile. "Please don't even try. At least, give me that respect."

After staring blankly at him for a few minutes, she walked over to him and placed the letters in his hand, closing his hand around them, kissed him on the forehead, and left the room. The Minister did not know how to react, and since she had not said anything to him, he waited for a few moments for her mother to come in and lay into him; he knew that she had heard most of the conversation. She did not say a word either, and all of them soon disappeared into separate parts of the house.

The Minister immediately went to his study and barricaded himself inside. With his elbows on his desk, and his hands covering his face, he cried like a baby. Finally, he reached into his drawer and pulled out his journal.

Dear God,

I'm sorry. My soul is black with pain, so much so that I don't think I can bear it. What I have done goes far beyond myself and I beg your forgiveness. If I can't go on, can you accept my soul? Can my life ever be repaired? Please save me. Please forgive me.

Amen

The Minister felt his eyes failing, and he wanted nothing more than to curl into the arms of his wife. He knew that he had been transformed, and his mind renewed, and if Alex had not come, they would have been able to enjoy a silent recovery, with Angie never knowing what had taken place in Chicago. But now, there was an additional blow to their lives, one that had hit harder than he would ever know.

The Minister knew that Angie was a smart and intuitive woman and that she could probably see that there was much more to Alex's visit than broadcasting the news about Gemma's assault even before his letters came into play. He had often prayed that he would never have to try to unravel the knots of history between them, to his wife. He would take his chances and try again to explain, having no idea where to start, definitely not from the beginning. Before taking a step, he fell on his knees and recited the words of a Biblical Psalm: "*Hear my cry oh God; attend unto my prayer. From the end of the earth will I cry unto thee, when my heart is overwhelmed: lead me to the rock that is higher than I...*" With his head still bowed, he stood and exited his office.

The hallways, of the house were quiet and seemed miles long, as he made his way to their bedroom. Each step seemed like a leap of faith on a fragile foundation, but he had to make the trip. When he entered the room, he looked at Angie who appeared to be strangely sleeping peacefully. He removed his clothes, preparing to slip between the sheets and hold his wife tightly until the whole nightmare went away, but when he reached for her, she woke up from slumber that had been induced by pain.

"What are you doing, Ed?"

"I'm coming to bed, baby," he said, hoping that she felt the miraculous spiritual healing that he had experienced the week before. She did not.

"Ed, you don't sleep here anymore. Goodnight." She turned over and pulled the covers over her shoulder.

"Angela, we can work this out, baby. This is the time we need to come together and stand as a force of one. The devil is trying to see how strong we are, and I know we're stronger than this. Alex is crazy and yes I did go to Chicago with the wrong intention, but something happened to me while I was there, sweetheart, and I know you can see that I'm not the man I was. I stood up baby; I stood up and faced some things that I had left untouched and un-addressed. I stood up then and I'm trying to stand up now. All that stuff in the past that has haunted me is not holding me like it used to; I've been freed. Baby can't we just try one more time to work this thing out?" His eyes were weary and his brow furled with chiseled wrinkle of stress, as he leaned over the bed. Finally she turned over to look at him.

"You know Ed; I love some of the scriptures that you use, especially the ones at the end of service for the benediction. You know the one in the book of Jude that you always use to close out and signify that every thing is over for the day? *'Now unto him who is able to keep you from falling, and to present you faultless before the presence of his glory with exceeding joy; to the only wise God our Savior be glory, majesty, dominion and power, both now and forever. Amen.'* I like that one, Ed," she said as she began to cry, "because everybody knows what it means; it means it's over, it's done, and it's time to go home. Well here's one for you, 'Now to my husband who keeps fucking me over and ever seeks to find new ways to disrespect me, his family and the sanctity of his marriage, and generally make me look like a fool. Yes, to my husband, whose secret sins so override his faith and whose lust has led his life, I hereby release you in the name of the father, son and holy ghost, which in your case are your eyes, your dick, and her ass. I release you to the satisfaction of your needs, whatever they may be, both now and forever. Fuck you!" With that, she got back between the sheets, pulled the covers over her head and began to cry loudly and uncontrollably.

The Minister left the bedroom without another word. He went to his study and collected his pocket-sized bible and journal, and left the house. Angie heard the door close and was not worried; she had a good idea where he was going. She would deal with her anger and disappointment in her own way, and as difficult as it was, right now, she would simply cry herself to sleep. There were things that he had said that she knew were correct. She could see something in his spirit when he came home from Chicago, something that spoke to her through her intuition, and told her that the same man who had left did not come back. The new man was home and conviction called on her to move forward with him as one, especially in this time of crisis. But she had to let her feelings run their course. She had to speak from the years of suppressed frustration and disappointment that were suddenly thrown in her face. She just was not ready to give him what she was almost sure she wanted.

The Minister would not be seen or heard from for the next two days, and what was about to happen would change him forever. Angie's mother watched in silence, from the kitchen, as her son-in-law headed out the front door. He knew that she saw him because he paused or a moment, making eye contact with her as she stood postured over the sink, drying dishes that were not wet. There would be no words now; she would say nothing to either of them. She loved them both and saw their pain, but healing was not hers to give.

CHAPTER 63

Miss Hattie Lee nearly had a heart attack when she heard the news about the recent events between the Minister and Gemma. She knew her granddaughter very well, mainly because she had never been the type of child to hide anything, even when it was something unpopular, but this was huge and completely out of character, even for Gemma. Ivy on the other hand, was not as shocked. She also knew her friend very well, and though Miss Hattie Lee was pretty well informed, there were several things over the years that she did not know; they were secrets that only sisters share. Ivy also did not have the ties to the church that Miss Hattie Lee and Gemma had, and to her, the Minister was just another one of Gemma's male blunders. She was only upset because she was unable to save her from this one.

The news had been broken when Ivy made her investigative calls to the Chicago police detective. The detective to whom she had been referred had not given her any solid information, but Ivy's own investigative tactics led to deciphering the fact that Alex *did* have a lead to check out, and that was why she had left so abruptly. She was also able to gather that the lead had something to do with a man from her hometown.

When Alex returned, Ivy confronted her immediately, asking her about whatever it was that she knew, and explaining that she and Miss Hattie Lee had a right to know. Alex had already intended to tell them, especially after her visit to the Minister had not gone as expected. She really did not know what she had expected by going there, but she knew that she had not gotten it. A consuming force of obsessive disappointment and anger had driven her, and now her demeanor was stoic and almost unfeeling as she explained to Ivy that the Minister was not a suspect, but he had been there, and involved with Gemma.

Miss Hattie Lee was being violently shaken by a mixed bag of emotions, and her heart was being ripped apart. That part of her that always wanted to see them together as children kept rising up inside her, but that dream had long gone and this was not at all what she had in mind. She loved Angie and hated to see her hurting, and she knew that she was most definitely in pain. She was a woman and knew the pain of a loving wife speared through the heart by the actions of a wayward husband. It was even worse, knowing that it was a part of her that was the culprit to the pain felt by the Minister's wife.

There was such an enormity of personal guilt that Miss Hattie Lee felt that she began beating herself up inside for pushing them together, remembering how she insisted that the Hebert's go backstage and meet her granddaughter at the play in Manhattan, but Ivy reassured her that she had nothing to do with it. It was who Gemma was and what Gemma wanted, and there was nothing she could do about it. Still, she could not fight the guilt of feeling, in some way, responsible for the deeds of her granddaughter.

Miss Hattie Lee was now becoming more angry and embarrassed than anything else, and knew that she needed to call someone. She was a great supporter of the Minister and the church, and felt some sense of being let down by everything that the Minister stood for. His sermon's on the virtues of chastity and the pain of adultery seemed meaningless all of a sudden, and she began to feel scarred, like those church members who defect from the fellowship, never to return, claiming emotional injury as a result of the indiscretions of their spiritual leader. But as she looked in Gemma's face and saw herself, she tried not to be completely judgmental, as she remembered the fragmented elements of truth surrounding the not so ancient rumors about herself and the former pastor of the Calvary Baptist Church, many years ago.

There were accusations tossed around the choir room, the kitchen and the usher board that placed Miss Hattie Lee in the arms of the former pastor, the Minister's uncle. She was always there and always available, and there was a sparkle in her eye whenever they looked at each other. And it was true; she had been in love with him for years, and had never denied the rumors because, though the details were usually incorrect and sometimes just plain lies, there was a core truth about her feelings that she shared with no one, and within her thoughts laid the unfulfilled fantasies of an old woman who lived somewhat vicariously through her child.

Ed Hebert was a reincarnation of his uncle, only a better model: more suave, more sophisticated, more charming, and more handsome. Evolution had treated him well. She completely understood how Gemma could have fallen for him, and the more she thought about it, the more she remembered her own love for his uncle. She gently stroked Gemma's face, as her tears were the manifested release of her bleeding heart. She stood what had brought her beautiful granddaughter to this tragic moment. In her heart she asked if it was her love for the young Minister, the nephew of the only man Hattie Lee Ross had ever loved.

Miss Hattie Lee had the benefit of wisdom on her side, when it came to her decision-making. She knew that she needed to talk to her pastor, because that was still who and what he was, no matter how dastardly he had been, and he still offered sage spiritual advice that was applicable and helpful to all who heard. She needed to speak to him, no matter how angry she was. But first she would make a much more important and truly difficult call.

"Baby, I just called to tell you that I'm sorry," she said as soon as Angie answered the phone.

"It's not your fault, Miss Hattie."

"But I feel so bad about it," she said sternly. "I just never would have thought that anything like this would have happened, and I'm just so sorry."

"Miss Hattie, don't blame yourself because you've done nothing wrong. We're talking about grown people here, not children. They did exactly what they wanted to do and now it's done, and it's over. And you know something; I actually wish I could thank Gemma. I don't know what she did for him, but he came back a changed man. I read the last letter that he wrote to her and when he came home, I could already see in him, that something had happened. I couldn't let him know that, but I knew it in my heart. He's not an evil man and he's not one who has ever been out to deliberately hurt me, and I guess that's what makes it so bad. If he can hurt me like this without even trying, I'd hate to be around to see what would happen if he really tried. I know that his desire has always been his '*thorn in the flesh*' and we've had to deal with some serious issues because of it, but I think Gemma did something angelic to him to help him remove it. I was hurt because of the way that it happened, and how it was brought to me, and that I was not the one with the power to do it." Angie spoke slowly and deliberately.

"Do you still love him, baby?" Miss Hattie Lee had tears in her eyes but she managed to speak clearly.

"I can't stop loving him. I hate him, but I just can't stop loving him."

"Then go get him and tell him. If you see that he's changed, by whatever the means, life is too short to go out hatin' and fussin' and fightin'," she said. "I know my baby was wrong for this and she's probably layin' up here dying because of it, but she taught me a lot by the way she lived, Angie. She didn't let one moment in time go by without trying to fulfill her dreams. She got hurt quite a few times and I'm sure she hurt a few people herself, but she never wasted time waitin' on nothin'. Y'all need to be together and fight for your blessings together. I'm gonna tell you something my grandmamma told me. She said, 'Don't let the devil ride; he'll ruin your happy home.' Go get your husband, baby before the wolves eat him, and before the devil rides y'all to death."

Angie was silent. She knew she had to fight through her pain to save a marriage that was worth saving. She knew, in her heart, that they belonged together and that she was staring through a brief window of opportunity. But the pain she felt behind this experience was severe and seemed relentless. It would take something greater than her to get through it.

"How's Gemma doing?" Angie avoided Miss Hattie Lee's last directive.

"She ain't gonna be here much longer, baby, and I'm going to let her go because I know I have to and I know that she can't live like this, but I want to ask you one more question, if it's okay."

"What's that?"

"Do you mind if my baby loved him? I'm not sure that she did, but I know there was something." Angie was silent for a while, and then finally matched Miss Hattie Lee's whisper.

"No," she said quietly, her voice cracking as she tried to swallow around the giant lump in her throat. "If she really loved him, her love might be the very thing that saves our marriage." She began to sob quietly.

"I'm asking you about that because I know about your precious baby, Shelby. Geraldine Williams called and told me all about it." She took a deep breath. "Gemma is brain dead, baby and they're just keeping her breathing with a machine. I want her to live on but I know that I can't have everything I want. She lived a beautiful life and a full life. You might say that it was cut short, but I say that she served God's purpose, and that was all she needed to do. The doctors say she still has some good organs inside her, and they've asked me a couple of times about taking them; I said no." She paused again and the split second silence seemed to go on for minutes. "I want your baby to have them. Whatever she needs, I want you to take it form Gemma. I want her to live inside someone I can love, someone I can touch, and someone I can hold. I want her to live inside someone who loves the Minister, and I know that baby loves her daddy."

"Miss Hattie Lee, I—"

"Baby, don't say nothin'; please don't say nothin'. Call your doctor and do what you have to do. Call your doctor and go talk to your husband. Don't wait, baby. Do it now because if you don't, that anger will set up like a disease and turn your heart to stone."

"Miss Hattie Lee, I love you," Angie said as tears streamed down her face.

"I know you do baby. I never thought you didn't, and I love you too."

CHAPTER 64

During those two cosmically transitional days while the Minister was gone, Gemma died and Shelby's life was saved. Her death was painful and tragic, but one would never know by the look on Gemma's face. She left the world in the true style of the premiere diva she was, and it was almost as if her smile simply transitioned from one grand stage to another. And then there was Shelby. The doctors had worked miraculously and had gone beyond themselves in terms of their abilities. Her primary surgeon even admitted after the eighteen-hour procedure that he felt a strange presence in the operating room that gave him unquestionable confidence and assured him that every incision was precise and every decision correct. He shared with Angie the fact that he had never felt so positive about such a high risk and delicate surgery. A multiple organ transplant had never, in the history of his career, gone so well. In most cases a surgery of this type would have never even been considered. Children's bodies reject adult organs almost all of the time, and most people are on waiting lists for organs until the damage is irreparable. But this case was strangely unique.

Gemma had a very unique birth defect of which no one was aware. Several of her internal organs had matured at a much slower rate than normal, making them not only smaller than most adult organs but also of better functional health than most people her age. The doctors explained that there was really no way to have discovered this issue without having taken the organs out of her body. Gemma was also one of the most physically fit specimens the doctors had ever seen. Her years of wheatgrass and purified water had paid off.

"All of her organs were functionally sound and there was obviously no reason to check on this condition if the patient never complained over the years," the doctor said with astonishment. "There's just no scientific way to explain it, and we would have never even considered the procedure without such a push from the senior medical team."

There had been specific instructions for the doctors to move forward with the surgical miracle, and what the press was not aware of was the extremely large financial donation from one little old church lady that had raced one severely injured little girl to the top of the patient transplant list.

The Press was all over the whole story like hungry scavengers, attempting to piece together the puzzle of information. The story had every interesting element that one could think of, and Gemma Kimbro, an acclaimed artist who had never received her fair share of news coverage in the states, was on every front page from coast to coast. There would be more to tell later, but for now, there was enough to substantiate any reporter's angle. Her death was tragic yet triumphant, and the spotlight was being shared by an unsuspecting little girl who would soon open her eyes from a nightmare to again view a fairytale. Her mother would also be stepping into the spotlight as well, and she knew that she did not want to be there without the man she loved.

Angie knew exactly where to find her husband. She knew that he was hurt, ashamed and angry, but she knew how much he loved his children, and that love would override all other aspects of his life. She walked down the long center aisle of the church to find him crouched before the altar, where he had been for almost the last forty-eight hours, straight. He had had nothing to eat or drink. That was the farthest thing from his mind.

She reached her arms around his shoulders and pulled him up, and when she did, she saw the pain on his face. His eyes were bloodshot and the frown on his brow looked as if it had been chiseled by a skilled sculptor. He had no words for her, and did not know what to expect from her, and before he could find the fortitude to make a statement of any kind, Angie took each side of his scruffy face and brought it to hers.

It was not his time to speak; if he had, the right words would not have come forward. This time was not about what he would say or do; it was about Angie, and knowing that, she gently placed her fingers on his lips. She whispered into his ear, a brief recount of what had happened with Shelby and the fact that it was Gemma's demise that had brought life to their daughter. He held her tightly and cried until no more tears would come. She let him cry about everything and for every reason he needed to, and she held him without consequence and without fear.

CHAPTER 65

It was over too soon for Ivy. Even though she routinely moved swiftly and decisively when it came to important declarations, she could not help feeling that Miss Hattie Lee had moved too quickly. She knew that there was virtually no hope for Gemma, and that her life had been taken away that early evening in the alley, but there was some part of her that wanted her back so badly that she could not bear it. It just was not right. She wanted to grieve longer; she wanted to cry harder; she wanted to scream louder, but it was done. It was over, and there was no appropriately appeasing emotion. She helped Miss Hattie Lee make funeral arrangements at home, and Gemma had already had a will prepared.

Ivy thought it was strange that someone so young had already prepared such a finite document, and as frivolous and spontaneous as Gemma was, she was surprised that she had taken time to have it done. It was one more thing that she did not know about her friend. Only Miss Hattie Lee knew, and when Ivy asked her about it, she reminded her that there are still some things that, "*only Mama knows.*"

Early on, she could see the pace of Gemma's life, and there was something that told her that it was not going to be long. It would be impressive, but not long. Miss Hattie Lee placed the document in Ivy's hand, when they got home, and asked her to handle it, and she promised she would. The funeral would be held in a few days, and she knew that Gemma would not have her moping around in sadness until then.

Ivy had to get back to work, and deal with another painful situation. She was ready to release every ounce of her frustration on Donovan before she left but, Miss Hattie Lee reminded her that, "*vengeance is mine, saith the Lord.*"

"I know you, Ivy Page. Don't you go doin' nothin' you know you shouldn't do," Miss Hattie Lee admonished.

"I'm not. Why do you say that, Grandma?"

"Because I can see it in your eyes," she said looking at her squarely.

She knew that Ivy was hurting and that she was not satisfied with the decisions that had been made. She also knew how intense Ivy was, and that whatever or whoever crossed her path in the next few days was probably in for it.

"Don't worry about me, Miss Hattie; I'll be fine," she said as she walked out the door.

She got in her car and headed downtown. All she could think about was talking to Gemma, and the conversations that they used to have. She needed her and was angry that she could not have her. Even though they would go for long periods of time without speaking to each other, when they spoke it was like they had never broken stride. They balanced and complimented one another and Ivy needed her spirit right then and there. Dealing with Donovan, in a professional capacity was going to be tough, but dealing with him emotionally, was going to be even more difficult. She needed the friendship that only Gemma could give.

When she got to her office, Yavonne was already waiting there for her. She could see the weight on Ivy's face but she knew that she had to push through her grief on her own. Yavonne knew Gemma as well, and was shocked to hear the news, but she was much more consumed with her career and the legal meeting she was about to have. Ivy's assistant directed her to the conference room, after having learned to read some of the expressions on her bosses face. She could see that Ivy was not ready to deal with Yavonne, and it did not take her long to see why. When Ivy came in, Yavonne quickly expressed her sympathy and then introduced the vice president of the magazine, who was there for the meeting as well, and to hopefully assist in reaching a compromise that avoided going to court. Timing was everything in the world of information and entertainment, and they wanted to move forward before their story got cold.

Donovan and his legal counsel were escorted to the conference room, as soon as they arrived, and before long, all parties were seated and accounted for. Ivy sat next to her managing partner, and when she saw Donovan, she did all she could to avoid eye contact. He still pushed her buttons; everything about him spoke to her and turned her on, and she could not deny her feelings. He was admittedly wrong for what he had done and he had called her and left several apologetic messages, telling her that she was the only woman who he cared for, and that he had no intentions of living a secret life anymore. He stopped short only, of telling her that he was gay and that loved her. She saw something in his eyes on this day though, and it was not love. He was ready to fight.

"Good morning everyone. I think we're all here so we can begin," Ivy said as she opened her file and placed it on the table.

"Excuse me Miss Page, but I think this meeting is over," Donovan's lawyer blurted out before she could say another word. "If you guys want to try to sue us, you'd better get another lawyer," he said looking directly at Yavonne and the magazine vice president.

"What the hell are you talking about?" Ivy stood to her feet and raised her voice. Her managing partner was stunned, as was everyone else on that side of the table.

"You're trying to prove that my client is a homosexual with a few photos, and he's not, and whether he is or isn't, is no ones business. Beyond that, he has had a relationship with Miss Page here for quite some time. She's a jilted lover and she's out to get him, therefore her opinions are biased beyond belief, and there's no judge in the state who's going to take her seriously. Mr. Davis has proof on tape, of her saying that she was going to get him after he dumped her."

Before another word was stated, a cassette player appeared on the table and excerpts of Ivy and Donovan's last conversation were played. The words and phrases had been edited to clearly prove the accusations Donovan's lawyer.

"Ivy!" Yavonne stood to her feet and shouted, as if her world had been crushed.

"Miss Page, is this true?" Her managing partner was on his feet yelling as well. "That's not admissible in a court of law!" He turned, after his statement to Ivy and directed his volume toward Donovan's lawyer.

"We're not in a court of law, sir and I don't think we're going to be, are we?" Donovan's lawyer calmly spoke. And then it was the vice president of the magazine's turn to shout.

"Miss Gaines, I knew it! I knew it all along! You've dragged us into a mess again; I should have never taken your word about this attorney friend of yours. I knew it!"

"Mr. Landcraft, please. I didn't know; I—"

"Well you should have known," he yelled.

Before long, words were being thrown around the room wildly, and Ivy said nothing, watching Donovan sit with a smirk on his face. Finally, she simply closed her file, took a deep breath, and left the room. Within hours of the fiasco, Ivy was in her office with packing boxes. She would fight later, but right then all her fight had gone along with any semblance of sanity.

Ivy was not fired; she was the best lawyer in the firm and her superiors knew that. But it was clear to her superiors that something had gone terribly wrong and that the whole scene needed to be severely addressed. After her reprimand for having not disclosed that information, they were still ready and willing for her to pursue the case, from another perspective.

The managing partner felt that he could smooth things over with the magazine executives and restore their confidence in the chosen representation. Further more, the firm brass had engaged some extreme investigative measures of their own without Ivy's knowledge and had acquired extensive information on the case involving the uncle of Donovan's lover and they saw large dollar signs around some level of involvement in the case. Ivy was far past angry and was surprised that they had not already come to her and implicated her in some level of professional impropriety and removed her from the case. They seemed to know so much; she was almost sure that she had been snagged in their dragnet. But it was not Ivy that they wanted. She was simply a pawn on a stage that had been played very well by the gamers involved.

Mr. Blum came to her office, not surprised to see her packing boxes but stunned her by offering her the opportunity to stay on the case. In his mind, it was an offered she could not refuse. Ivy had had enough though, and she shocked all who watched when she left the building without a second look and went home. She had no intentions of ever returning.

"*Game over*," she thought to herself as briskly paced to her car. "*Game over*."

CHAPTER 66

Gemma's funeral was the most beautiful service that anyone had ever seen. The 5,000-seat sanctuary was filled to capacity with all of the normally unused expansion areas wide open, and the total number of mourners easily rose to 7,000 when including those who waited outside. People came from all over the world to pay their respects, and Miss Hattie was proud to see that she was so loved. It had also become a media event, and one of the most unique stories of tragedy and triumph the world had ever seen. Even those who simply knew of her could not bottle their emotion when they approached.

The glorious light that poured in through the majestically elevated stained glass windows, the same godly light that captivated the Minister when he prayed at the altar, illuminated the radiant color of a spray of more than three hundred tulips that sat atop Gemma's mahogany casket. They were compliments of the Minister's wife, and when he saw them, he knew that she knew. For the last few days, there had been wordless communication between them, and the understanding had been paramount, greater and clearer than ever before. Angie had seen receipts that had been mailed, at her request, and even had a faxed copy of the bill from the Ritz-Carlton hotel, in Chicago. She wanted him to know that she knew, and that she was not angry. Whatever happened there would stay there and it was important to Angie, that her husband understood that concept. The woman who lay before them had played a significant role in the repair of their family and healing of their daughter. They had a fresh start because of Gemma Kimbro and it was something to be savored.

The Minister smiled humbly at his wife, loving her more and more with every glance. He had been broken in so many ways and needed to feel more than just her forgiveness; he needed her confidence, and with it came the revival of his spirit. Shelby's second chance at life was his redemption, and his reconnection to the fervor of his faith. There was an uncanny brightness in the sanctuary that filled every place that darkness would hide. Crawford pumped the choir into a frenzy of praise, and those seated in the congregation would soon follow. This day was essentially special for everyone in that place and an unexplainably awesome energy was fueling a unique movement in the individual hearts of those in the crowd.

Miss Hattie Lee sat in her same seat, rocking back and forth, wishing that Gemma were there to enjoy it with her, but being thankful that she would live on, inside little Shelby. Ivy sat right next to her and held her hand tightly. She glanced across the way and saw Donovan sitting with his wife and was puzzled by his presence, not knowing of Lydia's ties to the Minister. She expected to see Alex but she would not. She was there but she was not going to be seen, at least not by the congregation.

Ivy kept Donovan in her peripheral view and did not try very hard to fight the contempt for him she held in her heart. He had wronged her in the worst way and at the worst time, but that was how life was, at least how it had been recently. She was angry, tired and completely stressed out, and the recent events had caused her to re-evaluate her position in life.

Death has a strange way of causing the living to suddenly assume a posture of introspection, and Ivy muddled through her emotions to painfully journey to that point. She was called on to make remarks, and usually she was well prepared, but not this time. She approached the raised lectern that sat just to the right of her dearest friend's casket, with no idea what would come out of her mouth.

"I wish I had the right words," Ivy began slowly, looking down. "Usually, I do; I have note cards or an outline or something to help guide me through, but I don't have anything, today." She finally raised her head and scanned the audience. "My friend is gone, and she won't be back, and I have to be honest and tell you that I hate the reasons why she left." Ivy glanced in the Minister's direction. "She was a marvelous person and there are parts of her that I'm sure will live on forever, but I just wish there were something that I could have done. I wish I could have just talked to her one more time."

After a brief pause that seemed to go on for minutes as opposed to seconds, Ivy returned to her seat. It was clear that she was not a participant in the joy of the *Homegoing Celebration*, as it was being called. She was in pain, and becoming consumed with anger, looking at the men who she felt were, in many ways, responsible for her feelings. Ivy had not yet reached a point of mental and spiritual settlement, and her emotions were torturous. It would take a power well beyond her being to quiet the rage inside her.

Several others made remarks, as requested by Miss Hattie Lee, including Jason who was so broken up he nearly could not speak. Crawford blazed up the choir again, trying to lift the somber mood of the crowd, and then finally, the Minister stood behind the podium in the pulpit, looking noticeably different. He smiled before he spoke, looking down at the large photos of Gemma that had been placed on each side of her casket. The crowd sat quietly as they waited for the pearls of wisdom that would charismatically come. Still, he said nothing, scanning the room and looking through the crowd, locating the circle of participants in the most recent events of his life.

Brown sat behind him with softened, sorrowful eyes, feeling internally apologetic and not knowing why. The church was full and the faces spoke volumes. Many could not believe that they were there for such a purpose, while others focused their attention on personal issues. For them, Gemma's death was no more significant than the paltry dilemmas they would face within the next few hours, but it was a media event, a place to be seen. They would come and go, just like she did, but unlike hers, their lives would remain empty.

The Minister took extra time to study several particular faces as he continued to scan the room, and he wondered why he had been so fortunate. No one knew what he had been through in the last forty-eight hours, not even Angie. No one knew that he had raised a loaded revolver to his head, several times, and cocked the hammer while he was on his knees at the altar. He had come to the end of his strength and was ready to end it all, thinking that he would be more valuable to his family in death than life. He had felt that the mistakes he had made were unforgivable and his life, hopeless. But something had happened to him, something that he could not explain.

The last time he raised the gun to his head, he had the strange feeling of a soft hand intervening and taking it down. Every time he tried to put it back up, he felt a presence disallowing him. At the time he was unsure, but now he was convinced that it was some essence of Gemma.

"I know you all are waiting for me to say something extraordinary, but I can't. You're probably waiting for a good story that will make you feel better about losing this cherished jewel, but I don't have one. As a matter of fact, I don't even think I can preach to you today about this situation." There were a few *Amen's* in the audience, not because those persons followed where he was going, but because they were simply accustomed to blurting out the word.

"When I look at what I see today, I think I owe God an apology." *Amen's* rang throughout the sanctuary, and some of these really knew where he was going.

"Lord, I'm sorry," the Minister shouted, with his head tilted back and his hands lifted, "for every time I'm walked by a rose and didn't stop to inhale its fragrance. Lord, I'm sorry for every time watched a sparrow glide and a bee buzz by, and did not digest the awesomeness of your creatures. Lord, I'm sorry for all the times I went to the water front and watched your rolling waves and did not appreciate the complexity of your tides. Lord, I'm sorry for all the times you gave me time, and I didn't use that time to tell someone I loved them."

The crowd began to go wild as he continued his sermon and used scriptural support for his focus. As they settled down, he looked at all the faces of significance before he continued. He could see that their hearts were being stirred and moving in an unplanned direction, and then he quieted down, looking up toward the stained glass window that focused the light on him while he was at the altar. Turning back to address the crowd, he walked away from the podium and placed his hands in his pockets. To Angie, he looked to have aged ten years in the last two days, but he did not look older; he looked more mature, wiser and more understanding, and it seemed to have come from the hand of God himself. He was another Jonah, and he appeared to have been tormented in the belly of a whale of pain and uncertainty, but now he glowed after having been wrought into correction. He wore appreciation, gratitude and humility like a fine silk robe, and he would preach this day like never before.

"I was sitting alone in a hotel restaurant once, and I noticed a gentleman to my right who I'd say, was 'eating well,' and I don't mean that he had a lot on his plate. What I mean is that it was as if he had unique knowledge and a deeper appreciation for the value of his breakfast. He seemed to understand the need to taste; to chew; to digest; to eat, and to 'eat well.' "He appeared to be between sixty-eight and seventy-two years old, and this is only relevant because, as I watched him clean his plate, savoring every morsel, I noticed another table of apparent retirees in the same age group directly in front of me. The silver haired quartet seemed to share the same ideas about 'eating well' as the lone gentleman. The items on their plates had been knowledgably selected with an apparent adherence to its nutritional value: fruits, grains, dairy, and a host of other sensible items. There seemed to be a joyous camaraderie amongst the group as they engaged in light-hearted conversation, yet still focusing on the individual task before them, 'eating well.'

"Well, this sparked a quick survey of the patrons in my immediate area, and what I discovered was that the 'eating well' philosophy applied to almost all of the seniors around me, while tables with young families with children generally left an abundance of picked over food on their plates. What was the possible correlation? Of course there are medical and physiological inferences that are, I'm sure, correct and offer logical answers, but my personal analysis takes a different approach, and that's what I want to talk to you about."

The crowd began to stir as the Minister repositioned himself behind the pulpit podium. They were beginning to respond before he even continued.

"Many of these people grew up in the 20's, 30's, and 40's, in a time when hard work and hearty meals went hand in hand. And the devouring of a hearty meal gave strength and sustenance for a hard days work. In essence, an elementary ethic was developed during this time in which a deeper, yet primitively simple understanding of the nutritional value of 'eating well' paved the way for physical performance and a well developed immune system.

"When I imagine the dinner table dynamics back in those days, I don't see high-end metabolic and nutritional discussions of vitamins, A, B, C, or E, good and bad cholesterol, amino acids, vitamin complexes, etcetera. I see more poignant quotations like, 'eat all of your vegetables; don't leave those beans; eat your meat and all of your potatoes; drink your milk and eat your bread; and clean your plate.' In other words, take full advantage of every opportunity to be all you can be, and seizing those opportunities will be the very thing that makes you strong. Some households didn't have a full spread, and a whole lot of choices, so when you had a chance to 'eat well,' you took it, and from that, you learned the value of God's individual gifts.

"You might look at Gemma and say that she lived a life cut short, but it's not how long you live, but how you live while you live, and Gemma 'ate well!'" The crowd began to applaud and shout.

"It's unusual for a young person to understand the concept, but she did. Oh yes she did! She 'ate well,' understanding the value of every morsel of opportunity and every fork full of chance. I tell you, she 'ate well!' She seasoned the world with her gifts and talents, and taught those who watched her live how to bite from the goodness of life. I tell you, she 'ate well!'

"I'm glad that I had the opportunity to say 'thank you' to young Sister Kimbro, before she left. I'm glad that I got a chance to see her perform and light up the stage with the talent God gave her. I'm glad that

I got a chance to hear her melodic voice as it rivaled the sweetest praise of a swallow in the evening light! I'm glad that she helped me, and many others, to take hold to the most valuable things in life and not live bogged down by worry and indecision and pain. I'm glad that she lived a life in which she 'ate well!'"

The Minister continued with his complimentary sermon that admonished parishioners to take advantage of every moment in time and to be effective with their various gifts. Before long, both Miss Hattie Lee and Ivy were on their feet, applauding with tears streaming down their faces. They were both thinking of Gemma and how she did exactly what the Minister was talking about, leaving no questionable stone unturned, and loving without fail.

Ivy was especially impressed with the Minister and although she had previously stowed some animosity toward him for simply being there with Gemma, finding some way to place him in the arena of blame, she found what he was saying captivating, comforting and inspiring. She had never met him personally, but now there was some place inside her that he had reached, and she needed to follow his advice and not let the opportunity slip away. For a brief moment, she could see in him, what Gemma must have seen. He was strong, charismatic and beautiful. He preached with a conviction that she had never seen before in any man, even a preacher. She looked over at Angie, and though she had never met her before either, she knew that she was his wife. Her countenance was powerful and unforgettable, and Ivy saw in her, something that she saw in herself, a will to fight for what was hers and what she knew she deserved.

When the church service ended, and the mourners made their way out of the sanctuary, they were greeted by an unseasonably warm autumn breeze. The sun seemed brighter and closer than normal, warming people to such a point that the removal of coats and gloves was noticeable throughout the exiting crowd. As Miss Hattie Lee and Ivy got into the lone family car, they huddled close together, not to keep warm but to simply be close. Miss Hattie Lee rolled down the window and the air rushed in, stirring the papers on the floor and making her grab her hat. She leaned over to Ivy.

"You feel that warm breeze and you see that bright sun; that's my baby sayin' everything is okay."

"I know it is, Miss Hattie. I know it is," Ivy replied, her heart still stirring with a strange mix of emotions.

Gemma was laid to rest near a brook at an exclusive cemetery. Her headstone read:

SINGING AND DANCING THROUGHOUT ETERNITY followed by a quote from the 100th Psalm carved in intricate calligraphy. The Minister hugged Miss Hattie Lee tightly and again told her how sorry he was. Ivy looked on, as he tried to encourage her, admiring Miss Hattie Lee's strength at such a devastating time.

Even though Gemma was gone and had a beautiful service that respectfully celebrated her life, the situation at which they all looked was painful, cold and final. There were mysterious puzzles yet to be solved and the faces that surrounded the gravesite did little to hide the resounding questions that gnawed at grieving hearts. With their eyes filled with tears, they walked back to the family car, never looking back, holding themselves, holding their hearts.

Adhering to the traditions of most African-American families, the group made their way back to the church for the repast. The ladies had prepared a glorious meal and found ways even in crisis to comfort the bereaved. Baked and fried chicken, country ham, meatloaf, turkey wings, yams, cornbread dressing, cranberry sauce, green beans, okra, rice and gravy, pound cake, German chocolate cake, lemon cake and peach cobbler do great and magnificent things toward the healing of bereaved souls.

CHAPTER 67

It did not take long before Ethelreen Williams, one of the many church kitchen comedians, had Miss Hattie Lee laughing, and seeing her smile was worth more than anything money could buy. She had been through a tremendously painful experience, one that few would ever understand, and though her smile did not mean that everything was fine, it did indicate that she was willing and ready to heal. That was when Ivy slipped away. She wanted to meet and say something to the Minister, who had drifted away to his office after greeting a few of the mourners. He had left Brown in charge of the mealtime consoling.

Ivy asked around until she was directed to the corridor that led to his office. As she walked, she passed Angie in the hallway and introduced herself, explaining that she had been there before but never had the pleasure of meeting her, and what a dynamic speaker the Minister was. Angie thanked her for the compliment and told her that she was sorry that she could not stay and talk because she was on her way to the hospital to check on Shelby. The ladies exchanged words of sincere encouragement. She directed Ivy to her husband's office, and as she walked away, Angie watched her gait, knowing that she was looking at a woman who could make her husband salivate. Ivy was beautiful, with runner's legs, an athletic body, a flawless smile and piercing gray eyes. But Angie did not worry; she was too thankful for her miracle, so she took a deep breath, turned around and did not look back. The Minister would answer for his own discretions, and she had to find satisfaction somewhere in that truth. He had to make his own choices and the same righteousness that existed for others existed for him; whether or not he grabbed hold to it was completely up to him, and he would stand alone on that proving ground.

When Ivy knocked on the open door, she caught a glimpse of the Minister slipping out of his robe, and she noticed his muscular physique, even through his shirt. He was changing and preparing to join his wife at the hospital, but when he looked up and saw Ivy, he beckoned her inside.

"I just wanted to stop by and tell you how much I enjoyed and was moved by your eulogy," she said as she hesitantly entered, noticing the modernly appointed office. She tried not to gawk at the numerous citations and awards that hung on the walls.

"Thank you, Ivy. I feel like I know you," he said extending his hand. "Miss Hattie Lee has told me a lot about her 'other daughter' but she didn't tell me how beautiful you were."

Ivy could feel something that she was not ready for and did not want. She thought about how Gemma must have been ensnared in his charm, and she was determined not to have that happen to her.

"I came to pay you a compliment, not receive one, but thank you anyway."

"Relax Sister Page, I'm not out to hurt anyone, especially no one who is associated with a family that I have loved and that has loved me, as long as I've been alive. I don't know if Miss Hattie Lee told you, but our families go way back."

"She did mention that, and I'm sorry for snapping like that. Things have just been so difficult and there have been so many unanswered questions, and this just hurts so bad." Ivy began to cry and within seconds she was in the Minister's arms.

He held her and stroked the back of her head, allowing her to cry as much as she needed. She closed her eyes and had never felt so safe since the days her Uncle Henry had held her. She did not know if it was the Minster or just her overwhelming state of vulnerability that was in control. But whatever the case, she was enjoying being in his arms. Within moments, her hand was on his neck, then the back of head. She fought the urge to kiss him, as the scent of his cologne mixed with the sweetness of his light perspiration began to mesmerize her. He was so manly, just like she thought Donovan was, and his touch had the ability to take her places that she definitely wanted to be. The pace of her breathing increased slightly before he interrupted her traveling mind.

"Ivy," he said quietly, "everything is going to be all right, and if you need me, you're welcome to call me any time you like, but I have to go." She pulled herself back rather abruptly to see his smiling face, embarrassingly apologetic within herself for her wandering thoughts.

"I know you've heard about my little girl and the magnificent thing that Gemma did for us, well I need to go to the hospital to be with my wife, my son and my little girl. I'm sure you understand."

"Of course. I'm sorry, I didn't mean to keep you," she said wiping her eyes.

"It's okay, and I want you to call me. I think I'd like to get to know Gemma's sister."

"I'll give you a call some time," she said smiling, and then she left.

The Minister sat on the edge of his desk and watched her leave. She was beautiful and he knew it. Her eyes were fierce and blazing, and they touched him in a very special place. He went behind his desk and sat down. He looked at his pocket-sized Bible and journal that he had brought from his home office. He sat with his hand over his mouth, supported by his elbow atop the desk. His thoughts jumped wildly across a mental stage that flashed pictures of Gemma, remembering her touch and her scent. There was also Lydia with her fair complexion and supple skin, and he could feel something rising inside him.

And then there was his family portrait; he looked at Angie, beautiful, strong, pricelessly forgiving and faithfully supportive. Shelby and Junior were simply blessings from God and the jewels of his existence. They had been through more together than anyone knew, and Angie had been there with him all the way. She was like no other woman he had ever known, an angel. But his mind soon floated away from them and back to the beauty that had just left his office. He knew that she would be back and that he felt a spark in her bosom as he held her. Leaning back in his chair, he closed his eyes for a while and then reached for his journal, penning words committed to memory from the Song of Solomon:

Behold thou art fair, my love: behold, thou art fair: thou hast doves' eyes within thy locks: thy hair is as a flock of goats, that appear from mount Gilead.

Thy teeth are like a flock of sheep that are even shorn, which came up from the washing; whereof every one bear twins, and none is barren among them.

They lips are like a thread of scarlet, and thy speech is comely: thy temples are like a piece of pomegranate within thy locks.

Thy neck is like the tower of David builded for an armoury, wheron there hang a thousand bucklers, all shields of mighty men.

Thy two breasts are like two young roes that are twins, which feed among the lilies.

Until the day break, and the shadows flee away, I will get me to the
mountain of myrrh, and to the hill of frankincense.
Thou art fair, my love; there is no spot on thee.

The Minister tore the page out of his journal, placed it in his pocket and again closed his eyes, fighting tears that he hoped were not the same as those that flowed after his office encounter with Lydia. When he opened them, he put his coat on and headed for the hospital to meet Angie. He knew that was where he belonged, but he could not stop his mind from racing, as he drove. He felt as though there was a plate before him from which he could dine, and he knew that the option of *eating well* was completely left to him. When he got to the hospital and parked, he pulled the torn page out of his pocket, and wrote one last line.

I love you my darling; thank you for loving me...

When they met in the waiting area, he went straight to her, and without one word he embraced her, holding on like there was no tomorrow. Feeling the warmth of her intuitive body and restoring touch did more for him than she would ever know. She was healing him; redeeming him and giving him room to mend his brokenness. He took her hand, opened it and placed the torn page in her palm and then clinched her hand tightly around it, never daring to look her directly in the eye. Without even looking at the shriveled parchment, Angela placed her delicate hand on his soggy, dispirited cheek, and finding her husband's eyes through tears of her own, she said, "It's about time that I got a letter from the Minister."

THE END

(FOOTNOTES)

[1] *Soulmates*, Thomas Moore

Printed in the United States
69244LVS00003B/127-192